PLAY DEAD

PLAY DEAD

Bill James

CRÈME de la CRIME

This first world edition published 2013
in Great Britain and the USA by
Crème de la Crime, an imprint of
SEVERN HOUSE PUBLISHERS LTD of
9–15 High Street, Sutton, Surrey, England, SM1 1DF.
Trade paperback edition first published
in Great Britain and the USA 2013 by
SEVERN HOUSE PUBLISHERS LTD.

British Library Cataloguing in Publication Data

James, Bill, 1929-
 Play dead. – (The Harpur & Iles series)
 1. Harpur, Colin (Fictitious character)–Fiction. 2. Iles,
 Desmond (Fictitious character)–Fiction. 3. Police–Great
 Britain–Fiction. 4. Police corruption–Fiction.
 5. Undercover operations–Fiction. 6. Detective and
 mystery stories.
 I. Title II. Series
 823.9'14-dc23

ISBN-13: 978-1-78029-043-0 (cased)
ISBN-13: 978-1-78029-538-1 (trade paper)

All Severn House titles are printed on acid-free paper.

Severn House Publishers support the Forest Stewardship Council [FSC], the
leading international forest certification organisation. All our titles that are printed
on Greenpeace-approved FSC-certified paper carry the FSC logo.

Typeset by Palimpsest Book Production Ltd.,
Falkirk, Stirlingshire, Scotland.
Printed and bound in Great Britain by
MPG Books Ltd., Bodmin, Cornwall.

ONE

Harpur had what he regarded as some pretty good, bright information for Assistant Chief Constable Desmond Iles. But one of the central things about Iles was that he hated dependence on any of his people for good, bright information. Iles considered he was the kind who should already *have* all the good, bright information himself as of right – and have all other brands of important information, too, not just good and bright. He didn't want subordinates sneaking ahead of him in knowledge, and especially he didn't want Harpur sneaking ahead of him, in knowledge, or whatever else.

Over the years Harpur had come to realize it could be stupid to blurt straight out in a big-headed, smug way insights that Iles to date lacked. Instead, get deft. New facts should be offered one at a time and gradually, not all in a triumphalist lump. Eke them out. Harpur had learned how to eke, could have run a degree course in ekeing. And he would try to be deft and gradual today in this dodgy aftermath chat with the ACC.

One of the other core factors about Iles was he frequently went in for big self-blame. 'Big' meant allowing no excuses; 'big' meant bordering on suicide. With ruthless accuracy he'd weigh some part of his life in the balance and find it hopelessly wanting. Many would have been surprised to hear this about him, because he generally seemed so stiff-necked, feudal and tirelessly insolent. But Harpur had occasionally seen that other, confidential, cripplingly repentant side of the ACC. He saw it this morning. He understood where it came from. He thought he might have something precious to turn the ACC around, restore to him all that familiar brazen, Hunnish, startlingly talented obnoxiousness. The good, bright information should do it, but only if administered to the Assistant Chief with quiet dexterity and finesse, like a nurse with a suppository.

Not long ago he and Harpur had been sent by the Home Office to do deep checks on another police force where there was a possibility, and more than a possibility, of corruption at a middling, or upper-middling rank. For security reasons the force had been coded

Larkspur. An undercover officer brought in from a different force so as not to be recognized – Carnation – had been shot dead there. As it eventually turned out, the killer gunman was another officer who'd apparently feared a crook-police racket might be exposed by the spy from Carnation. But, until Iles and Harpur arrived, there had seemed to be no intense, committed investigation of the killing. It went nowhere. Blockages? The Home Office became uneasy. Were some people at Larkspur protecting themselves by neutering inquiries – the way inquiries seemed to have been neutered or sidetracked after the racist murder of the black teenager Stephen Lawrence in London?

Through good detective work Harpur and Iles discovered the marksman and arrested and charged him.[1] It stopped there, though. Who ordered the execution of the undercover man? Why? How high did the conspiracy go? The crook-police racket presumably centred on drug dealing – crook-police rackets usually did – but in what way, what ways, at Larkspur: the system, the connections? Harpur and Iles didn't find answers to these infinitely dark conundrums. The conundrums remained.

Iles and Harpur were in the Assistant Chief's double-room office suite at police headquarters in their own domain – encrypted Cowslip for that operation. They looked back and took stock. Colin Harpur had a red leather easy chair. The Assistant Chief paced, a habit of his, most probably meant to show off the straightness and slimness of his legs. He refereed rugby matches now and then, though he had gone off the game since it went professional. When younger he'd played at outside-half for police teams. He had that kind of unburly, lithe physique. 'I could jink off either foot,' he'd told Harpur once, and Harpur believed it. Jinking would come easily to Iles. 'Jink right!' 'Jink left!' Whichever the coach wanted, Iles would deliver.

'We failed, sir,' Harpur said. The approach with this fine new stuff – new to Iles – had to be oblique, roundabout.

'Absolutely, Col.' The ACC nodded in sad congratulations. 'Now and then you'll get things totally right. Maybe even oftener than now and then, despite your clothes and all-over appearance.'

'Thank you, sir.' Harpur did try, though, to fix a minor, preparatory lifting of the gloom. There had been pluses on their Larkspur

---

[1] See *Undercover*

visit. 'But I know some folk would say we didn't fail at all. The very reverse, in fact. That's why we were pulled off.'

'Who?' the ACC said.

'Who what, sir? Harpur said.

'Which folk would say we didn't fail?'

'Yes, quite a number. They'd argue that we nicked the one who actually fired the shots. He's doing life, minimum eighteen before parole possibility. Cop kills cop – that's evil.'

'We nicked a nobody. We fly-swatted, nothing more,' the ACC said.

'Many would dispute that, I feel, sir, with respect.'

'Who?'

'Many.'

'"With respect," tell me, Col,' the ACC replied, his voice wonderfully mild, conversational and dangerous, 'where do you come across them?'

'Who, sir?'

'The folk who say we did well.' Tone switch: 'Are they all fucking mad, Harpur?'

'They believe this is how policing *must* operate.'

'Who believe it?'

'Many.'

'How, then?' Iles said.

'How what, sir?'

'How *must* policing operate, in their folksy view?' the Assistant Chief replied.

'They'd say policing can cope only with the feasible, only with the achievable. There are tight limits. These have to be recognized, or frustration and distress result. Policing nails the villain it's possible to nail – nails the villain who *can* be nailed. In this case, it's the one who pulled the trigger, pulled the trigger twice: blew half a face away at night on a building site, as planned.'

'A cat's paw,' Iles said.

'A police officer, yet a killer.'

'But who instructed him to kill? Which superior, superiors, was he looking after – trying to shield from exposure?'

Harpur said: 'We're probably not talking about the Larkspur Chief himself, Rhys Dathan, are we, sir? After all, he asked for this undercover specialist from another force to come in. He needed a spy to penetrate a powerful, seemingly invulnerable, drugs firm on

Larkspur's ground, perhaps a corruptly favoured drugs firm by a clique of his officers. The Chief used standard tactics. He wanted someone unlikely to be recognized by any of the gang, so gets an officer from Carnation. The Chief acted properly. He wouldn't have done that if he personally was involved in a dirty game, would he? He'd be inviting exposure.'

'Smart, Col. Always I've loved the confident way you summarize the obvious.'

'Thank you, sir.'

'Of course, it could have been a ruse by Dathan, couldn't it? He must have realized his outfit looked dubious and had turned smelly. So, he invites undercover. Pre-emptive? Afraid undercover might be sent, anyway. By calling for it, he knows who the undercover is and can monitor and manage him, or her. Clever? Subtle? Anyway, Col, somewhere in Larkspur there was a secret, tainted syndicate,' Iles replied.

Harpur nodded. 'Still is? Regrettably, we never identified it.'

'Yes, regrettably, regrettably. We didn't even get near. Yet it's what we were sent to discover, Col – I, an ACC, and you a detective chief superintendent: a considerable, experienced team looking for evidence of a cover-up, evidence of a perversion of justice, but stymied, brick-walled.'

'Yes, this is where we missed out . . .' Harpur almost started his comforting news, then decided there should be a little more strategic delay.

'Obviously, matters can't be left like that, Harpur,' Iles said.

'Can't they? The operation is closed, sir.' Not exactly a lie, but in that area, though Iles wouldn't know this.

'Is it possible, Col – abandoned, given up on? Oh, God, no. No! OK, Harpur, policing deals with the – what did you say? With the feasible, the achievable. Is that *worth* saying, it's so trite? "Art of the possible" and similar jargon. But I'm one who believes the feasible and the achievable should be constantly extended, should be forcibly stretched by an officer of flair and grit.'

Iles paused. He did some very genuine work on getting modesty into his face and wordage. 'Please don't think, Col, these are terms I've suddenly and egotistically claimed to describe myself. No, hardly! But it's my mother. I'm indebted to my mother. She would joyously, wonderingly employ them about me as a child. "Desmond," she'd exclaim, "flair and grit – they are so brilliantly and resoundingly yours!" I wouldn't claim to *like* my mother, but she had perception and a kind of vocabulary.'

'Mothers can come out with all sorts,' Harpur said.

'In what sense, Col?'

'Remarks.'

'Which?'

'Remarks. They're what make mothers what they are.'

'In which respect, Col?'

'Often they mean well,' Harpur replied.

'Did *your* mother make remarks about you? Oh, dear, I'm sorry, Col. But at least it helped you develop a splendidly thick skin,' Iles said. 'Elastic and thick. You bounce back, regardless.'

'Regardless of what, sir?'

'Regardless, yes.'

The ACC continued to pace. Harpur could certainly spot agitation in this movement, but also observed resolve and a kind of cheetah-like, latent, on-tap energy. The two, big adjoining rooms had a connecting pair of doors. Iles needed these open to provide honest distance for his lopes. He passed through the gap now and went out of Harpur's sight for a while. Iles stayed audible, though. Both shouted a little when the ACC was at his farthest in there, trekking around a long conference table. Harpur kept to routine comments at this stage. It would have been off-key and unfair to bellow his special material while the ACC was yet a great way off, like the Prodigal, and absurd to phone him on his mobile. After a few minutes Iles returned, clearly still troubled.

He wore his pale blue dress uniform of magnificent material for some Lord Mayoral function he had to attend later. Iles didn't altogether despise these events and Harpur had heard he would even behave quite temperately at them, unless, of course, something or someone enraged him, which could happen. The office pacing slowed now, then ended. Iles lowered himself into another of the red, leather-covered easy chairs. The colours of his outfit and the uphol-stery contrasted, but more or less tolerably. 'I feel terrible guilt, Col,' he said. 'I, Iles, fell short.'

In an abrupt change from the slick grace of his recent in-house stroll, he seemed now to sit stricken, huddled forward around his shame, as if to conceal it; and yet, also, in a weird, masochistic, Des-Ilesian way, to cherish it – guard it, enfold it protectively, like a hen-bird with its eggs, because he, Des Iles, deserved it, had thoroughly earned it by what he would see as vast, unpardonable incompetence. *I, Iles, fell short:* that merciless pinpointing of his name, with the disturbing paired clangs of the 'I' sounds; *I Iles* – so poignant. 'Do you realize, Harpur, someone at Larkspur is laughing at me, at my defeat? Or maybe more than one. A dire, filthy phalanx of them, chortling at my bungling, drinking toasts to Iles's consummate ineptitude.'

'Laughing at both of us, sir.'

'Oh?'

'If it's to do with failure to net the organizer – organizers? – of that death,' Harpur said. 'I, too, was defeated.' By volunteering at once to accept his part in the shambles he longed to lessen the ACC's pain, divert a share of it. But, immediately he'd spoken, Harpur realized this was an idiotic, impertinent, lese-majesty error. Arrogantly, it presumed a kind of equality between him and Iles, a parity of suffering and self-disgust, whereas the ACC's suffering and self-disgust would be unmatchably awful.

'They'll laugh more viciously, more convulsively at me – a hierarchy aspect,' Iles replied. 'Just think of Hiroshima, Col.'

'True.'

'They needed a suitably significant target to drop the bomb on, not some outlying village, but a grand city. Targets have to be worthwhile, Col.'

'Very few would say you were not worthwhile, sir, whether as a target or anything else.'

'Which very fucking few, Harpur?'

'Maud has been in touch, sir,' he replied. Harpur knew, of course, this would agonizingly rile the ACC but it couldn't be avoided. Ultimately, progress had to take over from timid tact. Ultimately was here.

'Maud Logan Clatworthy? Home Office Maud? "In touch"? In touch with *you*?' Iles whisper-gasped these dazed phrases. The announcement had scattered his calm for a moment. He raised his left hand and stroked his chest in an instinctive twitch, as though trying to free up his lungs.

'I think you might have been difficult to reach at the time,' Harpur said.

'But she could reach *you*, all right, could she, Harpur? Naturally. In London, did you eventually get around to giving her something to remind her of you?' Iles recovered to ordinary speech level: an authentic, pedigree snarl, perfect for sarcasm. 'Home Office Maud,' was a whizz kid who had sent them on their anti-corruption mission to Larkspur. They'd spent a lot of time in Whitehall getting briefed by her. Iles had thought she showed extra interest in Harpur – little to do with the job, much to do with sex.

'She believes she can get the investigation "reactivated",' Harpur said. 'Maud's no more content than we are with the way it finished – finished without finishing.'

'She told you this? You had some nice, intimate prattle?' Iles sweetly feminized his larynx: '"Oh, it will be so grand and lovely, Colin, to team up again, don't you think? I'm really thrilled,"' he fluted. But then he reverted for a while to a normal, enraged male voice. 'She knows, doesn't she, because I told her at one of our previous meetings – you heard me tell her – I told her that not long ago you were banging my wife on the quiet in fourth-rate rooming joints, under evergreen hedgerows, in marly fields, on river banks, in cars – including police vehicles – and, most probably, my own bed? Yet this doesn't put dear Maud off, does it? What is it with you and women? Do they look at your garments and haircut and general air of decay and pity you – want to help you in one of the few ways available to them, such as letting you bang them in fourth-rate rooming joints, under evergreen hedgerows, in marly fields, on river banks, in cars – including police vehicles – and, most probably, my own bed? They find your clothes frightful, so prefer them off?'

Iles had now begun to scream, as he usually did when discussing Harpur and Sarah Iles. His voice went back to the high register needed to do Maud, and soon soared and quivered much higher. Minor froth appeared on his lower lip – minor in quantity, as compared to other foamings from Iles that Harpur had witnessed in the past, but not at all minor in quality, no: thick, throbbing flakes of spit, each a wet, glistening proof of his pain and disarray. His breathing became laboured and desperate, like a dog's half strangled by its lead and collar.

In a while he recovered and asked: 'Does Maud realize you have no respect for—?'

'As I say, sir, Maud would have spoken direct to you, but met unavailability,' Harpur replied. 'Daisy, her PA, tried repeatedly. Maud felt deep disappointment, but made do with talking to me. Very made-do. Possibly you were at another of these civic bean-feasts. Understandably you get so many invites. You confer on their little occasions what I think is known as cachet – brilliant distinction. They adore having someone of rank present in full but tasteful gear to bring undeniable class, don't they?'

'Well, *was* I at a function?' Iles said. 'When did she speak to you? This is easily checkable against my diary. Couldn't she have emailed, voicemailed?'

'Not regarded as secure. Think of the *News of the World* hacking scandal. Think of detectives trawling emails for evidence of corruption at *The Sun.*'

'So she goes to dearest Col whose ears and zip are always open. If he's not debauching my wife, he has this undergrad piece from the university up the road. Denise? That's her, isn't it?'

'Maud particularly wanted *us* to carry out any further digging at Larkspur, not have the matter handed over to some other combo,' Harpur replied. 'We already understand so much about the situation, the murder venue, the supposed hunt, the ambush, the blood spillage. And she was very insistent that I should let you know of this development soonest.'

'Should "let me know"?'

'Soonest.'

'Allow me into the loop finally?'

'Soonest.'

'Kindly,' Iles said.

'I think she has you very much in mind, sir.'

'Nice.'

TWO

Maud did get the operation 'reactivated' and Harpur and Iles went back to re-snoop and re-interview and re-dredge at Larkspur. Maud must have managed to convince her chiefs that sending the gunman to jail should be only the first move in a full Larkspur clean-up. He'd been very tidily scapegoated: loaded with all the blame for Carnation man's death. But who'd done the loading? Who'd given the executioner his orders? Who controlled him? Who, ultimately, hung him out to dry? Who could scare him so much he wouldn't talk, even for a reduced sentence trade? Who was money-doling and generally protecting his family as long as he stayed shtum? Who'd be making sure he got good stuff in jail, also as long as he stayed shtum? What dug-in crooked power group lay behind him? Did it still flourish?

This last she regarded as the crux question, touching now and the future. The murder and trial and conviction were the past. Or *merely* the past, Maud would probably say, in that brusque, now-get-your-ear-around-this style of hers. Maud thought big. Maud thought practical. Maud thought the present, but Maud also thought days and maybe years beyond the present. Maud thought the Home Office could often do with a kick up the arse from somebody who worked there and who despised non-interventionism – such as Maud Logan Clatworthy. She'd be late twenties, not more, maybe less. Daisy Fenton, her personal assistant, was at least twice Maud's age.

According to Iles, Maud would have a first-class Oxford or Cambridge degree in a very non-vocational subject, such as Philosophy or the Classics or both, and this should indicate true brain-bright scope. Also according to Iles, though, most of her superiors in the Home Office would similarly have first-class Oxbridge degrees in a very non-vocational subject. This ought to mean, didn't it, that they likewise should have true brain-bright scope? Just the same, Maud thought some of them needed a kick up the arse. From inside Maud knew the slowness and blasé languor and indecisiveness of the place. Maybe Maud had a *super*-first-class degree, a first-class degree with bells on, and therefore her brain-bright scope outscoped theirs. The kick up the arse might help them extend and revitalize their scope.

When Harpur and the ACC arrived at Larkspur for this second investigation and had booked into the same hotel as before, Iles decided there should be a bit of theatre. 'Let us go then, you and I, when the evening is spread out against the sky, and defy time, Harpur.'

'Time's always out there, sir.'

'That's a fact, Col. Time future is contained in time past, you could say.'

'And I do, sir. It's one of the chief things about time – it never stops. Even while we've been talking about time, time has moved on. Clocks can stop, but not time.'

'Don't go fucking ruminative on me now, Harpur. Look, Col, we'll re-create those rough, past circumstances and observe them as though afresh.'

'Which circumstances, sir?' Harpur said.

'A death, of course.'

'How?' Harpur said. They were in the hotel bar. Harpur had a double gin topped up with cider in a half-pint glass, his usual. Iles drank what he called 'the old tarts' drink', port and lemon, *his* usual.

'How what?'

'How re-create the circumstances?'

'We'll mimic the gunshot moments of the undercover man's murder.'

'Mimic?'

'Reprise. Closely imitate. Carry no identification, Col, just in case.'

'In case of what, sir?'

'Yes, just in case. We'll do it on location, where it actually happened. Authentic.'

'Play-act the killing?'

'Ah, you'll, naturally, be thinking of *Hamlet*, I know,' Iles said.

'Inevitably.'

'You'll have in mind, Col, the theatrical troupe who *portray* a murder, while Hamlet is considering a *real* murder, himself. It's eerie. I should imagine you've had many a shiver while watching this part of the drama from your seat in the gods.'

'Right. But what can we discover? We've already identified the killer and had him convicted.'

'We'll possibly learn something we previously missed – something in addition to the simple, limited shoot-bang-fire of the assassination, Col. We must seek its context, Harpur, its place in the overall villainous pageant.'

'Most probably the Carnation officer wouldn't have regarded the shoot-bang-fire as limited, sir. It finished him. But I suppose it *was* limited in the sense both bullets hit him, and nobody else.'

'He was just one step up from a nobody, Col, only a minor figure in a savage, wider scene. Our aim is to find the meaning of this figure among many others, some vastly more tasty and grand.'

Harpur accepted that Iles had a right, even a duty, to think and talk in this large, billowing, bullshitting style now and then. He was an Assistant Chief, for God's sake, and Assistant Chiefs always came with a cartload of wordage. And so, at what Harpur had called 'the murder venue', he took the part of the twice-shot man, and Iles became the sniper. There wouldn't be any Oscars. It was a building site of new dwellings, but hit by the recession and uncompleted so far. They'd be comfy, hygienic, executive-style villas with three bathrooms if they ever got finished – and if there were enough solvent executives around then to afford the deposit, and tell members of the household which bathroom they'd been allocated.

Harpur and Iles had come to look at the site previously, of course, on their earlier trip to Larkspur for Maud and the Home Office. Now, Iles wanted to sort of start from scratch – *re*start from scratch. They'd seek extra insights through a reconstruction; standard police procedure when a case grew uncrackably difficult. Iles didn't always fancy standard police procedures. He must be feeling daunted. His remedy was this atmospheric, *in situ* mock-ambush, a sketch: Iles to ambush, Harpur to *get* ambushed, as the undercover officer had also been ambushed from what might eventually be a front bedroom of one of the well-placed, detached property shells.

'Symbolism here, Col?' Iles said.

'In which respect, sir?'

'A society in accelerating decline, Harpur. No funds to build shanties for its people. Contrast this, would you, with heaven, Col?'

'Heaven?'

'"In my father's house are many mansions. If it were not so I would have told you." Notice that, Col: "I would have told you." In other words, high-grade accommodation for one-and-all is so much the norm there that any shortfall would trigger a warning. Impossible for us to match that. We lag and may lag more. Then, as if to add extra misery, extra grief, to this deplorable scene, the slaughter of a law officer among the blighted properties. Are we into breakdown, Col? Are we witnessing a slide towards chaos?'

It was night, to match conditions when Carnation man had been shot in that limited, focused, dead-on-arrival way. As part of the dramatization, Harpur would convulse, stagger, fall, get up somehow, then collapse again and finally, as if hit first in the face and secondly in the chest by successive, excellently delivered bullets from the upstairs. He would dread to tumble before that, though, by tripping over rubble and dumped litter. Following nightmares, Harpur had a long-time horror of lying among reeking, torn black plastic rubbish bags like some giant maggot in its chomping element. And up till now in real, waking life he'd been able to avoid that. If he saw a full, mysteriously bulging black plastic bag in the street, possibly fallen from a cleansing lorry, he would skirt it, but with no lapse into trembling or hysteria.

Although some light came from an adjoining street and a half moon, it was not much. Harpur stepped carefully. This would be pretty well exactly the way Tom Parry came on the night he got it: Thomas Derek Parry being his Larkspur undercover label. His true name, when home in Wilton Road, Carnation, was Detective Sergeant Thomas Rodney Mallen, married to Iris, father of two, Steve and Laura. And the funeral had been for Tom Mallen, of course, married, father of two. As Tom Parry, he'd managed to infiltrate the main and massive Leo P. Young Larkspur drugs firm, establishing himself as a valuable new recruit: a huge achievement, by any reckoning, and glorious if it had lasted. Disastrously, though, while Tom Mallen was still, on the face of it, totally and effectively Tom Parry, people at the top of the L.P. Young company had discovered his actual name and background: the Carnation detective sergeant; married to Iris; father of two, Steve and Laura; seconded, as someone not likely to be recognized in Larkspur, for undercover duties monitoring Leo Young's business; the aim eventual charges and elimination of the firm.

Consequently, as Tom Parry he had been tricked on to the building site that night and, as Detective Sergeant Thomas Rodney Mallen, executed with two 9mm rounds from a marksman cop in a potentially prestige setting, one or more of the bathrooms possibly *en suite*.

Undercover people tended to keep their first name, as long as this wasn't something freakish like Treasure or Breastfed. They'd had decades of automatically responding to it when called, so to stick with this handle made the identity-switch a fraction easier. Fractions mattered. 'Tom' was commonplace enough to suit a cop or a gangster. Tom, aka Tom.

Harpur felt thankful the funeral took place months before Iles and he had any involvement with Larkspur. Iles could get very emotional, violent and boomingly claptrapish at funerals, sometimes hijacking the proceedings from a vicar or minister by force, scrapping religiously for the pulpit like an example in miniature of all holy wars, yelling and blubbing his complex personal views, covering quite a range. The Assistant Chief would have been very upset and therefore dangerously bolshy at the service for Mallen. Iles disapproved absolutely of all undercover work because it brought terrible risks, and he would regard the death of Mallen as a flagrantly tragic and predictable instance. The ACC had once put an undercover officer into a gang, where he was rumbled and garrotted. Although some believed Iles subsequently garrotted the garrotters, he never properly recovered from the loss of his man.[2]

Harpur regarded such enslavement to one past incident, however grave, as sentimental and close to nonsensical. There would always be occasions when undercover was last-resort necessary. Iles refused to acknowledge that. Part of his splendid, tearaway brain had been shut down, like some mothballed frigate: a sloppy, posturing indulgence, Harpur thought, but would never say – or would never say to Iles, at least: garrotting was a painful death.

An inspired piece of plotting had been used for the wipe-out of police spy, Parry/Mallen, the object to make it seem Tom was shot in a routine pushers' dispute, and so make unnecessary any deeper speculation about the death. Drug dealers did regularly slaughter one another in the pressing interests of commerce. It came out after the murder that Tom had been conned into believing he was on an armed stalking trip with three fellow members of the Leo Young company, their supposed job to kill another member, Justin Scray, suspected to have turned rogue. The unforgiving word was that he secretly, persistently, operated his own profitable, self-contained business on the side, by siphoning off the best punters for himself – 'best' meaning hooked on the highest-grade substance, and easily able to pay for it from their stout profits, salaries and/or bonuses as stockbrokers, hospital managers, hair dressers, undertakers, cosmetic surgeons, plumbers, airline pilots, bankers, chiropodists, media chiefs, bishops, soccer stars, dentists. He apparently had a firm inside the firm, a classic drugs trade heist. Scray was still around, but apparently no longer maverick, his renegade outfit finished, and accepted back into the main outfit by Leo.

This imagined mission against Scray must have caused Tom sharp conscience worries. After all, he was still a cop, although seemingly something deeply different, and couldn't be party to a killing, not even to keep his disguise intact. Some criminality might be necessary and acceptable to give him cred, but not murder. He needn't have fretted about fine moral points, though. In fact, *he* had been the target, the quarry, without knowing it. As part of the concocted

[2] See *Halo Parade*

phoney trawl for Scray, the two-timing dealer, Parry was asked to take a course across this building site, where the gun waited behind what might one day be a glazed upstairs window on a comely housing estate. The south-facing house was famous and should have a special macabre interest when it came to selling. Television and newspapers had shown pictures of it during the trial.

Harpur, approaching the death spot now in the re-run – or, actually, re-walk – wondered whether, as Tom Parry began gingerly to negotiate this piece of supremely dodgy ground, he'd suddenly noticed how wide open he was here, and how convenient the place would be for anyone wanting to get shot of him. Yes, get *shot*. Undercover people lived non-stop with the fear of detection. They had to act relaxed while being anything but. Training told them to watch constantly for signs that their cover no longer covered. Did Tom ask himself whether being ordered by the firm's management to take a route through this secluded, half-dark slice of landscape might be one of those chill signs?

If he did ask himself, he got the wrong answer, and he hadn't behaved as the training said an undercover officer must behave in such circumstances: chuck the assignment at once – AT ONCE – and get out fast and back to base; put the undercover identity into meltdown. Instead, Tom had continued on this path. Did he tell himself he had no clinching evidence his game was known, and therefore to run would be panicky, unprofessional, yellow? Or had he reasoned that the spy role brought endless risk, anyway, so a little extra could be tolerated; *had* to be tolerated? Why get in a tizz about building works? Dim, Tom. You were in denial, Tom. The compulsion should have been to get home OK to your family and job in Carnation – detective sergeant, married, father of two – not to present yourself here as a blown, dumbo sacrifice.

Did he glance up worriedly at the window spaces of these would-be houses, trying to spot stealthy human movement or the glint of a weapon in the poor light? Harpur, on his choreographed version of the kill now, knew Iles lurked, with two fingers primed ready to simulate a handgun, and at which loophole-window. Harpur didn't gaze there, though. Wouldn't that have smashed the realism of the performance by giving Harpur as Parry/Mallen too much knowledge of the attack and where it must come from? Ambushes surprised their victims or they didn't rate as ambushes. And, for this present mimicking of the occasion, Harpur wasn't Harpur but Tom Parry, who'd actually been Tom Mallen. Harpur needed to stay in character while starring in this playlet, that character being Tom Parry, *en* sad *route* to becoming Tom Mallen; dead Tom Mallen. Iles had said he would give two popping sounds, to suggest a silenced piece as Harpur reached the right patch of un-made-up road in front of the house, embryo 14 Davant Road. Harpur listened.

The construction area had been fenced off when work was suspended as the economy dwindled, and 'Keep Out' notices posted. Naturally, these were treated as an invitation *not* to keep out, and the fencing had been vandalized. There were gaps – probably more gaps now than when Tom began his recommended attempt to cross; or than when Iles and Harpur first visited on their earlier Larkspur mission. The territory offered a short-cut from the Rinton shopping mall to Guild Square. Trial evidence had shown that Tom got Rinton as his area of search for Scray, but was summoned by mobile phone to the Square, where there'd supposedly been a sighting. But the only sighting that mattered was of Parry/Mallen displayed as an offering on the spooked Elms estate.

Harpur used one of the gaps now and made for the chosen house. It had originally been boarded up, but the vandals or firewood seekers had jemmied off most of this protection.

And, smack on cue, Harpur heard a muted, high-point explosion from Iles's mouth. It was not like real gunfire, but a theatrical version of real gunfire. The Assistant Chief made his skilfully formed, lippy popping sound and, after it, the whistle of a speeding bullet. The pop wasn't really loud enough for even the most efficiently silenced pistol, and bullets over such a short distance didn't whistle. But the general effect suggested menace, clear purpose and team hate and fear of a fink. These were what counted.

Harpur thanked God his ears usually functioned OK. If he'd failed to get into death mode – into a fold-down-into-the-mud mode – when Iles fired his cod rounds the ACC might assume Harpur found the whole exercise juvenile or even insane, and meant in his disrespectful, malicious way to fuck it up at the key denouement moment. Harpur could imagine the ACC muttering to himself, 'Col won't croak, the mean, selfish sod.' Suppose Harpur didn't respond as though hit, the Assistant Chief would have been sending his brilliantly fashioned fake bullets of good-grade compressed air out into nowhere. Dispiriting. Humiliating. To wait crouched and vigilant in that cold, token bedroom and then, eventually, get pissed about by

Harpur would really antagonize Iles and lead to very rough reprisals. Cooperative work on the current Larkspur investigation together into police racketeering might become more or less impossible.

Luckily, Harpur had brought two suits. The one he wore now would have to go to the cleaners after he tumbled to the filthy ground, theoretically struck twice by the 9mm Magnum lead. The first hit was scheduled for Harpur's face around the nose area, carrying through into the mouth and throat, probably fatal. He had never actually been hit in the face by a bullet of any calibre, so didn't know in full from experience how the victim would react in those moments before sinking. Would he lift a hand to check whether the layout of his features was still as it had been, sort of inventorying? Harpur couldn't be certain on this, but he did put his right up towards his nose, as a means of indicating to Iles in the property via an unspoken signal that he knew perfectly the script for this evening's interlude, loved it to bits, and would unswervingly follow it – face/head first, then chest. To butter the ACC occasionally seemed only humane because his mother was no longer around to extol and encourage him with comments. Harpur considered it strange that, despite her loyalty, Iles didn't like her.

Harpur keeled and went down, stood again and heard from above another terrific pop and whistle. This would be the later shot, ripping into his upper body before he reached the ground on a second visit, the old one-two. He lowered himself slowly, not a headlong plunge to the ground, which Iles might have preferred for dramatic impact, but which could have caused Harpur actual injury. Brick and wood fragments lay part-buried in the soil, liable to give an unpleasant jab. Harpur lay without movement for a couple of seconds on his stomach. He kept his eyes open and could have done a thorough itemizing account of the ground's make-up near his face – the brick and wood fragments, shreds of newspaper, an expired green ink Biro, a small cluster of defiant weeds, a metal ring-pull from a drinks can, what looked like small patches of spilled cement. Harpur reckoned the word for most of it – not the weeds – would be detritus. Had Tom noticed this array? Harpur felt a kind of detritus bond with him.

Then Harpur forced himself to crawl a few metres towards the front of the house, as Tom Parry/Mallen had forced himself to crawl, leaving a blood trail in the dirt. Harpur duly re-collapsed before he reached it though, as Tom had re-collapsed. Harpur tried to guess what Tom thought about as he lay there helpless and dying – if he *could* still think. Would he have gone over in his mind how he'd behaved and spoken lately, striving to spot what gave him away? But would there be any point to that? It had happened, and here was the plain, catastrophic result. Would he have spotted the larger aspect – the symbolism diagnosed by Iles?

Harpur did not budge again until Iles descended and came to stand over him. The ACC wore fine, Bowpark-Linden black lace-ups today. His trousers were long in the leg and swaddled the shoes generously. Harpur could examine them from his level, as he had examined the weeds and ring-pull and so on. 'I wept to see life leaving you, Harpur; actually, copiously, unstintingly, audibly wept,' Iles said sweetly down at him.

'I didn't hear that, sir, only the bullets.' No tears dropped on Harpur's skin from Iles, but possibly on to his clothes.

'Only the bullets. Only the bullets,' the ACC said. 'Oh, my God! Is life nothing but the pathfinder to death, Col?' His voice keened. He almost went sobwards.

Harpur didn't have an answer to the query and hoped it was the sort that contained its own reply, in this case, 'Perhaps.' 'You can stand now, Col,' Iles said. But, obviously afraid he might get soiled, Iles didn't offer his hand to give Harpur a tug up. The ACC had on a beautifully tailored light grey overcoat that would mark. Harpur could see his shoes and lower trouser legs were already streaked. He must have felt glad of the coat while he waited in the unheated room to do the vengeance chore. 'Others use this short cut, Harpur. We don't want to draw attention – you lying there like rat-arsed.'

Harpur stood. 'Did we learn anything new, sir?'

'Patience, Col. This is the kind of experience that must be mulled over and weighed. No rush into views and judgements. Did you get to feel you knew him? Did you sense your pulse gradually, irrecoverably subside? Yet you uttered no cry for help or of pain. Such courage, Col.'

'It was quality gunmanship, sir,' Harpur replied. 'Economical. No splattering, frenzied automatic barrage, just the two expertly slotted single shots.'

'Well, yes,' Iles said.

'Those bullets definitely had my names on – Parry, Mallen, Carnation, Harpur,' Harpur said. 'Each with the four, not split two and two.'

'You carrying anything, Col?' Iles replied.

'For this kind of operation, no.'

'Which?'

'Turning over another force. The armoury would refuse to issue, most probably. Protocol's involved – carrying an undeclared firearm on to someone else's ground.'

'Fuck protocol, Col.'

'Yes, sir, but—'

'Protocol, Col, is there to serve us, not mess us about.'

'But now and then we have to abide by—'

'Protocol, Col, is for flunkies and baggage men. You mean you couldn't browbeat that twerp in the armoury to issue, regardless of protocol, Col? Wallace Vayntor – an inspector?'

'*You* got something, sir?' Harpur replied.

Iles shrugged, meaning, Harpur knew, 'Of course I fucking did, Col.' The Assistant Chief undid the buttons of his overcoat, reached in and fiddled about under his left arm. Soon, he produced a holster with shoulder harness and an automatic in the pouch. 'It's a Walther, not a Browning, but will have to do,' Iles said. 'Strap it on, Harpur. We have to match Tom, or almost. We'll resume after the interval.'

'Resume?'

'You're not one to leave things incomplete, are you, Harpur? Thoroughness is your thing, isn't it? Not necessarily right, but thorough.'

'Incomplete in which sense, sir?'

'Culmination,' Iles said.

'"Culmination" in which sense?'

'Discovery, and then what followed,' Iles said.

'A couple short-cutting from the Ritson mall came across the body lying there.'

'Exactly, Col.'

'By that time, he was dead.'

'Or dying,' Iles replied. 'These were good, brave people.'

'Yes.'

'I'll do both voices,' Iles said.

'"Both voices" in which sense, sir?'

'I'll have to improvise their words as they approach the body on the ground, namely you as Parry/Mallen. What they said to each other didn't come out at the trial, did it? Not relevant, Harpur. Simply, the court wanted to hear how the officer was found – prone, hands and arms hidden beneath himself as if he'd been crawling and collapsed. Trousers knee-muddied, also suggesting a crawl, as did the blood track, in places a metre wide, moonshine on it, hence observable even in the dark.'

'A useless crawl,' Harpur said.

'In many ways a perverse crawl, Col. More symbolism here? I think so.'

'In which respect, sir?'

'Oh, yes, emphatic symbolism.'

'This is the thing with people of your staff rank, sir. They see beyond.'

'Beyond what?'

'The immediate.'

Iles expounded patiently, mentor flavour. 'We have to ask how the immediate came to *be* the immediate, Col. What is its genesis? What was it pre-immediate? This is our concern.'

'True.'

'Our shot sergeant, he regards a house – even an unfinished house – as a place of safety, a place of security and shelter. That's an instinct with most of us. Home – it's our castle. Walls, a roof, doors, cat litter, locks. But here, on that night, the house he longed to reach can offer only the opposite of all those comforting qualities. It is no place of safety, it's a sniper's eyrie. It is no place of security but one retailing deep danger. It is no place of shelter, except for a brilliantly capable, murderous, handgun lad. It's not Parry/Mallen's castle, it's an enemy turret. Do we observe disintegration of our most lovingly held, property-owning values, Col? Social break down? Chaos is come again, Harpur?'

'You produce some grand phrases, sir, despite standing out here in the symbolic, yet real, mud.'

'So, yes, the crawl is in the full meaning of the term, absurd. It is an attempt at escape but an attempt that makes escape less likely, shortening the distance, should the killer fire again. But, of course, it is also an inspiring, stirring glimpse of the dogged, unquenchable human spirit. He might tell himself that to crawl, to move at all, signified life. He could still, somehow, get his body to do it. This is the final struggle, a doomed, hopeless struggle, but a positive, thumbs-up struggle, against annihilation, Col. In his fading mind he might hear a voice cry out, "Do not go gentle into that good night", or "I was ever a fighter, so one fight more, the best and the last."'

'One he can't win.'

'When you're down there on the muck again, Col, post-crawl, post-more-or-less-everything bar snuffdom, I'd like you to have that kind of thought in place, just the same. Nobleness in defeat.'

'"On the muck again"?'

'What I meant about not leaving things unfinished,' Iles replied. 'The intervention of this couple brings a new, special element to the narrative. We have to include them and their reactions in our present recapping treatment, haven't we? I believe you'll accept, Col, that the dialogue I manufacture for them will be credible, likely, and as near to the actual as we can get. One of my flairs, Col, is quickly to know people through and through and, therefore, how they will articulate.'

'Did your mother mention that as remarkable in you, sir, at all?'

'Empathy, even though I haven't yet met the couple,' Iles replied. 'I can deduce from their actions what is their essence, Col. This is why I feel competent to do both their voices as they enter inadvertently and unbidden upon this crisis with their innocent mall carrier bags at five pence a go.'

'You'll display a remarkable range of mouth-lips expressions tonight, sir. First the bullets, then a two-sided conversation.'

'We know, don't we, that Tom was carrying a fully loaded Browning? The armament would have given the couple big worry, wouldn't it? Their testimony described the shock. They see someone laid out, inert, and think, maybe a drunk – a wino who squats in one of the to-be properties and hasn't quite made it back after a usual heavy night. Or maybe a stroke/heart attack for someone crossing the site. In their civically responsible way they come to the body and turn him over on to his back, maybe to give kiss-of-life, possibly expecting to see replenishment booze cans under the body.

'However, at this stage they get a view of his demolished face, and can tell this isn't just a piss artist or someone sick. The wound, blood and fragmentations would indicate the passage of high-velocity metal from close range. This is the first very unpleasant revelation. Then, they become conscious of the bulge near his armpit. They'd guess at once it was no abscess or roving goitre. They find he's tooled up. It confirms they'd farcically misread the situation earlier. They suspect – more than suspect – they understand they're into something very fucking hazardous and intemperate, Col. They'd think gang war, wouldn't they? Yes. They said so at the trial.

'Of course, they'd have no notion that he might be cop. They assumed a turf battle. Helping someone who took part in it could bring peril. But it doesn't stop them trying to assist him. These were fine people, Col. Kindly and responsible folk. I'm going to compose their dialogue as they see and then approach the body. Could you get down again, Harpur, and I'll as if discover you there – or, rather, *we'll* as if discover you there. We'll put our purchases from the Ritson on the ground and do what we can for you, admittedly not much. No alternative to my supplying both voices, is there, the man's and the woman's? It would ruin verisimilitude if you spoke one of the couple's words from the ground, taking two parts yourself – Tom and a shopper. They'd be discussing you as someone flat on the soil, but you'd be piping up as if you were one of them and standing, your actual voice coming, though, from below. Just lie there, destroyed, anonymous, would you, Col, please?'

THREE

Harpur went to ground again and got another deeply intimate view of the can ring-pull, thrive-anywhere weeds, and so on. He lifted his eyes, though, and watched the ACC walk off the site – walk off the site as simply Desmond Iles, an Assistant Chief, married to Sarah, father of one – and then spin around and start to come back, now representing within his creative self the two shoppers who'd found Parry/Mallen's body on that bad night. He picked his way out and then in once more over a flattened section of fence.

On his return he walked with a different rhythm from that familiar cheetah-like, easy, muscular stride, a conqueror's amble. Now, he held both arms stiff down against his coat, as though carrying bagged purchases from the Ritson mall shops, most probably food for the week, as well as other domestic items such as bleach, bog paper and shampoo. These imaginary loads affected his balance a little – *their* balance a little – when negotiating the wrecked fence and he took it gingerly, on the couple's behalf. If he fell it would be three people falling, a tripartite disaster. Harpur thought he could see a tolerant, wryish smile on the ACC's features, saying that, if you took forbidden short-cuts over uncleared ground, you'd better expect snags. Perhaps it also said that, if you took forbidden short-cuts over uncleared ground, you'd better expect to come across a deceased – a violently deceased, for instance – Col Harpur prone as Parry/Mallen.

Once on the site again, Iles looked ahead for most of the time, sorting out a safe route for the three of them – that is, Iles himself, plus the two Ritson customers, now played by the Assistant Chief in this evening performance of his own impromptu production. Flair? The word was made for him. Occasionally, he turned his head slightly left, to indicate a conversation with his – or her – partner. Then, after a few steps like that, he gazed forward again, navigating, and in a while angled his head slightly right. This would be the partner replying, of course.

They seemed to have quite a lively, talky-talky relationship, Harpur thought. Speech wasn't backed up by vigorous gesturing, however, because of the goods they both carried, or would have carried if they were real and present there, on site, instead of just Iles acting as them both. They *had* been real and present and very involved there, on site, during that murder night, and this was what mattered to Iles, as he devotedly dummied for both. Harpur could see his lips moving at these moments, but the distance was too great as yet to eavesdrop, or even to know which sex Iles might be in at a particular point, the man or the woman shopper. Gender-switches wouldn't bother Iles. He'd had some practice lately feminizing his voice when he lampooned Maud for supposedly chatting up Harpur. Again, flair – he embodied the word.

Occasionally, the man, or woman – whichever Iles might be at the moment – would laugh at something supposedly said between them. This was a louder sound, one that Harpur *could* pick up where he lay shot dead. Cheerfulness would be credible for the couple at these early moments, before they spotted the body. Possibly they'd had a successful session at the Ritson shops, taking advantage of special offers and discounts, stocking up very efficiently, negating inflation. It seemed to Harpur that most of the laughs – high-toned, bubbly, tickled-pink – came from the woman. The man appeared to be an entertaining, witty fellow, not just a packhorse for mall goods.

Harpur didn't understand where Iles had got this notion from. The court transcript showed both shoppers answering lawyers' questions about discovery of Parry/Mallen in a plain, forthright way. The laughter might be Iles's invention, to give them both some individuality, the he-figure a comedian, the she with a ready sense of humour. This was one-man theatre – one man playing two. Characterization counted. Harpur could imagine the kind of dating ad that brought these two together: 'Man with good sense of humour (jokesmith) would like to meet woman with good sense of humour (enthusiastic guffawer).' He wondered whether Iles's style of acting would be what was known in the theatre and Hollywood as The Method. Iles's Method was to nab both shoppers' parts for himself and cast Harpur as a carcass. This, too, was flair of a kind – the 'fuck you, Harpur' kind.

About 40 metres away from Harpur, Iles came to a gradual stop, as if startled, intrigued, by something off to his left ahead. He, or she, pointed at Harpur, heaped unmoving on the soil, as neatly targeted Parry/Mallen. Their chosen route would not have taken them to the exact place: again, too obvious and simple – unrealistic. They'd have to divert for a proper close-up. Iles did and began to approach. He came near enough now for Harpur to make out what was said. 'Someone there, Gerald. Look. It's not just dumped old clothes as I thought at first. Someone,' Iles stated, in his tense, emphatic she-voice. 'A man, sort of hunched. Injured? Ill? A tramp?'

Iles morphed into a man: 'Watch your step, Jane.'

'Something very wrong,' Iles-Jane said. 'I feel it.'

'Pissed out of his mind?' Gerald asked. Iles put plenty of male harshness and extreme non-empathy into his words for this. Gerald thought drunks were dross, anyone could tell that. He believed in orderly, probably routine, weekly shopping trips to the Ritson, part of a decently regular life, even if it did take in a bit of trespassing. 'Ill-met by fucking moonlight, and not much of it,' he said in more of the clangy Gerald voice. Harpur reckoned some of that must be quotation, which could help extend Gerald's personality further: he knew books and that kind of carry-on.

'Whether or not, we must try to help,' Jane told him.

Harpur shut his eyes, scared it would put Iles off if he felt he and his figment duo were being watched by a figment corpse, though an actual body. The suck-sound of the ACC's Bowpark-Linden black lace-ups on mud came very near again. It brought class to this dump.

'There's a blood trail, as if he crawled,' Jane said. 'More blood than from a simple fall, surely. And his clothes, so filthy.'

'That suit – bad enough when it was clean. A charity shop reject, I'd guess. Or joke garb for a clown. Is there a circus around? I'd be ashamed to lie here in a suit like that, dead or alive. It would put a blight on the housing, if it weren't already blighted.'

'The poor dear,' Jane replied. Iles gave her a tenderness missing in Gerald – avoided, even despised, by Gerald.

'We should phone for an ambulance,' he said.

'Perhaps in a moment,' Jane said. 'We must find what is the damage. I'll try for a pulse, shall I?'

As far as Harpur could remember, some of these exchanges were fairly accurately taken by Iles from their trial evidence. Iles would read something once and, if he thought it important, remembered it verbatim; though when the verbatim didn't suit him he'd jiggle it, of course.

'To me he looks a goner,' Gerald replied.

Harpur felt Iles's hand on his wrist, a tender, lingering, ladylike, hope-shorn pressure. 'I don't think there's anything,' Jane said sadly. 'Let's turn him over so we can see what's what.'

'Should we?' Gerald replied. 'Interference? This is a job for the paramedics. We don't know what we're letting ourselves in for.' Cagey Gerald, full of street savvy?

'It will be all right,' Jane said – a chancer, driven by human feeling and curiosity? Iles's acting could run the gamut. Move over, the shade of Alec Guinness.

'Wait, I'll put the bags on the ground,' Gerald said.

'Carefully. Remember the eggs,' Jane said. Iles would be proud of chucking in a background detail like that. It gave the scene workaday depth and authenticity. Fantasy eggs could get fantasy cracked and make a fantasy mess in the fantasy bag and so be unavailable for fantasy omelettes.

Harpur opened one eye for a second and saw Iles as if setting down the shopping so as to free his hands and arms. After a minute, he reached under Harpur and took a hold on the right lapel and surrounding material of his suit, regardless now of the mud. Gerald wouldn't be fussy: Gerald wasn't Iles, although, for the moment, Iles was Gerald. The narrative needed this flipping over of the body. It had actually happened on the night. Iles pulled with some gentleness but firmly and rolled Harpur on to his back. His hair as well as his clothes would need sprucing. Harpur had reclosed his eye. 'My God, what's happened to his face, Jane?' Gerald said, the horror intonation brilliant, of Gielgud standard. 'A ruin. This is all very strange, possibly very dangerous.'

It felt as though Jane came nearer and looked over Gerald's shoulder at Tom stretched out. If only Iles could have in fact been two people they'd have fallen into this configuration now. 'Shot?' she said, shrewdly.

'At least twice – nose area and chest. See?'

Harpur couldn't help them with any actuality for this, but kept his face blank.

'Feel for a heartbeat, Gerry,' Jane said. 'Sometimes the pulse is hard to read.'

'I tell you he's finished, Jane.'

'Please, just try once more.'

Iles's hand went *under* the lapel this time and rested on Harpur's chest. 'Nothing,' he said. 'Utterly still – stilled. But, hello. *Hello!* What's this?'

'What?' Jane said.

'Things get worse,' Gerald said. Iles unbuttoned the shoulder holster he'd given Harpur, took the Walther from under Harpur's jacket and must have held it out as if for examination by Jane, following the transcript.

'Heavens! Tooled up?' she cried. This was true amazement, almost.

'A Browning,' Gerald said. 'We use them in the Territorials. Excellent stopping power.'

'But why?' Jane said.

'Why what?'

'Why should he have a gun on him?' Jane said.

'Part of his normal gear, I expect, like shoes or a watch. He'll be carrying no ID, though. I told you, love – we're caught up in something very dubious. It's an innocent bystander situation,' Gerald said. Harpur opened an eye again. Iles was standing near, chatting very naturally into darkness as the two.

'What? You think a turf war – something like that?' Jane said.

'Something exactly like that,' Gerald said.

'But why here on such a dud bit of ground?'

'He might have been duped into choosing this route,' Gerald said. 'It's the chosen killing field. Ideal for that.'

'Duped how?'

'I don't really know, Jane. Set up by apparent friends? Some internal dispute in the firm? These people don't fool about. Or might he be a cop?'

'A cop?'

'Undercover.'

'But exposed?'

'They don't forgive what they see as treachery,' Gerald said.

'My God!'

'More important now, though, is the matter of where did the shots come from?' Gerald replied. 'The upstairs of one of the houses? We might be vulnerable here ourselves. Let's get clear and call emergency services. We've done our bit.'

'We can't leave him, Gerald.' Love of fellow humankind, regardless, was in her tone, possibly difficult for Iles to catch.

'We can't do anything for him,' Gerald replied. Male – practical, alert to hazard, icily logical.

'The BBC have been showing a public information film on how to help if someone has a heart attack,' Jane said. 'It's not kiss of life, but a hard pumping massage of his upper body. Useful here?'

'His chest's a mess,' Gerald said, 'and it's no heart-attack.'

'Just the same,' Jane said.

'All right, all right.' In fact, as Harpur recalled the trial transcript, the real Gerald *had* tried kiss of life on Mallen. Iles obviously couldn't face lips-to-lips with Harpur, and Harpur felt immeasurably grateful. Iles didn't have a monopoly on squeamishness. In any case, Harpur discovered that Iles wanted his lips free so he could talk abuse.

Harpur sensed Iles get down near him. He began to hammer on Harpur's chest. If someone else were crossing the site and saw them they might think a fight or a mugging. Iles must have put the gun away in his pocket. For a while, Harpur lay as if far-gone but possibly savable. He had the impression, though, that Iles wasn't following the BBC resuscitation method absolutely. The hands should be out flat on the victim's chest, surely, to provide a good area of pressure. Iles seemed to be using his fists and was giving short-arm jab punches rather than forceful massage: an attack, not a therapy. Harpur felt something, some *things*, damp and glutinous fall one-by-one in a small shower on to his face.

'Any response?' Iles asked in the Jane voice, but slightly winded from effort.

'Nothing yet,' Gerald said.

'Keep trying,' Jane replied.

'Yes,' Gerald said. The punching grew heavier, maybe of rib-cracking intent. Yes, it did make Iles breathless, and Harpur, as well, but Iles had big reserves of hate, malice and cuckoldry-resentment to keep him going OK. He was Des Iles now, not Gerald, and the blows were Des-Ilesian, unforgiving and deft. He stood for a few seconds so he could kick Harpur twice in the balls with the expensive black lace-ups. That, too, differed from the original Gerald's behaviour. Then Iles lowered himself and lay close again. The ACC grunted contentedly: 'Got you, you immoral, amoral, scruffy, smirking, lecherous sod, Harpur. Gotcha! I could see you off here – you realize that, do you? *Crime passionel*, recognized as just cause by the law. Terminate you. Why fucking not? No witnesses.'

'What about Jane?' Harpur replied. The punching abated for conversation.

'Who?'

'One of the shoppers – Jane and Gerald.'

'What the hell are you talking about?'

'Jane's watching *She's* a witness.'

'*I'm* Jane – *and* Gerald, you prat.'

'*You,* sir?'

'Of course.'

'You in person?'

'What's that mean?'

'You personally, sir, are Gerald?'

'Certainly. *And* Jane.'

'Both?'

'As agreed.'

'Agreed with *them*?'

'Agreed between *us*,' Iles replied.

'Which us?'

'Us.'

'You and me, sir?'

'Obviously, you and me. Have you gone nuts, Harpur? This is a performance.'

'Harpur? No, I'm Parry/Mallen, and dead.'

'Soon, yes,' Iles replied. He let his hands play on and around Harpur's neck, a possible garrotter's hands, governed by a possible garrotter's mind. He could probably amend to a simple throttle. 'Did you think when you were banging my wife on the quiet in fourth-rate rooming joints, under evergreen hedgerows, in marly fields, on river banks, in cars – including police vehicles – and, most probably, my own bed, that I'd get a lovely, heaven-sent opportunity to deal with you like this? Of course you fucking didn't, Col. You were driven by disgusting, traitorous, uncontrolled, uncontrollable fleshly compulsion. You had no time or inclination for thoughts about me, your superior officer and, in some senses, friend. "Think dick" was your mantra, which meant don't think at all, just have it away.'

Harpur realized that the droplets hitting his face were lip-foam from the ACC, often accessories to his frantic but well-structured rage episodes about Harpur and Iles's wife. 'Did you plan this, sir, just as it was planned to get Tom Parry/Mallen out here on a cooked-up mission? God, I've lost track of what's thesp and what's real, what's flashback and what's now. Have you, too, sir? If you kill me they'll get you from the type of construction site mud on your coat. The forensic people are good at that these days. Headline: "Did top cop murder love-rat pal in revenge spasm?" We're visible from the street and by anyone using the site.'

'Do I care? I'll have put things right, restored my pride in being who I am and was, Col – husband, father, law-officer of the Queen, guest at city hall functions, wholly unbribable rugby ref always up with the play.'

'*And* you're the two shoppers on their way home from Ritson. Very, very few would dispute your perpetual right to such pride in yourself, sir,' Harpur said.

'Which very, very fucking few, Harpur?'

'Well, never your mother among the very, very few, we can be sure of that,' Harpur said, with a warm chuckle of congratulation.

'Leave my sodding mother out of it,' the Assistant Chief replied. 'This wasteland is no place for someone's mother.'

'Sorry, sir. But you sometimes bring her into things.'

'I'm entitled to bring her into things. That's what being a son means. But not here where the dead properties give no shelter.'

'*I* don't do it.'

'What?'

'Bring my mother in,' Harpur said.

'I don't blame you.'

'Why, sir?'

'I don't. That's all,' Iles said.

'Thank you, sir.'

'I shouldn't think she'd want to be associated with you. Even mothers have to show some taste and discrimination.'

'Mothers have a lot to do – stair carpets to Hoover, measuring up for new curtains, feeding the goldfish. That kind of thing.'

'True,' Iles replied.

Harpur felt safer when they talked, even if it was mainly family and domestic topics. The conversation seemed to preserve a degree of normality, a tiny degree, but enough to give Harpur time to think of how to neutralize Iles quickly – how to bring him back to rational behaviour. No question, the ACC *could* manage rational behaviour for quite long, though unpredictable spells. Frequently Harpur had seen Iles more or less mentally normal, even for hours. Harpur wished he still had the Walther/Browning. Failing that, though, he moved his right palm in a sensitive, arcing sweep over the ground near him. He had come to think of it as *his* terrain. The Harpur writ ran here uncontested. These objects owed him dirty fealty.

His questing fingers homed in on the old, topless Biro, once able to write green. Almost certainly it could then have done something very lively and even vivid-looking on good white paper. Green was life – for a while. It said 'Go' at traffic lights. It showed in spring-time's new shoots. There was a Green Party, concerned with looking after the environment and, therefore, the health of the planet and its future. But Iles would most likely locate different symbolism in that green Biro – its decline into a cast-off, of no more use than the ring-pull from the can without the can. Iles tended to see many aspects of life as in decline. This pen could sum it up, not through what it wrote – nothing now – but merely through *being* a pen, a defunct pen, lying undegradable in soil that one day might be a road. Not yet, though.

But Harpur, still capable of thought despite the body blows and throat threat, would give the Biro a job, a positive job, not so much symbolic as plain, up-to-the-minute, potentially life-saving, and also thuggish. He took a good grip on it. Iles's hands went prospecting around Harpur's neck once more and felt increasingly committed and tempted. Harpur reached up and rammed the nicely pointed former writing end of the pen hard into the Assistant Chief's left cheek just below the eye, jolting against bone, as was only to be expected, given the skull's construction.

The Biro seemed to stay OK, didn't snap off leaving a section

poking out of Iles like a tyre valve, although not made for this kind
of work. Iles gasped. It might be a reaction to sudden bad pain from
getting roughly pierced, or hot admiration for Harpur's smart
improvising with local rubbish. The military said time spent on
reconnaissance was never wasted, and it had been close reconnaissance
of that square metre or so in front of the house that led Harpur to
recruit the Biro now, and bring it into bonny, offensive-defensive play.

Harpur pulled it out, causing a gurgling sound he was not keen
on, and didn't repeat the move as yet. The throat danger had passed,
at least temporarily: Iles needed one hand to get up to the side of
his face and investigate the wound. Harpur wanted the ACC to
realize there were his eyes themselves to be dug into, as well as
plenty of room in that cheek or the other, for more and maybe
deeper inserts, if he didn't get back to sanity. And get back also to
being the true Gerald and Jane of tonight's story, not his het-up,
betrayed self. He had a duty to the shoppers, a duty he'd formulated
himself. This early puncture of the ACC's chops was like the bomb
on Hiroshima he'd mentioned. It promised more and worse from
the same source if he didn't turn sensible: someone his mother
would have been willing to acknowledge as her son.

As well as the wrath froth, blood now also trickled on to Harpur's
skin and clothes from the nibbed nook in Iles's flesh. The blood
felt warmer and more runny. If the Biro had still contained liquid
ink, and some got released into the wound, Harpur thought there
would have been an interesting red and green mix in the outflow,
recalling colour use in some David Hockney exhibition pictures
recently featured on TV. The shaft of the Biro had green traces, but
long ago dried out.

Harpur's unusual role for the Biro now did cause him some worry.
Pens were certainly not made for this. It would be mad for Biro
manufacturers to advertise such secondary use in an emergency, say
when getting strangled. Lately, he'd begun to have a sort of
expanding respect for words and writing. He'd picked up that attitude
from his daughters. They did a lot of reading – actual traditional
books, as well as Kindle. They could get transfixed. Their mother
had been the same. Megan was dead now, murdered in the station
car park, off the last train one night,[3] but her influence might still
reach the children. Harpur had disliked Megan's bookishness – used

[3] See *Roses, Roses*

to feel excluded. But he'd come to recognize it must be a kind of worthwhile art to put ideas down on a page that people would want to read – not just instructions and manuals, but tales and descriptions of scenes and so on.

As a result, it troubled him to be adapting something intended to spell out stuff pleasantly via words and paragraphs etcetera – such as the Biro – yes, adapting it into a savage little combat item that could give the ACC a very timely, fuck-you-Iles spearing, possibly turning septic, and in quite a noticeable spot on his frontage. Iles liked to think of himself as refined-looking, polished and vigorous, and this would be difficult to maintain if he had a hacked-out concavity in his cheek, or possibly several. Harpur did suffer moments when he felt barbaric for changing the pen from its usual fine, communicating role into a lance-type weapon for use on a stalled building project. His daughters would be upset if they ever found out about it.

But Harpur had decided a long time ago now that to deal with Iles it was occasionally necessary to get barbaric, as answer to his own lofty, frequent, effortless barbarism. The Assistant Chief would understand this – consider it absolutely normal, in fact, required. Iles despised non-resistance. Perhaps his mother had said something to him about it as he grew up: 'Matador, bull, Desy. Likewise, you nobly honour your opponents.' She'd probably leave vague which of this pair – matador, bull – he was.

'Did we learn anything, sir?' Harpur asked again.

But Iles didn't answer. He seemed to grow very tense suddenly. Harpur thought, God, is this poisoned ground? Had the pen picked up some contamination over the months, years, lying here, that could kill instantly, like cyanide? 'You OK, sir? I mean, you as you, not Gerald or Jane.'

'What the fuck's this, Col?'

'What, sir?'

'Listen.'

Iles pulled back a bit to clear the way to Harpur's ears. Now, he could hear a police car siren, perhaps more than one.

'Some bugger saw what looked like a scrap or worse here and dialled nine-nine-nine,' Iles said. 'People will be sensitive about this spot after the murder.' He stood. Now, he did offer Harpur a hand and pulled him up, too. 'We disappear, Col. "There's blood upon thy face."'

'It's yours, then.'

'Don't get sentimental and possessive about that. Wipe it off.' He gave Harpur a handkerchief from his coat pocket. 'They'll come in as if from Riston. We withdraw the other way.'

'What'll we do with the shopping – leave it?'

'Stop pissing about, Col, will you?'

They ran. Harpur had some difficulty with that after the kicking.

FOUR

'Yes, as to your questions, Col, we learned something, didn't we, or half a something, anyway?' Iles said as they drove back to their hotel, Harpur at the wheel. The Assistant Chief sounded perky enough: able to distinguish between a something and half a something. A *Reader's Digest* article Harpur had come across not long ago said a person's intelligence level could be judged by his/her ability to see similarities and differences. The ACC's mental state must be OK or even OK-plus.

The Biro face incision was on the far side from Harpur and out of sight. Speaking generally, Harpur felt glad of that. Although he thought the damage had been necessary as a playful deterrent in case Iles went totally and murderously berserk from sex jealousy, he didn't want to spend much time looking at it, any more than he'd enjoyed hearing that wound lovingly try to hang on to the pen by flesh grip when Harpur pulled it out. Blood had rivuletted down the ACC's face, soaking his shirt collar and jacket lapel. He looked like a fencing slip-up – sabre fencing as a sport, not the building site, Keep Out kind of fencing. In the sport, someone on the end of a hit would cry 'touché' to acknowledge token contact from the other's foil. The delve into Iles's face by Biro went several millimetres beyond a surface touch, though. The Assistant Chief's mucked-up clothes could go with Harpur's suit to the cleaners in the morning, unless Iles objected to having his gear treated as a unit with Harpur's. He'd probably regard that as disgusting impudence, like being asked to use Harpur's comb. The front passenger seat would need some scrubbing.

'What actual *type* of thing did we learn, or half-learn, sir – its ballpark category?' Harpur asked. 'Just for clarification.'

'Fuck ballparks. That's not our lingo.'

'What actual type of thing did we learn, sir – its broad British category?' Harpur asked. 'Just for clarification.'

'I knew you'd get there eventually, Col.'

'Thank you, sir.'

'Off the beaten track, Harpur.'

'In which respect, sir?'

'Yes, off the beaten track.'

'New methods of looking at things, do you mean, sir – methods off the beaten track, so to speak? What's referred to, I gather, as "*lateral* thinking"? Escape the narrowness and clichéd response of the usual approach?'

'Off the beaten track,' Iles replied. 'This comes out of our little sojourn on the Elms Estate housing project tonight. You might ask, "Who is or was off the beaten track, and which beaten track?" That's an entirely reasonable question in the present circs, and a sign of your not by any means negligible acumen.'

'Which, sir?'

'Which what?'

'Well, circs,' Harpur said.

'These.'

'Who is or was off the beaten track, sir? I think that's an entirely reasonable question in the present circs.'

'Interesting, isn't it?'

'Which?' Harpur replied.

'Which what?'

'Which beaten track?'

'That's the heart of it, in my view,' Iles said. 'Certainly worth some consideration. You've put your finger on it, Col. I was convinced you would. People say all those things about you, but I think they're hasty.'

'Which things?'

'Malign.'

'In which respect, sir?'

'Don't let them depress you, Col. You have your positive aspects. They're not on palpable show but they're there somewhere in you. I tell these critics it's impossible and unfair to judge a man entirely by his slouch appearance and casual attention to hygiene.'

'Thank you, sir.'

So, after their little charade on Elms, flitting in and out of their

true selves, flitting in and out of their make-believe selves, alive
and dead – Harpur and Iles went next evening to call on the real
Jane and Gerald at their flat off Guild Square. It must be a weird
experience for the ACC to, as it were, hand back their identities to
this couple, Iles having been both of them less than twenty-four
hours ago in very memorable conditions, voice bang-on for each,
characters passably defined: she large-minded, bold; he cautious,
sceptical. 'But surely the case is closed,' Gerald said, smileless,
letting them in. 'The arrest, the trial, the conviction. We gave our
evidence then, dealt with cross-questioning, too. Does it drag on,
then?'

Harpur sympathized. 'And very valuable evidence. But some
tidying is still necessary,' he said.

'Tidying?' Gerald said.

'Several untouched elements,' Harpur said.

'Two very senior officers sent again from another force to do
"some tidying"?' Gerald said. 'Is it really so? Hard to understand.'

'An aftermath is like this sometimes,' Harpur replied. 'The exact
shape of an aftermath is often hard to figure. I don't know whether
you've had any experience of aftermaths, but pinning an aftermath
down is tricky sometimes.' He couldn't tell him that the Home Office
– or, at least, Maud Logan Clatworthy, star of the Home Office youth
team – no, couldn't tell him that Maud believed the conviction
reached only an edge of Larkspur's organized villainy and corruption;
was not much more than a token conviction, a fall-guy conviction.
She thought it required a serious, incisive, follow-up pry by the
original outside investigators, already knowledgeable about the area:
Iles and him. To date, the mission was based only on rumour and
loose talk. Maud possessed no hard information, and neither did he
and Iles. Maud had intuitions, though, plus, probably, that Oxbridge
first-class degree. It could give her intuitions a touch of credibility,
solidity and oomph.

'Yes, Detective Chief Superintendent Harpur has always been
one for a phrase,' Iles said. '"Some tidying" in an "aftermath". And
because it's an aftermath we might have to go over certain old
material again. A quick glance at it. Forgive us that, will you,
please?' Harpur could see both Jane and Gerald were fixated on the
Assistant Chief's face crack. Very dark bruising had gone up and
down: up to his eyelid and lower region of the forehead, and down
almost to the corner of his mouth. You'd often see women marked

like this in domestic violence courts. That comparison would probably please Iles. He liked to feel he had a link with all sorts across gender, religion, weight, class, education, medical state, race, as long as they didn't try to get objectionably close.

He said: 'Miss Matson – Jane, if I may – you declared in your trial evidence and statements earlier that you and Mr Beatty – Gerald, if I may – yes, you two were crossing the Elms building site between Ritson mall and Guild Square on the night of the killing, when you saw the body of Detective Sergeant Mallen about forty metres to your left.'

'I didn't know it was a body immediately,' she said.

'No, quite,' Iles said. 'A good moon but still fairly dark.'

'It was a shape, a heap, that's how it seemed at first.'

'You thought possibly a pile of discarded clothes,' Iles said. 'This is in the court narrative.'

'At first, yes. All sorts of litter on that site, the clothes possibly dumped as unwanted from a stolen suitcase,' Jane said.

'But then you corrected?' Iles replied.

Gerald Beatty said: 'Jane had drawn my attention to . . . to, well, something unusual over on our left. Yes, she thought just discarded clothes. I thought so, too. I joked that it might be an out-of-season Guy Fawkes.'

Iles chuckled for several seconds – no, Harpur realized it was more than several: say ten – a thorough-going, durable, entirely uncontemptuous chuckle. Iles said: 'Some jokes are all the better for avoiding too much subtlety.'

'But then she revised this,' Gerald replied, 'and said it looked like a man, sort of hunched on the ground, maybe ill, perhaps a heart attack. Possibly a vagrant. I wasn't sure, but she insisted. I suppose I felt reluctant to make the detour. We were each carrying two full carrier bags from Ritson.'

'Yes, and I expect they could put you off balance slightly,' Iles said, 'especially when negotiating around and over obstacles such as flattened lengths of fencing and so on.'

'The car was in dock,' Gerald said.

'Eggs?' Harpur asked. 'A need to be careful with the bags when you set them down.'

'And Jane had it more or less right,' Iles replied.

'Yes,' Jane said. 'I'd gone a few steps off towards whatever it was to cut the distance and could see him more clearly then.'

'But not a vagrant, of course,' Gerald said. 'A police officer, as we discovered later.'

'I expect you've been to the Elms site as part of your investigation?' Jane said.

'Well, yes, we've had a quick look around there, just to get the geography in our minds. That's basic,' Iles said.

'You'll know it's quite a big development,' she said. 'Not always easy to see accurately what's what far off.' Harpur could tell she tried to keep herself from staring at the unusual mess on the left side of Iles's face, but this was difficult. Jane's eyes would switch to it automatically for a half second, then get deliberately pulled away – then sneak back involuntarily for another short, appalled gaze, and so on. Gerald, the same, more or less. It was that kind of prominent, mysterious pit and widespread blemished vista. They'd be speculating in their heads about the cause, but would probably never think of a mock-up ribcage massage and the pre-emptive old Biro as explanation. These were fairly unusual events, not easy to imagine.

If Harpur and Iles were back on their own manor, and one of those important civic functions took place, Harpur felt sure the Assistant Chief would refuse an invitation because he looked such a deep-pecked calamity. Already, Iles detested his Adam's apple, considering it too glaringly prominent and gristle-craggy; and to have another defect in his appearance could make him very jumpy. The city treasurer, and/or director of parks and baths, shouldn't be allowed to see him like this. He'd realize they and others would be laughing in private about it, even if they didn't know the lesion was caused by a shagged-out bit of pen during a dramatization snippet on a stricken building site.

But Harpur and Iles were here now in Larkspur, not back home on Cowslip. They had easy chairs with tea and biscuits in the flat's large, very spruce living room. There were pictures, prints and photographs of animals and birds on the walls. Iles would be noting these as a guide to Jane and Gerald's tastes and characters. Iles had told Harpur several times in the past to be careful what art he displayed in his house because art told tales about the owner's psyche. 'Stick to watercolours of dinky little sailing boats on a calm, azure sea, Col,' Iles had said. 'They're so wishy-washy and slight they haven't got the strength to reveal anything but their individual triteness.'

'That Elms estate – an ugly nuisance now, really, so near the town centre,' Gerald said. 'Off-putting for visitors. And it can still be troublesome.'

'Oh?' Iles said.

'In what respect?' Harpur asked.

'I heard the police were up there again last night,' Gerald said.

'Really?' Iles replied.

'An incident?' Harpur asked.

'Possible mugging or a fight, a kicking, perhaps? Violence, anyway. Possibly not far from the area where Mallen died – Davant Road, to be, perhaps, perhaps. People can get so savage, given a chance,' Gerald said.

'Yes?' Iles replied.

'Oh, yes,' Harpur said.

'A colleague in the office was passing and watched the police activity. He didn't think the patrol found anything. The offenders had run off, alerted by the sirens. But you see what I mean,' Gerald said.

'Yes, a problem,' Iles replied.

'Last night?' Harpur asked.

'Yes,' Gerald said. 'Why? Is that significant?'

'Harpur's keen on dates, times, and suchlike,' Iles said. 'It's a sort of tic with him, a tick-tock tic.'

'Perhaps some folk are drawn there in a macabre way, knowing of the murder and, in a sense, trying to re-run the situation, repeople the scene, recapture the frightening atmosphere,' Harpur replied.

'In *which* sense would that be, Col?' Iles asked.

'Yes, in a macabre, bizarre sense,' Harpur said. He had his other suit on today. His daughters had told him never to wear it if he were with anyone he wanted to take him seriously, but he didn't have another with him.

'God, hooked on a killing! What a notion,' Gerald said. 'A sort of lunacy.'

'Right. A dark, obsessive fascination with the scene, regardless,' Harpur replied.

'Regardless of what, Col?' Iles said.

'Mud.'

'Obviously, we shouldn't have been there on that awful night, the night of the killing,' Jane said. 'But we weren't, aren't, the only

ones to use the site. A kind of unofficial set path has been made by
so many people crossing on the shortest, most direct route.'

'Ah!' Iles said. He smiled and the cheek bruising wrinkled, like
small, unadventurous waves in a murky patch of sea.

'Something, Mr Iles?' Gerald asked.

'Exactly what I want to talk about, as a matter of fact, the set
path,' Iles said. 'A beaten track?'

'Sort of, yes,' Jane said.

'And, as Gerald told us, you had to detour,' Iles said. 'You left
the beaten track because of what you'd seen, Jane?'

'Like that, yes,' she said.

'So, Harpur, you were right about the beaten track,' Iles said.

'Was I?' Harpur replied.

'Jane, Gerald, you go to him, this unknown man, and attempt
resuscitation,' Iles said.

'Gerald tried kiss of life,' Jane said. 'He's trained in first aid.'

'Of course, some authorities prefer chest massage these days,'
Iles said.

'Is that right, sir?' Harpur said.

'The BBC put out an instructional film,' Iles said. 'They had an
actor, a famous ex-footballer, demonstrate the procedure.'

'The BBC? Is that a health organization, then?' Harpur said. 'Is
the actor-footballer medically qualified? Which would you go for,
sir, if you met this kind of crisis?'

'Which what?' Iles said.

'Which emergency method?' Harpur said.

'But in vain, Gerald?' Iles replied.

'Yes,' Jane said.

'It was during this physical closeness that you found the holster
and pistol, wasn't it, Gerald?' Iles said.

'Alarming,' Jane said.

'In which respect?' Harpur said.

'We thought it indicated some kind of street warfare,' Jane said.
'And that turned out to be a fact, of course.'

'We'd accidentally become involved,' Gerald said.

'Involved?' Harpur said.

'Helping one of the participants,' Gerald said. 'As if we belonged
to his side in the battle. Dangerous.'

'Possibly,' Iles said.

A painting of the head and long neck of a cormorant was over

the fireplace in their flat. Harpur studied it, liked it – liked it because
he thought the artist had done the head and long neck of a cormorant
damn well. No doubt, that long neck helped with the fishing. Despite
Iles's theory, the bird couldn't tell Harpur anything about the minds
of Jane and Gerald, except they admired a picture showing the head
and neck of a cormorant and had a space for it over the fireplace.

'So, you had left the established path – unofficially established,
but nonetheless established – and done what you could for detective
sergeant Mallen, though, of course, not aware he *was* detective
sergeant Mallen – not aware of *who* he was. He didn't speak, did
he?' Iles said. 'These were admirably responsible reactions towards
someone you knew only as another human being, and rightly
commended by the judge.'

Iles raised his hand and skimmed it across last evening's skin
rip, maybe to test whether it had begun to improve; alternatively,
whether it had begun to erupt, cascading something colourful and
utterly unwanted. Iles hadn't so far asked what creviced him on
Elms, although he'd probably corner-eyed it when Harpur raised
the Biro from ground near him and swung it up in a bent-arm,
accelerating arc to give the ACC that invasive, warning poke,
Hiroshima mode. Or he could have glimpsed it on withdrawal. Iles
might consider it shaming to have been waylaid by a time-expired,
cheapo pen, and wouldn't want to discuss what happened. Getting
quelled by a Biro was not normal for Assistant Chiefs.

Iles said: 'Your clothes inevitably suffered blood staining, Gerald,
through contact with Mallen. I hope you were reimbursed for
cleaning costs.'

'Fine,' Gerald said. 'Only jeans and a donkey-jacket. My shopping gear.'

'Good. On the other hand, a badly marked suit can be a real
problem, especially if poor quality. Oh, yes, I'm afraid there's no
shortage of quaint suits around. The mud has to be removed,
certainly, but will such a ramshackle outfit stand up to getting
tumbled and pummelled at the cleaner's? That's so, isn't it, Harpur
– the anxiety?'

'About what, sir?' he said.

'Misshapen suits can come out even more misshapen,' Iles replied,
'shoulder pads gone knobbly.'

'But Gerald told us he wasn't wearing a suit at the time,' Harpur
said.

'I'm making a general point,' Iles said, 're: crap suits going from awful to very much worse.'

'General points are not my area, sir. They're too . . . too, well, is "general" the word I'm after? But I do recognize muddy suits generally are quite a topic for general discussion,' Harpur replied. 'It's a side of things I must catch up on – one of my blank spots.'

'You didn't notice an uncapped Biro among the detritus on the ground when you were down so close to Mallen, did you, Gerald?' Iles replied, in a smooth, sing-songy sort of friendly, hate-hiding voice. This tone usually indicated some kind of smart-arse shock was *en route* from the ACC. So, yes, he'd seen the pen as dagger on its way to or from him, or both.'

'Biro?' Gerald said.

Harpur noticed Jane swing another gaze over towards the pierced cheek. She was a tall, lean, shrewd-looking woman, long-faced, with brown eyes, hair fair-to-mousy with some grey over the ears. To Harpur she looked the sort who could make the connection between a hole in someone's face and a former working Biro. He would trust his own estimate of her rather than follow Iles's teaching and look for clues to her personality in the cormorant.

'Traces of green ink on the pen,' Iles replied.

'Some people like to brighten up their writing,' Harpur said. 'The content might be dull, so they go for vivid, vitalizing ink, like bright wrapping paper around a dud pressie.'

'That's another of Col's phrases, you see – "vivid, vitalizing ink",' Iles said. 'It's quite impromptu, yet his schooling was pathetic. The alliteration and vowel music are entirely of his own make, uncribbed. He's what's known as an *autodidact*, meaning he looked after his own education. Unfortunately, he isn't satisfied with *autodickacts*, meaning keeping it to himself, self-pleasuring.'

Although viewing Iles's injury obviously unsettled Jane and Gerald, it seemed to Harpur reasonably OK now: clean and dry at the centre of the bruising, with small furls and fronds of ruptured skin around its rim, like a springtime campion flowering pink in black soil. The Biro obviously had a very considerable rarity among Biros as species. Throughout the whole country there surely wouldn't be many of them that a senior police officer, lying in rough terrain to rehash a murder, had used on an Assistant Chief Constable's cheek bone, to stop the ACC strangling him in a vendetta convulsion away from home.

Iles had seemed to need the elementary, though understandable satisfaction – even joy – from getting his fingers terminally around Harpur's windpipe. He'd had the loaded Walther in his pocket but didn't draw it, to scare or use. He must have wanted the intimacy of flesh on flesh, to parallel the behaviour of Harpur and Sarah Iles, in fourth-rate rooming joints and so on, that her husband aimed to avenge. In any case, bullets could be matched to that pistol, which was booked out in Iles's name. It would be flagrant. Did he have the Walther aboard now as they talked to Jane and Gerald?

Gerald had obviously been thinking about Iles's last question. He repeated the query. 'Biro? Near the body? There was all sorts of small-scale trash on and in the soil,' he said. 'Is it important?'

'It came to Detective Chief Superintendent Harpur's – that is, Col's; he allows the familiarity – yes, it came to Col's knowledge,' Iles said. 'Don't ask me how. He has avenues. Someone phones him and whispers "Biro" or "pen", then cuts the call, but it's enough to get Col's brain going. Oh, yes, there's a kind of brain there. I'm not sure whether he'd consider the Biro important.'

'Important in what sense, sir?' Harpur said.

'Yes, important,' Iles replied.

Harpur said, 'Well, a building site: when it was still active, brickies, plumbers, surveyors, roofers moving about all day, so we should expect such thrown-away items. Perhaps a ring-pull from a can, shreds of an old newspaper – that sort of thing. Higgledy-piggledy.'

'Very true,' Iles said. 'Possibly a sample in miniature of our disordered civilization, if it deserves that term.'

'Which, sir?' Harpur said.

'Which what, Col?'

'Which term?'

'Civilization,' Iles said.

'This is a theme of yours, sir – the withering of standards, then looming chaos. The Biro has touched it off,' Harpur said, 'to its credit.'

'Anyway, let's get back to the established path, the beaten track,' Iles said. 'I know Colin believes we should be focusing our thoughts on that by-way over the Elms site.'

Of course, it was the Assistant Chief who'd first emphasized its possible relevance. Iles did this sometimes – credit Harpur with one of the ACC's ideas, as though Iles himself would regard it as vulgar and pushy to tout for possible praise, possible recognition: what he called 'tuft-hunting'. He didn't require praise, thank you very much, you condescending sod. He knew his value. He despised most people, anyway, and would regard their praise as worthless, and possibly presumptuous. He didn't require recognition from others, thank you very much, you kowtowing creep. *He* recognized his genius. His mother had helped with that. Harpur had no idea what the hunted tufts were, but, whatever they might be, Iles didn't want one. Tufts were a no-no. He hunted crooks. Nobody did it better.

'Plainly, Mallen was not on that beaten track,' Iles said. 'Many metres off course. The question Col would ask is, how come Mallen went so far adrift – so far off the most direct, quickest route from Ritson to Guild Square? We were told he'd been called by mobile to an urgent rendezvous in the Square. Why had he wandered off like that, apparently chosen such a devious approach?'

'Of course, there was *no* urgent rendezvous for him in the Square,' Gerald said.

'But Mallen didn't know this at the time, did he – or ever, come to that?' Iles said. 'The supposed rendezvous was part of a plot to get him on to ground where he could be efficiently and secretly executed, a proven spy.'

'On to the Elms, yes,' Gerald said. He and Jane were both in their early thirties, Gerald about as tall as Jane, more heavily made, with ruthlessly cropped fair hair, and a boyish, confused look on his face most of the time. That might not be permanent. Iles often had this effect on people, whether they appeared boyish or otherwise. Harpur had never heard anyone actually ask, 'God, is he real?' about Iles, but he thought plenty would like to.

'Not simply on to the Elms, was it, though, Gerald?' the ACC said.

'Oh, I see the point you're making, Mr Iles,' Jane said, a kind of awe at his cleverness in her tone.

'Yes?' Gerald said. His mixed-up-kid face became more mixed-up. He obviously didn't like being corrected by Iles, nor getting left behind by Jane. He had a middling-to-big job in IT.

'What Col has observed, in his acute style, is that Mallen had to be steered away from the usual track so he would enter the pot-shot precinct in front of the property that might one day be number fourteen Davant Road; in front of this property and specifically and exclusively this property,' Iles said. 'Elms, yes, but here, exactly, on Elms. Number fourteen Davant had a dedicated function that night – turret. The gunman was already installed upstairs there and prepared. But he could act only if Parry/Mallen occupied the ambush zone – a very limited zone. Accurate pistol shooting is not easy, not even for a skilled marksman. He needed Parry/Mallen to present himself as target in a very precise and predictable spot. There might have been rehearsals. They'd certainly have to come over to Elms pre-op and sort out the right incomplete house for their gunman – one with the staircase, manageable locks, and a bedroom window that gave a view of the appointed slab of terrain: from a view to a death.

'Of course, the house they picked would determine which *was* the appointed slab of terrain. Maybe one of them had done a previous, preparatory stroll through Elms towards number forteen, pretending to be Parry/Mallen, so the lad in the house could check angles and range. Then, fine, it's all set up – or as much as it could be without Parry/Mallen actually included yet. But, these are perfectionists. The stand-in victim is told to make the approach just once more, double or treble checking. And what if he has a Biro in his pocket, the top section long lost, and puts it on the floor as a marker for the re-run or re-re-run? Instruction to himself: "Get to the Biro, get mock-hit, get mock-dead, get an Oscar." There'd be enough moon-light for it to be seen – maybe even for it to glint a little, like a navigation buoy.

'Naturally, when Tom Parry/Mallen came that way on the actual slaughter night, he wouldn't know he should seek out the exactly right bit of ground. But our pal with the gun does know which is the exactly right bit of ground and, having this as reference point, can adjust his aim and angle to suit any slight variation. Thorough planning and timetabling had gone into this termination project, this cleansing-of-the-firm project, but it did require some cooperation from Parry/Mallen – unconscious cooperation, obviously. He has to be in what Harpur would probably call "the right ballpark".' Iles sat back in his chair and drank a little tea. Then he said, as though deferentially: 'I believe that's a fair summary of your thinking, isn't it, Col?'

'Along those lines, yes,' Harpur said. He felt a kind of buddiness with the supposed gang member who, before him, might have done what Harpur had done last night – acted as Parry/Mallen on his appointed way to destruction. And had the sniper launched some

Iles-type shoot-bang-fire pop sounds to imitate the blasts due for Parry/Mallen soon? Perhaps this Parry/Mallen replica keeled over as if twice struck in key regions, the way Harpur did later. The 14 Davant corner of Elms could figure as a training base for the Royal Academy of Dramatic Art, or a commando unit.

'We're going at matters arse-backwards,' Iles said.

'In which respect, sir?' Harpur replied.

'We've placed Jane and Gerald in front of the house, attending to Tom Mallen on or near the special location. But we haven't worked out why Tom left the normal path – the path Jane and Gerald had been following until she saw the chucked garments that turned out to be Mallen – left the normal path and drifted over towards fourteen, a drift of forty metres.'

'You're right, Mr Iles,' Jane said.

Gerald edged his way into things. Getting talked down to by cops in his own living room might badly piss him off. The conversation had gone away from him. He seemed to resent the enthusiastic way Jane agreed with the Assistant Chief. She said, 'You're right, Mr Iles,' as though it meant, 'You're always right, Mr Iles.' This was, though, the type of accolade the Assistant Chief might dismiss as stupidly redundant. He already knew himself to be always right, and expected others to know it, too; know this as so plainly a feature of the ACC that to hail it like a discovery was offensive, a kind of impertinence.

Gerald said: 'Excuse me, Mr Iles, but one is bound to notice that on the left side of your face you appear to have sustained—'

'The Assistant Chief is very hands-on,' Harpur said. 'Some of us try to get him to take fewer front-line risks, but he's not made that way. For him, leadership is leadership. I heard that in a previous posting he was known as "Audacious Desmond".'

'No mere backroom pen-pusher?' Jane replied. 'Though some do say the pen is mightier than the sword.'

'A pen *can* give a nasty dig when pushed,' Iles said.

Gerald said: 'Your injury, Mr Iles, is one that—'

'If there's trouble, the ACC is as likely to be personally involved as any of his people,' Harpur said.

'But you – you're one of his people,' Gerald said. 'You're not injured.'

'I could show you,' Harpur said.

'What happened?' Jane replied.

'I'm very glad you asked,' Iles said.

'Yes?' Jane said.

'Oh, yes,' Iles said.

'Mr Iles wouldn't want it thought that this wound and contusion suited his face so well that they were not noticed – or at least not considered worth mentioning,' Harpur said.

Jane said, 'Simple politeness might have stopped us from—'

'Mr Iles is man enough to know when he has become exceptionally unsightly, and it's not in his frank and open nature to ban all comments on this outstanding, if not unique, ugliness,' Harpur said.

'Thank you, Col,' Iles replied.

'But who could have done this to him – to an Assistant Chief Constable?' Gerald said. His tone had mellowed. 'The injury – so near his eye.'

'Yes,' Harpur said, 'as if calculated.'

'How?' Gerald asked. 'Who?'

'So, Tom Mallen comes in at the flattened bit of fence just like Jane and Gerald,' Iles replied, 'and for a while, say fifty or sixty metres, follows the direct path, as almost everyone would. But then he swings away. What does this seem to indicate?'

Jane said: 'Well, it could be that he—'

'It indicates extreme caution,' Iles said. 'Or even a touch of panic.'

'In what respect, sir?' Harpur said.

'He'd seen something,' Iles said.

Jane said: 'But couldn't it be that he was called to – the gunman shouts through the window space to him by name, suggests he should come that way, past fourteen Davant?'

Iles put a bent hand up to the side of his mouth as if to make his voice carry better. 'Over here, Tom, so I can nail you, you treacherous, ratfink bastard,' he cried. He lowered his hand. 'Is that how you think it went?'

Jane ignored the put-down. 'Just calls his name. That might be enough, surely. Tom would want to find out what was going on – perhaps a change in the plan. After all, it's a very fluid situation.'

Iles said: 'This is an undercover officer, aware continuously that his cover and his life could get blown. Don't you think he'd be wary of wandering off to a comparatively lonely part of the site because someone yells his name? This is not like a lad's mother fondly calling him home from vandalizing a parked car to have his tea.'

'He's used to risk. He can't be over-careful. It's not that kind of job. After all, going on to the site in the first place carried risk, didn't it?' Jane said.

'And he wouldn't want to add to that,' Iles said.

'We don't know his thinking,' Jane said.

'We guess. We deduce,' Iles said. 'We fix on what's likely.'

'Subjective,' Gerald said. 'People will guess differently, deduce differently, fix on different factors as likely.'

'Mr Iles is remarkably tolerant and definitely always conscious that some people don't see things as he does,' Harpur replied. 'He pities them unstintingly. On the whole he considers it best to ignore their views. That's a fair summary of your thinking, isn't it, sir, positive, though with a negative core?'

'Tom leaves the normal route to *avoid* risk, not increase it,' Iles replied.

'I don't understand that,' Gerald said.

'He's on the path and then, suddenly, doesn't want to be on the path,' Iles said. 'Indeed he eschews the path. It has become a hazard for him, rather than a safe beaten track: something to be escaped from at once. Why? None of this came out at the trial, of course. The prosecution was interested only in the death outside fourteen. How he got there didn't matter to their case.'

'You say he's seen something,' Harpur answered.

'But what, Col?' Iles said.

'Not some*thing*, some*body*, perhaps*?*' Harpur asked.

'Good, Col,' Iles said.

'Somebody ahead of him on the path he doesn't want to see?' Harpur said. 'Or be seen *by*.'

'Good again, Col.'

'But who?' Gerald said.

Jane gasped slightly. 'Ah, I think I get it,' she said.

'Good,' Iles said.

'Get what?' Gerald said.

'He's been ordered to take a route across Elms,' Jane said, 'because this makes a fine killing field, as they see it. They know, though, there's what you're calling the "beaten track", Mr Iles – the usual path followed on Elms by nearly all the short-cutters. Parry/Mallen is likely to take this. But getting him on to the site is only half the job. They've decided that one property gives the best billet for their marksman, and it's reasonably secluded. Parry/Mallen has to be directed, persuaded, tricked, pressured, shepherded into going that way, rather than continuing on the standard track. So, they arrange for an obstruction.'

'Good,' Iles said.

'An obstruction?' Gerald asked. 'Part of the fence?'

'The somebody already mentioned,' Jane said.

'This somebody is an obstruction?' Gerald said.

'The somebody doesn't actually, physically, obstruct but makes Parry/Mallen divert,' Jane said.

'Who could do that?' Gerald said.

'Ah,' Harpur replied.

Jane said: 'I don't know why, but my feeling, my instinct, is that this must be another police officer, or perhaps more than one.'

'Excellent, Jane,' Iles said. Harpur guessed the ACC would be thinking of that long neck on the cormorant. Jane didn't have an unusually long neck, but might have a less obvious affinity with the bird. The cormorant could scoop out fish from well under the river or sea surface, whereas Jane could brilliantly retrieve instincts and truths from her subconscious. It was always a mistake to dismiss altogether an Ilesian theory, not only about art – about anything, including cormorants, although they were currently suffering a cull.

'Yes,' the ACC replied, 'a police officer or officers on the path, possibly coming from the Square towards Ritson and therefore about to meet Tom face-to-face.'

'These are bought police, on the take? They belong to the firm?' Jane asked.

'Certainly,' Iles said. 'But Tom wouldn't know whether they were or not. He's inside the firm by now, yes, but not familiar with all the intricacies of its workings, all the low-level contacts and contracts. That's his job as undercover man – to discover the whole extent of the corruption. He's only just started. And, of course, the firm would be aware which bent cops he did know of. They pick one or two that are strangers to him and tell them to get on the path at the right time and uniformed, walking in the opposite direction to Parry/Mallen.'

'To scare him?' Jane said.

'To make him switch. Tom's *en route* to the killing of the maverick trader, Justin Paul Scray, or believes he is. He probably wouldn't be keen on this. OK, an undercover cop might have to take part in some criminal doings of the host firm, to preserve cover, but involvement in a murder is too much. Perhaps he's glad to be delayed. The supposed killing could take place before he arrives, and he'd have a quotable excuse for his lateness on the scene. In any case, he doesn't want to get spotted by what might be straight cops. He'd be remembered. If Scray is killed in the Square, or near, there'll be a trawl for anyone seen close to the scene at the right time that night. Tom might get traced and pulled in. Of course, he could explain his way out of that – he tells them he's an undercover detective, and they can verify it. But there are crooked officers in this police force. What should be secret information regularly leaks from headquarters to Leo Percival Young's firm. Tom's mission would be critically weakened, perhaps sunk.

'He is a responsible, conscientious officer and sees he must prevent that. In case the police he spots ahead of him are not part of the conspiracy, Tom realizes he must get off the path, avoid this oncomer, or these oncomers, and take another approach to the Square – an approach brushing against the nascent fourteen Davant. The firm would have calculated he'd behave like that if he felt threatened. Therefore, they supply the threat, and supply the sniper for fourteen's bedroom window.'

'Yes,' Jane said. 'It might be.'

'And only might be,' Gerald said. 'Speculative. Strained?'

'"Might be" is the best we can do,' Iles replied. 'As in so much of our work. What we do know, and what's no "might be" is that Parry/Mallen was killed and the shots came from the future fourteen Davant.

Harpur said: 'If we can identify this "oncomer", these "oncomers", we have a way into the whole Larkspur racket.'

'Good yet again, Col,' Iles said.

Harpur naturally recognized this as semi-slur done up as praise. Perhaps two-thirds slur. It was Iles treating him like a dim pupil whose tiny achievement in seeing the obvious had to be extolled to keep his morale up. Occasionally, Harpur wondered how and why he stuck with loyalty to Iles. But he did. There was compensation to be offered, of course, for what had happened between Harpur and Sarah Iles, the ACC's wife. Maybe it went further than that, though, and further than Harpur could understand. For instance, he found his behaviour with the Biro after that Elms encounter more or less inexplicable. Harpur hadn't thrown it away.

This was not because he thought the pen might help with self-defence again some time. That would be an absurd idea. Its uses as a weapon were limited. For instance, you wouldn't have one of those warriors in the Japanese combat film *The Seven Samurai* armed with a Biro, even if they'd been around then. No, he'd decided it would be disrespectful to Iles, flippant, even callous, to leave the pen in the muck with his blood and possibly bone fragments on – a kind of betrayal, *another* kind of betrayal. The incident on Elms was private between Harpur and the ACC. It must be kept like that. No part of it should be casually ditched where it could get trampled, maybe crushed, in the indeterminate soil of the stymied property site.

Harpur felt no need to say he still had the Biro. No need? It went further than that. In Harpur's view to admit he'd kept it would be a kind of gloating/crowing. And he'd avoid iconizing it: no reverencing the small plastic tube like a holy relic. Harpur had washed the Biro and placed it in one of the sealable cellophane envelopes he carried for items of evidence. It was in his suitcase back at the hotel. He thought there might come moments ahead when he felt down, depressed, and would bring out the Biro to restore his spirits by recollecting its special, adapted service. Ultimately, though, the pen was just something that figured in an episode, a sort of theatrical prop. But it should not simply get discarded at the end of the performance.

If Iles ever did grow curious about it, Harpur would be willing to let him see the Biro in peaceful conditions, such as at the hotel or back home in the ACC's suite; and fine if Iles wanted to make something profound and emblematic of the Biro and its odd transformation, from workaday green communicator to chiv. Harpur wouldn't ridicule or even interrupt that kind of mouthing. ACC rank meant jabber. Iles was in a great, continuing tradition. Harpur always tried not to carry over grudges against him. He accepted that Iles had good cause for his occasional husbandly rages, even to the extent of brutal violence.

After the 14 Davant shoeing, Harpur's balls had swollen up pretty well equally for a time, but they'd begun to subside nicely, also at level pace. He reckoned he must have a sweetly balanced metabolism. It no longer hurt so much to piss. He could have bicycled without saddle pain. Perhaps Iles had aimed to neuter him once and for all, as a generous aid to chastity. Harpur was more or less certain that wouldn't work.

FIVE

I n the London newsroom of the *Epoch,* one of its star investigative reporters, David Lee Cass, was talking to his boss and editor, Philip White.

'Daisy says that her infant boss—'

'Meaning Maud? Maud Clatworthy?'

'Maud, yes. Daisy says Maud doesn't think much of the way things ended up in that building site case – execution of the undercover lad. She's asked the same pair of cops who did the previous dig to go back and dig some more. But deeper. Or, to put it another way, higher. They're already there.'

'You want me to send *you* back, too?'

'If it comes to new prosecutions, everyone will have the story. We might be able to break it sooner. Potentially a very juicy exclusive, Philip – high-rank police corruption, *cwtching* up for gain to one of the drugs gangs.'

'So, Daisy's still leaking, is she?'

'With discrimination, as ever.'

'Why hasn't she been panicked into silence?'

'By what's happening at *The Sun,* you mean?'

'By what's happening at *The Sun* and thereabouts. James Murdoch and Rebekah Brooks resign from big boardroom jobs. Staff arrested for bribery. Dawn calls at their homes by troupes of detectives. Or *alleged* bribery – paying police and other public officials for confidential stuff. "Entrenched criminality" and "a culture of illegal payments" – that's a couple of the milder phrases I've heard to describe it. The bribed as well as the bribers are in the frame.'

'We're not *The Sun,* though, are we, Philip? We're *Epoch,* a decent, well-behaved broadsheet national newspaper run by honourable editors such as yourself.'

'And its decent and well-behaved broadsheet national newsroom houses a reporter who criminally buys Home Office secrets from a section head's personal assistant. How d'you word the *douceur* on your expenses sheet, Dave? Or perhaps it would be better I don't know.'

'"Gratuity to special source."'

'Will that fool anyone, if the shit starts to fly? You'd have to cough names.'

'Reporters don't cough names of special sources. It's why special sources are called special sources.'

'*Sun* management handed over all sorts of information about *their* special sources to the police.'

'Management here wouldn't do that, Phil, would they?'

'Who knows?'

'You?'

'No. I can't tell what our lawyers would say. *The Sun* boardroom obviously had the jitters, scared they'd get done for hiding evidence. It could happen here.'

'As a last resort, we'd plead "in the public interest". That's genuine. Daisy wouldn't do it otherwise. She believes disclosure is a kind of holy duty. And we have a duty to respond, don't we? In the public interest.'

'Magic phrase.'

'But legit.'

'Maybe. A "public interest" defence works for disobeying the Data Protection Act. I'm not sure it does for bribery. Isn't it that dodgy proposition, the end justifies the means?'

'Some of that, yes. Plus, admittedly, Daisy's getting old. She frets about her future. Huge government cuts in civil service funding. It's no longer "Sit on your arse for fifty years and hang your hat on a pension". Or not such a grand pension, anyway. Hers is possibly OK, but she'd like to build a reserve, just in case. Salaries are frozen and her job's not entirely safe. She's on her own since hubby hopped it with the nursing sister. Daisy follows ice hockey here and abroad – Canada especially. It's her substitute for sex. But dearer. Pucks not fucks.'

'They managed a conviction for the undercover murder, didn't they?'

'Not one that satisfies Maud. Small potatoes. I've got a download here of her report up the line to the Home Secretary. It details where the original investigation fell hopelessly short, in her view, and suggests the reopening of inquiries. It's headed, "Larkspur: Stage Two". You can see she's thinking of it as a continuing operation. There might be additional stages. And she sticks to the name coding. It's still active.'

'But Daisy, her sidekick, doesn't give a monkey's about security and coding, does she? Crazy.'

'Public interest takes precedence.'

'Ah.'

'That's how she sees it. How *we* should see it, Philip, surely.'

'I'll try.'

'We mustn't get left behind. We might not be the only paper Daisy talks to.'

'But you said exclusive.'

'Of course, I hope so, but—'

'That's the trouble with sources.'

'What?'

'They can spout in all directions.'

'We've had some good page-one tales from her – the double adulterous Minister of State; the MI6 woman's suicide.'

'Were those in the public interest?'

'Well, the public were interested in them.' Cass liked to get mildly jokey with White. There was a danger of some pretentiousness and pomp infecting the tone when newspaper men or women began to talk about 'investigative' assignments. They liked to kid themselves they were hard-edged, indomitable, relentless and, of course, incorruptible. Some of them behaved as if they were born only for such work, committed to it, destined for it, from the cradle, like Mozart with music. David Lee Cass believed in this kind of reporting, and liked it, but he didn't kid himself that it invariably brought any good and notable changes to the world. In fact, he didn't ever feel sure his inquiries would yield enough to get published, let alone improve prospects for the human race.

There were obstacles: the law of libel; the editor's taste, judgement, caution – above all, caution; the ability of those being investigated to keep their secrets secret from even the most brilliant investigative operator. Investigative didn't mean lucky. When Cass was going off on one of these stories not long ago, his wife, Louise, a nurse, had snarled: 'There's investigative reporting and investigative surgery. I know which digs deeper.' She hadn't said anything of the kind this time. Repartee shouldn't be re-reparteed. But she might be thinking that way again.

White said: 'If you trust Daisy, *I* have to, because I have to trust *you*.'

'How journalism works.'

'How journalism can come unstuck. Ask Rupert Murdoch.'

On the train to Larkspur, David Cass looked again at Maud's Stage Two notes, as forwarded by Daisy Fenton, acting (1) in the public interest, and (2) in Daisy's private interest, keen to swell her auxiliary retirement pot and ice-hockey fandom fund. Maybe (2) should be (1) – her priority.

The conviction of Courtenay Jaminel for the murder of Detective Sergeant Tom Mallen closed the most pressing aspect of this case but, in my opinion, must be regarded only as a minor and very limited advance.

Courtenay Jaminel was a detective inspector in the Larkspur force and a trained marksman. It is improbable that he acted alone. However, he consistently refused under questioning by Assistant Chief Constable Desmond Iles and Detective Chief Superintendent Colin Harpur to provide information about others involved in the Mallen killing. It is assumed he feared reprisals against his family if he spoke.

ACC Iles and DCS Harpur had been assigned as outside investigators to Larkspur following what appeared in my own and departmental colleagues' judgement to be undue delay and an absence of commitment in dealing with the death. It was known that Mallen, under his cover name of Parry, had been lured on to the Elms building site, and to a specific area of the Elms building site, by an elaborate, well-prepared plot involving at least three members of a drug-dealing firm. Some kind of cooperative understanding therefore seemed to exist between a criminal gang and certain police officers, including Jaminel. Possibly it still exists. In any case, further investigation is required. I believe that Assistant Chief Iles and DCS Harpur are the best suited officers for this task. They made themselves familiar with Larkspur and had a success in finding the evidence to convict Jaminel, though their success went no further.

One possible caveat to the selection of ACC Iles and DSC Harpur should be put on record. Although they are capable of working harmoniously and very fruitfully together, there is considerable animosity at times from Iles towards Harpur owing to an affair in the recent past between him and Iles's wife, Sarah. This animosity can express itself in fits of fierce rage, bordering on what could be mistaken for foaming madness. Mr Iles is particularly vehement about what he regards as the undignified locations where their extra-marital love-making took place, such as 'fourth-rate rooming joints' and 'marly fields'. He seems to feel these tacky settings degrade him, personally, and not just his wife.

I have witnessed one of his disturbing episodes. There is, perhaps, a danger of physical violence from the ACC. And Harpur would no doubt try to defend himself. A totally innocent word in a conversation can set off one of these spasms. Mr Iles will bring his own, poisoned meaning to it. Sensitive questioning of suspects and witnesses may, it's true, be pushed askew if the ACC starts upbraiding Harpur during interviews of others and using unusual terms like 'marly'. Obviously, this tension between the two men could occasionally make combined, effective work difficult or temporarily impossible. However, the fit I witnessed lasted only minutes; this might be typical. And, regardless of these moments of imbalance in Mr Iles, I feel he and DCS Harpur are the best officers to handle this complex and very challenging inquiry.

And, according to Daisy, this recommendation was accepted, despite the troublesome caveat, and Harpur and Iles had been back at work in Larkspur for at least several days.

SIX

For the second time, Cass took a room in the same hotel as Harpur and Iles. That could be a help. It showed harmony of choice: they were the same sort of people as to taste and should therefore get on together OK. That is, if those two didn't feel hounded and tracked down by him, as reporters did hound and track down. He hoped he might bump into one of them or both in the bar or dining room and engineer a conversation. Cass could switch on smarm, charm, deference, croneyness, radiant integrity, or a couple of these, or three, or four, or a combination or permutations of the lot – whichever seemed most likely to further the blessed cause of an eventual page one David Lee Cass exclusive – 'see also pages 6-7-8'. The tall headlines, prominent byline and space allocated would impress even Louise, though she'd offer no flattery. 'God, the wordage,' she might say, 'and to think the discovery of DNA took only one page in a mag.'

Cass had checked with a local reporter and found Iles and Harpur were installed as before in the Mayfield. Cass had met them then, though he wouldn't say either had been very friendly. He recalled that chats with the pair were likely to see the apparent main topic – say, murder of an undercover cop, and detectives' failure to investigate it properly – yes, this apparent main topic would get chucked while, as in Maud's note, the Assistant Chief screamed and frothed about Harpur having it off with Iles's wife in unsavoury, conspicuous settings such as a canal tow path, but pronounced 'carnal' by Iles. Besides, Harpur and Iles had arrived in Larkspur to take its police force to bits, and they hadn't wanted some questing, mission-driven, snooping journo to foul things up by trying to do ditto. Those circumstances might be pretty similar now. But Cass took the room in the Mayfield just the same. *'Well, how pleasant to run into you like this, Mr Iles, Chief Superintendent Harpur. Are we on the same kind of project?'*

He didn't really know how he'd order his programme of inquiries, but there were two contacts he'd certainly have to make fairly early on. One was with the local reporter who'd told him about the hotel. She acted as a 'stringer' for the *Epoch,* feeding the paper with information and rumour that might turn out strong enough for national coverage. Second, he must see the Larkspur police Press officer, an inspector, to get the approved line on what was happening. This would almost certainly turn out vastly useless, but protocol had to be followed, and occasionally, by accident, one of these designated mouthpieces would say something significant that could be followed up. Very occasionally.

Cass could anticipate the kind of responses he would get: 'extremely happy to have the situation examined by the two distinguished officers from outside'; 'will finally clear the air'; 'nothing to hide'; 'certain to draw a line in the sand and enable us to move on'; 'full and positive cooperation with the two officers'; 'sometimes a good thing to be given a fresh, uncluttered view of what might be overfamiliar matters to members of the host police force'; 'assurance that if any faults are found there would be immediate and wholehearted corrective measures applied.'

In other words, more or less total bureaucratic, self-serving bollocks and obfuscation, but you couldn't expect an appointed spokesperson to admit their outfit stank and would be doing everything it could to conceal all rottenness and blight from those two professionally intrusive, virtue-touting, integrity-boasting Cowslip fuckers. And, of course, also from that other professionally intrusive fucker, David Lee Cass, who, however, knew the politesse wrinkles and came in to act sweet and obsequious, pretending that neither he nor the Press officer regarded the meeting as a farce though, in fact, both did. Investigative had its seemly, diplomatic rituals, its creepy arabesques.

Before seeing anyone, though, he hired a car and went out to take an update look at 14 Davant on Elms. Of course, he'd been here several times during the previous visit. He needed to get, or re-get, what he thought of as the 'ambience' of the spot. If he did ever find out enough to write about the present situation for the *Epoch* he'd want his wholesome prose to evoke the dismal, stark murder setting, most likely alongside a picture of it. Louise would probably admit he did dismal very well, and might agree to stark also, if it was put to her.

He stood again at the spot on what should some day be a flagstone pavement where Tom Mallen, known as Tom Parry, had lurched when shot, had fallen, had somehow got back to his feet, staggered a few more steps, then took another bullet, had fallen once more and died. It was mud and rubble now, with an occasional small, brave flourish of weeds, just as it had been previously. He bent to look more closely at their leaves. If they'd been there on the night of the killing, might they show some blood stains? That would make a good line in any article he wrote: the classic, observant eye of the reporter fixed on a telling factor; the taint of human villainy on innocent Nature.

He realized, though, that the idea was mad. Would they be the same growth of leaves now as then? A botanist might be able to tell him, but he had no idea himself about the life cycle of weed leaves in harsh terrain. And, if the leaves *had* caught some of Tom's blood, it would have been noticed at the time and the plant dug out, perhaps as a possible exhibit to help prove the detail of his final tumble.

But then – good God! – he saw a gleam on one of the leaves, a wetness, a bright red streak. Incredible? The leaf was part of a small clump. When he tried to separate it from the rest with his fingers for a better view, he found his hand was smeared not just from the targeted leaf but some of the others in the clump. The plant sort of closed matily on his whole fist and lower arm, like one of those machines to self-measure blood pressure, as if it wanted to declare all-round comradeship – and what did a bit of blood matter; wouldn't it lubricate the cheery, fellowship gesture? And could this really be Mallen's blood, out here decorating low-grade foliage for months – unwashed off by rain, untrampled into the ground, still liquid? Had he, Cass, got right through to the, as it were, heart of the murder?

Cass remembered that, when killed, Mallen had been wearing an 'I Love Torremolinos' T-shirt as part of his assumed identity, with the 'love' not spelled out but represented by a picture, a picture of a red heart – a picture for the gunman to draw a bead on with his final shot, that *coup de grace*: a virtual heart but real cascading blood.

'Excuse me, sir, what is it?'

When Cass stood straight again he saw a woman and a man watching him. It was the woman who had spoken. Cass said, 'Nothing, really. The leaves, you know.'

'No, I don't know. What about them?' she asked.

She was blunt and commanding. 'How they survive in such ground,' Cass said.

'You've hurt your hand, sir,' the man said. 'We have a first-aid kit in the car. Shall I go and get some antiseptic and a bandage?'

'I think I'll be all right,' Cass said. 'But thanks. It's not much. A thorn.'

'That kind of thing interests you, does it?' she said. 'You're into flowers and weeds?'

'Environmental matters can be fascinating,' he replied. He gave this thought some lavishness. '*So* fascinating.'

She said: 'I'm Detective Inspector Laverick.' She had on a dark woollen suit, the skirt to calf length, a navy blouse, tan half-heel shoes. She'd be mid-thirties. She gave a little wave towards the man. 'This is Detective Constable Ure.' He was younger – early twenties, maybe. He also wore a suit, grey, two-piece, single-breasted, with a county style, bold, crimson, yellow and tan check shirt and mottled, mauve tie with black lace-up shoes. She said, 'There was an incident here last night. We're keeping an eye,

hoping to run into witnesses who might be using the estate short-
cut today.'

'What kind of incident?' Cass said.

'We're not sure. It's why we're here. May I ask who are you,
sir?'

'Cass,' he said. 'David Lee Cass.'

'The journalist?' Ure said. 'I've seen some of your reports, haven't
I? Investigative? Some just after the death of Tom Mallen?'

'Were you here last night?' Laverick asked.

'Because of the leaves, or anything else?' Ure said.

'What happened?' Cass replied.

'You're saying, are you, that you weren't here – if you didn't
know of the incident?' she asked.

'No, I wasn't,' Cass said.

'You weren't here?' Ure said.

'What happened?' he replied.

'An incident,' she said.

'Yes, I got that,' Cass said. Might this explain the blood? Perhaps,
after all, it didn't date back to Mallen. How the hell could it, idiot?

'Possibly some sort of violence. A member of the public made
an emergency call,' she said.

'You weren't in time to deal with the incident, whatever it was?'
Cass asked.

'The people concerned had run off, scared by the two-tone, probably. We're looking for them,' Ure said.

'You say you were definitely not here last night?' she asked.

'Definitely,' he said. 'I'd remember.'

'Please don't get smart,' she said.

'But we don't know why you're here now,' Ure said.

'The house might be an important element if I write something
for my paper,' Cass said.

'Number fourteen as murder house?' she asked.

'I'm afraid that's how it's branded, yes,' Cass said.

'Because of operators like you,' she replied. 'Continually feeding
people with references to it.'

'But all that's old, isn't it?' Ure said. 'People have heard everything there is to be said about the house.'

'It's germane still,' Cass said.

'Germane to what?' she asked.

'The current scene,' he said.

'Which?' Ure said.

'He means the two visitors,' she said.

'Oh, them,' Ure said.

'But this doesn't explain you and the weeds,' she said.

'When you mention "some sort of violence", what, exactly?' he replied.

'Possibly fighting – fighting on the floor, where we're standing,' she said. 'Two men. One on top of the other. Almost certainly not sexual. Fully dressed. Not particularly young. One wielding what looked from a distance to be some sort of small weapon.'

'The weapon not really glimpsed at all, but deduced from the arcing movement of the attacker's arm,' Ure said. 'Probably too miniature to be a dagger.'

'Just the same, there might have been injuries,' she said.

Blood? 'But they were able to run off,' Cass said.

'We'll take your address, please, in case further inquiries are needed,' she said.

'I'm at the Mayfield,' Cass said.

'Oh, like those two,' Ure said.

'Have you got them under surveillance, then?' Cass said.

'Are you in cahoots with the pair?' she replied.

'Cahoots?' he said.

'Looking after one another,' she said.

'Looking after?' Cass said.

'Do you have to echo?' she asked.

'But they're police officers. I'm a reporter. We don't *look after* each other.'

'Sometimes there are relationships. You have nice chats with them, do you?' she said.

'What sort of relationships?' Cass asked.

'Mutuality,' she said.

'Mutuality?' he said.

'Oh, hell,' she hissed. 'Like, you put only favourable stuff in the paper about them – Harpur, Iles – to help with *their* careers, and they'll favour you, on the quiet, with information they've collected, which will help *your* career. Looking after each other, you see.'

'There's a proper procedure for information given to the Press and media,' Cass replied. 'Every police force has an official Press officer.'

'Wow!' she said.

'You probably have a Press officer,' Cass said.

'Sure,' she said.

'I'll be seeking an interview with him, or her,' Cass said.

'Her. About the indomitable leaves?' she asked.

'One can rely on the material from a Press officer,' Cass replied.

'The horse's mouth. But this horse can only give you and the other Press folk what has been OK'd by the management. And everyone gets the same. No scoops,' she said.

'Accuracy is more important than the hunt for scoops,' Cass said.

'Wow!' she replied. 'But just in case there might be something exclusive flying about, you get into the same hotel as those two, right?'

'A coincidence,' he said.

'Wow!' she said. 'If you should change hotels – *so* unlikely, but just in case – you'll let us know, won't you? You'll have the number of the nick – same as for the Press officer. I'm on extension three-four-one, Inspector Belinda Laverick. Or Detective Constable Gwyn Ure.'

'I might get pulled off the story, of course,' he said.

'I doubt it. Not now you've got yourself close to Harpur and Iles. No boss is going to waste that. And anyway, which *story*?

'Whatever develops,' he said.

'This *story* could cause terrible damage to a good police force,' she said. 'Do you ever think what harm you might be doing when you're chasing your *story*, and then writing it up in a style to dish out as much harm and injury as you can?'

'I hope your wait's not fruitless and you get some leads to the people who were scrapping here last night,' Cass replied.

'The wait hasn't been fruitless,' she said.

'Oh?' he said.

'No, we've learned you're here, in the city, doing one of your trawls again,' she said.

'With a concern about weeds,' Ure said. 'And weed?'

'We know you're under the same roof as the two scrutineers – by a slice of good luck, we hear,' she said.

'Yes,' Cass said.

'What we still don't know is *why* you're around again,' she said. 'Harpur or Iles told you they were coming?'

I'm here following a tip from Daisy Fenton that Maud Clatworthy of the HO wanted to reopen the inquiry. But Cass didn't say this.

'Things elsewhere were quiet. The paper doesn't like me idle,' he replied.

'Quiet?' she said. 'A banking crisis. Terrorism frights because of the Games. Hacking and bribing scandals.'

'The *Epoch* has specialists to deal with each of those,' he said.

'What's *your* speciality, then?' she asked.

'He's investigative,' Ure said.

'Investigative of what, though?' she said.

'In general,' Ure said. He bent down to the leaves. 'You've lost quite a bit of blood from that thorn puncture. The weed is soaked. Are you sure you don't need a bandage?'

'It's all right,' Cass said. 'But thanks again for the offer.'

Back in the hotel, Cass checked both bars but didn't see Harpur or Iles. He asked at Reception if they'd been about and the girl said no. She thought Mr Iles might still be recuperating.

'In what sense?' Cass said.

She said that the night before when Mr Harpur and Mr Iles came in, Mr Iles seemed to have been injured. 'How injured?' Cass asked. The girl said possibly something to the side of his face. 'What to the side of his face?' Cass said.

'An incision,' she said. 'He was holding a handkerchief to it, so I'm not certain.'

Blood? But again he only thought this; didn't say it aloud. He'd sound ghoulish. 'Did he or Mr Harpur mention an incident?' Cass asked.

'What kind of incident?' she said.

'Any kind of incident,' Cass said.

'I don't think so,' she said.

'Did either of them speak at all about what had been happening?' Cass said.

'Mr Harpur saw I was concerned about Mr Iles's wound. Mr Harpur said Mr Iles believed in confronting troubles personally and was a leader who led.'

Or bled. But Cass didn't say that, either. He rang home, to tell Louise he'd arrived and was installed at the Mayfield. 'I get a feeling the police here don't much like me,' he said.

'Never mind, Dave, the children and I do,' she said. 'You'll go carefully, won't you?'

SEVEN

Helga Ormond, the *Epoch*'s stringer here, was in her early to mid seventies. Cass had met her several times before and during Jaminel's trial. There was much more to her than emphatic jewellery, but she did go for emphatic jewellery: big circular ear rings like doubloons, hefty medallions on stout hawsers around her neck, notable brooches, usually representing musical instruments – say a four-centimetre-long piano, or tiny helicon tuba in gleaming mock-brass, for a Lilliput band.

Today, she wore a green tam-style hat on her dyed auburn-to-vermilion hair, and a yellow silk suit, the skirt with five parallel golden lines around the base, as if to calibrate progressive grope limits. The matching yellow jacket had a kind of halter at the back, like a naval rating's, but deeper, and embroidered with what on a quick count Cass reckoned as half a dozen parallel golden lines, similar to the skirt's, though on a comparatively neutral part of the body. She had a sharp, slightly masculine face, a straight nose and no-nonsense chin. Cass stood her lunch in The Platter, a fish restaurant alongside the River Vaze, and not far from the handsome Vaze Upper stone bridge, famous for those drownings in the so-called Midsummer Riots of 1817, forerunners of the Peterloo massacre further north two years later.

Cass agreed with Kingsley Amis that some of the most depressing words in the language were, 'Let's go straight in, shall we?' They downed a couple of double vodkas and tonic in the bar before tackling the meals. Helga took the tam-'o-shanter off. She had a fish soup starter and main course halibut. Cass never found restaurant fish soup fishy enough and chose whitebait instead, then crab. They drank a New Zealand Chardonnay, solid and aggressive, like the country's All Blacks rugby team.

Customers at other tables greeted her. Helga had been in local journalism a long time and knew a lot of people. That's what stringers were for: their established strings to the citizenry about them, and especially to the important and/or notorious citizenry around them. Her bling-boosted outfits and her hair announced there was nothing sneaky or furtive about journalism. You couldn't imagine someone so uproariously flashy secretly hacking into voicemails, a solitary vice. The waitress called her 'Helge' and seemed to know what food she would order.

'You discovered Harpur and Iles were returning before I did, Dave,' Helga said. 'Don't care for that, not a bit. Makes me look switched-off and indolent. I'm outflanked. Vibeless. You got a Home Office tip, did you? Do I recall there was someone called Maud, much concerned with the situation here on the last investigation? She breathes into your ear still? Or perhaps she has a secretary or clerk who does. They're worried about their pensions up there, aren't they? You can contribute a little extra for them, I imagine, to go into a private, back-up pot. They're pleased to be on the *Epoch*'s "special contact" pay roll, despite all the hoo-hah lately about bribery by the Press.'

'The feeling in *Epoch* from right after the guilty verdict was that it didn't count for much – except to Jaminel and his family.'

Helga broke some bread into fragments and scattered them on the soup, like feed for goldfish. 'I heard you were out at fourteen Davant again on Elms and ran into Belinda Laverick and young Gwyn, one of her very fit sidekicks,' Helga replied. 'Or, rather, *she* ran into *you*.'

'I gather there'd been an incident the previous night,' Cass said.

'Yes, an incident.'

'A call to the emergency services. Violence.'

'And then twenty-four hours later Gwyn says you'd done yourself an injury.'

'Nothing.'

'No, I've been studying your hands. Undamaged.'

'A bit of blood, that's all.'

'It *was* yours, was it?'

'Who else's?' Cass said.

'Exactly,' she replied. 'Someone hurt during the "incident"?'

Yes, probably. He didn't answer, though. Did the blood come from Iles? But, of course, Cass hadn't known enough to suspect this at the time. It was the hotel receptionist's words that started the idea. And it remained only speculation. Because Iles had a face wound, it didn't necessarily follow that he got it on Elms. Who on Elms would stab him, and why? It was a journalistic habit to keep findings private until they could be put into a piece for publication, and so Cass had pretended the blood was his. Gwyn Ure seemed to have accepted this. Had he really? Had his boss, Belinda Laverick? At any rate, for the moment, Cass would continue to abide by his trade's practice of hoarding and non-disclosure.

'Isn't it just like police?' Helga said. 'They have what they call "an incident" one night. They don't get to it fast enough, so put a patrol out at the same spot as if they think it's going to happen again. They're ruled by the past. I understand you were into a leaf-hunting forage, as almost anyone might be on a standstill building site at night. "I'm popping down to Elms, dear, to bag a leaf."'

'Just looking closely – amazed at the weed's power to grow, to survive, on such terrain. Some seed fell on stony ground, but never mind, it makes the best of the situation.'

'Nature's quite a thing, isn't it? A lesson to all of us. Adaptability.'

'Well, yes.'

'There are people in and out of the house, you know.'

'Which people?'

'Dossers. Crime scene tourists. Jaminel.' She finished her bread-stiffened soup. 'As to "the incident" it could be crime nuts – people fascinated by murder locations and acting out the death. They get off on the recollection and imitation of lethal rough stuff.'

'But these two fought on the ground, according to Belinda Laverick. Mallen was shot,' Cass said.

'The floor-level wrestling, if that's what it was, might have been a bonus. Dickheads get taken over by their dreams and need to ginger up the brutalities. It starts as charade but can turn real.'

Did Helge mind, but there was no broccoli today, so would asparagus tips do? the waitress came over to ask. Asparagus tips would do, though they were difficult to pronounce without spitting, after the vodkas and wine.

'Belinda believes there might have been some sort of weapon in the incident, according to a witness – but a witness quite a way off,' Helga said.

'Yes,' Cass said.

'A dirk? Are dirks in fashion? A Stanley knife? We're all guessing. That's why I queried the blood,' Helga replied.

'Queried it in which sense?' Cass asked.

'Whose was it?' she said.

'Mine. I explained: a thorn,' Cass said. 'Not worth making a major issue of, but mine.'

'Yes, you explained, but not how your hands are unmarked.'

'What I'd like to focus on is the Leo Young side,' Cass replied.

The main courses arrived. Cass asked for another bottle of Chardonnay. He'd come by taxi and didn't have to worry about driving. Helga lived just over the Vaze Upper bridge with her partner and had walked. Cass might have to walk her back. They ate and drank for a while in silence. The asparagus tips looked to be right up Helga's street, an excellent piece of luck. She asked the waitress for another portion. The waitress seemed troubled. This would be two changes and would require substantial reprogramming in her memory for the future: asparagus tips instead of broccoli and not just that: a doubler of the asparagus.

'The museum committee,' Helga said and stopped. She spoke as if, because of booze, she needed the firmness of a general topic heading first, and she could then, possibly, move into a detail or two, gently incremental, each point leading on to the next by small, negotiable advances. Rome wasn't built in a day and neither were items of chit-chat. 'Yes, the museum committee.' She sounded triumphant. She'd picked a parameter and, as parameters went, it was a comely and robust parameter, deserving repetition. She said: 'This is an aspect that will repay attention.'

'Right,' Cass said.

'I'm well in with quite a few people around the museum. They want a bit of publicity now and then for this and that. They pick up the phone to Helga. I've even got stuff about the museum into *The Times* for them, and the *Guardian*, not just locals. So, they're grateful. So, I'm owed. So, some recip . . . so some recip—'

That was too big a step. 'Reciprocity,' Cass said. Drink hit women harder and more quickly than men. Nothing to crow about: just a gender difference. Advantages equalled out. For example, Cass thought women better than men at taking offence.

'Recip . . . Yes, that exactly,' she said. 'This committee – there's some know-all, straight-talking people on it. They have an eye for conditions around, conditions now, *prelavent* . . . I mean, not just ancient, as you'd expect, it being a museum.' They both ordered sticky toffee pudding for dessert, and as finale, coffee and Tia Maria.

'With Emily Young, Leo's missus in the chair,' Helga said.

'Quite. I remember that from before.'

'You say, "Quite," as though that's normal. But think about it,

Dave. There's members of that committee with gongs – up to and including CBEs. These are people of what could reasonably be called discernerment.'

'Discernment.'

'Yes, yes, discernerment.'

'Yes, discernerment,' Cass replied. He'd come to feel it was wrong, cruel, snooty to correct her, had already let 'prelavent' go. Surely someone of her age, in that kind of gear, and three-quarters pissed, should be entitled to temporary dyslexia. Bevies could liberate one from the tyranny of faultless vocab. In any case, he was beginning to be undermined by the alcohol himself and if put to it would agree with Helga that 'discernerment', though longer, was easier to say than the rather terse and unrelaxed 'discernment'. Then he had a couple of panic moments when he realized he didn't know any longer which was correct, 'discernment' or 'discernerment', 'prelavent' or 'prevalent'.

He found himself craving the Tia Maria, which hadn't been served yet. He reckoned he needed something stronger than white fucking wine to clear his brain, though his unclear brain was clear enough and platitudinous enough to advise him that Tia Maria on top of the rest of it would most likely super-fog his brain, not clear it, and possibly end in an abrupt puke.

He sorted out, fairly efficiently, he thought, the quickest way to the gents' lavs, or to any lavs, in case of emergency. If he got this wrong there might be a bit of an eventuality at the post-liqueur stage. The route he charted should cut the risk to others' clothes and/or meals and, if he did throw up, it would be on to vacant tables – easy for staff to get into rubber gloves and change the cloth, cutlery and condiment jars. He'd put the tip up to 20 per cent, from his own cash, or the paper's expenses people would kick. As it was, they might query the double asparagus on the bill.

'When I say conditions prelavent, what do I mean, Dave?'

'Contemporary. Of the moment.'

'Contemporary. Of the moment. Correct. So, what conditions of the moment have I got in mind?'

Cass felt unsure whether this showed she'd forgotten what she was talking about, or, like a good teacher, wanted to prompt a pupil into providing the answer. He said: 'Emily Young.' This answer seemed to cover both, and he was proud of it. These were names easy to say and, at the same time, appropriate.

'Emily, educated, cultured, tremendous CV – so what's she doing with a shady, hamster-faced object like Leo?' Helga asked. 'People on that committee must have been wondering that for yonks. And now the puzzle gets really strong. The rumours about Leo have always circulated, but lately they're in regiments. They're in regiments because Harpur and Iles are here, you're here, and Dathan, the Chief, is edgy. Some on the committee have important connections in London and might have heard that Maud is warpathing again and wants you to write up the situation for the *Epoch*.'

'With the massive and unstinting help of Helga Ormond.'

'What I can, I will.' Helga pursed her lips, frowned, winced, bared her teeth, which looked like her own, projected her chin. It was as though she wanted to check she still had control of her entire face and features, despite the tipples. And Cass thought that, if she could manage this satisfactorily, she would assume her mind behind the face and features must be in normal shape, too. For whatever was coming next she wanted to sound cogent, not addled: wanted to *be* cogent, not woozy. She said: 'Noreen.'

This sounded like another of those helpful section headings. 'Someone called Noreen?' Cass asked.

'Noreen, yes.'

'On the museum committee?'

'Noreen Laucenston-Isson. Family money through kitchen design. Lineage traceable back to somebody minor but definitely there in the court of Victoria. An hon. Noreen is the sort who'd have views about Leo. Well, of course, many have views about Leo. Noreen might voice them, and voice them to Emily. I don't say Noreen would be insulting or rude face to face, but she'd have a sort of classy way of commenting which would get the insults and rudeness over to the listener, such as Emily, without actually spelling them out. Emily's perceptive, sensitive. She'd pick up what was being said while not being said.'

Perhaps all those phizog contortions really worked and helped restore Helga to accurate, well-ordered speech. She'd got the Noreen surname right, as far as Cass knew; done 'perceptive' and 'sensitive' OK; and could outline quite well the difference between explicit insults and rudeness, and oblique insults and rudeness. Cass said: 'You think Emily will start wondering about Leo herself, because of Noreen Whatever?'

'Because of Noreen and others,' Helga said. 'We're discussing something as grave as murder of a police officer here.'

'But, as grim topic, the murder of a police officer has been around for a long while. Emily seemed able to live with this suspicion, didn't she? And the conviction of Jaminel would help her do that, wouldn't it?'

'Maybe. But I can imagine Noreen pointing out to Emily, without seeming specifically to point it out to Emily, that the Jaminel conviction was a *start* to the clean-up campaign, not its *end*. An overture. Noreen would most likely play at sympathizing with Emily, calling the revived investigation "a bore", for her. When people like Noreen dub a situation a bore it doesn't mean that it's boring. Emily would probably *like* the situation to be boring – that is, going along as untroublesome and ignorable as ever. When Noreen brands something "a bore" she's saying it's a pain in the arse, is frightening – very – a threat, a potential catrostrophe.'

She'd got through what came before 'catrostrophe' very well, and Cass continued with his benign policy of non-correction. It was brave of her to make the shot at a blatantly tricky word that could lead to catastrophe in speaking it, or catrostrophe. She could probably have done 'disaster' or 'holy fuck-up' instead of catastrophe, to perfection. He felt strengthened by her and downed the Tia Maria without qualms. He said: 'You think Emily could be the means to get Leo, do you?'

'Big pressure on her. This is a woman not without morality, though hitched to a high priest of villainy. She might want to change things.'

'Will Harpur and Iles realize this?'

'Iles sees plenty, doesn't he?'

She stood, seemingly without difficulty. Cass paid and followed her out, and was also all right. 'Shall I walk back with you?' he said.

'I'll be fine.' She put the tam back on, as if to prove she was equipped for no matter what conditions Fate or Life or both might fling at her.

'Right. And thanks,' Cass said.

He called for a taxi and sat on a low wall outside The Platter, waiting.

EIGHT

Harpur said, 'I had a quick look around the room of David
Lee Cass, the reporter who's booked in here. Top-quality
Samsonite luggage and not just one but three electric toothbrushes. Nothing of any significance, though, really, except a note
to himself, neat copperplate, reminding of an appointment he's fixed
with the Larkspur police Press officer later today. This lad knows
about protocol.'

'Those card-in-the-slot hotel room keys are pitifully easy to fool,
aren't they, Col?' Iles said.

'Lockbust Ferdy back home.'

'Ferdy? Yes?'

'Showed me how to work a card, before we sent him down for
doing a complete corridor in The Angel. Luckily I saw Cass's name
in the hotel register,' Harpur replied.

'You had a quick look at that, too, did you?'

'I suppose we could have guessed he'd come to Larkspur again.'

'*How* could we have guessed it, Col?'

'A sort of follow-up to his previous. As soon as he heard we're
back here he'd see possibilities. They're driven, these investigative
stars. Driven.'

'But *how* would he hear?' Iles said.

'These things get about.'

'How do they get about?'

'Oh, yes,' Harpur said.

'Maud leaks? Purposeful leaks? You have a weird affinity with
her, don't you? Does she seem the leaking kind?'

'Or someone close.'

'A secretary?'

'I suppose Maud would have a secretary, even several. Maud's
big stuff, isn't she?'

'I don't know what kind of stuff she is, Harpur. You?'

'This Cass. He's formidable,' Harpur replied. 'Stickability.
Intuition. That kind of approach. And, yes, driven. International
Press awards for furthering the human cause.'

'Which?'

'Human.'

'D'you think he sees the perils here?' Iles said.

'Routine for them. Danger's built in to that kind of job, isn't it?'

'Has he got family?'

'There were framed pictures of kids in his room.'

'Wise to put himself at risk?' Iles asked. The ACC could get like this sometimes: motherly. Harpur found it disgusting.

'And there was that game old bird, Helga, who helped point him in the right direction last time,' he said.

'The sun shone out of her medallion – reflected. We'd better sit in on Cass's interview with the mouthpiece.'

'The Chief won't like that.'

'No, he won't. Hard cheese, as Orwell might say.'

'He came out with all sorts, didn't he, sir?'

'Who?'

'The one you mentioned.'

'Orwell?'

'That's the one. It's a river, isn't it – like they call a Welshman, Taff.'

'Have you heard of him, Col?'

'Some of these people – they know the exact phrase to hit on in a situation,' Harpur replied heartily. 'Because, you see, sir, hard cheese is still indisputably cheese, but not very pleasant, especially for those who like their cheese soft, as with, say, ripe Camembert. Hard cheese has to be put up with, though, from time to time. Those two words "hard cheese" contain all that meaning!'

'No need to dot the i's and cross the t's, Harpur.'

'Ah, that's another of those spot-on phrases, sir.'

'Fuck off, Harpur. That's another.'

At the headquarters meeting, Dathan, the Chief, also sat in. The Press officer had a spacious room with a long, impressive, solid oak conference-style table. Harpur thought it was probably all meant to show the force took relations with the media seriously and that only the double-checked truth would be put before them here. They sat in chairs around the table, the Press officer at the head. She introduced herself as Inspector Ruth Bowles and said she would read a statement first and take questions from Cass afterwards. She was plump and friendly-looking, probably not far off retirement age, obviously knowledgeable about what could and could not be said, and aware that the people in front of her today, and on other days, knew she was bound by the unyielding rules of what could and what could not be said. Truth had to be sanitized, redacted. Her voice for the statement was conversational, matter-of-fact, take-it-or-leave-it, as if she recognized this was not great oratory, but so sodding what, and roll on pension day.

She said: 'I know I speak for the Chief when I say how happy we are to have the present unsatisfactory situation on our ground examined and, I'm sure, remedied, by the two distinguished officers from outside.'

Dathan muttered, 'Indeed,' and gave an endorsing nod each to Iles and Harpur, an unflamboyant 'Thank you, pals,' for striving to drop him and his outfit in the shit.

'But perhaps I should state what I mean by an "unsatisfactory situation",' she said. 'Unsatisfactory in the sense of aftermath.'

'So true,' Dathan said.

'This aftermath stems from a past, grave crime – a murder – for which a police officer was found guilty and sent to prison,' Ruth Bowles said. 'Although that would have seemed to close the matter, some felt certain aspects of the case stayed unresolved. A shadow of doubt fell, unsettling, even demoralizing for all in the force.'

'True, again,' Dathan said. 'Yes, beyond unsettling. Demoralizing.'

'Morale, an item to be cherished, protected,' Iles replied.

'And so, we are grateful and relieved to have the two officers who helped us with the original case return now and recommence their investigation, though with perhaps a wider remit,' she said. 'We trust that – but, no, we are *confident* that their second intercession will have as result a final clearing of the air. Fortunately, we have absolutely nothing to hide.'

'Nothing,' Dathan said. 'Fortunately. This is not to criticize those who have commissioned the new inquiry, not in the least, but I think we are bound to feel unthreatened by it, unresentful of it – though not smug or complacent – because we know that nothing but good can come out of it for us.'

'There are times when it is a very positive matter to be given a fresh, blazingly impartial view of what might have become over-familiar factors for those in the host force,' she said.

'Certain shortcomings might be tolerated because they have taken on a kind of time-blessed status unrelated to their real value. Such complacency can be identified and swept away by the likes of Mr

Iles and Detective Chief Superintendent Harpur. For this necessary service we shall be extremely thankful.'

'Extremely,' the Chief said.

'Ultimately, they will draw a line in the sand and enable us to move on,' she said. 'To that end, we shall offer full and positive cooperation with the two officers.'

'One hundred per cent cooperation,' the Chief said. 'To put this at its most selfish, it is in our interests to make such an offer, for it will remove the traces of taint and guilt that have quite unwarrantably lingered here too long.'

'Harpur will get at these traces, believe me,' Iles said. 'He's famed for giving short shrift to traces. It's coded on his personnel documents: SSTT.'

'Any faults that may be found will be immediately and vigorously corrected,' Ruth Bowles said. 'Though we expect nothing of that sort to come to light, because they do not exist.'

'And would already have been dealt with if they *had* been located earlier,' the Chief said.

This seemed to Harpur an exceptionally powerful description of nothing at all: there were no faults and, even if there had been, they'd gone now. Was Maud wasting her own time as well as his and Iles's?

Cass said: 'Although it is obviously a pleasure for you to have Mr Iles and Detective Chief Superintendent Harpur here again, I believe you didn't actually suggest this second visit, did you?'

Dathan had a big, worldly, charmless laugh. 'Now isn't that just like a newspaperman? He listens to our version of things and as a first response tries to pick holes in it! Well done, Mr Cass. You admirably abide by the precepts of your trade.'

'Not to pick holes,' Cass replied, giving a very pleasant smile, to match Dathan's geniality. 'It's just that I need to see the sequence of things.'

'Sequence! Oh, sequence. Who did what and when, d'you mean?' the Chief said.

'This can be important in some instances,' Cass said.

'Possibly, possibly,' the Chief said.

'What I mean is, the push for the second investigation came, didn't it, not from you, Chief, but was ordered by the Home Office, and you . . . you, well, concurred, as you would be obliged to?'

'You've been talking to Maud Clatworthy, have you, up there in

London?' the Chief said. 'Or more likely listening to. Or – another or – more likely listening to that PA of hers, Daisy Something. Daisy Fenton. A famed carrier of tales for a fee.'

'Daisy Fenton?' Cass said. Harpur thought it a pretty poor pretence at ignorance – the bafflement in Cass's voice and on his face badly overdone. Then he said: 'It would change the complexion of the investigation, wouldn't it, if you had suggested to Maud that the case should be reopened, rather than Maud ordering in the two outside officers as a personal initiative.'

'Complexion?' the Chief said. 'In what manner?'

'Well, as Inspector Bowles said, you have nothing to hide and therefore would have no objection to a second look at the situation.'

'But if we have nothing to hide, as is, indeed, the case, we would hardly call for another investigation, would we, because we wouldn't be aware of anything that *needed* investigation,' Dathan replied, with what Harpur considered damn grand phoney logic, the kind all Chiefs should have ready when keen to get out of a rotten spot.

'Subtle points, sir,' Iles said. 'You show that police work can move beyond warning people to cancel milk deliveries when going on holiday so it doesn't pile up on the doorstep, inviting burglars. No, there are also complicated, virtually philosophical issues to be dealt with.'

'So, I can take it that the decision came from Maud and the Home Office,' Cass said.

'Since you've obviously been briefed by her, or whispered to by Daisy Fenton, you will have arrived here with your views on that issue already formed,' Dathan said.

'I'm open to correction,' Cass said.

Dathan had discarded his amiability for the last few moments but resumed it now, not with a full-on guffaw or chuckle, but a definite grin. 'This hair-splitting is . . . is hair splitting! Wherever the first move in this second inquiry originated, it is now under way and it is under way with our enthusiastic approval and with our stated intent to assist it.'

'Bravo!' Iles cried. 'What's that lovely old Welsh song, "We'll keep a welcome in the hillsides"? We're not in Wales, but Harpur and I have felt what is probably the equivalent of that welcome – or even warmer – here, haven't we, Col?' Iles sang softly for a while, substituting Larkspur for Wales in the lyrics where necessary, regardless of scansion.

Iles gestured to Harpur to join in, but Harpur said: 'Remarkable hospitality,' and left it at that.

'I'm intrigued by the Leo Young side of things,' Cass said.

'"Intrigued" in which particular?' the Chief said.

'It's the aspect where Inspector Bowles's remarks about the effectiveness of a fresh viewpoint comes into play, I feel,' Cass said.

'I'm not sure I follow,' Dathan said.

'That Young and his companies should continue along their successful business path as though they were in no way involved,' Cass said. 'And this is apparently accepted. How can that be?'

He was looking at Ruth Bowles, directing the question there, but she did not answer. Although she'd said she would field questions from Cass, Harpur could tell this was one of those areas where the limits on what could be said and what couldn't came into play – specifically what couldn't.

'But no connection to Leo Young or the Young companies was established at the Juminal trial,' Dathan said. 'I think Mr Iles and Chief Superintendent Harpur will confirm that.'

'We failed,' Harpur replied.

'And it's because you failed that you have been sent back now by Maud Clatworthy?' Cass said.

'There was a conviction,' Dathan said. 'I wouldn't call that failure. But Maud does, does she? You've been given a privileged account of her thinking, have you, Mr Cass, possibly with Fenton as conduit? Perhaps Maud Clatworthy actually put her up to whispering to you, so you'd think you had something special, something exclusive, and would move in on it urgently.'

He paused and changed tone again – grew brusque and authoritative. 'I'm going to speak off the record for a minute or two, Mr Cass, and I know you will respect this. The Home Office doesn't get much favourable publicity, so where there's a chance of some, people there grab at it – and particularly favourable publicity in one of the daily broadsheets, the *Epoch* and/or the *Telegraph*, two heavy, serious-minded papers. Television and radio trust them and are likely to follow up their stories. The main dread in the Home Office is not that it will make errors but that it will be seen as a do-nothing, a *fainéant* department, slow to intervene where it should intervene, and even fail to intervene altogether. Therefore, there come panic moments when *any* kind of activity is regarded as a plus, as a virtue, even though it might turn out eventually to be disastrous, or sooner than eventually. Maud, like all of them at or near the top there, is affected by these sudden spells of corrective restlessness. Hence the return of our two investigative friends.'

This shrewdness and easy word-flow surprised Harpur, after Dathan's earlier display of semi-bonkers reasoning. Momentarily, it was possible to see why he might have made it to Chief. He had the indispensable, evasive, bullshit side, but also a sharp, cogent side. Of course, the central question now should ask whether he was sharp and cogent enough to realize that some of his people were on the payroll of crooks. And to take it a huge step further: was he sharp and cogent enough to lead a police force whose apparent only task was to do the law and order bit, while also being personally signed up in a fine, prosperous and murderous alliance with a thriving drugs firm, for instance, Leo Young's?

Cass said: 'Is Young untouchable, legally? That's how it might appear.'

'Appear to whom? You? Maud? Your boss at the *Epoch*? Nobody is untouchable. But nobody is touchable when we lack evidence,' Dathan said.

'Mrs Young.' Cass replied.

'What of her?' Dathan said.

'Has she been interviewed, questioned?' Cass said. 'Mightn't she be of help?'

'Help in which way?' Dathan said.

'This is a classic case, isn't it? The family financed by illegality and the wife/mother keeping herself deliberately ignorant of where the money comes from? Michael Corleone's Kay in *The Godfather*.'

'We don't look to fiction for guidance,' Dathan said.

'Mrs Young, a distinguished scholar, prominent in the community, she must have some uneasiness, surely, about her husband's business. Businesses.'

'Ah,' Dathan said, 'it's not just Maud who whispers in your ear, but one of our local ladies – though rather older. This is Helga Ormond's line you're taking, isn't it? She's always nagging us about the need to get at Emily Young. That's what your lunch was about, was it?'

Ruth Bowles hadn't spoken since doing her statement but now said: 'The Platter, Tuesday last.'

'God,' Cass said, 'you keep Helga under surveillance? An ageing woman who does something now and then for the papers?'

'No, no, not surveillance,' Dathan said, giggling at this absurdity. 'But you weren't exactly inconspicuous there. In fact, is Helga ever inconspicuous? Somebody eating in The Platter noticed her and recognized you from byline pictures in the *Epoch*. He mentioned it to someone, who mentioned it to someone, who mentioned it to someone in CID – the way so much information comes to us, isn't it? Libations? Vodkas to start, two bottles of Sauvignon—'

Ruth Bowles glanced at some notes: 'New Zealand Chardonnay, I think, sir.'

'Then Tia Marias,' Dathan said.

'This sounds like surveillance to me,' Cass said. 'A nasty, thorough job of it.'

Harpur agreed.

NINE

C ass rang his editor, Philip White, at the *Epoch* office in London. White had been a subtle and supreme investigative reporter himself – broke that famous Blue Ciel scandal tale, and the Orbit Major fraud exposure – but he wasn't brilliant as an editor. He veered bewilderingly between super-caution and acute impatience. He could be robotic, he could be frenetic. The trouble as Cass saw it was that if White relaxed his cautiousness by just one degree he would be hit by this stupid, galloping impetuosity, and expected the reporter out in the field to 'velocitize', as he called it, even if that meant getting crudely blatant and/or accepting mad risks. White lacked sensible balance. It was either stay cosy and secure in barracks, or the ballsy, barmy charge of the Light Brigade. But they weren't his balls.

He must have applied a careful mix of the gradual and the decisive when stalking Blue Ciel's chairman and Chief Executive, and Jimmy Devonald-Lade at Orbit Major, but seemed to have forgotten those subtle means of progress now he'd been granted a chiefdom. Responsibility messed him about. Cass couldn't ever know in advance how White would be at any stage. Cass reckoned that one of the flairs vital for an investigative reporter was how to manage your manager, counter his or her complexes.

'Nothing publishable as yet, Philip,' he said. 'But there's possibly some movement.' At early, feeling-out moments in a conversation, Cass liked to give a dollop of negative and another dollop of unspectacular positive. He'd decided to hold back, or even leave unmentioned altogether, his suspicion that his hotel room had been frisked. This information could drive White into a disabling panic or a ferocious urge to retaliate: confront and accuse someone. Which someone, though? Cass might sense there'd been an intrusion, but he couldn't tell who by – possibly only routinely, by a maid or cleaner. The door lock had not been forced, so the visitor must have a card-key, either Reception's or a master, or a clever, illegal replica. But Cass couldn't have said with certainty what told him there'd been an interloper. Nothing was out of place except, possibly, his toothbrushes, as though the guest had been astonished to find three and had slightly fanned them out in his toilet bag to count.

'I did the standard call on their Press officer, Phil, and for once it had a useful item or two.'

'What! Really?'

'She recited the customary kind of claptrap statement, but Larkspur's Chief as well as Harpur and Iles were there. In fact, the Chief more or less took over after the statement, obviously scared Madam Press Officer might say something beyond formula. Hard to tell whether he's worried about the reputation of his force and wants to protect it; or is he worried because he's personally involved somehow in the Mallen death, and the Leo Young business scene?'

'But hadn't we decided, Dave, that it could hardly be Dathan himself racketeering? Would he have invited "undercover" into the system?'

'A bluff? Did he want to appear intent on virtue and lawfulness? He'd probably realize Maud could have important doubts about him. He might have thought they could cope with the secret invader. The undercover man had a local handler, didn't he? That came out at the trial – an Inspector Howard Lambert, if you remember. Mallen, like anyone in that kind of work, would report his findings to the handler. What if Lambert were in on the scam? They could monitor whatever Mallen discovered.

'Dathan possibly decided he'd prefer to have an undercover officer he knew about rather than one he didn't. Pre-emptive. This way he could keep tabs on Mallen-Parry. Lambert, the handler, gave evidence at the trial, of course, but said Mallen had not come up with much at the time of his death. True? Perhaps he had, and they realized the bluff wasn't working. So, get Mallen on to Elms and annihilate him in good time.'

'Possible,' White replied. 'Harpur and Iles were at the Press officer meeting, you say. They've got an understanding with Dathan?'

'They're *investigating* him, aren't they?'

'Are they? They're all police, Dave. They stick together.'

'Yes, I had thought of that,' Cass said. 'Loyalties? Why they didn't nail Young last time, maybe. Iles has a wound.'

Cass heard a gasp from White at the abrupt subject change. 'What sort of wound?'

'Facial. Could be from a screwdriver or bradawl. That sort of hole. Or a skewer.'

'Facial where?'

'High on his left cheek. Near the temple.'

'Prominent?'

'Very.'

'Self-inflicted?' White said.

'I wondered.'

'He's liable to strange fits, isn't he? Don't I recall he gets scream-prone and froth-flecked now and then because Harpur was giving it to Mrs Iles?'

'In low-grade settings,' Cass said. 'Fleapit rooming joints. He sees it as an insult to himself, his rank, the legal system, the police profession worldwide, as well as to her. He probably visualizes the crummy duvet and rickety wardrobe with its gaggle of wire hangers.'

'Perhaps he's into a different kind of pain now – torn between a career bond with Dathan, and the need to expose him as corrupt. In this turmoil he reaches out and grabs something to do him some showy, pitiable hurt. He invokes sympathy, like Saint Sebastian punctured by all those arrows. Iles is normally vain, isn't he?'

'*Ab*normally, except about his Adam's apple. Apparently he despises that, thinks it wrecks the lovely smoothness of his outline. He believes he has an obligation to be beautiful – a duty to numerous, widespread communities.'

'Stress makes him want to diminish himself, disfigure himself – almost see himself off, if he hit the temple,' White said.

'Could be. I won't be asking him, though. Or not yet.'

'No. You're so right. Do you feel . . . well, do you feel safe, Dave?'

'They're alert to any unwanted activity.'

'Such as you?'

'Such as nosiness from anyone. It looks as though they've got the local stringer under close, continuous watch.'

'What! Old Helga? She's given us good tip-offs for years.'

'Which is why they've got surveillance on her. They deny it, of course,' Cass said.

'Watch your back, Dave,' White said.

'Dathan didn't like my interest in Leo Young's missus as a possible means of getting to him. He tried to spike that ploy by complaining I'd been briefed by Helga.'

'Had you?'

'Of course. Doesn't Helga usually gets things right? She wouldn't be able to buy all that junk jewellery if papers didn't trust her, and stopped her retainers and fees.'

'So, is *she* safe?'

'I've been wondering,' Cass said.

'Yes, well wonder, but look after yourself.'

'I might try to talk to Emily Young later.'

'You'd better let me know in advance,' White said.

I've got three electric toothbrushes in my toilet bag – holiday kit, one for me, one for Louise, one spare. I think someone moved them slightly to check the number. But Cass didn't say this. He thought White sounded close to the jitters. It would be callous to shove him nearer still.

'Mrs Young, I'll postpone,' Cass said. 'I'll see if I can reach the handler, Inspector Lambert.'

'You're going to get a stone wall there, Dave. This is someone who helped run a secret operation. Whether he's bent or not he's hardly likely to welcome the Press. He said his bit at the trial and that'll be it.'

'Maybe. But I'll give it a go. He might have stuff he didn't realize the significance of at the time.'

'I ought to overrule this. But, yes, it could help velocitize things,' White replied.

TEN

Harpur got two messages along the same disturbing lines. He'd told most of the people they'd talked to on the new inquiry so far where he was staying, in case they heard something fresh, or recalled something they'd forgotten to mention. Jane Matson, with her partner Gerald Beatty, had found Mallen dying on Elms, and she turned up alone now at the hotel where Harpur and Iles were having evening drinks at the bar, Iles with his port and lemon; Harpur the large gin – Old Raj if available – in half a pint of cider. He considered that this mixture, if taken aboard twice or three times at a session, gave him a clearer view of life in general: politics, the job, his daughters, Denise, anthropology, religion, Iles, travel, interior decorating. He knew some would dispute this.

Jane Matson said she would take bourbon on the rocks. Harpur could see Iles approved: it brought an international tone. He disliked ostentatious temperance in women, and even worse, teetotalism, though he also shunned two-pot screamers, women who got loud after a small amount of booze. 'This is how things *ought* to be, Jane,' he said, 'relaxed, friendly, leisured. I expect you remember the scene in one of George Borrow's books about gypsies and his journeys where he meets some glum-looking people but finds that after a drink or two they all perk up, seem more cheerful, so sucks to the anti-alcohol lobby.'

'Well, yes,' she said.

'And so with us,' Iles replied, 'though I'm not saying you look glum, Jane. Not a bit.' She had a long, naturally glum face, now laced with anxiety, but Iles handed her the glass and watched with pleasure as she sipped. 'Grand!' he said, though Harpur saw not much change in her features.

'There's a London journalist,' she said.

'They get everywhere,' Iles said.

'Cass. David Lee Cass,' she said. 'He gave us his card. He's well-known.'

'He has a room here,' Harpur said.

'Yes, I know,' she said. 'He said we could find him in this hotel if necessary. I don't mind if he sees me talking to you.'

'Good,' Iles said.

'In a way I *want* him to know I'm in touch with you.'

'This is flattering,' Iles said. 'Harpur doesn't usually get that kind of compliment.' His voice grew tremulous and sharp, like a two-pot screamer's. 'The way he conducts his private life, and particularly his private life as regards women, whether or not they are married, possibly to a colleague, and a colleague of superior rank, is hardly likely to result in general public esteem, is it, Jane, I . . .?

'Cass has been to see you lately, has he?' Harpur asked her.

'He has our names and so on from the trial, of course,' she said.

'Probably you'll say "it takes two to tango", Jane,' Iles replied, 'and that my wife was as much a part of it as Harpur but—'

'Cass and his paper are interested because they've heard Mr Iles and I are here and that there might be further developments in the Mallen-Parry situation,' Harpur said.

'I gathered as much,' she said, 'but we want no further part in it.'

'I can understand that,' Harpur said.

'We did what we had to do for the trial – gave evidence of the discovery,' she said. 'That was stressful enough, but inevitable. This, we hoped, was the end of it. We don't want to get drawn into anything further. We don't want to appear in the Press again.'

'Harpur, opportunistic, sly,' Iles said. 'I would be away on a staff course, perhaps. My wife, lonely, isolated. He sees his damn chance, doesn't he, Jane? He can be ingratiating and—'

'I don't think there's a likelihood of anything appearing in *Epoch* at present,' Harpur said. 'Cass can know nothing because there is nothing to know.'

'He's talking to people all over, he told us, as if that would be some kind of comfort! Does he realize that this is a very dangerous area? Who knows who's watching him, and watching those he calls on? You tell me there's little immediate possibility of publication, but that's not the point, is it? We have no wish to get involved in it at all, now or later. We don't want him leading a trail to us. Gerald is furious that this reporter should be stirring things again. Can't something be done to stop him, and those behind him?'

Home Office Maud might be behind him, in a devious, confidential way. It wouldn't be wise to tell Jane Matson that, though. Harpur went for truism instead: 'He's the Press. He's the *free* Press, greatly prized in our country, despite its occasional massive slip-ups.'

'Can't he be warned about how hazardous it is – for himself as much as for those he implicates? We've tried to convince him of that. It would be more effective coming from two senior police officers.'

Iles said: 'Of course, my wife and I now, subsequently to the Harpur episode, find it more or less incomprehensible that she should have allowed herself to be tarnished by him – *her*self and *my*self. Many's the hoot we have when looking back on the preposterousness of that situation, hoots in concert with each other.'

'Hoots in concert are often cited as evidence of a successful marriage,' Harpur said.

Next day, he and Iles had an arranged interview with Inspector Howard Lambert at the headquarters building. Lambert had been Mallen-Parry's handler. A burly, mock-genial detective, he met them in his room in the CID wing of the building. He, like Jane Matson and Beatty, had given evidence at the trial of Jaminel and there probably wasn't much more for him to say now. The meeting was not a lot above a formality, but it gave an uncomfortable echo of the conversation with Jane Matson.

At the trial, Lambert said Tom Mallen-Parry hadn't been in place long enough for him to have gathered much information. Lambert had met him secretly twice and Mallen-Parry had talked mainly about his method of infiltrating the Leo Young firm. Lambert's evidence might be accurate, or not. Their meetings had no witness, of course. His room was extremely tidy, the furniture a workstation and screen, a small bookcase full of what looked like manuals and abstracts, a secretarial, revolving chair at the work station, four straight-backed metal chairs stacked against a wall, a cork notice board near the work station with schedules and graphs displayed. Lambert unhooked three chairs and they all sat down.

Iles said: 'Your evidence at the trial was exemplary – as one would expect from an experienced detective – but it was properly concerned with the immediate circumstances of Tom Mallen-Parry's recruitment to undercover and his couple of briefings to you.'

'That's all I could offer,' Lambert said.

'But while you were very rightly focused on those factors, did you push to one side other matters, so you could concentrate on what then was relevant, and only on that – a quite commendable way of getting to the nub of things, as the nub at that stage was defined?'

'What kind of matters, sir?' Lambert replied.

'Stray, tentative, insubstantial observations Mallen-Parry might have mentioned, almost unnoticed.'

Lambert gave a sort of token whistle: 'Do you know, sir, this is the second time lately I've been asked that kind of question.'

'Oh?' Iles said.

'Cass?' Harpur said. 'David Lee Cass?'

'You know him, do you, Mr Harpur?' Lambert said.

'Heard of him,' Harpur said. 'He called to see you?'

'Phoned.'

'Did you tell him anything?' Iles asked.

'I don't have anything to tell him,' Lambert said. 'Like you and Mr Harpur, he had the trial records, and like you and Mr Harpur he wanted to know if there was anything more – anything I might have neglected to mention in my trial evidence because it would not have been deemed relevant.'

'How did you answer?' Harpur asked.

'As I've answered you and Mr Iles,' Lambert said, unbothered, unvexed. 'Nothing. But one facet was different from this talk today. I told him that he should be careful.'

'Careful in what sense?' Iles said.

'Well, if he's going about our ground making implications and looking for more, he should be wary,' Lambert said.

'Implications of what?' Iles said.

'I'm not sure,' Lambert said.

'Implications that might suggest a link of some kind between one of the firms and police officers?' Iles said.

'Of that order, yes,' Lambert said. 'Absurd. I rang off.'

'Excellent,' Iles said.

'Yes, I rang off,' Lambert replied and stood. The interview was over.

ELEVEN

Almost all national newspapers carried a report of the murder of investigative journalist David Lee Cass. Harpur read each of them, plus the locals. Cass's own paper published a full obituary with head-and-shoulders picture, as well as the page-one account of the place, time, circumstances and method of the killing ('at least four knife blows'). Colleagues' tributes made up part of the obituary, on page 18. The longest came about halfway down. It began, 'Philip White, Associate Editor (News) writes,' and Harpur guessed this would be Cass's immediate boss:

> David Lee Cass was a brilliant investigative journalist – thoughtful, persistent, accurate and with a charm that won him many confidential sources, so crucial in his type of work. They knew they could trust him to use the information in a measured, considerate way, disguising, as far as it could be disguised, where and whom the secrets came from. It is one of the most difficult skills in exposure journalism. A reporter naturally wants the full impact from what's been uncovered. But the published story mustn't betray its source. That can bring him or her trouble, possibly dire trouble and, if nothing else, make further disclosures unlikely.
>
> David Lee Cass began as a junior reporter in the Midlands but, after two years of describing charity walks and local council spats, felt an appetite for tougher tasks and came to London. He adapted swiftly to the requirements of investigative work: its concealed purposes, its subtle but binding rules, its patience, its use of sophisticated and ever-improving technology, its tactical finesse in, say, deciding whom to approach first with questions, then second, third and so on. And its occasional quaint and specialized humour. For instance, this police area where he'd most recently worked, and where he was killed, had been given a befogging title by police to hide its location, its identity: Larkspur. Originally, an undercover operation there had to be protected, and the name stuck. Another police force,

who'd supplied the undercover officer, was labelled Carnation,
and another, Cowslip. David would have a smirk at such prim-
itive ruses. He said he was glad to know they hadn't used
Pissabed, the dandelion.

He'd gone to Larkspur lately to chart the aftermath there,
following the murder of undercover officer Detective Sergeant
Tom Mallen ten months ago, and the subsequent trial and
conviction of a local police inspector for his killing. Before
this visit, Cass had made inquiries and found that some aspects
of the case were never satisfactorily dealt with, possibly very
substantial aspects. A deliberate, unholy ploy? It was the kind
of dubious, complicated situation he relished, and he went to
see what he could find. The barbaric nature of his death suggests
he had begun to unearth features of the aftermath that someone
– or more than one – did not want revealed. He has been
silenced before he could find more. The gentle, serene coding,
Larkspur, seems now, after two killings, sadly inappropriate.
This paper and journalism generally have lost in David Lee
Cass a remarkable, brave and principled representative,
possessed of what every investigative reporter must have: an
abiding thirst for truth.

The moments of clanging rhetoric made Harpur uneasy. He'd come
across a lot of journalists in his career and some of them certainly
had an abiding thirst, but not necessarily, or exclusively, for truth:
vodka and tonic, maybe, or claret, or both, and in any order. For
God's sake, who said 'abiding' these days? Or 'possessed of'? Did
a 'barbaric' killing indicate more than a *non*-barbaric killing – if
there was such a thing – that someone had to be prevented from
talking? And perhaps Cass really had 'relished' some of his assignments, but it seemed a puffed-up word to Harpur. He thought 'sadly
inappropriate' about the name Larkspur a showy, wet and irrelevant
attempt at sensitiveness. 'Principled representative' sounded like an
anti-scam salesman: a very rare species.

He went back to the straight, factual account of Cass's death on
page one. 'At least four knife blows' must be based on someone's
immediate view of the body where and when it was discovered.
There had been no post-mortem yet. Four separate patches of blood
on his clothes? Or maybe a neck wound and a face wound as well
as those to the torso.

The report said Cass's body was found by a routine police patrol at just after 2 a.m. near the junction of a couple of minor country roads at the western edge of the city. A parked, silver Ford Focus stood nearby. One of the local papers carried a photograph of the spot, though the Focus had been removed before the picture was taken. An invoice in the glove compartment apparently showed the car was signed out to Cass by a local hire firm a few days before. It had no satellite navigation, but a road map, open on the front passenger seat, might have helped him locate the junction. It raised the possibility – probability – that he had driven to this secluded spot by arrangement, secretly at night, to meet a contact, or contacts. This would probably be the normal way people in his kind of skulking job functioned. They'd pick somewhere remote or somewhere shelteringly crowded for their rendezvous.

The report said it was unclear whether more than one person carried out the attack. 'Cass was over 6 feet tall and around 220 pounds. He might have seemed a risky target for someone acting alone, even someone armed with a knife.' But the paragraph added that Cass wouldn't have been expecting violence at what rated for him as a business meeting; and, if there *were* only one attacker, he, or she, would have the advantage of maximum surprise.

It seemed likely Cass had taken several steps from the Focus, possibly to go to talk to someone, or more than one, in another vehicle. Police would be examining the ground for tyre tracks. The news item ended with a brief biography and a list of important investigative stories Cass had previously handled, including a charity fraud, a pimping organization across six counties, club protection firms in Manchester, Leeds and Nottingham. He was 29 years old, married to Louise, 31, a former nurse, and with two children, Zoe, four, and Timothy, two.

Harpur turned again to the obituary. *Before this visit, Cass had made inquiries and found that some aspects of the case were never satisfactorily dealt with, possibly very substantial aspects. A deliberate, unholy ploy.* This sounded as though there had been a discussion, or discussions, between White, the associate editor, and David Lee Cass, about the current Larkspur state of things. To be expected: Cass couldn't just clear off to Larkspur without an OK from his superior. Cass would presumably have argued the case for renewed inquiries there, and White must finally have agreed.

Harpur felt a lack in White's summary, though. *He went to see what he could find.* It sounded so offhand, so autonomous. This should have read, shouldn't it, 'I sent him to see what he could find'? It wasn't just David Lee Cass who targeted Larkspur, it was David Lee Cass as hack, emissary, bellhop, for a major British newspaper. How had Cass convinced him there might be a story? *Why* did Cass decide to make inquiries so long after the jailing of Courtenay Jaminel seemed to close the case satisfactorily? How and why did Cass get to suspect calculated neglect of these *possibly very substantial aspects. A deliberate unholy ploy?*

Philip White's tribute contained no explanation. He wrote as though Cass had been given a sudden, supernatural signal. From Sunday school at the Gospel Hall when he was a child, Harpur recalled that King Belshazzar in the Book of Daniel watched a hand write in capitals on the wall of his banqueting hall, 'YOU HAVE BEEN WEIGHED IN THE BALANCE AND FOUND WANTING'.

Harpur felt the obit's tone suggested Cass might have had something similar: 'VERY SUBSTANTIAL ASPECTS IN LARKSPUR HAVE BEEN CLEVERLY BLIND-EYED, DAVE – A DELIBERATE UNHOLY PLOY, SO SADDLE UP.'

But, of course, Maud Clatworthy – Home Office Maud – had also come to wonder whether some 'very substantial aspects' of the Mallen case were left uninvestigated, despite the conviction: calculatedly uninvestigated. Harpur and Iles had secured that conviction, and this was as far as they'd been asked to go then. Over the months, though, Maud had obviously decided on another objective and the ACC and Harpur were sent back. Had Maud known David Lee Cass and been so affected by the famous integrity and charm that she became one of the *many confidential sources, so crucial in his type of work*? Cass might have had contact with the Home Office and Maud during an earlier investigative case, or cases. Did she resolve to make sure Larkspur got a really good going over this time, by briefing and assigning not just Harpur and Iles, but also an accomplished, wide-ranging Press muckraker?

Harpur took this as a possible slight on him and Iles – as if they couldn't conduct this new inquiry without help. Maybe, though, it had not been Maud personally who prompted Cass but, as Dathan had suggested, one of her staff, familiar with Maud's thinking and willing to pass it on for a dab in the hand; maybe even on a retainer, like many of *The Sun*'s payrolled whispering officials. Who said broadsheets were above all that? Answer: those who ran broadsheets. Who believed them? Answer: only their mothers.

The obituary – and especially White's contribution – was very coyly phrased, perhaps with some of that *measured, considerate* method it referred to, so as to prevent undue clarity. White would know all the tricks of investigative journalism – its *concealed purposes*, and areas needing *tactical finesse* – as thoroughly as Cass, including how not to over-blab in print. Harpur realized when analysing this obituary that his young lover, Denise – 'the undergrad piece' as Iles called her – had taught him quite a bit about dissecting a slab of writing. Her university courses trained her in the skill, and now and again, when she was stopping over, she'd bring some academic work with her and chat to him about how to get at its essence. Harpur's divorced sister was looking after the children while he was away, and Denise would probably call in when she had time and help.

Silenced before he could find more, the newspaper article said. More? More than what? Had he begun his explorations and discoveries? And had he told White what the discoveries were, to prove progress, and reassure him that the rail, hotel and car hire expenses he'd have to wave through would ultimately be justified by at least a double-page show in their paper and big-deal, unignorable headlines?

TWELVE

Harpur was in the downstairs lounge of their hotel with the newspapers and a post-breakfast coffee. He and Iles had been asked to call on the Larkspur Chief Constable as a formality this morning at the force headquarters – standard protocol for officers working on a patch not their own. This would be a private meeting, not like the five-sided session with Ruth Bowles, the Press officer. Harpur and Iles would, of course, be loathed as Home-Office-hired snoops and stirrers by many Larkspur people. That kind of contempt, plus possible obstruction, always came with the job of scouring another force, and possibly dishing out blame. The proper rituals had to be gone through, though, and the Chief treated as if he himself were spotless.

The headquarters were not far from their hotel and they would walk.

Iles came in to the lounge now and sat down. He wore one of his double-breasted, custom-made grey suits. Harpur thought the cloth radiated a kind of smugness, as though it had lain waiting hopefully in the tailor's bale to be cut and stitched for a wearer worthy of its excellence, and could now glory in the fine luck that brought Des Iles. Harpur reckoned about a thousand quid's worth, the shoulder padding totally right for Iles's shoulders, and only Iles's. There had been a time when Harpur foolishly tried to gauge the Assistant Chief's state of mind by what he wore. It was a hangover from Harpur's school days: he'd noticed that one of the teachers always seemed in an evil rage when he turned up in a tartan waistcoat. For a six-month spell Harpur diaried Iles's garments – other suits or blazers and flannels – as against mood. He'd daily filled in a chart pinned to the back of his office door, and disguised as a breaking-and-entering record of incidents and methods. But he'd failed to find a relationship between outfits and temper. Destructive malice, for instance, could spring vibrant and hale from Iles, regardless of any fashion choice. Likewise, something very close to sanity and reasonableness might show, also regardless of kit. On Harpur's chart the acronym 'BSB' might appear, indicating, on the face of it, 'Bell System Buggered' – i.e. the alarms of a warehouse had been totally neutralized by the thieves before their pinch. In fact the letters meant 'Blazer (Single Breasted)' and referred to Iles's garb on the day. Against the BSB entry could be a couple of capital Bs, signifying the ACC had been a 'Bloody Bastard' while in this garment; or S & S, short for 'Sweet and Saintly', although in the same single-breasted blazer.

Iles glanced at the *Daily Star*. He carried a cup of hot water, from which slight trails of steam rose, and sipped it with loud enjoyment now and then. Iles never took breakfast, said he'd been put off it eternally as a kid by the scatter-gun way his father ate baked beans on toast. On the day Iles told Harpur this, the Assistant Chief had, for a moment, reverted to childhood and instinctively raised a hand as if to wipe daddy's mouth missiles from his face and hair. 'Maud sends us here to look at the background and origins of an *old* murder and as soon as we arrive we get another, Col, most probably related,' he said. 'Fucking reporters. Why can't they stay in the newsroom hacking celebrities' voicemails, or fixing up big bribes by phone? What's he doing out on a nothing road in the night?'

'Cass was investigative.'

'And?'

'It happens with investigative journos.'

'What?'

'I think it's like this, sir, investigative journalists feel they have to get out and investigate. It's what makes them investigative.'

'Lying dead alongside a Ford Focus is not very investigative.'

'They follow their nose, like us.'

'And it leads them to a knifing.' In a similar movement to the baked beans response as a boy, Iles raised his hand to his left cheek, as if reminded of his own nose region. 'How do you think it looks now, Col?

'What, sir?'

'The impairment.'

'Well, I expect you've examined it in the mirror.'

'But I want *your* view, as its architect.'

'It has a plus side.'

'In which respect?'

'Neatness.'

'In which respect?'

'It's a perfectly rounded wound, not an untidy, crudely jagged skin rip, which would suggest a barbaric, wholly uncivilized attack.'

'Would you say the way it was given was *un*barbaric, then, Col, and civilized?' Iles put his index finger on the hole. 'Yes, it *feels* round. There's a definite shapeliness.'

'That's because it reproduces the shape of the . . . well . . . implement.'

'Which . . . well . . . implement?'

'The one that did it.'

'What *was* that?'

'I thought you'd have got a glimpse.'

Iles sipped again, sending his mind back in the pause. 'I had an impression of something green – yes, a greenness swinging in on me at the end of your arm, like a scythe tinted by chlorophyll from brambles.'

'That's very perceptive.'

'I was a detective. I perceive. At Staff College they called me "Des, the ever-open-eye".'

'A fine commendation.'

'If something, of its nature, can be seen, I, Iles, will see it. What was green?' Iles replied.

'A Biro with faint old traces of green ink in its barrel.'

'Yes, I thought a Biro. But difficult to believe. You actually carry one as weapon – no gun but a Biro?'

'I—'

'Previous to this use, did you write green messages to that undergrad Denise with it? Intimate, hot green messages? Does green turn her on? Do I want that kind of horny, pleb excess in my blood stream, Harpur?'

'It was there.'

'Where?'

'There. Under me.'

'There? Latent? Ready? You're telling me God or Fate or Fortune or What-have-you made it available so you could break into my face despite rank?'

'Chance.'

'Some will find it hard to understand this injury, Col.'

'Yes, it could be difficult for them to guess how and where it happened – the Elms mud and a role-play episode. It's not the sort of thing that comes up every day or evening.'

'In a way, a blemish of this kind takes away some of one's self-confidence, Harpur.' His voice had gone flaky, his tone shrivelled and pitiable. Occasionally, Iles could suddenly get like that: all the bombast, vanity and cockiness suddenly lost. Hadn't it happened through self-condemnation not long ago in his suite back home?

Harpur hated it when the ACC glissaded into uncertainty and weakness. If Iles could be reduced like this, anyone could. Harpur found the idea alarming, a step towards universal disintegration. Iles's usual arrogance, iron unmeekness and mighty brain power helped keep the world, or this bit of it, reasonably OK. It was damned irresponsible of him to turn frail and humble: self-indulgence through abasement. His customary roaring offensiveness must be allowed to flourish. It was offensiveness in a good and vital cause. Now, though, the face jab seemed to have punctured him, deflated him. As face jabs went, Harpur considered this one had been exemplary for timing, location and sheer power.

He said: 'Yes. I see the awkwardness. You can't very well announce you've been penetrated by a ballpoint. Oh, sure, Jane

Matson mentioned that mot stating the pen is mightier than the sword but this probably wasn't to do with an ex-Biro poking its way through skin.'

Iles thought about things for a while, then said: 'What I'd like you to do, Harpur, is go ahead of me, on your own, to the meeting with the Chief.'

'Certainly, sir.' Harpur yearned to help him back to full cantankerousness and true Des-Ilesian disdain. Although his suit might be brilliant, it couldn't on its own hold him together.

'Then I'll come in later,' the ACC said.

'Right. He didn't seem to notice the wound in Ruth Bowles's room. Or might have been too polite to mention it. In case he didn't notice, do you want me to forewarn him, alert him to it, so he's not surprised into uncontrollable giggling? I could explain its cause – the intense tussle at very much ground level on the housing estate, you out of your mind with jealousy; me as Tom Mallen/Parry; then you as the gunman and, I suppose, as Death.'

'Death, yes. If you open your gob like that I'll kill you.'

'Right.'

'This might be too subtle for you to understand, Harpur, but what I wish to give is a lively demonstration of carefreeness, suave blandness on my part. I *will* show up – that's necessary politesse – but I show up when I feel like showing up. Autonomous. I'm not bound by his holy Larkspur timetable and agenda. OK, I, without question, do display, quite prominently, a temporary unsightliness, but that doesn't mean I'm going to turn all crushed, unbuoyant, diffident.'

'Few would ever accuse you of being crushed, unbuoyant or diffident, sir.' Harpur realized at once he should have phrased this differently. His mind had momentarily gone slipshod again. Often Iles had rounded on that kind of attempted compliment, treated it as a blazing insult.

'Which fucking few, Col?'

'Yes, I'll do the warm-up for you,' Harpur replied. 'You'll be able to make a really worthwhile, debonair entrance, like David Niven in old movies, despite the Biro pit.'

'Thanks, Col.'

'What excuse shall I give?'

'Excuse?'

'For your absence.'

Iles smiled a large, tolerant smile. 'You don't understand, do you, Col?'

'Don't I, sir?'

'I have no need to offer an excuse. That's the kind of man I am, you see. Excuses are for serfs, subordinates and minions. Mine is an independent, cheerfully casual approach to things. It will become apparent to him when I arrive. Probably he already realizes as much from our previous visit. This will confirm. I defy adversity. I have a wound, yes, but what care I?'

'I'll just say you'll get there as soon as you can.'

'Not as soon as I *can*. As soon as I *wish*. Let him see that neither you nor he can corral Desmond Iles.'

'They don't build corrals able to achieve that, sir.'

'Who don't?'

'In general.'

Iles gargled unostentatiously with the remaining mouthful of hot water and then spat it back into the cup. 'A corral is a pen for animals, isn't it, Harpur?'

'Well, yes.'

'I've been penned but in a rather different sense.'

'Rather.'

'When I arrive, Col, smiling in an unapologetic way as I enter the room, I'd like you to say in a pleased, enthusiastic, spontaneous tone, "Oh, here's Mr Iles now! I'm so glad he's been able to fit you in, Chief".'

'Right, sir. I'll bone up on the spontaneity.'

The ACC went back to his room. Harpur wondered whether he needed some private time to polish up his free-spiritedness. Harpur had a couple of hours before the meeting at 11.30. He left the hotel and set out down the main road, past police headquarters, to the shops. He wanted to get something to send his sister as thanks for looking after Hazel and Jill. She often helped out when Harpur was away. The kids got on fairly well with her.

As he came near to the headquarters building, a man who'd been standing on the pavement outside turned towards Harpur and raised his hand in a kind of greeting. Harpur didn't recognize him. He had on a new-looking Barbour all-weathers jacket, a green and gold cravat, a Royal Enclosure brown trilby, green corduroy trousers and brown brogues. On the floor near him was a large zipped-up holdall. 'Mr Harpur? It is Mr Harpur, isn't it?' he said. The accent seemed local. 'I was intrigued by that conflict you had on the floor at Elms with your colleague, Mr Iles, presumably.'

'Oh, yes?' Harpur replied.

'Or rather more than presumably.'

'Oh, yes?'

'I thought you or he or both would come to this police building at some stage to, shall we say, "clock-in" on your repeat visit, much buzzed among the cognoscenti of such matters, so I waited around. You'll ask, "Waited around to what purpose?" And the reply is, I sought contact. That, though, is possibly not a satisfactory explanation, for you might well than ask, "To make contact with what purpose?"'

'This *is* puzzling.'

'Clarification comes! Well, you see, depending on one thing and another in the flow—'

'Which flow?'

'Of life, obviously. Depending on one thing and another in this flow, I sometimes move in for the night at one of those uncompleted houses on Elms. Hence I could audience your, as it were, recent contretemps. This appeared all-out savagery, correct me if I overstate. Now, you'll say to yourself, no doubt: "This man looks much too smart and clean and, in fact, fashionable, to be a dosser. His garments are of a county family mode." It's not the first time I've run into that type of reaction. Hardly so! But my answer is – always is – spruceness and a sustained style are even more required by someone leading what could admittedly be considered a somewhat unstructured life than by those in a more, shall we call it, without prejudice, yes, we'll call it a more *normal* existence.'

He nodded towards the holdall. 'In there, besides a sleeping bag and toiletries, are what could be termed more rough-and-ready clothes for when I'm in a setting such as Elms for an *in extremis* short period. This is a turn-and-turn-about arrangement. If I'm in those rough-and-readies, my more impressive outfit will be in the bag. Then, before I come to a spot such as this and in these circumstances – conversation with a distinguished police officer – I can take this *more* presentable stuff from the holdall, where it is then replaced by the *less* presentable garments, and so, having duded up, appear bandbox fresh and tidy as I trust you'll agree I am now, as if scheduled to visit a polo match later or that type of exclusive outdoor gathering.'

'First rate,' Harpur said.

'The rumour was certainly around among the said cognoscenti that you and the Assistant Chief would return, or had returned, and this, obviously, helped with identification during the mud shindig, providing, as it were, a longlist of possibles.'

'Right.'

'My resting place, not in *the* house, not number fourteen, you understand. Of course you understand. I'm not a superstitious or over-nervy person, but there are certain limits, I think you'll confirm. So, to sleep in a house where the shots came from – this is beyond the acceptable, even for someone who, on a temporary basis, is seeking a crash-out lodging. That house might have been fine for me before, but not since. I could *see* that house – the gun lair as previously mentioned – yes, I could see it from the dwelling I'd picked, number eighteen. Well, obviously, or I wouldn't have known about those antics of you and him in battle, would I?'

'That's a fact,' Harpur replied.

'It was dark and a bit of a distance, but nevertheless.'

He stopped. Harpur could have helped him out and asked, 'Nevertheless what?' But one of the most elementary rules of interviewing or interrogating was you let the subject fix his or her own pace, his or her own punctuation. He'd be about fifty, Harpur thought; thick fair hair protruding under the trilby, a round, unlined face, lively blue-grey eyes: he seemed someone who'd had plenty of good sleeps, on Elms or elsewhere. His complexion went well with the countrified clothes. You could imagine him at his ease among polo ponies and chukkas.

'Nevertheless,' he said. 'Yes, now what was that "nevertheless" about, though? Oh, dear! This is an adverb, but what was the verb it's adding to? Ah, I remember. "Make out" – that's the verb. Like so, then – nevertheless, I could make out it was definitely you, supine, and I guessed the other must be Mr Iles. When you were here last time, relating, eventually, to the arrest of Inspector Jaminel you both had your pictures in the local press and on TV quite a bit, and the reports said you were on an investigation into how the situation was being dealt with after the murder of the undercover man. So, most folk around here know how you look, but I admit I'm having to speculate that the one lying close to you in the rough stuff on the ground was Mr Iles. He had his back to me.

'And Mr Iles – if it *was* Mr Iles, which I think it must have

been – Mr Iles – and I say this with full appreciation of its serious-
ness, believe me – Mr Iles, he seemed to be trying to throttle you
as you lay on your back there, like you'd had a quarrel, that kind
of thing, an important quarrel if it made him want to kill you on
the very place someone else got killed, name of Parry or Mallen,
depending which end you're coming from, as it were. Usually, an
attack as all-out as that – strangulation of a friend or colleague – is
about a woman, referred to by the French, who sort of excel at this
kind of crisis, as "crime passionel". I don't know if you had been
giving it to Mrs Iles and he found out, maybe caught you on the
job, or *in flagrante delicto*, to hop from French to Latin. Revenge,
like a vendetta, could bring on that sort of violence.'

'Number eighteen suited you, did it?' Harpur replied.

'Obviously, what one looks for in this kind of venue is a property
with the roof definitely on and weatherproof and the flooring
complete, able to give a decent, consistent surface for the sleeping
bag. A sleeping bag without a floor under it would not offer a good
night's rest, would it?' He had a deep laugh about this and the cravat
quivered, bringing some silver spots in the design out from where
they'd been hidden among its folds. They gleamed mildly in the
morning sunlight. When he'd recovered, he said: 'Access through
a front window where the boarding up had been part removed. This
is so with several of the properties, if we can call them properties
at this non-completed stage. As a matter of fact, I was downstairs
trying to re-secure the boarding from inside so there'd be no intru-
sions while I slept when I saw the disturbance close to the house
two along, the killer house. It's grand to have a room of one's own.
Someone wrote a book about it. If you think of the Elms development, it's a kind of crescent, isn't it, like those famous terraces in
Bath, giving the house where I was a good angle to view the possible
throttle scene to the right.

'You'll ask, why didn't I do anything to stop this dangerous tussle,
such as shout or even get back out through the window and try to
pull the two apart before terrible damage was done, namely wipe-out
of you by him. Well, this is two big-time police gladiatoring. Do I
stick my nose into that? Or maybe not my nose, but at least my
voice. I don't think so. Mr Iles – if it *was* Mr Iles – has got some
grievance and he's not going to feel sweet about it if someone from
outside, such as self, interferes in a private brutality. What often
happens in that kind of imbroglio is the two stop trying to hurt each

other and turn on the third party, peacemonger, together. They – that's to say, you, plus Mr Iles – didn't know they – you and Mr Iles – were being watched by self and I decided it was better like that, safer like that. I was in my other, low-class, non-polo-match clothes. You and Mr Iles might think I must be some kind of tramp, and wouldn't care to have your behaviour questioned by such a one. I didn't exactly pass by on the other side, as the Bible says. I stayed put. But by staying put that's what I was doing – passing by on the other side. Or turning a blind eye.'

'You seem to be saying there'd been previous *"in extremis* short periods" when you looked for shelter on Elms,' Harpur replied.

'You're wanting to ask whether I was in one of the houses for a kip-down the night Mr Undercover got the bullets.'

'Were you?'

'No. That's what I wanted to discuss.'

'What's to discuss?' Harpur said. 'You weren't there.'

'I can understand why you turn abrupt, Mr Harpur.'

'Sorry. But if you weren't there you weren't there. You're no witness.'

'That's too simple. What's the *reason* I wasn't there? Have you pondered that, Mr Harpur? It's like in the Sherlock Holmes story, the dog that didn't bark. This negative was the clue nobody spotted except Sherlock himself. Similarly in this case. My name, though, is Hill-Brandon. Ivan Gladstone Hill-Brandon.

'*Why* weren't you there?'

'Exactly.'

'In what sense?' Harpur said.

'Because of one thing and the other, such as getting here to outside the nick at the start of the day, in case you and Mr Iles showed as a politeness matter towards this Chief, I seem to have missed breakfast,' he replied.

Harpur looked about. 'There's a caff open up the road.'

'Ah, so there is.' They walked towards it, Hill-Brandon carrying the holdall. 'This is the kind of situation where it's important to have on a becoming outfit, or they don't let you in, won't serve you. They're afraid of odours and/or lice. Their priority is their other customers, the regulars. I can sympathize.'

'Mr Iles doesn't have breakfast so it wouldn't affect him even if he was in scruffy clothes,' Harpur replied. More interrogation technique: to soothe the target you tried to follow up topics raised by him/her, even if it made you sound inane. They took a table. Harpur ordered two full Englishs although he'd had eggs and bacon at the hotel. It was necessary to achieve a kind of bonding: knife and fork comradeship.

Hill-Brandon said: 'I don't think I've got this wrong, despite the dark, but my impression was you stabbed Mr Iles in the upper-left cheek with what seemed to me a small, dirk-type weapon, small, yet able to cause quite a wound. I didn't know where on your person you'd been carrying this blade, but your arm came around in an arc as if you'd pulled it from a hidden sheath and administered a very corrective blow, corrective of his attempt to strangle you, possibly owing to a woman who'd put herself amiably – too amiably? – in your direction. If you'd been fishing in his pool it would be understandable you'd carry a knife in case he found out about it and went for you in extremely conducive circumstances, such as an unpeopled building site at night, unpeopled except for me, which neither of you would be aware of. Conducive, also, in that you were flat on the ground, helpless, apparently, as part of a re-enactment of the Jaminel pot-shot night. But only apparently. Somewhere about you was that defensive dirk.'

The food came. Hill-Brandon ate very systematically, no gobbling and no splutter of particles here and there as with Iles's father's beans. Hill-Brandon got more or less equal amounts of mushrooms or bacon or black pudding on to his fork every time, and gave each load a matching long chew. Harpur kept pace. There could not be bonding and comradeship otherwise. To peck at the meal would suggest superiority, as though Harpur had reserves of nourishment aboard and never fell into troublesome hunger, as Hill-Brandon might, owing to an unstructured existence lately.

He kept his trilby on, not to conceal lice, but because it had become a crucial part of his present image. Staff here might think that after a hearty, very British, sort of Empire-building meal from the old days he would be off to watch one of those traditional polo games he'd spoken of, or to buy another racehorse at auction. He said: 'That assault on Mr Iles's flesh seemed to work fine. I think there was a groan and then sighs from him and his hands fell back from around your throat. It was impossible for me to tell how far in the dirk went, but I had an idea it might have severed something important in his nervous system causing partial collapse of intent. A fraction of his morale could leak out through that kind of hole.

'Of course, I wondered if you would try another stab, on the principle of never let an enemy recoup, Mr Iles being, at this juncture, an enemy through possible cuckolding, though in general a colleague and boss. It's said Hitler lost the war because he didn't wipe out British forces in 1940, but let the bulk of them get away via Dunkirk, and eventually become fighting-fit again. So, I thought you might re-strike. Then, though, I heard police sirens. They approached fast, the din increasing. Perhaps someone else had witnessed the squabble on Elms and called nine-nine-nine. You two also heard this new factor in the situation. Both of you stood and then ran off together so as not to get caught, taking a direction away from the sirens. That made me think differently of you from what I usually think of the law, which is not favourable, owing to some unpleasant encounters.

'But people who start a bit of theatre, such as you and Mr Iles pretending to be the main folk in that murder, and then it turning really bad, followed by the frantic scarper because of the police arrival – it made me realize you were not so unlike the rest of us. I thought to myself, and still think to myself, I wouldn't mind giving a couple of adventurers of that sort a bit of help – which I didn't fancy previously, on account of me being one type of individual and you and Mr Iles being another. But anybody looking in through the window now would see you and me together with a spread and coffee and they'd decide we must be friends and in true accord.' He mopped up some egg yolk with half a piece of fried bread and Harpur did the same on his plate, to prove fellow-feeling and team solidarity.

'Thank you, Ivan.'

'I don't require thanks, Mr Harpur. I'm just describing a changed attitude on my part, which has been brought on by events. It is an inevitable development.'

'But thanks all the same,' Harpur said. 'And please drop the Mr, would you, Ivan? I'm Colin, or Col.'

'You ask how I can talk usefully about the undercover murder if I wasn't actually on Elm that night,' Hill-Brandon replied.

'It does seem a bit of a poser. I'll admit to being perplexed, Ivan.'

'Perhaps. But I'd like you to consider, Col, *why* I wasn't there that night. This will open up a new vista, and one by no means irrelevant.'

'Well, you've said you only went to Elms for *in extremis* short periods. I think I'm remembering that right.'

'You are, you are. But this *was* one of those short periods of *extremis* for me when the usual procedure would have been to hole up on Elms for a night or two, the first of those nights being the very one Mallen got it. Or got hit. Yet I did not proceed.'

'Proceed? So, you did start?'

'You're quick, Col. You know how to pounce.'

'You started but changed your mind – gave up?' Harpur said.

'Exactly that, Colin.'

'Something intervened?'

'Somebody. Some*bodies*.'

'In which respect?'

'I want you to think of the scene, Col – the scene that night, the night of the death. Well, of course, you and Mr Iles were trying to imagine – to act out – that night when you were down on the mud, as if shot in front of the house. But please broaden out your idea of that evening.'

'In which respect broaden out, Ivan?'

'Re me. Where am I in that visualizing? Where is Ivan Gladstone Hill-Brandon?'

'*Are* you in it? You said no, you weren't sleeping on Elms then.'

'Correct.'

'How can you be in the visualizing?'

'I was *approaching* Elms, Col. Approaching.'

'You were intending to sleep there but it didn't happen? Is that it? This was one of your *extremis* periods but—'

'Let's say I was *between* spells in various other accommodation units, some of a far more conventional nature than a half-finished house – yes, other accommodation with proper running water, hot and cold, a bed, even central heating. Invitation to the rooms of a recently met girl, for instance, or a friend's place.'

'But not available on that night?'

'Not immediately available in any of the locations where it sometimes was. So, I'd decided to take what in French is known as *faute de mieux* – something instead of the very best, but fairly OK, such as an empty property.

'For convenience, I'll term it a property. I thought I must make do with Elms until the situation elsewhere improved. This is what I mean by "unstructured". There can't be a set pattern to my life, due to an absence of certainty as to billet. I've had to adapt to these conditions. Previously I enjoyed a very regular existence, owning a shop, and a family home for my wife and two children. The shop went in the "downturn" as the slump's called – making it sound not quite so bad, though, really, it's terrible – and the house went with it and then my marriage came apart. I've had to get used to *faute de mieux*, haven't I?'

'You couldn't reach the house on Elms?' Harpur replied.

'This would be quite early in the evening, before the shooting. If I'm thinking of a sojourn in quarters available to anyone of the general populace I like to arrive there soonest – install myself satisfactorily, getting settled before any competition. There are plenty of people with unstructured lives these days who might want free shelter on an interim basis. I read in the Press of someone who lived in a bus shelter on a main road in Wales and had decorations up for Christmas. We are an expanding group requiring what is referred to officially as "domestic substitution at a rudimentary level".'

'How far towards the property were you, Ivan?'

'That's the point, isn't it?'

'*You* tell *me*.' This was the impulse behind all questioning, all interrogation: *you* tell *me*. There could be occasional prompts, though, if things seemed to be moving OK. 'You were using the sort of unofficial path through the estate?'

'Sharp again, Col. I'm on the path, coming from the Guild Square end, not the mall end, when I see ahead of me two figures in uniform.'

'We'd wondered whether Mallen-Parry had wanted to avoid someone, or more than one, on the path. You're saying they were police?'

'Who'd wondered?

'Myself. Others. So, definitely police?

'Police.'

'They're going in the same direction as you?'

'Well, they are, but very slowly. Sort of loitering? Yet alert with it. Looking about.'

'As if waiting for someone?'

'That's what I thought at the time. So, obviously, I was worried.'

'In what respect?'

'Are they there to stop people getting into one of the estate houses – and to catch anyone trying to get in? Most probably it's against the law to break in to those properties, removing boarding and so on. Maybe there have been complaints. I've had bother in similar environs previously. Some areas will put up with squatters at least for a while. Others won't. So, you'll see why I felt disturbed seeing them there.'

'I think they were present for a different purpose,' Harpur said. 'Not at all to do with you.'

'Well, of course, I think so, too, now. But now is not then.'

'You stopped, did you?'

'They had their helmets on. That puzzled me.'

'Why?'

'It made them so conspicuous – I mean, if they were trying to surprise someone getting into a house.'

'They *wanted* to be conspicuous.'

'Yes, I realize that now. Hindsighting.'

'Descriptions?'

'Too far off in the dark. And the helmets gave some concealment to their faces.'

'Build? Physiques?'

'One maybe six feet. The other slightly shorter and thinner. I stopped and turned back.'

'Why do you think they were there?' Harpur said.

'Why do you?'

'Where did you spend the night?' Harpur replied. *He* was the one who asked the questions. 'You couldn't stay in an Elms property and nowhere else was offering.'

'Not quite true. Luckily, I have another address, not too far away.'

'A different on-hold building project?'

'No. Some might regard this one as even more *faute de mieux*. But, again, all right for a crisis. It's walkable.'

He went into one of his silences again as if wondering whether to disclose a secret – disclose a secret to a cop. Harpur waited. He drank the remains of his coffee and then signalled to the waitress to bring a couple more. He wanted to suggest patience and relaxation.

Before they arrived, Hill-Brandon said: 'There are some big metal recycle bins, like skips but with a hinged lid, in the Tesco car park. Some for newspapers only.'

'Yes?'

'Half full are the best, obviously. You can usually find one like that. Newspapers make good blankets. And under you they are as soft as a mattress, nearly. They call the Press "the fourth estate". But newspapers are the second estate for me, the one after Elms.' He had a further laugh at this, and Harpur joined in. It was more comradeship. It recognized lateral thinking and the difference in outlook of those with an unstructured life and a special attitude towards the Press. 'Holdall as pillow. Close the lid, against the weather. But no claustrophobia because there's the sort of letter box on the side where people can push their papers through if they don't want to lift the heavy lid. Nobody's going to come dumping papers in the middle of the night. Important to get away early in the morning, but, in any case, newspapers falling on you wouldn't do much damage.

'It's not a twenty-four-hour Tesco but it opens at six a.m. I get into my good gear and go in and buy some fruit for breakfast. That way they can see I'm a genuine, very valid customer, so I'm entitled to go into their Gents to give myself a bit of a clean-up etcetera and shave.' He sat back in his chair. 'But you don't want to hear all that, do you, Colin? You're interested in the Elms.'

'The stuff about the recycle bin is an eye-opener.'

'How I see the night of the death is like this: Mallen-Parry, we heard from the court or local gossip, was coming back from the mall to help knock off Justin Scray, the dealer. Or so he thinks.' He paused while the new coffees came. He took a good gulp. When the waitress left he said, 'Mallen-Parry is an undercover cop and has to keep his cover so, although he's a cop, he doesn't want to run into these uniformed cops, just as I didn't, but for a different reason. Suppose the Scray hunt was genuine – as Mallen-Parry thinks – not just a ploy. Scray gets killed. There's a trawl for people who were in the vicinity. The two uniformed cops remember meeting head-on a man making for Guild Square on the path. They can give a description. Mallen-Parry is pulled in. He has to say who he really is. End of undercover operation, if not something worse. This is how he would calculate, anyway.

'Of course that's not how it really was, not a bit, because there's no Scray hunt. Parry-Mallen himself is the target, and the two uniformed officers have been sent to help with that. Parry-Mallen believes he has to get to Guild Square to maintain his cover. He decides to skirt the two officers, find another roundabout track to the Square. Which is why the two have been sent in their look-we're-police-officers-helmets. Tom turns off, and walks into Jaminel's killing range.'

'Yes, it could be like that.'

'You'll ask why I didn't mention all this at the first investigation. Answer: I'm not sure. But, as I said, when I saw the throttle attempt and the stabbing, I thought, these are not your ordinary police. These are human beings with their own human anxieties and their own games. I felt what's known as "rapport". Plenty of French today.'

'Good, Ivan.'

'You'll ask, did I recognize either of the uniformed men? This would give you a way into the conspiracy, wouldn't it? The word around is that you and Mr Iles are here to expose – that is, expose if you can – an "arrangement" between some drugs people and some police, such police taking backhander salaries for their cooperation and protection. You'd like to prove that Jaminel was just the fall-guy ordered to kill Mallen-Parry because he was a spy and might get to know too much about the "arrangement", maybe already knew too much about it. You yourselves, or someone above you, have, has, come to realize that getting Jaminel done and locked up is only the easy bit, the insignificant bit of the job. Those two men on the Elms path were probably part of the "arrangement", weren't they? It would be a big advance if you could discover who sent them.'

'And *did* you recognize either?'

'No, but I could work on it.'

'Work on it how?'

'Work on it,' Hill-Brandon replied.

'Keep very alert.'

'You're thinking of the dead journalist, are you, Col? Was he here to probe this post-Mallen situation, too?'

'It's possible.'

'Likely?'

'Possible,' Harpur said. 'You'll ask will there be something monetary for you in this.'

'Please, Colin. It's a matter of what I've already referred to as rapport.' He put a hand up and set the trilby more firmly on his head, probably to suggest four-squareness and a contempt for lucre in their new relationship.

Harpur paid for the breakfasts. He said: 'I'll talk to Mr Iles. There might well be a reward packet available. Get in touch again if anything shows. Or can I reach you? Have you got a mobile?'

'Yes, but can't always get it charged.'

'I'll take the number, anyway.' Hill-Brandon gave it and Harpur made a note. 'It's good the killing hasn't put you off Elms altogether, or you wouldn't have seen that little playful episode. Those houses might get completed once the economy picks up. I'm glad to hear there's the fallback pad at Tesco.'

'Tell me, Col, do you carry that dirk as standard?'

Harpur ignored this. He was the one who asked the questions. And, in any case, to say the stabbing had been done with an old Biro would take away much of the drama and raw humanity of those minutes. Hill-Brandon seemed keen on humanity, and Harpur didn't want him disillusioned.

THIRTEEN

Harpur watched Iles watching Rhys Dathan, Chief Constable of Larkspur. Harpur found it as hard to read Iles's face as it was to assess his feelings from the clothes he chose each day. The wound made it even trickier than usual to learn anything from the ACC's expression. The wound, of course, remained pertly, pinkly constant, no matter what might be happening elsewhere to Iles's features. Or might seem to be happening. Despite the difficulties, though, Harpur thought it would be reasonable to say Iles looked as if he didn't swallow all they were hearing from Dathan. The snag with this, of course, was that Iles rarely looked as if he swallowed everything from anybody – *any*thing from anybody, more like it.

He had arrived exactly on time for the Larkspur HQ meeting, dropping his original scheme to make a delayed, gloriously uncowed, smirking entrance to Dathan's precinct; no call in the event for Harpur's cry of rapture that Iles had somehow managed to fit Dathan into his schedule. Typical Iles, this switch of plans. Although his actions and words often seemed to defy what would be expected of a very senior police officer, ultimately that's what he was, a very senior police officer. He accepted this – had to and probably wanted to. The rules and customs always finally took him over. He believed in these rules and customs. But he'd flout them temporarily now and then, and do some of his freewheeling, soaring, unfettered soul stuff, just to show he could. Also, he liked to upset and confuse those he regarded as enemies: many.

And although very senior he wasn't at the top, and perhaps recognized he never would be. A Chiefdom, full-out and unadjectived, not an Assistant, was possibly beyond Iles. Occasionally this would infuriate him and he'd describe himself as an Asssissstant Chief Constable, the extra, crawly S sounds to emphasize his job's high-grade, bum-sucking servility. But Harpur thought Iles knew he needed a presence above him. He had to operate inside a frame, a frame fashioned by someone else. Iles was part of a hierarchy and must take his due spot in it. A Chief was a Chief, Dathan included, here at Larkspur. If he arranged a meeting you turned up when he said you should, even if you'd claimed you wouldn't on account of your freewheeling, soaring, unfettered soul. Hierarchies and souls didn't fit together very well.

They were in Dathan's office at headquarters. Because of the second breakfast with Hill-Brandon, Harpur had been forced to postpone his trip to the shops and he'd arrived in the headquarters foyer at the same moment as Iles, right on 11.30. The ACC had said in the lift on their way to Dathan's suite: 'Col, of course he's going to tell us again how happy he is to see us back, and that he'll make sure we get maximum cooperation, but I wonder. True, he accepted Maud's decision to send us in last time – not that he had an option. But, in any case, a second visit is something else. This makes it look as though he's presiding over a snake pit. How is it he's allowed things to develop like that? Now, he's got the dead reporter to make the scene even darker. He's going to worry that Maud and those above Maud in the HO will think he's lost control of this manor, and should be chucked.'

In his conference area Dathan pointed them to blue upholstered easy chairs. 'I'm so happy to see you again, Desmond, Colin,' he said. 'And as ever you can count on maximum cooperation from all of us here.'

'Thank you, sir,' Iles said.

'But you are injured, Desmond!' The Chief spoke considerately, no trace of a giggle. Perhaps he really hadn't noticed previously. Or there might be some tactical reason for postponing his sympathy.

'An old wound playing up, as it will, occasionally,' Iles said.

'When did you suffer it? How?' Dathan said.

'We've chosen a profession that has its perils, sir,' Iles replied.

'We do not succumb, dare not succumb, because of those who depend on us for quiet enjoyment of their lives. Enforcement of the law must be "in good hands", as George Savile, first Marquis of Halifax, said all those years ago, didn't he? From time to time the possessors of those good hands are subjected to attack and harm in other parts of their bodies. We decline to bleat or whimper. We display our wounds as red badges of service.'

'Oh, quite,' Dathan muttered. One of his staff brought tea. The Chief said: 'I had hoped the conviction of Jaminel marked the end of the case, you know. Maud Clatworthy thinks otherwise, and Maud . . . well, Maud is Maud.'

'Harpur also considered we'd failed here,' Iles said.

'You're hard on yourselves, surely, Colin,' Dathan said.

'Col is like that,' Iles said. 'His way is unflinchingly, utterly unflinchingly, even ruthlessly, to examine a situation and his part in it. If he sees faults or inadequacies he will say so, he will act.'

'And your own view, Desmond?' the Chief said.

'A quite interesting relationship has developed between Harpur and Maud, and may develop further, I believe,' Iles answered. 'She seems prepared to overlook what might be regarded as rather grossly, cruelly, libertine aspects of his, shall we call it, form?' Iles's voice began to rise screamwards, and a little froth lined his lower lip. 'For instance, without decency, shame or compunction he—'

'What Maud is disturbed about is the possibility that a whole network of sophisticated crookedness and corruption lay behind the shooting of Mallen,' Harpur said. 'A network we have touched only the edge of. It is powerful enough to demand, and get, silence from Jaminel despite the standard offer of a lighter sentence if he gave names and details of others in this probable complex criminal conspiracy.'

Iles said: 'You might think, sir, that a woman like Maud, wonderful brain, fine teeth, extremely capable lips, endearing arse, would not find herself drawn to an ageing, comically dressed, dick-driven—'

'We have, of course, some possibly useful leads from our previous investigation which were not proceeded with when the Jaminel conviction seemed, as you mentioned, sir, to close the case,' Harpur said. 'Maud believes it closed a *section* of the case, and potentially not the most important section.'

Iles seemed to have subsided. He brought a handkerchief from a jacket pocket and wiped his mouth. These fits never lasted very

long and Harpur liked to shepherd him away from his fury before
he began to list the locations where he believed Harpur and Sarah
Iles had betrayed him. As the ACC frequently made plain, the
sordidness of some of these spots especially enraged him.

The three discussed for a while the direction of these new
inquiries. Dathan listened, asked the occasional question. Iles
answered one or two of them and batted the others away. Dathan
said: 'And now this murdered reporter. We've spoken to his department head in London, who was very guarded, I gather. He claims
to have had no contact with Cass since he arrived here, but admitted
he was on what this editor called "a general investigative assignment". We can guess what that means, I think. There's a lot of
media interest – one of their own killed. We'll hold a formal Press
conference tomorrow.' The Chief was burly, square-faced, strong-
jawed, wide-necked with a good mop of grey hair worn fairly long
and pushed up at the front in what Harpur saw as a 1950s' style
quiff: it was boyish and historic. He seemed defensive and very
uneasy. Harpur could understand that, almost sympathize. Dathan
had survived the indignity of seeing one of his senior people nailed
by outside investigators – Iles, Harpur – and sent down for murder.
Now, this pair of troublesome invaders had come back, aiming to
prove that things in his domain were rotten all through; possibly
more rotten now than they'd appeared at the Jaminel trial. And, as
the Chief said, the Press were on to it, and would be on to it in
numbers following the slaughter of one of their gifted and best-
known colleagues.

Harpur and Iles walked back to the hotel together. As they passed
the breakfast cafe Harpur recalled a remark of Hill-Brandon's. He'd
said that anyone looking in through the window would see him and
Harpur together with the meal and coffee and they'd decide the two
of them must be pals and in true accord. Just after that had come
the mutual mopping up of egg yolk with fried bread, perfectly
synchronized eating, a picture of considerable, all-round buddiness.
Harpur's memory of part of Hill-Brandon's statement might not be
verbatim, but the resounding last phrase 'in true accord' certainly
was.

Hill-Brandon had meant this in a positive, heart-warming sense
that helped show his change of attitude towards police. Harpur
thought of it differently now, though. Somebody looking in might
decide this was an informant cascading what he knew to a cop over

an on-expenses meal: the cop's expenses. As Hill-Brandon had pointed out, Harpur's face was familiar following media coverage of the previous investigation. Hill-Brandon, due to his homeless wandering around the city, his holdall and alternative garbs, might also be familiar. Perhaps among those looking in were officers on their way to or from the HQ across the road. And among *these* might be profit-sharers in the 'arrangement' between police and drugs dealers that Harpur and Iles had been sent to expose and destroy.

Harpur wished now he'd been more emphatic and more thorough in warning Hill-Brandon to go carefully when he began to 'work on' the identity of the officers he'd glimpsed ahead of him that night on the Elms short-cut path. Hill-Brandon wasn't trained in the skills of sensitive research, where 'sensitive' meant hazardous. He'd been a shopkeeper. He lacked elementary wariness. Hadn't he possibly made himself conspicuous by hanging about outside the nick scheming to intercept Harpur or Iles or both? Such clumsiness and maybe new instances to come could be . . . yes, hazardous. Someone, or more than one, might see the link between his nosing activities and the level-pegging, mates-together breakfast.

At the hotel when he was alone for a short while Harpur tried the mobile number Hill-Brandon had given him. No contact, though. You couldn't recharge a battery in an unwired shell of a house on Elms, or in a recycle bin at Tesco: the supermarket's slogan, 'Every little helps', didn't include free use of power points.

FOURTEEN

Apparently, in one of the local papers Iles had noticed a theatre advertisement for a play called *The Revenger's Tragedy*, by somebody centuries ago he had heard of, or by somebody else he'd also heard of. One of the things about Iles was he'd heard of quite a few people from the past, not just the obvious like Nelson or Moses, but less familiar folk. This play was on at The King's theatre in the city centre. He said: 'As you'll know, Col, some give the authorship to Tourneur, spelled with two U's, not just the one as in "turner and fitter", but many claim it for Thomas Middleton, and others say others. There are scholars who earn a fair screw by saying, "I'd bet on Cyril Tourneur with two U's", or "I'd bet on Thomas Middleton", or "I think X or Y or Z because of the unique way he uses the word 'and'." The piece has killings, rape, seduction, procurement by the hero of his sister – really zestful, joyous, lip-smacking evil. The hero talks to his very dead mistress, calling her "the bony lady", meaning not that she's anorexic but a skeleton. You probably didn't realize there were people called Cyril so long ago.'

Iles proposed he and Harpur should relax by going to see the tragedy together this evening. Harpur didn't fancy that. Although he greatly liked some of the plot, as vividly summarized by Iles, Harpur always tried to keep social contacts with him to the minimum, as distinct from unavoidable contacts through work. There had to be a limit. Possibly this guardedness on Harpur's part dated from that time when Iles, flourishing his crimson scarf, would make a play for Hazel, Harpur's elder daughter – elder, but still under age. Iles seemed to have given up on that now, but Harpur's caution had become built-in, permanent.

Of course, the sexual tensions between Harpur and Iles were complex and not at all one-sided. There'd been Harpur's daughter, but there'd also been Iles's wife. Revenge could be a tricky topic. Something in a play of this sort would probably set off one of the ACC's uncontrollable resentment spasms about Sarah Iles and Harpur, and he'd start shouting the location and frequency details of the love-making, and perhaps noisily blubbing from massive self-pity, messing things up for the rest of the audience and for the actors, and looking especially awful even in the theatre's subdued lighting because of the Biro face cleft. From what the ACC had said about the play's violence, Harpur thought that, if there'd been Biros about in those days, there could easily have been a similar stabbing. Extreme drama ought to stay behind the footlights.

Supposing Iles did one of his rants, he'd probably be asked to leave and, naturally, wouldn't, not peacefully. There might be fighting in the aisle, with Harpur and usherettes or management trying to quell the Assistant Chief, who had a PhD in head-butting. Some might feel amused, thinking it a deliberate, scripted 'happening', designed to give a sort of updating and parallel to the rough stuff on the stage. But most people would be annoyed, perhaps scared, and might demand refunds, calling Iles a loony or piss-artist or a loony piss-artist, though the Assistant Chief could, in fact, create this kind of shambles without the help of drink. He had enormous bedlam reserves. Harpur hated getting caught up in such public, Des-Ilesean, essentially sad disturbances. And Rhys Dathan wouldn't think much of it, either, if word got back. There seemed something rather off-key about an ACC fucking up a very worthwhile literary occasion.

'You go, sir,' Harpur said to Iles. 'I'll have a prowl around.'

'Around where?'

'Yes, around. The purlieus, I think they're called.' His fears for Hill-Brandon remained. Harpur ought to try to find him and make sure he was all right and understood the hazards and threats. People got snuffed in this domain. Harpur and Ivan Hill-Brandon had been on dangerous show in that breakfast cafe.

'Are you sitting on some information, Col, in your customary, festeringly stealthy mode?' the ACC said.

'Which kind of information, sir?'

'The informative kind.'

Harpur thought he wouldn't mention the Hill-Brandon meeting and egg and bacon conference for the present. Harpur liked to time carefully any briefing of Iles and this was not the right moment to bring him up to speed on Hill-Brandon. Often Harpur loved to confer ignorance upon the ACC. In any case, Harpur realized he might not be up to speed on Hill-Brandon himself. This was what fretted him, and when Iles had left for the theatre and it grew dark Harpur went to the Elms site again. He hoped that if the more usual and comfortable accommodation remained unavailable Hill-Brandon might have moved into one of the estate bedrooms for the night, though not the one Courtenay Jaminel had fired his two death shots from: squatting observed its own special, goofy etiquette.

Hill-Brandon had said he liked to come early to grab a favourable spot for himself and his sleeping bag. Harpur carried a torch to use in the properties and try to find outside where the boarding might have been interfered with to allow entry. This couldn't be a foolproof process because Hill-Brandon had said he actually went downstairs to re-fix boarding in number 18 so he would have a place to himself. Harpur remembered the location Hill-Brandon had given of the house he was in on Biro night and his account of the way he'd got access. It had been by loosened boarding at the front, whereas Jaminel had used a rear door and sprung a lock in the other house.

The Jaminel property was two to his right, Hill-Brandon said: Jaminel's turret, his fortress. Harpur had taken his daughters on holiday recently to the Mar Minor region of Spain south of Alicante, and they'd stayed briefly – not briefly enough – in a ghastly town called San Javier, full of big villas built to look like medieval castles with towers, battlements and loopholes, done in pink or orange. The Elms house was only that – a house, a part-completed house – but it had more warlike qualities than any of that stupendously naff Spanish architecture. Hill-Brandon had been trying to patch up the front access point from inside when he'd spotted Iles and Harpur in the mud. That suggested the boarding had not actually been removed or seriously damaged; perhaps some of the wall screws taken out, allowing the wood to swing sideways on a surviving screw like a pendulum, if you knew about it and gave a push. And Hill-Brandon would know about it: he was an *habitué*.

As he approached the houses, Harpur tried to guess at and follow the exact route taken by Tom Mallen along the established pathway, then diverting from it. According to Hill-Brandon, that was because Mallen wanted to avoid the two helmeted and obvious police officers hanging about on the path ahead of him; the same two officers who had also caused Hill-Brandon not merely to divert but go to alternative, downgrade lodgings in the Tesco recycling and stopover facility. Harpur couldn't know exactly the spot at which Parry changed direction but thought he had it reasonably right.

In a while, he crossed the small rectangle of ground where the body had been found by Jane and Gerald on their way back from shopping, and where Harpur and the ACC had fought. Harpur felt this tussle brought a flavour of farce to things now, despite the crafted tragedy of the sergeant's death. He stopped in front of the house sometimes used by Hill-Brandon and had a good gaze at the downstairs boarding. He thought he could detect something slightly adrift at one of the bay windows to what might some day be a top-of-the-range lounge. When he went closer he found it as he'd imagined: a couple of the planks had been freed from all but one wall plug and could be pushed right and left to make a gap, like opening a pair of curtains. He put his head through and called out at good, friendly volume, 'Ivan, Ivan Hill-Brandon, are you in here? It's Col. Just a social call. I happened to be in the vicinity. Nothing serious.' No reply and no sound of any movement.

He bent double and stepped over the sill into the room. He was wearing a brown leather jacket and he took this off now, folded it and placed it where it would hold the two planks slightly apart. From burglars over the years he had learned always to leave yourself a quick and obvious exit from a property. It had become for him a more or less automatic drill when entering a problem building, perhaps illicitly, perhaps illegally now and then. Although he had the torch to help him find his way back, he still felt compelled to follow the rigmarole. The ground floor was woodblock, scattered with a lot of brick and timber debris.

Harpur kept the torch on and picked his way across the room, out into the hall and stood at the foot of the stairs. He called Hill-Brandon again, but without any answer. Harpur began to climb the stairs. He took them quickly, another ingrained habit. Police training taught that you were at your most vulnerable when on stairs. Gunfire could get you from below or above, so don't loiter. True, Hill-Brandon wasn't likely to be armed, wasn't a gangster but an ex-shopkeeper, wiped out by the Coalition's 'we're all in this together' policy, though government ministers seemed to keep their heads above water OK. Hill-Brandon might be harmless, but Harpur still moved fast on the stairs.

There were six doorways off the first-floor landing, with as yet no doors. They opened on to what in due though uncertain course would be bedrooms and bathrooms. He gave priority with the torch beam to the two front bedrooms, the biggest. In time, one or other of these might be known as 'the master bedroom' and Harpur had the notion this would appeal to Hill-Brandon who had been used to some status as a home and shop owner, particularly as the floors of these two main bedrooms were in place and would very adequately provide a base for one's sleeping bag. It was in the nature of floors to give support.

Hill-Brandon was not in either bedroom, however. Harpur saw traces of previous use in each. Rats and mice would have seen off any food remnants but in one room the torch lit up wrapping paper that might have held bread or cold meat, and a couple of Heinz soup cans, the contents presumably taken cold, beef broth and tomato. The sight of these tins heartened Harpur. They would bring sustenance. Heinz used to boast of 57 varieties of their soup flavours, and perhaps there were more now, so anyone living on them could have a change of daily diet for at least eight weeks and then revert to the beginning.

He was also pleased to find no ciggy ends, though he didn't have any special views about smoking. Denise got through what might be half a twenty pack a day and he enjoyed seeing her jet the fumes from her nose after they had done a good, swift inner tour of her chest. But for someone like Hill-Brandon, reduced to a comparatively deprived kind of life, tobacco smoke might do extra-swift damage, especially if he'd unhygienically picked up the butts in the gutter and reclaimed the remaining half centimetre to the very last of the possibly infected tip. So far Denise had no cough and didn't gasp, except when she should be gasping. She probably had a spliff now and then, but mainly she went for tobacco. He didn't like to think of her having a fag with some male acquaintance – say another student – and their outgoing smoke mingling damn intimately in the air around them. He didn't like to think of it but he did think of it, and it niggled him. He saw this as only a step away from merging their bodily fluids.

Harpur was taking big, self-righteous pleasure from his session of sympathy and large-mindedness towards Hill-Brandon when he thought he heard movement behind him downstairs. He couldn't place it exactly. He switched off the torch. He considered calling out to Hill-Brandon again, but then reconsidered and didn't. Harpur reasoned that if Hill-Brandon came here for the night he would, as he'd said, arrive early to get his spot on reliable floorboards. This was not early by the standards of someone looking for an untroubled and secure kip. Harpur needed a minute in the dark to adjust to the possibility of meeting someone else – most probably someone he didn't know, and whose behaviour he couldn't foretell.

A woman said in a chatty, jaunty tone, 'Ivan, Ivan, dear, what is it with your coat?'

'How do you mean, my coat?' Harpur said, aiming his voice down the stairs and trying to keep the same genial intonation. The woman must have entered the house deftly, quietly, through the adjusted planks. She seemed to be standing at the bottom of the stairs. Harpur had the impression of someone in, maybe, her late twenties and possibly wearing a navy or black jogging suit.

'You're not Ivan,' the woman said.

'No.'

'But it's your coat – the brown leather job?'

'Yes,' Harpur replied.

'I come back to the original question, then: what is it with the coat? I saw it folded and carefully placed, and decided somebody must be in here. Ivan might have been in any of the houses, except that tainted one, "the bullets house", as he titles it. When I saw the coat, it sort of narrowed things down, though, clearly, I didn't know he had a leather coat, which, in the event, turns out to be accurate, because the coat's yours.'

'Right. It's to signal an exit. Luckily it's not cold tonight or I'd miss it, obviously.'

'Alternatively, I took it as signalling an entrance,' she replied.

'It's the polar opposites in the very same article. This can happen in life. Think of two sides of the same coin, or that saying, "My enemy's enemy is my friend".'

'I'm not certain either of those is a match,' she said.

'This is not the kind of setting for mere verbal quibbles, surely – a half finished house in the dark.'

'Who *are* you?' she replied. 'I seem to remember your face – in so far as I can see it.'

'Like you, I was looking for Ivan Hill-Brandon.'

'Why?' she said.

'We could each ask the other that, I suppose,' Harpur said.

'We could, and I'm asking you,' she said. 'Do you think he might be in some sort of danger?'

'Is that why *you're* here?' Harpur replied.

'I saw the folded coat there, holding the two planks apart, and this was bound to prove a kind of pointer.'

'Which?'

'Which what?' she replied.

'Which kind of pointer?'

'Some planning has gone into your visit,' she said. 'There's a purpose to it.'

'To find him.'

'For all I know, that might mean to do him some harm. This whole area has a disturbing reputation.'

'And yet Ivan liked to bivouac here.'

'Not much choice.'

'How about you?' Harpur said.

'How about me in what sense?'

'*You* might have been here to do him harm. In that case, the folded coat would have been a mistake. A big one. It would draw you into the house and if he were here you would have found him, possibly surprised him.'

'But he isn't here, is he?' she said.

'No. My name's Harpur, spelled with a u. It's Scottish, I think.'

'Well, I noticed this name in the Press when that killing took place near here. And a photograph. Ah! It's why I thought I recognized you. You're police, yes? That means you think he might be in some peril.'

'He might be.'

'Well, not from me,' she said.

'No, I don't imagine from you. I think you, also, fear he might be in peril and have come to try to help.'

'Are we both here for that?'

'Probably. Who are *you* then?'

'It scares me,' she replied.

'What?'

'The fact that both of us, quite independently, feel he's got possible trouble. We've each picked up what I've referred to in connection with the folded coat as pointers. Occasionally, he'll stay with me.'

'Yes, I understand that.'

'He's a good person. He shouldn't get pitched into an evil situation without in any way choosing that kind of involvement.'

'I agree.'

'I've been away working and I come back and hear about the killing of this journalist now. We already had that other death a while ago. I think of Ivan, living the way he does, and exposed.'

'Yes, that's how it could be.'

'And you're here for the same matter, aren't you? This is frightening. We endorse each other.'

As if to underline that idea, the doubling of the message, this house gave an echo to the words, 'We endorse each other.' No doors had been fitted anywhere so the echo had plenty of routes to chase itself on. He let the beam bounce off the stairwell walls and take her in. Auburn hair to just below ear level, perhaps its natural colour. About twenty-seven, twenty-eight, and in a dark jogging outfit, as he'd thought. Good, considerate/worried face, fresh skin, small, inquiring nose, rounded, nice chin which would fit very comfortably between Hill-Brandon's thighs. He would do all right here when she was available, which would be less often than he wanted, but, to his credit, he'd made himself adaptable in at least a couple of

fall-back pads. He didn't get all distressed and shattered when she
was absent. He had mental resources and notable creativity, which
enabled him to see opportunity in a Tesco bin. She obviously valued
him, and he might deserve it. Harpur kept the torch on and went
downstairs. 'I'm Veronica,' she said, though without holding her
hand out to be shaken or offering her cheek to be kissed.

'Colin, Col.'

'I feel as if I've let him down twice,' she said. 'Once, obviously,
when the undercover man died. Ivan set out to come here because
I wasn't around in Kitchener Street and couldn't give him a place
to sleep and so on.'

'Well, you have to go to work.'

She shrugged, as if the obvious was the obvious, but it still didn't
excuse her. 'He might have *been* seen and noted by cops on the
path. That gaudy cravat. You'd be interested more in what he saw
than in whether he'd been seen, wouldn't you? But it's a clear
possibility, isn't it, that he was spotted? He wouldn't speak of it.
He'd regard that as alarmist.'

'You'll see office blocks with notices on declaring, "This building
is alarmed". Sometimes it's right to get alarmed.'

'Of course it is, but Ivan isn't the sort who'd want to cause worry
by suggesting he might be living under a threat. He told me about
giving up on the path because of what he'd seen. I personally worked
out that he, himself, might have been seen. And then I come back
this time and hear a journalist who possibly knew something about
the real situation here had been killed. Silenced? A reporter who'd
only recently arrived, but with a reputation for digging out stuff.
Well, Ivan knows something about the situation here, too, doesn't
he? He must, or why would you be stalking him? And, I'm not on
hand to keep him off the streets, where he's so damn conspicuous
with that holdall for his alternative costume.'

Harpur found this term 'costume' strange as a means of describing
a man's clothes. He wondered whether it told something about her
work. He could imagine her running karaoke on a holiday ship and
switching costumes for each show. That pleasantly rounded, friendly,
multi-purpose chin would help get passengers into a party mood.

'In the Tesco bin – I mean, what chance would he have, shrouded
with newspaper, if someone came looking?' she said. 'Lift the lid,
and there he is, like a prisoner in a dungeon. A gunman speaks the
Tesco discount vouchers motto down at him, "Every little helps"

and adds, "So here are a couple of rounds for you, Ivan, neither bigger than point-thirty-eight inches wide but able to tear suitable holes in you at very short range, anyway."'

'I've thought about that Tesco slogan myself. We should go over there,' Harpur replied. 'We could knock gently on the lid so as not to shock and terrify him.'

'I've been earlier. It's on my way. He's not there, either.'

This area where they talked would justifiably be called a hall when the house was finished. It would be about twelve metres square. The squareness mattered. Harpur's mother would always refer to the equivalent feature in the house he was brought up in as 'the hall', spoken with a mild clang of pride; whereas most of the neighbours called that section of their homes 'the passage'.

As a child, he used to think this description about right. It wasn't square but like a thin corridor with doors off to the living room and sitting room and reaching the kitchen finally. But his mother considered that to dub it 'the passage' was humiliatingly basic and low class. There'd been a barometer in their hall and every day his father used to tap the glass with his knuckles, not hard but persuasively, to get the latest atmospheric pressure reading and forecast. His mother and father obviously thought that such a relationship with Nature's workings needed the proper kind of setting: a hall. In other words, that hall had a climate function. It was not just an indoor alleyway and rat-run. Halls set the tone of a house. His mother would undoubtedly have regarded this potential hall on the Elms development as brilliantly suitable for the discussion of something perhaps extremely serious, such as the disappearance of Ivan Hill-Brandon. Harpur continued with the torch beam, not directly and offensively on Veronica but to the side, fixed now on a patch of wall that would be ideal for a barometer. 'Are you to do with karaoke at sea, such as on a cross-Channel ferry?' he asked.

She held up a hand as though about to begin some sort of performance in witty answer. But after a moment he realized her signal meant they should be quiet. He heard what she might have already heard, footsteps on the dirt outside, nimble but less than assured footsteps, like someone pretty certain he or she was in the right general area, but not exactly, absolutely, where he or she wanted to be. That was the thing about Elms: it offered quite a degree of choice. Harpur sensed movement near the coat fender. He shifted slightly and put the torch ray on to the gap in the front room. They

saw Iles, crouched and squinting into the property. It was not the
squint of someone examining the house because he might one day
want to buy it; no, this squint showed he thought an individual or
individuals might be in there and he wanted to know who and why.

The focused beam made his Biro wound glow reddish, like a
level-crossing warning light. He had on civilian clothes, of course,
and no hat. To Harpur, the ACC looked like somebody who'd been
having a fine and educational time with fiction lately, such as *The
Revenger's Tragedy*, but now demanded the real, and would examine
it ruthlessly. 'Is that you behind the glare, Col?' he said. 'I recognized the coat, bought cheap when they were putting down many
cattle diseased by badgers, so oodles of leather available. I thought
you'd be around here – a secret carry-on that you'd prefer to the
theatre.'

'How was *The Revenger's Tragedy*, sir?' Harpur replied. 'You're
the sort who would pick up the theme of a drama, whether you
were in the stalls or the dress circle. Did they have intervals – to
cater for your quite manageable complaint?'

'I'm Veronica Pastor,' she said. 'You must be the other one.'

'That depends on your starting point,' Iles said. 'But, in principle,
no. Harpur is the other one. I'm more towards the supremo
position.'

'Do come in. We mustn't keep you on the doorstep, must we,
Col?' she replied. Iles climbed through. 'Two police officers from
a different force came to examine the situation here after the undercover murder and now, bingo, you both seem to have come back,'
she said.

'It's necessary, Veronica,' Iles said. 'Not only Harpur and I realized this, but a girl called Maud, very ready to put out for Col, in
my opinion. Reading all that ancient Greek soft porn at Oxford
makes them exceptionally questing and inventive sexually. Maud
didn't like what she saw here, and what she still sees. How are you
connected with the killings, Veronica?'

'She frequently accommodated someone named Hill-Brandon,'
Harpur said, 'but in a catch-as-catch-can mode. To her he's Ivan,
skint, and implicated oddly, interestingly, in the Mallen narrative.'

'How did you find that out?' Iles said.

'I'd have given Ivan a key,' she said, 'so he could use the flat
when I'm not at home, but my sister lives with me and was afraid
that if I wasn't there neighbours would think Ivan was fucking both

of us on a turn-and-turn about schedule. If it's Tuesday it must be
Veronica. I should have ignored her prissy objections. Ivan's safety
should be prime. A really urgent need, this. My sister isn't the sort
he'd fancy, anyway – those thick legs, like a larder in her stocking.'

'This Hill-Brandon is involved how, Harpur? I don't recall the
name,' Iles said.

'In mainly a negative sense,' Harpur said. 'He wasn't here on
the night, but almost here. This is crucial.'

'How?' Iles said.

'I've got nothing against theatre,' Harpur replied, 'old or current.
But this evening I felt a yen to get down here to the Elms, even
though this yen was founded mainly on the negative aspect I've
mentioned.'

'You felt a yen, did you, Col?' Iles said. 'He felt a yen, Veronica.
Did you feel a yen, also? Were plenty of yens getting felt around
here?'

'A yen like that comes unexpectedly out of nowhere but is very
compulsive,' Harpur said. 'Clearly, I might have had a yen to see
The Revenger's Tragedy, which would have been more positive, I
admit. But this was not the yen that took hold of me.'

'The thing about leather in a coat like that, although folded and
set down in a packet on ground hardly spruce, is that once it's been
uncrumpled by wearing, or hung up in a wardrobe, it will soon
recover its proper shape and smoothness,' Veronica said.

They left the house. Harpur recovered his jacket and put it on.
The planks fell back into place, seeming to shut off the prospective
dwelling, yet providing an entry method if you knew where to look
and how to operate the movable panels. Veronica said: 'I can't help
noticing that facial lesion, Mr Iles, which is definitely not leprosy.
Did Col Harpur organize the wound?'

'Why do you say that, Veronica?' Iles replied.

'The non-reference to it between the two of you, as if it's an
embarrassment, because you're supposed to outrank him, yet you've
taken a rather picturesque degradation,' Veronica explained.

'That's what Harpur would passionately like it to be, but it isn't,
can't be, can it?' Iles remarked.'My core remains my core, intact,
robust.'

'Isn't it this disagreement that puts any discussion off-limits,
censors it, redacts it?' Veronica said. 'There's a very gentlemanly,
unspoken treaty to avoid talking of it.'

'I don't see Mr Iles as a gentleman,' Harpur said at once.

'No, I wouldn't want to be herded into that shit flock, ta very much,' Iles replied. 'Curtailed. Restricted. I'm fiercely interested in Harpur's coat. It has a massive bearing on the Mallen case and subsequently, such as now.'

'My jacket to do with all that?' Harpur asked. 'In which respect, sir?'

Veronica said: 'The main part of your evening was at the theatre, yes, Mr Iles? Virtually an afterthought brought you to the Elms. You wouldn't want any delay in your search. Sight of the coat helped speed things for you. It directed you to the desired spot.'

'Yes, but that's not what I mean,' Iles said. 'Likewise the discussion of the wound and the concept of gentlemanliness. These are very significant. Incidentally, on the matter of gentlemanliness and class generally, Harpur's family is in Berks' Steerage.'

'You're telling us that all this is relevant to the Mallen case?' Veronica said with a small laugh. 'Soon, you'll claim the play was relevant, too!'

'In a way, yes,' Iles said.

'Which?' Harpur said.

'Which what, Col?' Iles replied.

'Way.'

'*The Revenger's Tragedy*,' Veronica said. 'That's ages old. Jacobean? By Tourneur with two U's, or Middleton?'

'Mr Iles has already told me that,' Harpur said. 'My name's with one U, not er at the end.'

'And yet the play's not totally ancient and passé,' Veronica said. 'A friend of mine who worked for the BBC said that when they were adapting a drama called *House of Cards* for TV the writer was told to "think Jacobean", meaning, I suppose, evil as humour and nods and winks to the audience, to help out the dialogue.'

'But that's not what I'm getting at. Not at all,' Iles said.

'Oh?' Veronica sounded snubbed.

'I'm thinking of time,' the ACC replied.

'Which time?' Veronica said.

'The time it's taking us to get back to the path,' Iles said. 'We've been able to discuss my injury, gentlemanliness, the Jacobean period, the BBC, and Harpur's coat. That coat has sorted itself out, as you promised it would, Veronica.'

'Well, yes, but so what?' Veronica asked. 'Leather does that.'

'So you instructed us,' Iles said. 'It's fascinating to see it happen, though, given adequate time. It makes me realize how far off the path we must have come. And how far Mallen must have come. That would seem to indicate he'd had a real fright of some sort on the path. Considerable avoidance tactics. Harpur and I tried to mock-up the events of the death night, but we became distracted by some mutual, extremely lively hatred, and had to leave before we'd learned very much.'

'We knew he'd come off the path,' Harpur said.

'But I hadn't realized the full distance, the massive urgency,' Iles said. 'Stupid of me.'

'It could be important, yes,' Harpur said.

'You were on to it already, were you, you selfish, dissembling sod?' the ACC replied.

'He saw two police officers ahead,' Harpur said. 'Helmets. They're unidentified.'

'I'd suspected this, hadn't I?' Iles asked.

'I haven't finished my inquiries into that side of things,' Harpur said. 'I couldn't confirm.'

'Why you came down here tonight?' Iles asked.

'Yes. Veronica *has* confirmed, but it was good fortune, not pre-planned.'

'So, I can be told at last, can I, Harpur, because I got halfway there myself, by noticing how long the chat took and the leather progress?' Iles said.

'True, it has substance now,' Harpur said. 'I wouldn't bring you something merely speculative, would I, sir? No names for the officers on the path yet.'

Of course, he wondered whether Hill-Brandon could have done better with a description of the two but was holding back for his own, hidden reason.

'Harpur aims to keep ahead by any Jesuitical trick and sophistry possible, Veronica,' the Assistant Chief said.

'But he would never comment on that disgusting cheek hole, no matter how prominent,' Veronica said. 'He has deep consideration for you.'

'He has fucking *what*?' Iles said.

'He'd be ashamed to serve you incomplete info,' she said.

'We need to go through all the job assignments and rosters for that evening,' Harpur said.

'We do, we do,' Iles said.

'There you are, you see,' Veronica cried delightedly. 'It all works out harmoniously regardless.'

'Regardless of what?' Iles replied.

'Regardless in a general sense, yet also very specific,' Harpur said.

FIFTEEN

Most of the time, Emily Young felt like one of Bin Laden's wives, or Diane Keaton, as the fictional Kay, married to Michael Corleone in *The Godfather*: they suspected, of course, that their husbands' careers had mysterious, even dodgy, aspects. These were intelligent women, hardly stooges. They'd learned not to get obstreperously inquisitive, though. Tactfully preserved fog hung about. Kay Corleone lived – lived well – on the proceeds of Mike's mysterious, even dodgy, occupation, and this tended to inhibit curiosity about the source of the considerable family money. It wasn't so much mercenary as an acceptance of the seemingly normal: their household ran like this and had run like it for a long while. Kay took it as natural. And, as one of Bin Laden's wives said, some of his activities were Bin's concern, not hers, and she didn't interfere. Quite. Emily had heard Leo, her husband, praise a Mrs Bin Laden for that wise demarcation.

Just the same, Emily Young had lately begun to feel an exceptional unease about Leo's income and overall business status. As she understood it – as she required herself to understand it – this overall business game centred on profitable investing which was not a loll-back-and-enjoy-it position, but needed positive, day-to-day, hands-on nurturing. Leo had to be out and about, directing things. Occasionally he spoke of hedge funds, takeovers and salvage potential, which she assumed meant asset stripping of tottering companies bought cut-price; not a very wholesome way to profit but entirely legal and genuinely entrepreneurial. There would be business folk who did operate like this – make a living like this – though she didn't feel totally sure Leo must be one of them. Was there something else?

Occasionally, she'd become aware of distaste for Leo among her acquaintances, but she'd schooled herself to put up with that, especially as many successful, seemingly respectable business roles had their dubious, even shady, aspects. Some of her colleagues on the city's museum committee were seriously Socialist anyway, and talked like that caricature Leftie, Dave Spart, in the satirical magazine *Private Eye*. They took a hostile, suspicious view of all private enterprise, particularly successful private enterprise, which she'd heard them equate with theft: Marx? Emily had the chair of the committee for a two-year spell.

Naturally, the killing of the undercover detective, Tom Mallen or Parry, had brought real darkness. He'd worked his way into Leo's firm, masquerading as an ordinary would-be staffer and had, in fact, strongly impressed Leo; had also, though, fooled him thoroughly. Tom was a guest at their house, Midhurst, several times. Emily got on well with him. One obvious question nagged her. Why had the spy targeted Leo and his business? Who'd decided the firm should be infiltrated, and to what purpose? Although these certainly remained deeply troublesome questions, the ultimate point was, wasn't it, that Mallen had been executed by another police officer in what appeared to be a skilfully planned attack? The gunman was caught and jailed. Naturally, the police had interviewed Leo, because of the undercover detective's role as a supposed member of the firm. Nothing had ever been proved against Leo or his companies, though. Inevitably, he was deeply shaken by what he saw as a betrayal, but any head of a business would feel like that about being spied on. The conviction of the officer, Courtenay Jaminel, had seemed to end matters, even if Emily never heard a satisfactory explanation of why one police officer should kill another. She had been intent – half intent – on letting the mystery of that death *stay* a mystery.

But now rumour said that the two outside investigators who nailed Jaminel were back, apparently in an attempt, blessed by the Home Office – perhaps even demanded by the Home Office – to discover who had masterminded him, detailed him to make the hit. The government involvement scared her, made things look ominous and very major. Gossip said Jaminel was picked for his excellent shooting. Who did the picking? Who did that skilful planning? And the suggestion was that a conspiracy had existed between certain local police and certain eminent and protected local criminals, barons in the drugs hierarchy. So, Emily felt disturbed, and sensed that some folk wondered about her husband. So, Emily felt disturbed and wondered about her husband.

Or perhaps she didn't have to sense others' reactions. People sort of accused by cod-commiserating, such as bitch-gob Noreen at the museum committee: 'This must be a bore for you again, Emily.' A bore in Noreen's kind of underplayed, upper-crust vocab meant something between a slight nuisance and paralysing fright.

'So kind of you to worry, Noreen, but of no concern to us,' Emily said, in a splendidly casual voice. 'Naturally I heard those same two Paul-prys have returned, but this doesn't really touch me, touch Leo and me. How could it, for heaven's sake? Everything was gone into so thoroughly last time, to nil purpose, nil effect. As far as Leo and I are concerned, that is. Obviously there were dire effects elsewhere – for Jaminel and his family.'

'Well, yes, thoroughly, but someone has decided not thoroughly e-bloody-nough,' Noreen said.

'Busybodying.'

'Brave of you to take things so calmly.'

'I really don't know how else I should take things.' But Emily thought she observed in Leo an unusual jumpiness, plus a kind of resignation, as though he'd guessed, feared, dreaded all along that the Jaminel sentence might be only a start, a stage, in the Mallen postscript. Leo had an ability to look far ahead. A leader needed this. It could make for discomfort, though.

Noreen said: 'That whole building site death sequence seems to me to carry a much greater impact than we'd realized. This is not a mere self-contained incident.'

'We mustn't get obsessive about it, surely, Noreen. That's all a long while ago now.'

'But, actually, I'm talking about the present. Oh, very much so. Do you know, Emily, some friends of mine short-cutting on the path the other night, thought they saw a woman – young, late twenties, say – this woman crouched down and talking through a gap in the boarding to someone inside. Apparently, her posture put them in mind of a religious ritual, like someone consulting the Delphic oracle. They didn't leave the path, so were at some distance, but they think they got it right. Not the Jaminel house, but close – two or three away. There might have been a light on in there, a moving beam. A torch? They believe she climbed in. Emily, it's as though that estate has become sort of totemic in some way.'

'Oh, Noreen, please.' But at home, in what Leo liked to call the drawing room of Midhurst, their big, converted Victorian farmhouse, Emily said: 'I was talking to Noreen, whom you know, Leo – and know what she's like – and she thinks the Elms properties have become sort of totemic – that's her phrase, "sort of totemic".'

'Sort of *what*?'

'Totemic.'

'Meaning?' Leo said.

'Significant.'

He laughed. It sounded put on, bogus. 'Well, obviously it don't need a genius to see the Elms was significant, love. A killing there.'

'Is significant now?' Emily asked.

'How?'

'She says people were in one of the houses the other night.'

'Squatters?'

'That's what I thought. But, inevitably, Noreen being Noreen, sees drama.'

'What kind?'

'These people investigating again.'

'How's that to do with the Elms and Noreen?'

'I don't know. But is it bad, Leo?'

'Is what bad?'

'Have we got a new situation here?' Emily said. She saw a startled look hare across his small-featured face. He smiled and for a moment seemed pleased, grateful, comforted. Then the startled reaction came back. It would be that word 'we'. It meant, didn't it, that she considered herself with him in his troubles, whatever they might be: would stand by him and strengthen him as ever? An ally, as ever. As far as she could, she'd help him cope, help him survive, even against the Home Office, the government. But, at the same time, or almost, he clearly felt shocked and alarmed that she should know anything at all about those troubles. The holy and convenient convention was that she stayed blind to some of Leo's business activities, particularly those that might bring, re-bring, the police here; activities possibly linking to a murder, or to a couple of murders now.

And, true, she didn't actually *know* about current stresses, but could make some sort of guess, for a moment could stop kidding herself; could switch from happy, dopey faith in Leo's commercial purity and instead . . . instead, what? She imagined Noreen saying to some other member of the museum committee: 'Poor Emily. She married her bit of rich, anti-grammatical, pinheaded rough, and now the pain really begins for both of them. But she had it coming, didn't she?'

Midhurst was on the side of Cold Hill and looked out over a gravelled yard toward the city and then the sea. There were restored outbuildings at the side of the main house. They sat with a glass of white wine each in brown leather easy chairs, Leo as almost always with a fine, custom-made three-piece, dark suit on, Emily wearing jeans and a crimson V-necked sweater. 'Might they have some new information, Leo?' she said.

'Who?'

'This pair – Iles, Harpur: the names were often in the media back during the first investigation.'

'What new information?'

'Well, I don't know. But do you hear anything?'

'How would I hear anything, Em? Whatever they're here for it don't affect us. Why should it? How could it?' Bluster: that's how she'd have described Leo's tone. But then he sharpened, and this worried her more. 'Which house was she talking about?'

'Noreen?'

'The house the sniper fired from?'

'No. Near it. Is that important?'

'Did she see this herself – some woman in her twenties messing about at one of the houses?'

'No, friends told her. They said it was like someone quizzing an oracle.'

'What oracle, for God's sake? What's this about?'

'Delphos.'

'What?'

'The classics.'

'Oh, that. Them.'

'Apollo looks all over the world for a place to put his oracle.'

'And the Elms wins?' he replied. 'Which friends of Noreen saw all this?'

'She didn't say, Leo.'

'They reliable?'

'Noreen seemed to accept what they said.'

'But like you mentioned, she's fond of a bit of drama.'

'This was just a description of what they saw. They wouldn't make a mistake over something so plain.'

'Plain? What about the oracle? Flimflam. Come on, Em. Where were they?'

'Who?'

'The friends.'

'On the path.'

'That's quite a way from the houses, I think.'

'Not too far for them to see, apparently.'

'Apparently, yes.'

'You believe they'd get it wrong?'

'Why did she tell you, Em? Why you? Why did she think you'd be interested in something like that?

'It was just conversation.'

'It'll be squatters, that's all. Definitely. And nothing to do with us, anyway, is it?'

What she'd just now identified as bluster had returned. A thought she recognized as unkind and disloyal came to her. It was that bluster registered in his small face very nicely. Emily had noticed before how full-scale anger wouldn't work properly there; seemed out of proportion to the mini setting. But the frowns, reddening patches and the twitches that came with bluster looked OK and natural to Leo: made-to-measure, the measure being quite limited. That 'definitely', that 'nothing to do with us', sounded like blatant efforts by him to close the subject, dismiss it as not worth discussing. 'Flimflam.' His lips got around those f's very capably, giving them excellent, wipe-out power. Most probably Leo would have liked to extend the alliteration to 'fucking flimflam'. However, he rarely swore in Emily's presence. 'Flimflam' did a good job on its own.

Yet there was an intensity to Leo's queries that neutered any effort to rubbish Noreen's account: exactly which house had been concerned, Jaminel's or another; how reliable were the people who watched; who were they; how well placed or not were they to see the woman and her performance; why did Noreen think Emily would want to hear about this odd behaviour on the Elms? He'd expected serious answers, perhaps above all to that final question. Did he suspect that Noreen saw a link between Emily and the building site, and with the murder there: the link, of course, via Leo, her husband?

Also in her head, and despite herself, Emily found she was fixated on Noreen's word 'totemic'. It was an outlandish idea – such an extravagant and silly term, such a fanciful Noreen-type term. But, just the same, perhaps those half-done properties did hold valuable

answers to a few very chewy, very enduring problems. She felt a
weird and possibly senseless urge to see at first hand those half-done
Elms houses, see them in place and actual, not merely as media
photographs. Perhaps they'd say something to her. What? She had
no answer. As a secondary aim, though, she might be able to demystify the Elms houses, bring them back to a kind of ordinariness, not
items able to put Leo into a panic; and set off some of Noreen's
deluxe hocus-pocus and gibberish. Emily decided she'd nip down
to Elms alone one night when she had a chance and get her notion
of these jinxed and maybe doomed bits of property back into matter-
of-fact, sane, possibly informative shape.

SIXTEEN

Iles told Harpur he'd enjoyed *The Revenger's Tragedy* so much
he thought he'd 'get along there again for the final performance'
before it moved on to another city. The Assistant Chief said he'd
'like to give certain nuances in the drama a re-run' because he might
not have appreciated them fully on his first visit. He maintained
that, when a writer or director or actor had clearly taken care over
nuances, it was surely an obligation for audience members to respond
gratefully and, if necessary, with a second, belt-and-braces attend-
ance, particularly when the nuances had survived for so long. To
treat them offhandedly would amount to a kind of contempt for
history and for the nation's precious cultural stock.

'What kind of nuances, sir?' Harpur said. Naturally, he wondered
if they centred on revenge methods and might suggest to the Assistant
Chief new, gaff-proof ways of paying back Harpur for that lovely,
loving, illicit interlude with Iles's wife, Sarah. Harpur didn't want
to get deballed or strangled by a nuance.

'You ask what kind, Col, in your thorough-going, fact-obsessed
style. Answer: nuances of a theatrical kind, this being, you see, a
play in a theatre.'

'Ah, yes. That seems to follow. I can imagine Tourneur with
two U's, or Middleton with two D's, saying to himself as he
worked on the script, "I believe there ought to be a nuance just
here in Act Three," and putting one in with his quill. He'd think:

"Good box office. People will keep coming back for another chance to enjoy it.'"

The ACC's plan for a repeat experience at The King's gave Harpur several worries, of course. Iles's earlier trip there had apparently gone off peacefully enough. Harpur hadn't heard of any disturbance, neither heckling nor assaults and/or breakages. But there would be possible trouble from renewed contact with the play and the players. Iles might come to feel a special closeness to them through this familiarity and decide he must, as a compelling *esprit de corps* matter, take part in some fashion – incorporate himself and his Biro gash into the violent stage action, with his own added dialogue and cuckold's near-screams.

It would be comparable with his famous behaviour sometimes when attending in an official role the funeral of someone killed by criminals. He could become moved to such a pitch that he'd try to take over the service, so it could benefit directly from his total personal involvement, occasionally manhandling a vicar or minister or rabbi or priest to the side, or down pulpit steps, if they resisted and attempted to keep control. He'd told Harpur once he always felt uneasy about having to duff up someone in robes but it could be unavoidable 'should a fucking holy Joe get uppity as though he or she had a suzerainty over the realms of death.'

This evening, while Iles was at The King's, Harpur went alone to the headquarters room they'd been allocated by Rhys Dathan, the Chief, and on the computer screen began to scroll through the Incidents and Duties Log for the night Mallen-Parry was killed. It might help get an identification of the helmeted officers glimpsed in the distance by Hill-Brandon on the Elms short-cut path. The machine's memory held a data file for each twenty-four hours, with names and brief notes of assignments and outcomes for all on duty. Before Iles left for the nuancing top-up he told Harpur not to dwell too long on any log entry. 'They'll probably have our computer linked to another and will be tuning in on your search and noting what interests us. We don't want to forewarn them, do we?'

'Which them?'

'Exactly, Col. Them.'

The sift would not be simple. Harpur couldn't expect the log to record an order for two officers to install themselves on the Elms site's illegal but established path between Ritson Mall and Guild Square. This ploy would be coded, disguised – supposing it had been included at all, and supposing Hill-Brandon's memory of events accurate. Harpur figured that what he should be looking for were task descriptions notable above all for their vagueness, and their freedom from need to make traceable contact with members of the public, because there shouldn't be any contact. The descriptions would be deliberately concocted to lead nowhere much, and to bring no awkward repercussions from any inquiry; from any post-killing investigation; from any post-killing investigator, such as Harpur.

So, although the two officers would have been very specifically ordered on to the path to frighten Parry-Mallen off it, that's not how their role would be labelled in the log. Whoever gave them the order was part of the villainy and committed to that evening's murderous deception. The two officers would also be in the plot and aware of the awaiting, off-piste ambush.

There'd been these two uniformed men on the path together, but this didn't mean a single mention in the log would cover both, and a single opaque, fictitious summary of their job that night. The pair would most likely appear in the list separately, with entirely different supposed undertakings, and in locations nowhere near each other. Police who'd often cracked crooks' conspiracies during their careers had seen where the flaws and weaknesses might lie, and knew how to guard against them. The planning had to be smart and unskimped.

Harpur reckoned he could ignore some categories on the log. These would include any call to a domestic disturbance when a full, checkable address would have to be recorded. Arrests could also be discounted because if the entries had been real, all kinds of subsequent detail and paperwork would follow. Likewise motoring offences, pub fights, grievous bodily harm incidents, rapes and noise complaints. He excluded all entries involving women officers. Hill-Brandon had spoken of the two on the path as male, and even in the dark and at a distance, he surely wouldn't mistake gender. Women officers didn't wear helmets.

The work was tedious but to some extent it heartened him: here was an anatomy of one police force's constant guardianship of the citizens on its patch in a multitude of ways during a typical twenty-four hours. It was the whole police function in miniature. The service had developed quite a bit since the days of those early law enforcers, the Bow Street Runners. And yet a police force could still be corrupted, and the exhaustive, seemingly impressive log might hold major, disguised elements of that corruption.

Harpur had to crack these disguises, if he could. The name was given of the sergeant or inspector or above who handed out each assignment on the night and signed it off. This would obviously provide an important lead if the two officers on the path, and their supposed job, or jobs could be identified.

Harpur got what he regarded as the possibles down to seven. Three were security surveys on commercial and industrial estates; two ordered patrols of tarting activity in a district where, apparently, there'd been complaints from householders; two wanted examinations of vehicle licences on street-parked cars to ensure they were present and up-to-date. These were duties that would entail full reports eventually, but all of them could have been carried out before or after the Elms path stint; or even done under the assumed names of the path two by off-duty personnel who were in on the racket, and on the slaughter tactics. Because of Iles's warning about possible electronic snooping, Harpur didn't linger on the seven but made quick notes of the names and the listed objectives.

Did any of the task descriptions sound phoney, made-up? Back at home a few weeks ago Denise had tried to teach him those skills in seeing what might lie hidden in a group of words. She called this 'deconstruction'. It was the kind of thing she did on one of her university courses, apparently: the breaking up of bits of literature to discover what they really added up to behind the obvious. Harpur had never fully trusted words to do the job they seemed made for, and he'd been glad to hear from Denise that in this particular game they weren't even called words but 'signifiers'. That is, they were letters on a page or sounds in a voice and didn't have much to do with meaning at all. He tried this now on some of the seven log items. Did *Kerb crawling abated notably on my perceived arrival in Stapleford Road* sound right? How could he know it 'abated notably' if he'd only just arrived? He wouldn't have seen what it was like previously. What made him sure his arrival had been 'perceived'? His evidence for this must be the alleged drop in kerb crawling. But this wasn't a certainty. What you had here was two very dodgy statements trying to prop each other up.

This kind of coaching in language tricks by Denise amounted to only one of her strong aspects. Obviously, the greatest of these was that she fancied Harpur. Also, (1) her snoring hardly ever reached a decibel level that kept him awake, and (2) Harpur's children adored her, regarded her as family and took special delight when she was present in the house at Arthur Street for breakfast. They reckoned this proved she belonged. Breakfast for them was a signifier, especially when she'd cooked it herself, but even when Harpur had done it.

He thought Iles might want to start the next move in his investigation with a face-to-face call on the Stapleford Road officer, PC Alan Silver, and with the officer who sent him, Sergeant Graham Quick. It was the kind of potentially tough interviewing the ACC liked and excelled at. However, the sergeant had initiated one of the other expeditions, too, and the result was described in words so much like standard police jargon that it might be genuine. This concerned a security tour of the Patterson-Nelmes industrial estate and the summary concluded *very satisfactory enhanced outer overhead lighting units in both number and wattage since previous inspection when eleven vulnerable shadow areas were identified.* So, maybe this was an authentic policing visit and Sergeant Quick and his boys authentic, too, untouched by the kill-Parry scheme, ignorant of it, intent only on kerb crawlers and enhanced security lighting numerically and wattagely.

Harpur was into more scrolling when someone knocked gently on the door. He had locked it from the inside. Perhaps Iles had changed his mind about the theatre. Or the play might have been sold out. Harpur shouted: 'Be with you now,' and cleared the screen. He crossed the room, unlocked and opened the door. Rhys Dathan, the Chief, stood there, solid and grave. He had on chino-style beige trousers, blue and white training shoes, a check shirt, no tie, a navy pea jacket and rat-catcher's flat cap. Harpur thought he looked like a debt collector or bailiff, and one hale and muscled enough to carry away an onyx table if you failed to pay up now, on the spot. Most probably he didn't greatly like having to knock on a door in his own headquarters and wait while someone inside considered opening it; and someone not even part of his outfit – in fact, someone sent to do his outfit big, radical damage.

'I heard *you* were here, Harpur,' the Chief said.

Reception could have informed him. Or, as Iles had suggested, there might be another computer somewhere in the building following Harpur's work on the log. But, in that case, would Dathan have come on this visit and made the spying obvious? Perhaps Reception had orders to let him know whenever Harpur and/or Iles went to their headquarters room. His clothes suggested Dathan had been called from home and had picked up the cap on his way out. In his right hand he carried what looked like a sheet from a stationery pad with several lines of writing in ink on it. Harpur felt that the stress on 'you' – 'I heard *you* were here' – seemed to show Dathan had tabs on him, but wanted, also, to know where Iles might be, and doing what. This was a totally wrong interpretation of Dathan's meaning, though. He already knew Iles's whereabouts and activities: knew more about Iles's activities than Harpur did. 'I've had a bell from The King's theatre,' he said.

Oh, God. 'Yes, sir?' Harpur said. He smiled a cooperative smile, to signal he felt happy to take part in literary chat, if necessary.

'I know the manager there – run into him now and then at cultural things and so on. He has my private number since we both helped run a charity campaign last year. The phone message was to do with Mr Iles. The manager recognized him from previous media publicity.'

'Yes, a lot of publicity then.'

'The manager thought it best to get through to me personally and I'm damn glad of that. Damn glad.'

Oh, God. 'Something sensitive, sir?'

'Uncomfortable.'

A deliberately non-alarmist reply? Oh, God. 'I believe Mr Iles was going to the play at that theatre this evening,' Harpur said. 'A work by Tourneur. Or possibly Middleton. Scholars squabble about the authorship. I've heard there's the same kind of dispute about Shakespeare – did he do the stuff or Bacon?' Harpur gabbled, needing time to get himself ready for whatever came next.

Dathan stepped into the room and glanced about. There were two beige moquette-covered easy chairs and three adjustable, armless secretarial swivel perches. The computer and four telephone sets stood on a metal table that occupied the centre of the room. Two grey, lockable filing cabinets were against one wall, with a vase of artificial dahlias on top. Harpur thought they must have been provided, perhaps on Dathan's orders, to make the room look a little less stark. Harpur considered them pretty good imitations. He detested the smell of real dahlias, anyway.

Dathan had his back to Harpur for a minute or so, but then turned and put his gaze hard into Harpur's eyes. Harpur felt very conscious of a squareness theme: Dathan's face generally, his jaw especially, and even his neck, eye-sockets and nostrils. The stance he took reminded Harpur of nose-to-nose encounters between two boxers at a televised weigh-in, trying to outstare each other, and so suggest a grudge match, to boost ticket sales. He must have been great at interrogation when a detective. Dathan would shove that massive, ungenial phiz forward and grunt at a suspect, 'I don't like you.' And the suspect would feel he'd better try to change that, and so he'd sing.

'An incident. Or, more accurately, incidents,' Dathan said, very clipped, very definite.

Oh, God. '*The Revenger's Tragedy*,' Harpur replied. 'Mr Iles is very interested in the period, regards it as remarkably fruitful. All drama is dear to him, but that century's in particular. It's been so since he was a boy. He had quite an education. And the theatre is often his way of unwinding after a tough day. An escape into his favourite fiction with costume and wigs and buskins.'

'The manager said there's a line early in Act One about a character's abused heart strings being turned into fret.' Dathan glanced at the piece of paper and read for total accuracy like consulting his notebook in the witness box: '"Turns my abused heart strings into fret".'

Oh, God. 'Mr Iles likes these plays for their directness and force of language. He finds the drama more substantial than, say, *Coronation Street* on TV, successful though that might be of its own kind; and possibly generations in the future will look back on *Coronation Street* as someone like Mr Iles looks back on *The Revenger's Tragedy*.'

'He stood up, in the stalls.' Dathan consulted the paper again. 'Row Four, central where there'd luckily been a single unsold seat. Just stood there, unmoving.'

'Spoiling the view for those behind him. I can see that might be an irritation,' Harpur said. Oh, God, let this be the whole story.

Dathan said: 'But then he called out in response to the abused heart strings into fret line, "Ah, don't I know how you feel – don't I though? However, is anyone going to write a play about *my* heart strings, *my* fret? Some sodding hope!"'

'Mr Iles can get caught up in skilled storytelling. It's as if he's taken over momentarily. He sees and hears nuances that might not be obvious to others. In a way, it's a gift.'

'The actor speaking the line – playing a Duke, I believe – the actor was, as you'd expect, thrown by this interruption. But, very creditably, he gathered himself and came what they call, I think, "out of character". He addressed Mr Iles direct.' Dathan read again: '"Sit down and shut the fuck up, sonny boy."'

'Some of these old plays, and the shape of the stage, actually invite participation from the audience, I gather,' Harpur said. Denise had spoken to him about that not long ago. 'An apron stage, it's called, jutting out.'

'Perhaps Mr Iles was himself thrown by this rejoinder,' the Chief replied. 'He did resume his seat and became quiet. The play proceeded.'

'These moments of aberration are generally only that – moments,' Harpur said.

'As you would expect, the manager and others kept a watch on him from then on. I'm not clear at which disturbance the manager recognized Iles.'

Oh, God. There was going to be another disturbance, or other disturbances. The Chief had said 'incidents', plural. Incidents, the plural, were more likely than an incident, singular, from Iles. One of Harpur's children had mentioned the word 'exponential' to him the other day and he'd discovered from Google that it meant increasing at a more and more rapid pace: exactly how incidents could be for Iles.

'Does Maud Logan Clatworthy know about this kind of thing, Harpur?' Dathan asked.

'Home Office Maud?'

'Do we have another Maud Logan Clatworthy?'

'Which kind of thing are you referring to, sir?' Harpur replied.

'These aberrations. These seemingly ungovernable spasms. Is she sure this is the type of person to conduct a very complex, delicate investigation of another force – to have actual *charge* of such an investigation?'

'I think she'd be prepared to put up with Mr Iles's minor foibles and eccentricities as long as she and the Home Office have the use of his remarkable brain and mind.'

'So she doesn't, as yet, know about these strange fits?'

'I couldn't say whether she does or doesn't, sir. What I—'

'Perhaps she should. And the wound on his face, for instance. There's never been a proper explanation of that,' the Chief said. 'A sculpted hole. It looks as though it was inflicted by a Biro. Does he go in for self-harm, grabbing anything near as a weapon? This "fret" he picked up on: perhaps he deliberately seeks causes to fret, such as prominent injury? Was he going for his eye, the fret magnified into frenzy?'

'It's healing well,' Harpur replied.

'Yes, yes, but where, how – all right, he, you, choose to be unfrank about that. It's the past, anyway. I'm more concerned about tonight.'

Oh, God. 'Once he was into the swing of the play he'd be fine, I think, sir.'

'We need to get over there, Harpur.'

'To the theatre?'

'You're familiar to him. That could be important – a sort of liaison function. I don't think it would be wise for me, on my own, to confront him. Too *de haut en bas*.'

Oh, God, but a Harpur-hate must be what set Iles off. Harpur was the one he'd accuse of abusing his heart strings into fret. He wouldn't be yearning for liaison with Harpur.

'I've a car outside,' Dathan said. 'This is something I want settled internally – not the Press, and not an official call-out to us, the police, or an ambulance.'

Oh, God. 'An ambulance?'

'Later in the play he seemed to find something totally unbearable. He stood again but this time didn't contribute dialogue. He forced his way urgently out to the aisle. My friend, Liversidge, the manager, thought he must be ill and, with another of the staff, took him to the theatre bar, sat him down and gave him some water. That's as far as my information goes. Liversidge doesn't want the fuss of a nine-nine-nine call either. I said we'd come at once.'

Harpur switched off the computer and locked the room behind them. The Chief drove him in an unmarked Audi to The King's. Harpur said: 'Sometimes I think Mr Iles should give up drama, as some people give up drink or smoking. He's a victim of his own empathy with the cast and their supposed emotional agonies.'

'Don't talk shit,' Dathan replied.

Iles, very pale, was still in the bar, seated on a stool and occasionally sipping from a glass of water. His hand trembled. A couple of barmaids waited for the next interval. An elderly, bald, paunchy man in denim stood close to the ACC. Dathan introduced him as Paul Liversidge. Iles pointed the index finger of his free hand at

Harpur and chuckled with very deep wryness: 'You're responsible for this, you inveterate bastard, aren't you?'

'What?' Harpur said.

'This play.'

'Tourneur with two U's wrote it,' Harpur replied. 'Or possibly Middleton. You can check authorship on the Internet.'

'I don't mean you wrote it,' Iles said.

'Right,' Harpur said.

'You could hardly write a laundry list,' Iles said.

'What laundry list? Are you OK in that respect?' Harpur said.

'Getting me here,' Iles replied.

'Where?' Harpur said.

'To this fucking play,' Iles said.

'You said you wanted to go back because of possibly missed or under-appreciated nuances,' Harpur replied.

'I can confirm that Harpur mentioned the nuances to me,' Dathan said.

'I dare say he did,' Iles said. 'He's using nuances as a smoke screen. It's a blatant trick of his. Show him a nuance and he'll turn it into a smokescreen. I've seen it happen frequently. Why I said "inveterate".'

'A smokescreen to disguise what, Desmond?' Dathan said.

Liversidge said: 'He seems . . . he seems . . . well, I suppose the word is obsessed . . . he seems obsessed about a line in the play.'

'Yes, you spoke of that – the fret,' Dathan said.

'I'm glad *someone*'s spoken of it,' Iles said. 'These people on the stage act as if they're the only ones who've got frets, poncing about with their moans and threats. They're probably at it in there now.'

'Yes, the play's still running,' Liversidge said.

'I'm not going back,' Iles said.

'That's understandable,' Harpur said. 'You've probably nailed all the nuances.' He hated to see Iles like this, malevolent and diminished. Malevolence on its own would have been OK. Malevolence came naturally to him. That was Iles. But to see him shaking, ministered to by this old denimed twerp, and sipping water as if he'd just been rescued from the desert frightened Harpur, made him feel the whole proper order of things had come adrift.

'No, I'm not talking about the fret line,' Iles said.

'Oh?' Dathan said.

'Harpur knows the line,' Iles said.

Oh, God. 'Which?' Harpur asked.

'Don't play the fucking innocent with me,' Iles said. 'It's why you sent me here, to suffer and cringe and despair at that line while you are somewhere laughing full out and uncontrollably at the pain and humiliation you've fixed for me in the stalls.'

'Which line, Desmond?' Dathan said.

'*He* knows,' Iles said.

'I'm not very up on *The Revenger's Tragedy*,' Harpur said. 'Never heard of it until a couple of days ago.'

'And I suppose you're going to tell us – tell the Chief, the manager, other members of the staff here – tell us, them, without compunction, that you've never, either, come across the line that sums up so exactly your rotten behaviour in a certain quarter?'

'Which quarter, Desmond?' Dathan asked.

Harpur said: 'I think what Mr Iles is getting at in his discreet way is that—'

'Which quarter? Which quarter?' Iles semi-shrieked. 'Well, my wife, of course.'

Liversidge looked at his watch. 'There's the final interval in five minutes and the bar will get crowded. We ought to try and clear this up soon.'

Harpur said: 'I don't think there *is* anything to clear up. Mr Iles has suffered some stress brought on by the forcefulness of the drama, that's all.'

'Listen to him, listen to him!' Iles yelled. '"Nothing to clear up!" The effrontery! The callousness. Are these the words of a colleague and, yes, of a friend, a kind of friend?'

'Why did you return for a second viewing, sir, if the play upsets you so much?' Harpur said.

One of the barmaids, small, sharp-featured, mild-voiced, a little apologetic, said: 'Lust.'

'Yes,' Liversidge said.

'I don't follow,' Dathan said.

'The line,' the girl said. 'Mr Liversidge and I were watching him because of the previous, and we both thought it was lust. It's a harsh term, but this is a play with some very adult material in it. If they do a DVD there'll have to be parental warning.'

'Adult?' Dathan said.

'Like adult mags. Top shelf. Explicitness. Private areas. That kind of adult,' she said.

'Lust, yes,' Liversidge said.

'"The insurrection of his lust,"' Iles replied in a snarling, hissing, very audible whisper. '"The insurrection of his lust." Can you feel the filthy, intransigent heat?' He looked all around the bar, as if quizzing everyone present – could they feel the filthy, intransigent heat?

'Is that the line?' Dathan asked.

'Isn't that enough?' Iles said, normal voiced. '"Insurrection." So entirely the word, isn't it? I, Desmond Iles, am an Assistant Chief (Operations) and therefore, clearly, Harpur's superior in rank and much else. I have been put above him by those who know what there is to know about command requirements, schooling, degree, sheer social class. And yet he gets his furtive, soiled paws and other working parts in contact with my wife. I won't list the kind of locations. They are hardly believable and I don't wish to sicken you with disgust. Yes, perhaps I could tolerate it once – that first visit to the theatre. But the second time, I am nearer the stage, better placed, and what I heard was not insurrection. A twitch of the tongue and what did it become? I believe it was spoken of as insur-erection.'

'No, no,' Liversidge said.

'As, of course, Harpur knew I would. Has he got some sort of arrangement with the actor? Money passed? You forced me back to experience that, didn't you, Col?'

'As I've said, you wanted to re-run nuances,' Harpur replied.

'And you doctored one of them,' Iles said. 'Turned it to your own vindictive use.'

There was the sound of applause from the auditorium. The Act had finished. A rush of people appeared and Liversidge went behind the bar to help the two girls. A woman summing up her impressions of the play so far, said to her companion as they waited to be served, 'Such malice, such mercilessness, such utter rawness.'

'Yes!' Iles cried out. 'Yes, but I, Desmond Iles, can take them all – malice, mercilessness, rawness – can undergo them, yet not, as it were, go under.'

'So true of you, sir, so true,' Harpur said. 'Those who have your services are, indeed, fortunate.'

'Thank you, Col,' Iles said.

SEVENTEEN

Emily Young left home an hour early for an evening session of the museum committee. She wanted time to fit in first the Elms visit she'd promised herself, to take a quick look at what she thought of as 'the Jaminel property', and what others would probably think of as 'the sniper's nest' or 'the gun emplacement'. Those conversations not long ago with Noreen at the committee, and then with Leo, still troubled her. In Emily's head that area of the Elms had lately come to assume a depressing, frightening symbolism. She aimed to put a once-for-all stop on that, demystify it, prune away all the symbolic nonsense, by going there and viewing, in their useful, banal reality, bricks, tiles, walls, windows or window gaps, downpipes, gables, mortar, guttering, doors, 'Keep Out' notices, security boarding, garden gates, fencing. She usually thought of herself as businesslike and practical, a born chairperson. How she felt now, though, didn't square with that, not at all. The change scared her – panicked her?

The fact that she kept this little detour secret from Leo, and lied about the museum committee start time, showed why the mere notion of the Elms could worry her so much – could bring her such awful uneasiness, could, yes, symbolize. Could symbolize what? Could symbolize the gap, the distance, that seemed to have developed between her and Leo: an information gap, a moral gap, a right and wrong gap. In an attempt to stay businesslike and practical she continually put a harsh question very bluntly to herself: did he have some connection with the death of the police undercover detective? She felt proud of this plain, brave thinking. Boldly she'd refuse to blind-eye. She wasn't Kay Corleone or Mrs Bin Laden, tactfully cocooned against the full, difficult truth.

But the plain, brave thinking, the bluntness, the boldness, went no further. She knew she should have followed up and asked, OK, if there's a connection, what is it? Never mind the fancy, inflated woolliness of symbolism. What actually, factually, literally is it? The possible actual, factual, literal answer, answers, crash-balled her, made her doubt she remained as nitty-gritty capable as she claimed. She shied away from this spiky question, her bravery ditched, the boldness punctured and chucked. She'd decided, instead, to get along to Elms and see it for what it was and nothing more: a cash-strapped dump, waiting, and waiting and waiting, to be an executive spread.

But nothing more? Of course it was something more. The mighty caveats got at her again. She'd been shoved off her perch. An appalling murder had occurred on the Elms; absurd to hope she could forget it. What she'd try to forget, though, or ignore, or cancel, or expel was the intolerable, badgering notion that Leo might have had a part in it. Might have organized, initiated it to safeguard himself and the firm? Oh, God. She realized that a curt, psycho-babble, mind-state term could define her attitude: 'in denial'. That wasn't a state she would have considered remotely feasible for herself, until now. It meant there were possibilities you didn't much like the look of, so you simply *didn't* look, or not properly. You self-deluded. You acted as if they didn't exist, although you suspected they did; maybe more than suspected, because self-delusion had limits. You regretfully, ashamedly, opted for blackout, for ignorance, for a kind of peace, quite probably a phoney kind: back to blind-eyeing, perhaps. How else to handle the notion that her husband accessorized a killing in the cause of continuing trade profits, and continuing avoidance of clink? *Hi Kay! Hi Mrs B.L!*

She left her Mini in a Ritson Mall supermarket car park and took the short-cut path across Elms towards Guild Square. This was the beginning of the murdered policeman's route, an area pictured by the media many times just after the death and during the trial. At some point she knew she must branch off towards the Jaminel villa. As far as she could remember, none of the reports had explained why he made this diversion but, obviously, he did. She took a torch although for now it was a clear evening with a good moon.

The house was one of two or three nearest completion when the money ran out, and banks took against lending. That would be in the first dip of the recession. The second confirmed it. Once she could see their roofs clearly she switched course and made her way towards them. If Noreen and Noreen's pals had things correct, this section of the Elms was becoming a sort of pilgrimage venue. Emily had turned groupie. The track grew muddier and was littered with debris. She had to be careful not to trip. These hindrances pleased and comforted her. This was how a building site ought to be, carpeted with lumpy bits, jagged bits, soil, furls of discarded, rusting barbed wire, muck, stones, half bricks, wood fragments, glass fragments, all of it real and ordinary, not part of a horrifying nightmare fantasy. Occasionally, on some particularly rough stretch of ground, a piece of rubble would jab at her shoes and hurt one of her feet. Good. In fact, excellent. The pain confirmed the reality and told her she should have put on hiking boots. What had Tom Mallen, the dead detective, been wearing on his feet? Well, not three-quarter heels.

Following his footsteps, she tried also to follow his thinking. What made him divert? Had he seen something, somebody, on the path he didn't want to confront – didn't want to get spotted by? Or had he simply made a mistake, taken the wrong direction? He wasn't a local officer and might not be familiar with the geography. This seemed an unlikely answer, though. The short-cut had been so well-trodden that anyone could see the usual direct trail. Even if he were half asleep or half drunk he should surely have felt the change of terrain underfoot.

Had he, perhaps, glimpsed something in or near the Jaminel house that made him curious? She thought the distance from the property to where Mallen had probably left the path too great for that. It had been dark at the time, of course, as it was now. Had someone called out to him from the house? But surely he wouldn't respond – would suspect some trickery, some hazard. He was an undercover cop and no doubt alert always to hints he'd been rumbled. He'd interpret a shout from one of the houses as a possible invitation to catastrophe and, of course, he'd have been right, dead right.

Ahead of her now, and very near the Courtenay Jaminel property, Emily made out a woman – navy anorak, jeans, short green wellington boots – not moving much but crouched forward, as if searching for something on the ground. Another Elms pilgrim? She must have heard Emily's footsteps and straightened suddenly, then turned towards her. She'd be in her late thirties, Emily thought, a longish, wary, but not unfriendly face, short fair to mousy hair cut short, the anorak hood not in use.

'I suppose one day they'll finish all these and there'll be a nice, tidy estate, instead of this no-man's land,' Emily said.

'Oh, are you thinking of buying here, then?' The accent was not local.

'No, no, we're very settled. But I find it so sad to see properties like this. Well, hardly properties at all, yet.'

'On the news they said the economy is picking up slowly. Soon, there might be activity here again.'

Emily thought she didn't seem to favour the idea. 'You're wise to put on wellies,' Emily said. 'I'm foolishly unprepared.'

'This isn't the first time I've been here,' she said, 'so I know the conditions.'

'The place has a hold on you?'

'Yes, I suppose you could call it that.'

'In a weird fashion I can't explain, it has a hold on me, too,' Emily said.

'Oh, I think I could explain why *I* come here,' she said. It was spoken in a cut-and-dried, statement-of-the-obvious, no-choice tone, a tone Emily herself, the natural chairperson, could often take.

'Yes? You have some special reason for visiting?' Emily replied.

'Certainly.'

Nothing came, though. She seemed to think Emily should be able to work out the answer for herself. And perhaps she could. Her brain was whirring. What would bring a woman repeatedly to a grim place like this and give her the habit of wellingtons? Emily could think of one answer. Only one. She would go gingerly, though. 'Excuse me,' she said, 'and excuse me particularly if I've got this wrong, but are you . . .?'

'Iris Mallen,' she said. 'My husband, sometimes Tom Parry, was shot here. Two bullets, one in the face, one in the chest.' That same clipped, almost offhand style.

'Oh, God, I'm sorry.'

'It's a while now.' She pointed up to a front bedroom. 'From there. A widow-making window. But I expect you know the story. Tom had what Andy Warhol would term his fifteen minutes of fame, the bulk of them posthumous.'

'Well, yes – the Press and TV.' Emily reckoned Iris Mallen had deliberately toughened herself, at least in conversation, as a way of making things tolerable. Her plain speaking was of a different sort from Emily's.

'He had an "I love Torremolinos" T-shirt on, except the word "love" was represented by a heart, in that way you see stickers on car windows,' Iris replied. 'One of the rounds, the second, went through that red picture to his actual heart, a neat merging of the figurative and the real. Of course, he'd never been to Torremolinos – not our type of resort: Blackpool with sunshine.

This was part of his assumed character – the Parry aspect of him, not the Mallen.'

'I don't remember reading about the T-shirt,' Emily replied. She did, but it seemed kinder not to say so, kinder to herself as well as to Iris Mallen. The first shot knocked him down, but he'd stood again and made himself a target for the next. Emily had met Mallen-Parry several times when he was part of Leo's firm. She'd liked him and would prefer not to revisit too thoroughly the details of his slaughter. She'd leave that fullness to Iris Mallen. Possibly, talking about it without constraint had become a sort of therapy for her. People dealt with their setbacks in all sorts of ways.

'You wanted to have a look at the location for yourself?' she asked Emily. 'Not the right shoes, but with a torch.'

'It was a terrible time back then.'

'You can see why I wouldn't greatly want the Elms to become . . . to become . . . what did you call it, "a nice, tidy estate", everything concreted over, including this sliver of soil where it happened. This will be a pavement. The milkman will step on it every morning.'

'Yes, I see, I do see your thinking,' Emily said. So, the Elms, and this house on the Elms, and this small stretch of ground, did combine to make a symbol – a grief symbol for Iris Mallen. 'But you live elsewhere, don't you?'

'A different police manor, yes. That was important – so Tom wouldn't be recognized here. A wise precaution, of course. Routine in that kind of spy job, he said. But also, of course, sometimes the routine doesn't work. It's not all that far for me and a fair bit of it is fast motorway. I can get here and back in less than four hours. I'll be home around half nine. The children are at friends' houses.'

Emily thought there might be two, a boy and a girl, the boy a teenager. It must have come out at the trial and been reported. Obviously, Tom Mallen-Parry wouldn't have told her that, or anything else about his real background. His real background had been an absolute secret. Evidently it had become not so absolute at some point.

'I don't know who you are,' Iris Mallen said, chattily. 'We share an interest, are both, as you put it, held somehow by this house and slice of ground, and yet you haven't told me why you're here.'

And Emily couldn't say, could she, couldn't admit she was married to the outfit who might have done for her husband, Tom, also known as Tom; the outfit who had put him down on to the mud and then put him down again via his Torremolinos heart after he'd somehow managed to stand once more? 'It's not of any significance,' Emily said, in her coolest chairperson voice. She was used to editing meetings into the shape she wanted.

Iris Mallen shrugged, didn't show annoyance or resentment. Maybe, married to a spy, she'd learned that many of her questions would go unanswered.

She'd be doing some guesswork. Emily couldn't edit and shape that. 'You seemed to be searching for something when I first saw you,' she said.

'I was. It's missing. A Biro. An old Biro. I stuck it in the ground to mark where Tom lay, in case after a spell away I got confused about the location.' She paused, shook her head. 'No, that's rot. I'd always know the couple of square metres, wouldn't I? The pen was a sort of symbol, I suppose. It used to belong to Tom. Green ink. He liked green ink. One of the last things he wrote with it was a birthday message to our son, Steve – tied to a mountain bike Tom had bought him. I heard these rumours about construction picking up and was afraid the Biro might disappear under tarmac. So, I would have liked to reclaim it, a memento. No luck.'

She began to walk swiftly away, the wellingtons making a gentle flapping sound against her lower leg, like driving on a flat tyre. She turned her head and called out: 'Nice to see you, whoever you are, expensively, inappropriately garbed and shoed. Don't take that wrong. Please. I'm sure you have your reasons. You're involved in all this somehow, aren't you? On the distaff side?'

'Look where you're going. You'll trip,' Emily replied.

'I must get to the multi-storey in Guild Square and hot tail it. Perhaps we'll meet here again. It might be a neighbourhood by then, though, the house alive with lights and a family, and all the shit families can run into willy-nilly.'

Yes, families could, couldn't they? Emily stayed. She had another fifteen minutes or so to spare. This expedition hadn't turned out as she wanted, not so far. She might still salvage something. She'd come here to get comfortingly acquainted with the solid, honest, temporarily skint basics of property building, and instead had been shanghaied into Iris Mallen's terse but heavy sentimentalizing of the Torremolinos T-shirt, her boy's birthday mountain bike and an old green Biro. Yes, poignant and graphic, but not what Emily sought. In fact, they were the kind of emotive items she didn't quite trust: too many bloody overtones. Overtones should be kept under.

She switched on the torch and walked across the front garden, as this stony, brambled oblong should one day be, and put a hand on an immaculately pointed area of wall beneath a boarded downstairs front window. This was going to be a house, just a house, with charmingly antiqued, factory-made brickwork, and a black damp course let into it near the ground, guaranteed to keep the rooms weatherproof and snug. She felt better for the simple contact. She patted the wall three times and thought, 'Well done, house.'

She moved her hand up to get similar contact with the window boarding and was surprised to find it shifted slightly under this minimal pressure: surely damn useless if it gave way so easily. She played the torch beam on to where the screws should have been keeping it in place and saw instead that all the bottom ones had been removed and, at the top, only a single screw plugged each board to the wall. It meant a wooden panel could swing on it; could be pushed aside, like a curtain. This was probably the same for each nearly completed house. They'd probably all have unofficial guests squatting in them now and again. Some might not fancy sleeping in number 14, the actual murder house.

Emily realized that maybe she should have given more weight to what Noreen had told her. Then she wouldn't have been startled to find the boarding here so adjustable. This must be the spot where the woman seen by Noreen's chums had been talking to somebody inside the house – as if in a chinwag with the Delphic oracle, as one of them had suggested: Noreen would have that sort of mouthy, bookish mates. Emily eased a board aside and lit up part of the room. The floor was wood block and almost as littered with rubble as the ground where she and Iris Mallen had talked. It didn't smell as Emily would have expected an oracle to smell. Just the same, Emily thought she should get through the gap and have a look around.

She had come here to prove to herself that a building was a building and not much else. And buildings had interiors to be taken account of, as well as outsides. It would be chicken, wouldn't it, to turn away now. To retreat after finding this entrance might suggest the house husk really did represent a special, forbidding symbolism.

Getting in required some gymnastics. She pushed one of the

boards back on its fulcrum screw, leaned over the sill and put the torch, alight, down flat on the inside, because she needed both hands free. With her left, she held the board open, then used her right to help lift and drag herself up and over, taking care not to kick and possibly dowse the torch. As Iris Mallen had said, Emily wasn't really dressed for clambering about on a construction site but she'd give herself a good brush down with her fingers before she arrived at the museum committee meeting. She had on a dark woollen suit – pricey, as Iris Mallen had also said – and any creasing should fall out of such quality material all right.

Of course, when she stood in the room she had to let go of the board and it slipped back into place behind her, clunking against the other one with a noise like a door blown shut in the breeze. That shook Emily for a moment; more than a moment, although she ought to have foreseen it would self-close: gravitational pull. She should have put something there to prop the board part-open so the gap was easy to identify when she wanted to get out, and she might want to get out in a rush.

She felt enclosed, trapped, too dependent on the torch. It would have been sensible to put new batteries in before starting all this. She couldn't remember how much use the present ones had had. She picked up the torch, turning the beam on to where the entrance gap was, and tried to get a picture into her memory of the exact location in the bay window space. The light seemed OK, no flickering, no fading from white to yellow. She let it linger on the board for a few moments, scared to give it over to darkness and perhaps make it unfindable – particularly if she were panicked. Then she became ashamed of her timorousness and brought the ray around to the other side of the room and to the door space leading from it, though no door was hung yet.

She could see part of the hall and the foot of a wide, curving staircase. Once complete the house would have some style and spaciousness, for this category of dwelling. Yes, some. She considered it very suburban and ordinary, though, when compared with where she lived and its grounds. You needed Leo's kind of money to buy and develop a place like Midhurst: converted and extended farmhouse, gardens, outbuildings, driveway, paddock. This moment of snobbishness meant she was hit by the big question again: how did Leo get his kind of money – the ample, splash-around kind? Where did the loot come from that entitled her to sneer at this house and the rest of the Elms' future billets for the *nouveaux*? Leo was 'old money' – five or six years at least – and slump-proof. Not investigation-proof, though. Should she ask herself whether Leo had actually come to this address to judge its suitability for an assassin? Oh, hell, no! He wouldn't be hands-on to that degree, would he? *Would he?* Was something like that what these two ferreting pry-guys from another force hoped to prove? Mrs Mallen, too, would no doubt like this possibility looked into by impartial, invasive eyes.

Emily took a couple of steps towards the hall and the scraps underfoot crackled and popped. She paused. Had those little explosions almost drowned out another sound, perhaps coming down the stairwell from one of the upper storey rooms? It was a much slighter, softer noise than the crunching caused by her shoes, but she thought she'd heard something – perhaps a small, infinitely careful slither movement and very brief. Had an occupant been alerted by the torch gleam and the mild but definite racket? She wanted to switch off the torch, because it gave away her location, but she feared the darkness: feared she might stumble and fall, but also just feared the darkness as darkness.

She decided she'd done enough, had enough. A range of funks gripped her, one – the most minor – a dread that something could happen here to make public she'd broken into an Elms house – *the* Elms house. How could she explain it to Leo and others? This was no proper setting for the joint owner of Midhurst, and no situation for the chair of the city museum committee. 'Something might happen.' What something? This was where the real terror lay. Who was slithering about upstairs? Who might come downstairs to find her? She swung the light back around to the loose boards, located them absolutely OK, shoved one hurriedly aside, exited and made for her car. She'd get her breathing and heartbeat back to reasonable on the drive to the museum.

Just before the meeting started, Noreen said: 'Gosh, Emily, don't mind my mentioning it, but your shoes! Well, they've obviously taken a hammering. Have you been gardening in them, or what?'

Yes, 'or what' would cover it. Emily said, 'Geraldine's going to give us an evaluation on that Nantgarw china collection first, isn't she? We must make sure we get it.'

EIGHTEEN

As was normal for these police-on-police inquiries, Maud had fixed for a special, dedicated, secure, private phone line with an extension to be installed in 3V, the room allocated to Iles and Harpur by Rhys Dathan at his headquarters. Iles said: 'Maud's Oxbridge-brill, Col, and could tell you instantly the difference between the Peloponnesian War and a G-string, yet she really believes a special, dedicated, secure, private phone line in a place like this is going to turn out to be secure and private. In its quaint way, such innocence is charming, particularly, you'll say, when combined with a fine arse and effulgent tits. But there are those in a place like this who have worked out how to eavesdrop on calls to and from a special, dedicated, secure, private phone line in a place like this.'

Maud rang now on the line. Iles answered. Using the extension, Harpur listened in, and occasionally spoke. 'Desmond,' she said, 'Dathan has been in touch with the Department here about some incident – has been in touch at a level above mine and not much below the Minister himself.'

'Incident?' Iles said in a voice that hinted incidents were right up his street, but she would have to specify.

'He felt he had to – yes, *had* to – take it up with us. I've been told to put it to you.'

'You're going to put something to me?'

'Since I'm your point of contact with the Department,' she said.

'Might I caution you?' Iles replied. 'This line, although, ostensibly special, dedicated, secure and—'

'It's to do with a theatre play,' Maud said.

'A theatre play?'

'*The Revenger's Tragedy*, by Cyril Tourneur.'

'Do you remember that Barbara Streisand mot in *What's Up Doc?* when she hears of someone named Eunice? "There are *people* called Eunice?" she queries. I'd adapt that to "There are *people* called Cyril, even in the seventeenth century?"' Iles replied.

'Or Thomas Middleton,' Harpur said.

'Something of a display,' Maud said.

'Oh, really? In which respect, Maud?' Iles said.

'Two displays,' Maud answered.

'I believe I know what you're getting at,' Iles said.

'Featuring in the first incident, a lead actor telling you, as I understand it, to "Shut the fuck up."'

'Vendici,' Iles replied. 'Aka Vindici.'

'Not a play I know,' Maud said.

'You'd have been preoccupied with the Peloponnesian War,' Iles said.

'Totally unlike a G-string,' Harpur said.

'I took that coarse language from the actor in very good part,' Iles said. 'This is their livelihood, after all, performing these works. They're bound to feel protective of the whole shemozzle, so the expletive is pardonable, possibly inevitable.'

'The theatre manager recounted things to Chief Dathan, and we have no cause to doubt their veracity. Dathan is presenting a serious issue – or so it is viewed here. To do with your fitness for the task in hand. To do with your fitness, or lack of fitness. Jointly.'

'Jointly? No, no, Col wasn't a part of this. Admittedly he'll shag other people's wives, but theatre *qua* theatre is rather beyond him, except for, say, pantomime – *Mother Goose*, although he thought that meant incestuously fondling a parent and left, disappointed, before the interval. That's right, isn't it, Col?'

'I can't make up my mind between Tourneur and Middleton,' Harpur replied.

'Jointly in the sense that Rhys Dathan doesn't believe the two of you can work effectively together,' Maud said. 'He sees these troubles at *The Revenger's Tragedy* as springing from an abiding enmity between Col Harpur and you, which makes wholehearted cooperation unachievable. Certain parts of that play touched off in you this intense hostility towards Colin.'

'There are some quite acceptable aspects to Harpur,' Iles replied. 'I'd be the last to deny that. Well, among the last.'

'And I've often heard Mr Iles praised by quite sensible people, on the face of it,' Harpur said.

'Which people?' Iles asked.

'What we're getting from Chief Dathan is pressure to shut down this inquiry owing to the clear unsuitability of the investigating team,' Maud replied. 'There are colleagues here, some higher placed, who regard the operation as unnecessary and even malicious. They argue that the killer of Tom Mallen was convicted and jailed, and consider further interference redundant, even *ultra vires* – exceeding legitimate powers. They see in your *Revenger's Tragedy* behaviour a sign that the difficulties – impossibilities – of the assignment are such that they have destroyed mental balance.'

'Meaning that, if we were pulled off, it would be unthinkable to send different investigators to look at this *impossible* conundrum,' Iles replied.

'The Chief maintains that the antipathy between the two of you is perhaps at its most blatant in a facial injury suffered by you, Desmond, probably done with the writing end of a Biro, judging by the injury's dimensions, which he puts at five millimetres square, and almost certainly inflicted by Col.'

'"Probably", "almost certainly" – is this the language of the factual?' Iles said.

'Hardly,' Harpur replied.

'Several here agree overall with Dathan's attitude and conclusions,' Maud said.

'We'll stand by you, won't we, Col?' Iles said.

'This is our mission and we'll stay committed to it,' Harpur said.

'The Chief argues that you, Col, are unforgiven for having it away in low-quality settings with Mrs Iles, and this will always undermine any attempt by you and her husband to function as a successful unit.'

'What do you say to that then, Col?' Iles asked.

'This is certainly one of the most complex cases I've ever met,' Harpur replied. 'We did get Jaminel.'

'There you are, Maud,' Iles said.

'Yes, obviously, but what about Dathan's comment that—'

'Many, many angles,' Harpur said.

'There you are, Maud,' Iles said.

'Yes, yes, but how do I convince my superiors here that—'

'These many angles require patient, systematic attention,' Harpur said.

'There you are, Maud,' Iles summed up, unwaveringly.

NINETEEN

Harpur continued to worry over Ivan Hill-Brandon. His whereabouts remained unknown, supposing he still had whereabouts. Harpur went and did the obvious – checked the Newspapers Only skips at Tesco, and the house on Elms. Negative. He felt a sort of impoliteness in just throwing back the bin lids at Tesco without warning, like breaking down someone's front door in a Nazi-style raid. But to knock on the metal and wait for a response as if on a doorstep would have prolonged things, and he might get spotted by the store's security people going from bin to bin and mistaken for a scavenger. He could flourish his warrant card, of course, and explain his purpose, but he'd rather keep this side of the investigation confidential. He didn't want Tesco alerted to the lodgings role of the bins in case Hill-Brandon needed to come here on the quiet some time in the future.

He didn't have an address for Veronica Pastor, who sometimes gave Ivan shelter, but recalled she'd said something about living in Kitchener Street with her sister. Harpur got the electoral register and found an entry for Veronica and Jeanette Pastor at 26B, probably a flat. His local map gave Kitchener Street in the Arabella district of the city and he drove there now. It looked a quiet, keep-one's-self-to-one's-self area, with what appeared to be a couple of Housing Association apartment blocks among semis.

Number 26B was on the second floor of a building with its name board outside: Ashley Court. When he rang the bell at 26B he was conscious of being examined via a one-way judas hole in the door. Then he heard a man on the other side laugh aloud and cry out, 'It's Mr Harpur, would you believe? In person.' The door was flung open and Ivan Hill-Brandon in shirt sleeves and wide red braces stood there grinning. Always fresh faced, he radiated extreme good cheer now. Harpur thought Ivan could have advertised a brand of pick-me-up tonic wine, or a bracing seaside holiday resort in the Hastings area. Behind him were Veronica and another woman, older, plainer, bulkier, tighter-lipped, who must be Veronica's sister, Jeanette.

Hill-Brandon said: 'Well, some surprise, Colin! I was going to
get in touch, but now, here you are.' His voice suited his hearty
appearance – warm and booming; the voice of somebody who had
beaten bad times and would beat any more that arrived. Harpur
remembered from school the title of a poem, 'The Song of a Man
Who has Come Through'. It could have been about Hill-Brandon
today. One line from the poem had stuck: 'Oh for the wonder that
bubbles into my soul.' As a child, Harpur had liked that notion of
a soul with bubbles in. He had understood bubbles and they'd made
the soul a less mysterious and difficult item. Hill-Brandon might
have bubbles in his soul now.

'Come in, do,' Veronica said. 'But how did you find us?'

'He's police, isn't he?' Jeanette said. 'They know the lot, but
don't always tell it, or half of it. They have their methods, some
legal.'

They went into a large, very tidy, square sitting room. 'I'll make
tea, shall I?' Ivan said. He seemed to bubble with confidence – yes,
bubble, at ease with his new status as man of the house/apartment.
Perhaps this ability to adapt fast to new surroundings came to people
who spent a lot of time in unfinished houses or bins of old newspapers. They'd learned how to take command of the accommodation,
like victorious troops settling into a captured town. There wouldn't
be much to challenge their authority, at least as far as the bins were
concerned; and the same for houses on Elms, as long as you got
there early.

Veronica looked delighted that Ivan felt so comfortable in 26B.
Harpur saw something sweet and exhilarating in their partnership.
The braces and shirt sleeves proclaimed happy domesticity, especially the harsh redness and crude width of the braces: at 26B Ivan
could forget about appearance and Barbour jacket smartness. He
belonged. He could relax, have a laugh, make the tea. OK, so
Jeanette might not like it. So, fuck Jeanette. Or not, even when
Veronica was away running the cross-Channel ferry karaoke, or
whatever, and Jeanette and he had the flat to themselves. Harpur
found it hard to see any family similarity between Veronica and
Jeanette, either in features or attitudes. He hated the cliché notion
that plainness caused crabbiness. But Jeanette *was* crabby.

'Where have you been, Ivan?' Harpur replied. 'We were worried.'

'I met someone,' Hill-Brandon said.

'Yes?' Harpur said.

'That can happen when I'm making one of my walks across the city,' Hill-Brandon said. 'I'm something of a well-known sight.'

'Certainly,' Harpur said.

'Ivan tells us something bizarre happened to him on return,' Veronica said, as though he needed help with his story – might be too shy and hesitant. She wanted to care for him. Harpur thought again that they'd built a nice relationship.

'You'll ask, "Whom did you meet, Ivan?"' Hill-Brandon said.

'Yes,' Harpur said, 'whom did you?'

'This is a guy from my shop days,' Hill-Brandon said. 'Someone I sold electrical stuff to and fitted for him. Now, he wanted to rewire. Could I handle it? I'd be cheaper than some of the others. He'd get all the necessaries. Of course, I couldn't supply them now – no shop. But I can do the work. So, I go. He can put me up in the spare room for a couple of days. All meals free.'

'Congratulations,' Harpur said. 'You were quick to spot a chance.'

'Work over, rewiring complete, I leave his home. Veronica wasn't here till today, so naturally I went to Elms last night,' Ivan said.

'I looked there the night before,' Harpur said.

'No, I was still at my customer's house then.'

'You had money for the work?' Harpur asked.

'Yes, of course. What is it the Bible says – "the labourer is worthy of his hire"?'

'But you still slept in the Elms house?' Harpur said.

Ivan looked sheepish. 'I've got so I don't like paying for lodgings or bed and breakfast. I hang on to the cash for when the weather gets really bad, when I might need to pay for a room.'

'You mustn't worry about that any longer,' Veronica said. The words came out terse and definite and affectionate. 'You're installed here now, Ivan, rain, sun or snow and whether I'm at home or not. Jeanette won't mind.'

Harpur was uncertain of that.

Jeanette said: 'I'm not averse. If there's real need. If he's genuinely in possible danger.'

Yes, he was genuinely in possible danger. He had some information and might have been seen hobnobbing with Harpur in the caff near police headquarters. And Hill-Brandon would be spottable easily enough on Elms or climbing into a Tesco Newspapers And People Only bin. 'Why we felt troubled,' Harpur said.

Unpleasant surreal prints in silver frames decorated the sitting room's walls, blatant mauve a sort of theme colour, linking all of them. Possibly when Hill-Brandon had absolutely established himself here he could have these mistakes dumped, if possible retaining the frames for saner pictures. Harpur wondered which of the sisters chose this dud stuff. He assumed it must be only one of them. No two or more people could deliberately and jointly favour it. He hoped Jeanette picked the art and that, out of kindness and some pity, Veronica had allowed her to display them, perhaps for a very carefully defined, limited period.

The furniture was a mix of styles, and OK. Perhaps the two of them had lived separately for a while and then decided on merger. Their beige Victorian or Edwardian *chaise longue* stood next to a white, assemble-yourself, chipboard book case. Harpur glanced at a few of the titles. They appeared to be mainly about self-analysis, self-improvement, self-assertion. Harpur approved of these kinds of books. They had an obviously positive purpose, not like some of the volumes his late wife had in *their* sitting room with off-putting names on their spines such as *Urn-Burial*. Did he have that correct? He had disposed of all the books a decent time after her death, except for one on boxing, *The Sweet Science*, and the diary of some writer called Orton. Harpur's daughter, Jill, wanted them both kept.

Hill-Brandon made the tea and he, Jeanette and Harpur sat in chintz easy chairs. Veronica took the *chaise longue*. Harpur said: 'Veronica mentioned that something bizarre occurred when you returned, Ivan. What was that?'

'Yes, very bizarre,' he said.

'People walking about on a building site in the night, I fail to comprehend it,' Jeanette said.

'I'm sure this was not arranged, planned, between the two women,' Hill-Brandon replied. 'Fluke.'

'I don't see how that matters,' Jeanette said.

'A fluke bringing them together at the house, and a further fluke that I should be sleeping upstairs, when for several nights I'd been elsewhere,' Hill-Brandon said. 'And the fluke went further, would you believe? I couldn't get into eighteen or sixteen Davant – people already there. So, this was fourteen. I didn't like that, but it was necessary.'

'We were concerned,' Harpur said.

'Yes, I'm sorry I couldn't have let you and Vron know,' he said. 'But it was quite an unexpected job offer. My mobile's uncharged.

I felt I had to go. These are rather constrained times in the job market. We freelances have to grab what comes. In the police, different. A career structure.'

'The public purse,' Jeanette said.

'Which two women, Ivan?' Harpur replied.

'Early evening, though dark,' Hill-Brandon said. 'I wasn't asleep but—'

'You like to get established before any rush,' Harpur said.

'In a property, yes.'

'But this time some other squatter had beaten you to eighteen and sixteen.'

'I had to make the best of things. I didn't feel like trekking across the town.'

'To Tesco,' Veronica said.

'Right,' Hill-Brandon said.

'That's very much the past now,' Veronica said. 'Both. Either.'

'Thanks, Vron,' Hill-Brandon said.

'If it's necessary,' Jeanette said.

'The two women?' Harpur asked.

'Talking,' Hill-Brandon said. 'At first. Yes, talking,'

'Talking near the house? You could make out what was said?' Harpur asked.

'The situation seemed very like that time when you and Mr Iles were there, though not the scrapping, of course,' Hill-Brandon said.

'Scrapping?' Jeanette asked. 'Two police officers? Two high-up police officers?'

'They weren't high-up that night, were you, Col? Ground level.' Hill-Brandon chuckled a while, fondly. 'Like a tussle, though of possible serious intent. Not a punch or thump fight. Mr Harpur was underneath. There's a little gap for looking out from the bedroom where someone has broken off a corner of the boarding. Of course, there was *no* boarding when the shooting took place.'

'You'll never have to peep from there again, Ivan,' Veronica said.

'Thanks, Vron.'

'It's undignified,' Veronica said. 'You're worth so much more than that.'

'They were down, fighting on the mud?' Jeanette asked.

'Yes. But, mind, I don't mean the two women were *this* time,' Hill-Brandon said.

'No, I understand that,' Jeanette said. 'But what was Mr Harpur doing on the ground on that earlier occasion?' Jeanette said. 'You described it as "underneath". What does that mean? Underneath what? Whom?'

'Yes, underneath,' Hill-Brandon replied.

'Underneath Mr Iles?' Jeanette asked.

'Both fully clothed, obviously,' Hill-Brandon said. 'Throughout.'

'Did you recognize either of the women?' Harpur asked.

'Not at first,' Hill-Brandon said.

'But later you got a better view, did you?' Harpur said. 'Who, then?'

'Not a better view. I could see both of them OK. A moon. One quite a bit older than t'other.'

'How old?' Jeanette said. 'We've only had an outline of these events previously.'

'One late thirties, the other forties,' Hill-Brandon replied.

'Mature women! What are they *doing* there at all?' Jeanette said.

'That's the point, isn't it?' Hill-Brandon replied.

'What point?' Jeanette said.

'As to why they were there,' Hill-Brandon said.

'Why were they?' Jeanette said. 'Veronica and I have heard some of the tale, Mr Harpur, but I still can't fathom it all.'

'After a time you recognized both?' Harpur asked.

'One,' Hill-Brandon said.

'And you didn't actually recognize her as such, did you, Ivan?' Veronica said. 'Not as such.'

'As such?' Harpur said.

'Assisted. Very much so: she spoke her name,' Hill-Brandon replied, 'and then I remembered pictures of her in the Press and on TV at the time.'

'What time?' Harpur said.'

'The murder on Elms,' Hill-Brandon said.

'So, what name?' Harpur said, but he could guess.

'Mallen. Iris Mallen. She told the other woman who she was, and then I recalled the pictures,' Hill-Brandon said.

'The undercover officer's wife, widow,' Veronica said. 'And she was there for a purpose, wasn't she, Ivan, a quite definite purpose?' She obviously felt proud of his sudden, accidental connection with the case, like congratulating a child on its first swimming strokes. This was more than a bit patronizing, but Harpur still sensed, all the same, that the two had developed an exceptionally happy relationship. Good for you, Ivan!

'Purpose?' Jeanette said. 'Well, of course there'd be a purpose if she drove all those miles. But what *species* of purpose? As Ivan tells it, a stupid, pointless purpose; in fact, no real purpose at all, just sentimentality and gush.'

'Oh, I wouldn't say that,' Veronica replied.

'Naturally you wouldn't,' Jeanette said. 'For your own reasons, Veronica, you want to squeeze every drop of drama out of this incident. It's absurd. It's slightly pathetic, if I may say.'

'You *have* said,' Hill-Brandon replied.

'Surely some things can take on a significance beyond their actual, obvious self,' Veronica said.

'We're into semiotics, are we?' Jeanette said.

'A sort of symbolism,' Veronica said.

'Oh, my!' Jeanette said.

'What was it?' Harpur said. 'Symbolic of what?'

'This won't sound very significant,' Hill-Brandon said.

'Because it isn't,' Jeanette said.

'Never mind. What?' Harpur replied.

'A Biro,' Hill-Brandon said.

Harpur, shocked, did full-scale puzzlement while he rallied his wits. 'A Biro?'

'Symbolic because it used to be the undercover man's, didn't it, Ivan,' Veronica said.

'Fatuous,' Jeanette replied.

'She put it there not long after the trial, I imagine, partly to remind her of the exact spot where her husband was found by the two shoppers, as reported then,' Hill-Brandon said. 'Stuck it into the ground like a little flag pole, without the flag, or a surveyor's peg. A green Biro.'

'Green?' Harpur said.

'She said he liked writing in green,' Hill-Brandon explained. 'Some do, I know.'

'Affectation,' Jeanette said.

'Apparently, he'd written a green ink birthday gift message on their son's new mountain bike,' Hill-Brandon said. 'Bikes *are* green in that they don't pollute.'

'Oh, blimey,' Jeanette said.

'I can see why she'd want to recover and keep it,' Veronica

replied. 'The estate won't be in that delayed state for ever. The pen would get buried under a road covering.'

'But Ivan has told us it wasn't there, anyway,' Jeanette said.

'No, it wasn't there,' Hill-Brandon said. 'Or she couldn't find it.'

'So the trip was doubly daft,' Jeanette said. 'It would have been ridiculous to come all that way to reclaim it – suppose she had. And the journey and time wasting are even more mad when the Biro can't be found despite all the effort. And of course it can't be found. People would have trampled it under: people coming to see the murder house, or just wandering around the estate in case they might want to buy a property one day, or vandals and thieves. The pen would have been in fragments, probably, even if she *had* found it.'

'I haven't spoken about one extra aspect to Vron and Jeanette yet, Col,' Hill Brandon said. 'I hope you won't mind if I do.'

'Which?' Harpur said, knowing, and minding, and ready to shut the sod up if things got really difficult.

'What interested me when she said the pen had gone was – well, in that tussle, as I've called it, you and Mr Iles on the ground – in that tussle you seemed to reach down for something and give Mr Iles quite a jab with it in the cheek. This put an end to the struggle, didn't it, and I was wondering if—'

'What about the other woman, the older one?' Harpur replied.

'Jabbed, stabbed, another officer in the face?' Jeanette said. 'So, *you* had the Biro, Mr Harpur. Still have it?'

'Col might have been strangled otherwise,' Hill-Brandon said.

'My God,' Jeanette said. 'And you're talking about two high rankers who are supposed to be here on a clean-up mission, instead of which they're trying to kill each other in the mud.'

'This seems to have been play-acting that was carried too far,' Veronica said. 'A mock-up situation devised to imitate how things might have gone on the murder night, and this drifting into actuality – near actuality.'

'You mean these two couldn't tell the difference between theatre and real life?' Jeanette asked.

'Mr Iles is very keen on theatre, but he can get over-involved in the action,' Harpur replied. 'In some ways, it's an endearing, child-like quality.'

'This child wants to strangle you? This child gets his face gashed?' Jeanette said.

'I'm only guessing that Col used the Biro to resist Mr Iles,' Hill-Brandon said.

'Well, Mr Harpur should be able to tell us whether you guess right,' Jeanette said.

'It's very touching to find that she wanted to mark the area of ground in that way,' Harpur replied.

'She went for her car in Guild Square, saying she had to "hot-tail" it from there, meaning, I suppose, that she had to get back to her children.

'And the other woman?' Harpur said. 'Do we know who she was?

'She stayed for a while longer,' Hill-Brandon said. 'No, I don't know who she was, but you might be able to find out, Col. You have the means not available to me.'

'You got a car registration?' Harpur asked.

'God, Col, you're quick,' Hill-Brandon said.

'No, not quick,' Harpur said. 'Just well used to finding identities through cars.'

'So like the police,' Jeanette said. 'They understand cars better than people. But, a car on Elms? How can that be?'

'The other woman – the older one – she's doing a little pace about, although her shoes are all wrong – all wrong but very pricey, I reckon, like the rest of her gear,' Hill-Brandon replied. 'Her shoes, heels, yes, all wrong for the muck. Well, she said so herself – said the other was wise to come in wellies. This seemed to show Iris Mallen knew she was making for Elms and prepared for it – familiar with the scene and conditions. But maybe the other is there from a kind of accident. Or maybe she had to fit this trip in before or after some different visit where she'd need the sharper clothes. And anyone could see she was used to these sharper clothes from the way she moved, and the way she held herself. They were natural to her. Being at Elms in the dark and the mud wasn't. I suppose it wouldn't be natural for almost everyone. Anyway, this was a woman who had a place in the world, and the place was not a half-finished house on a building site. I wouldn't say she had class, but she obviously lived where loot also lived and had its generous being, slump or not. I'm an expert on slumps and I can tell you she has no part in them.'

'You ought to be a detective, Ivan,' Harpur said.

'I've got the car reg,' Hill-Brandon replied. 'You can ask the police computer about it, can't you, Col?

'I still don't see how a car could be on Elms,' Jeanette said.

'I'm watching her and think I can work out what's going on in her head,' Hill-Brandon said. 'Presumptuous? Maybe. But in my kind of present career – that is, no career at all – you get accustomed to reading signs in people. Have to, because they can't be bothered talking and explaining to a nobody like me.'

'Oh, Ivan, don't say that!' Veronica cried.

'Wide, vivid, exceptionally ugly, coarse braces, like those you have on, Ivan, are often worn by men of exceptionally strong personality – for instance, bookies or boxing promoters, certainly not by nobodies,' Harpur said. 'Those braces state, "This is me. Take it or leave it. I am totally, autonomously, comfortable in my skin and braces."'

'Her pacing and general nerviness – I could interpret them,' Hill-Brandon replied.

'Don't tell us *she* was looking for the Biro, too,' Jeanette said.

'She's glancing at the house all the time during her parades, really giving it scrutiny, like it was a challenge which, so far, she hadn't dealt with. I had the idea she wanted to come inside,' Hill-Brandon said. 'It's as if she's thinking to herself, "I've made the decision to attend here" – which might have been a tricky one – "and now I'm present in this unfamiliar environment, I ought to do the job properly, which requires entry, something beyond this outside gawping." I'd never claim these were the actual words of her musing, but with this general drift.'

'I don't follow,' Jeanette said. 'What does it mean, "do the job properly"? Which job? Why should it be part of her job to get into an unfinished house? Why is entry required? Who requires it? What *is* her job? Does her job demand the expensive shoes and clothes? *How* expensive? It's a comparative term. What's expensive for some would be ordinary, even cheapjack for others.'

'Then, a development,' Hill-Brandon replied. Puzzlement touched his voice.

'Yes?' Harpur said. He would have liked to yell, 'Get on with it, you wordy prat,' but that would be brutal. And Jeanette could provide all the brutality needed today.

'She stops pacing in the area around the house and comes nearer to the property itself,' Hill-Brandon explained. 'When Veronica says "bizarre" she's spot-on, Col.' He paused and gave Veronica a smile of congratulation plus a thumbs-up, to mark her cleverness.

'Bizarre?' Harpur said. He trowelled the bafflement on, to encourage Hill-Brandon and prove he had a rapt listener, gasping for more. And he did.

Hill-Brandon put down his cup and, leaning forward in the chair, stretched out both arms in front of him and began to work his fingers in a kind of gentle but intense kneading action. 'The woman is handling the brickwork, feeling it, like testing a bike's tyre pressure, as though she wanted to make sure it was really there, and actual, solid, real. A kind of reverent ritual, worshipful, slow, loving.'

'Is this dame barmy?' Jeanette said. 'Of course it's real. It's not a true house yet, but what there is of it is real. What else could it be?'

'She seemed to want reassurance on that. To crave it,' Hill-Brandon said, 'as though coming out of a nightmare and taking comfort from the ordinary, safe things around.'

'You mean like Dr Johnson kicking a big stone to destroy Bishop Berkeley's theory about the non-existence of matter?' Jeanette said.

'Is that Johnson with an h?' Harpur asked. Denise had a room in a student block called Jonson Court, without an h, though she spent most of her nights in Arthur Street with him, Arthur Street and him both having an h. Harpur knew there were two separate people in literature with similar sounding surnames but different spellings. Denise had explained the difference to him. Ben Jonson did plays and poetry, and Sam Johnson said deep things like he wouldn't want to talk to someone who'd written more than he'd read. Harpur felt that kicking large stones would be more like Sam Johnson with the h.

Hill-Brandon said: 'And then I think she put a hand on some of the boarding, to check on that for solidness, too. She's tactile. That the word? She's literally hands-on. But – big but – but it might be the shiftable boarding, the gateway boarding she fondles. And when she touched it there'd be some give. It yielded. *Not* solid like the bricks. So, if she was thinking of getting in, and was blaming herself for staying outside so far, this would persuade her to have a go. I heard one of the boards move. When I say "move" I don't just mean move marginally because she'd put a little pressure on it, seeking solidity. No, this was the sound of a boarding plank pushed aside on its solitary wall-screw and grating against one of the other planks as it swung over it and made slight contact. She had a torch with her, which could, perhaps, show she knew she was coming to Elms, even if she hadn't put the right shoes on. Or she might always keep a torch in the car for eventualities.

'She switched on and the light shone into the hallway downstairs and moved around, sort of casing the place. Preparatory. Reconnaissance. Then came a faint clinking and I thought she must have bent over the sill and put the torch on the floor of the room, so she'd have a hand free to help her climb in while holding a board back with the other. The light stayed on, its beam now fixed and still because the torch lay flat. I picked up the noise of some hard breathing, a minor grunt and the rustle of clothes, and I guessed she'd clambered in. This seemed some determined lady. She was a lot more than just chic clothes and shoes – that is, chic in suitable surroundings. She'd gone out of my sight now. I remained near the front bedroom boarding and tried to stay totally quiet. The board swung with a bump back into place. After a couple of seconds the torch light moved about again, so I knew I'd been right. She must be inside, standing, examining some of the downstairs.

'Most likely, Col, you'll say what was I bothered about, she's only a woman in the wrong shoes and with a torch. She had some objective, though, didn't she? What was it? I wanted to know. And did someone send her? Who, then? This was all a mystery, a conundrum I must solve, and I thought the best way to solve it was not to call out a greeting to her, like a gentlemanly host, but to wait and see what she did next, without her knowing there was somebody else present in the building as well as herself.'

'"Masterly inactivity", to borrow some words from history,' Veronica said.

'Mackintosh, about the House of Commons during the French Revolution,' Jeanette said. 'In *Vendiciae Gallicae*.'

'Quite a read, that one,' Harpur said.

'I could be more or less certain this wasn't another homeless looking for a sheltered kip. The clothes and shoes weren't right for that, nor the conversation with Iris Mallen,' Hill-Brandon said. 'I had to think of something to say in case after her tour at ground level she came upstairs. The point was, wasn't it, that in this house the upstairs had always been the interesting part. Where the bullets came from. The exact location for the trap. So, if she was connected somehow to the case – and I considered she had to be – I mean, what else would make her behave like this? – the estate at night, an unfinished house, and inviting herself in – yes, if she was connected with the case she'd come up to the front bedroom soon. For her, this would be getting to the core of things. I'd need to have a pleasant chat line ready, owing to the unusual circumstances of the meeting, however you looked at it.

'Something like, "Well, hello there. Sad about these potential homes, isn't it, particularly when there's such a demand for new housing? The construction industry has suffered disproportionately badly during the recession. Recessions. Four per cent reduction while the rest of the economy flatlines. That flatlining is bad enough, in all conscience, but a four per cent drop much worse, I think you'll agree. Myself, I come here fairly often. I wouldn't argue there's any special charm or beauty about these surroundings, but they can offer a service of, admittedly, an emergency nature. Although it's difficult to see you properly through the torch dazzle on my face, I believe you must be new to this area. I quite understand why you would need the torch in what might be strange, not to say, alien, surroundings for you. Even someone such as myself, truly familiar with the layout and strewn rubbish, can occasionally come quite a cropper. I would respectfully speculate that incursing yourself into blighted housing is not consistent with your usual lifestyle, neither as career, nor hobby. But perhaps your interest in this property has to do with the death of the undercover police officer whose widow you spoke to outside? It's an extremely complex, multi-aspect situation, isn't it?"'

'This sounds to me a very reassuring start,' Harpur replied.

'Gabble, hot, strong, cliché-rich, and pitiful, I would respectfully speculate,' Jeanette said, 'in all conscience.'

Harpur thought that in its snarling, wallflower way this was correct. What else could the words be but a verbose, creaking fantasy spiel? Now and then, though, gabble could soothe and then move on to something meatier. Harpur wondered whether Jeanette had spent too much time among the spruce-up-your-personality books, with special emphasis on the importance of self-assertion. Harpur didn't mind self-assertion as long as the self being asserted was tolerable. This could exclude Jeannette.

The idea upset Harpur. He'd hate to see anyone, and particularly any woman, isolated by their own inner clumsiness. For this reason he approved of Denise's smoking. When she inhaled – at every drag, naturally – she did it in fine, powerful, ferociously thorough style, sometimes chaining. The fumes seemed to get hurtled urgently, comfortingly, to all her interior recesses, providing a balm that helped Denise bring vivacity, vitality, lovely good nature and sexual energy to her life, and Harpur's. He loved her mouth when it was acrid with charred Marlboros. This seemed such a worldly, unfancy, dependent taste. They knew about the health dangers, and occasionally Harpur would feel guilt for not lighting up and sharing the risk. Although invasive closeness to her entailed some passive smoking, this couldn't qualify him as an equal addict. But she often said she'd be stopping the ciggies any day soon, and Harpur accepted that she might. Or might not. Denise told him some writer in the past had composed *A Farewell to Tobacco*, and this showed it could be done. She was an undergraduate and believed in literature. Harpur had a very good verbal memory and recalled some of the lines she quoted about the weed. There was the basic contradiction:

> For I hate, yet love, thee so;
> and thoughts on the sweetness of the smell:

> Sidelong odours that give life,
> Like glances from a neighbour's wife.

Denise said she expected him to recall the second example, particularly.

Hill-Brandon said: 'Of course, talking to this woman about the Elms house wouldn't reveal *why* the death of Mallen interested her, if it did. What connection? Was she just one of those people who got a sick kick out of crime scenes? Or could she be part of that complex, multi-aspect nature of things I mentioned?' He paused and smiled encouragingly, like someone running a discussion group, and considerately giving members time to mull these questions.

He went on, though, before anyone else spoke: 'Why had she rejected a names swap with Iris Mallen? Wasn't that unfair, offensive, rude? Did she want to keep this Elms visit a secret? Why? I thought that if, perhaps, I could find the right kind of approach when she came upstairs there might be additional progress in making matters clearer. Plainly, this was an odd place for a meeting and some subtlety would be needed at the start.'

'Sensible,' Harpur said.

'Ivan has a very understanding way of dealing with people,'

Veronica said, 'dating, obviously, from his time as a business owner.' She could reach him from where she sat and leaned over and patted his bare arm a couple of times in praise.

'Well, he's certainly put some of the fluence on *you*, Veronica,' Jeanette replied. But she grinned as she said it, seemed almost amiable, after all. Maybe she had come to recognize a bit late that something authentic and good existed between Veronica and Hill-Brandon and that nothing Jeanette said or spat would alter it. An intelligent woman. She knew when she was beaten. Strategic withdrawal.

'My only regret is I was rather slow responding,' Veronica said.

'That's natural,' Hill-Brandon said. 'I was just a tramp, though with two sets of clothes, including a Barbour.'

'W.H. Davies wrote a well-received book called *Autobiography of a Super-Tramp*,' Jeanette said.

'I've never thought of you as a tramp, Ivan, ordinary or super,' Veronica said.

'Thanks, Vron, but, really, that's what I was,' Hill-Brandon said.

'If so, no more,' she replied. 'You have come home.' Harpur thought she got a kind of solemnity and grandeur into the last two words. He knew his daughters would have giggled and given Bronx cheers to the phrase, just as they did when a dog film they found disgustingly mawkish, called *Lassie Come Home*, invaded the movie channel.

'Thanks, Vron,' he said.

'So, were you able to make your introduction to the woman, Ivan?' Harpur said.

'Ill-met by torchlight,' Jeanette said.

Harpur guessed this had a witty reference to something.

'Col, I think I might have moved very slightly, just to vary the way I was standing, to ease some muscle strain,' Hill-Brandon said. 'Or possibly I breathed too loudly once or twice.'

'She heard?' Harpur asked.

'The house is very quiet – far from the traffic,' Hill-Brandon replied.

'Did she speak – ask who was there?' Harpur said. 'That's what I'd expect.'

'The torch beam seemed to get pulled away,' Hill-Brandon replied. 'I could still make out a small glow of light up the stairwell, but it seemed to me she'd turned it and herself back towards the entrance/exit boards.'

'She wanted out,' Veronica said.

'That's how it looked,' Hill-Brandon said.

'She'd taken fright?' Harpur said.

'She's in a scary situation,' Veronica said.

'I reckon she'd worked herself up to the quite brave act of coming into the property alone during darkness, but that was as far as this bravery would go,' he said. 'She's a woman with limits.'

'Credible enough,' Harpur said. 'She hears something, yet nobody speaks – it's a very chilling moment. She doesn't know who's up there, nor how many.'

'This is a house with overtones, extremely unpleasant overtones,' Veronica said.

'What the devil is she doing there, in any case?' Jeanette said, but mildly, genuinely puzzled. 'She's plainly not a vagrant, even less so than you, Ivan. As a scene, this is totally wrong for her. Yet it obviously has some sort of compelling fascination.'

'I think she might have been nervy about finding her way out,' Hill-Brandon replied. 'I'd guessed from the way the board thumped back when she let it go after entering that she hadn't propped the gateway open a little, making it simpler to find, an elementary ploy. The torch beam had been redirected to locate the movable boards, and hardly any of the light would reach other parts of the house now.'

'And she was successful?' Harpur asked.

'Successful in retreating, if that's success,' Hill-Brandon said. Strategic withdrawal.

'I heard one of the boards get yanked aside. I lost the light altogether then. I assumed she must have done more or less the same with the torch as when coming in, but reversed – leaned out now, and put it on the ground in front of the house. It was probably switched off. I'd have been able to see the light through the spy hole up there if it was still burning. Then, the same sounds of effort as she got clear of the house while holding back a board with one hand. Soon, that bumped shut. In a couple of seconds I could see her outside. She had the torch unlit in one hand and with the other brushed herself down and straightened her clothes, a dark tailored suit, a business suit, I'd say.

'She began to walk quite swiftly in the opposite direction to Iris Mallen's route. It seemed like she had to keep up with a timetable. As I said, she'd probably given the Elms house visit a set duration in her programme. She appeared to be making for Ritson Mall. I expect you can imagine, Col, that all this intrigued me. It was like seeing half a mystery solved, but not the other half. I felt I had to get things complete, or as complete as I could.'

'This was a remarkable, eminently positive decision by Ivan,' Veronica replied proudly.

Hill-Brandon shrugged, as though to say anyone would have done what he did next – or, at least, anyone who frequently camped out in uncompleted houses. 'I'm not trained in tracking,' Hill-Brandon said.

'Well, no, you wouldn't be, would you?' Jeanette said. 'You were a shopkeeper, not a Mohican.'

'You followed her?' Harpur said.

'This is why I called it a remarkable, positive decision by Ivan,' Veronica said.

'I had a torch of my own, naturally,' Hill-Brandon replied.

'Basic,' Veronica said, 'but no longer vital.' She waved a hand, taking in the flat and its foul art work and happy jumble of furniture styles. 'This is your haven, your continuing haven.'

Wide, red braces were right for havens.

'Thanks, Vron,' Hill-Brandon said. 'I had a torch, but, obviously, I didn't use it while she was in the building. Now, with that light to help, I got quickly downstairs, selected the familiar swing-back board and was soon out into the front garden, as it will eventually be if the Coalition saves the economy. She's a good way ahead by now, but I can still make her out. Luckily, there weren't many people using the short-cut, so she wasn't obscured.' He turned towards Harpur and shrugged again. 'But when I say I don't know much about tracking, what I mean, Col, is the working odds.'

'Working odds?' Harpur asked.

'The competing risks,' Hill-Brandon replied.

'I think I see what he means,' Veronica said.

'In this kind of situation, do I lie well back, in case she turns her head to check behind, or do I get up close so as to be sure I don't lose her, but with the increased chance I'll get spotted?'

'I'd say there's no formula answer to this,' Veronica replied.

'Ad hoc,' Jeanette suggested. 'Pragmatism.'

'Right,' Harpur said.

'What your instincts tell you is best at the moment,' Jeanette said.

'Right,' Harpur said.

'I had the notion there'd be a car parked somewhere around Ritson, and if I could connect her with that I'd have something really hot for Mr Harpur.'

'This is constructive, under-pressure thinking,' Veronica said.

'Certainly,' Harpur said.

'I decided on the up-close option,' Hill-Brandon said.

'Probably correct,' Harpur said.

'My reasoning is, that call at the Elms was an on-the-side element in her programme, sort of in brackets, if I can put it like that.'

'There's a famous twentieth-century work called *In Parenthesis*,' Jeanette said. 'It's ironic.'

'Definitely,' Harpur replied.

'I didn't think she'd look back because she was urgently getting on to somewhere else,' Hill-Brandon said. 'Getting on, that is, to the main engagement of the evening. And she'd have no reason to think she might be followed, anyway.'

'This strikes me as a very cogent appraisal,' Veronica said.

'Absolutely,' Harpur said.

'Getting on to that main engagement in the kind of clothes and shoes which would probably be appropriate for it,' Hill-Brandon said. 'I asked myself, might there be deception involved here, by which I mean, was this main engagement supposed to be the *only* engagement she was attending this evening, and she slipped the Elms visit in secretly? I'd wondered previously, hadn't I? But a secret from whom? Husband? Partner? These seemed the most likely. And so, another "why?" What made her think the secrecy was necessary? It wasn't as if she came to the Elms for a romantic, maybe adulterous, meeting. All she did was talk to Mrs Mallen outside, and then conduct a small survey of the house downstairs, abruptly terminated.'

'Ritson,' Harpur replied. 'What happened when she reached there?'

'If I'd lain back she'd have disappeared and I'd have failed,' he said. 'But as it turned out, I was just in time to see her go into a multi-storey car park.'

'Excellent work, Ivan,' Veronica said.

'Very difficult for surveillance – tracking, as you call it, Ivan,' Harpur said. 'At least, for undisclosed surveillance – too many floors, too many lifts and vehicles cluttering the view, either moving or stationary. You have to stay very near, and, if you're very near – say, in the same lift – the target is likely to sense there's something wrong.'

'My solution?' Hill-Brandon replied. 'Get to the way out. It should be possible to see this "target" in her vehicle as she left. That was the objective, wasn't it – note the car reg?'

'This is real single-mindedness, real focus,' Veronica said. 'A remarkable grip on relevance, a cutting through to the essential.'

'It's one of those car parks where the driver pays into a machine and gets a receipt ticket to insert, which lifts the barrier. It takes a little while. I could watch her for a full minute. She's in a Mini Cooper, yellow lower body, black top.' He brought a folded piece of paper from his shirt pocket and handed it to Harpur. 'The reg,' he said. 'There's a little kiosk office near the barrier and I'm behind that, hidden pretty well. The overhead lighting very good. To me, she looked miserable, dissatisfied, as though she felt chicken at giving up on the house inspection – maybe contemptuous of herself for being suited to whatever situation she was driving to now, but poor if she tried something else, something wholly new and strange.'

'You ought to be a psychologist as well as a detective, Ivan,' Harpur said.

TWENTY

'We hear from a number of theatre aficionados about strange happenings on Friday last at the staging of that blood-soaked and bawdy Jacobean play, *The Revenger's Tragedy*, at the King's.'

The local paper – *Alert* – carried a weekly gossip column called 'Talk of the Town', a title borrowed, apparently, from some American magazine. Harpur read the lead story in it across the table to Iles fairly *sotto*. An *Alert* archive head and shoulders picture of the ACC, taken on the previous clean-up visit, was let into the bottom half of the column.

'When we refer to strange happenings we do not mean strange happenings within the play itself,' the writer said, 'though there are

certainly enough of those. No, this concerns the audience, or, more
exactly, one member of it, Row 4, *fauteuil* 12.

'As we understand it, there were two incidents. In the first of
these, 4/12 suddenly stood, obscuring the stage for several folk
behind, and started an impromptu conversation with one of the
play's characters, the Duke Vendici, or Vindici. The Duke had been
complaining in bitter style about his abused heart strings getting
turned into fret, the way Dukes do in some dramas.

'Up pops 4/12 to say that, as a matter of fact, he knows just how
the Duke feels, and to ask, very ironically, very peeved, whether
anyone will write a play about *his* heart strings, *his* fret? His answer
to his own question requires some tactful dots in a family newspaper,
"Some so . . . ing hope!" The Duke, or, rather, the actor cast as the
Duke, finds this unscripted, yelled contribution to things very unnecessary and, speaking out to the stalls and gallery, says (more dots
are needed) "Sit down and shut the f . . . up, sonny boy." Sonny
boy did, apparently, and the Duke went back to being a Duke. The
play proceeded.

'But then comes a second moment of crisis, brought on it seems
by a particular line in the play: "the insurrection of his lust." Upon
hearing this, 4/12 barges urgently out into the aisle. He is helped
to the bar by staff and given some water in case he is ill. Here,
though, he begins to shout about his wife, about nuances, and about
an alleged conspiracy to get the actor to give a suggestive, crude
mispronunciation of the word "insurrection", so as to upset 4/12.'

'Col, it has to be either that fucking manager or one of the
usherettes who's leaked this,' Iles said. 'Only they knew what went
on in the bar as well as in the auditorium. I'm certain nuances were
not even hinted at during that early discussion of abused heart strings
suffering fret.'

'I don't know, sir. I wasn't at the theatre then,' Harpur said.

'Use your common sense, Harpur. Am I likely to disrupt a very
moving dramatic sequence in a justly esteemed play by shouting
about nuances?'

They were having breakfast in their hotel's large, crowded dining
room. Iles took only warm water again. He had on one of his brilliantly tailored navy blazers and a foul puce and turquoise striped
tie, probably the colours of some elite London club, or a rugby
referees' association. Although Iles often wore this tie or another,
just as bad, but featuring yellow and crimson circles, Harpur never

asked about them. He knew to do so would be lunacy. He recognized that Iles wore these bits of insignia only to give instant offence. And to react with even the slightest trace of dismay and nausea would tell the ACC his ploy had worked. Maybe he'd sensed in his extraordinary way that something rough might turn up today and had put the tie on this morning to repel anyone who might try to get awkward. 'Talk of the Town' got awkward, but couldn't be repelled.

'There's a photograph,' Harpur said.

'Of course there's a photograph. If you're doing someone damage you want everybody to know who the someone is. Maud will hear of this publicity. Maud's bosses will hear of this publicity. Are they going to let her keep me on the investigation? They were already giving her pressure merely on that ponce Dathan's second-hand description of what happened. Now, it's from the rooftops.'

'Bungalow rooftops. It's only a local paper, sir. Maud and her superiors are in London. The tale probably won't get picked up by the nationals. It's not weighty enough.'

Iles took the decibels up a degree or two. 'What's not weighty enough?'

'These incidents.' Harpur had known he was gambling: he wanted to assure Iles there probably wouldn't be wider publicity, but the only way to do it was by suggesting he didn't count for much. Iles might choose to accept the offered comfort. He might not: impossible to turn back now, anyway. Harpur said, 'The London papers are concerned with very hefty topics at present – Syria, the Greek shambles, B Sky B television, the Chancellor of the Exchequer, the Afghan war, for instance.'

Iles waited until Harpur had finished this list, then said, 'We are talking, aren't we, Harpur – I hope I haven't made an error on this – we are talking, aren't we, about Desmond Iles, an Assistant Chief Constable, top of his intake at staff college, yet made a monkey of in the backstreet theatre of a shit-hole provincial town by disguised but very present insults in a mercilessly savage play? You say this is not an adequately important topic to interest the national Press? Is that really your view, or are you only misguidedly trying to comfort me?'

Harpur read some more of the *Alert* article: 'What makes these extraordinary events even more extraordinary is the identity of 4/12. He is an Association of Chief Police Officers member here on a mission to investigate and report on the condition of our own police force, his name—'

'Dathan will make super-sure Maud or Maud's bosses are informed of this grossly disrespectful, indeed, lampooning write-up,' Iles said. He glanced around the room to see whether anyone else was reading the *Alert* or eavesdropping on them. Harpur didn't spot any special interest in the ACC. People might be scared to show it, though. Iles could produce that effect, whether he had on a stuff-the-lot-of-you tie or not.

But now, in a pleasantly conversational style, he said, 'I don't imagine when you were debauching my wife, Harpur, often in degraded and degrading settings, that you realized this would lead one day to difficulties for a work such as *The Revenger's Tragedy*, rightly deemed a valued item in the British literary canon.'

'Regardless of doubts about authorship, sir,' Harpur replied.

'They'll shut us down, Col,' Iles said. 'Or shut me down. The investigation's dead. We fail to advance. I've had a go at those two officers on the path that you identified, Alan Silver and Graham Quick, and more absolute brick wall. They've been expertly terrorized or expertly coached in saying nowt.' He leaned over his own plate and Harpur's and gently took the copy of *Alert* from him. Now, Iles did the reading aloud, as though he knew an indictment of some sort must be coming at the conclusion of the piece, and meant to face up and speak the judgement himself: 'His name is Assistant Chief Constable Desmond Iles (pictured) – it says that, "pictured", like a Wanted photo – Desmond Iles, present on this ground to rectify and purify. Some will no doubt ask whether he is altogether suited to this task, given his tendency to get pushed drastically off balance by nuances and frets. Who polices the police was a traditional tricky question. Now, it's a lot trickier – who polices the police sent to police the police?'

A man of about fifty, well-barbered, thick grey hair, beige slacks, ginger suede jacket, approached from a breakfast table across the room and stood smiling alongside them. Harpur hadn't noticed him earlier. Maybe he'd come from one of the rooftops. 'Forgive, do, the interruption,' he said, 'but a question. I, too, have been reading the "Talk of the Town" piece, which I see in your hand, and I'm defeated by one remark therein. This crude mispronunciation of the word "insurrection". What on earth can that be?'

'Prick,' Iles replied.

'Prick? But that's nothing like the sound of "insurrection". It could hardly be called a mispronunciation. A substitution, perhaps.'

'No, I mean *you* are a prick,' Iles said.

The man's smile fell away. 'It was a valid query, I think. There's surely no need for rudeness.'

'Yes, there is an acute need for rudeness,' Iles said. 'Bugger off back to your eggs Benedict.'

'Have you been pushed drastically off balance again?' the man asked.

'Do you want to get thumped drastically off balance?' Iles said. When the man had gone, Iles said: 'Do you pity me, Col? Do you see me as a target for lurking prats in suede like that? Am I diminished?'

'Never! Believe me, I regard you, sir, exactly as I always have.'

'Oh, God.'

TWENTY-ONE

But Iles was right about Maud and those above Maud. He and Harpur had arranged to see Leo Young at his home, Midhurst, this morning and they were in Iles's car after breakfast and about to leave, when Harpur's mobile phone rang. 'It will be Maud,' the ACC said. 'She wants to talk to you privately. She wants to talk to you privately because it's about me. You and she have an empathic understanding, don't you, Col?'

It *was* Maud, wanting to talk to Harpur privately. Iles, who would be doing the driving, didn't switch on. They stayed in the hotel car park. 'Can you speak all right, Colin?' she said. 'I wanted to catch you before your day really began. You're alone for a moment?'

'Absolutely.'

'It's delicate.'

'Right.'

'Dathan's been talking to us again.'

'Rhys?'

'The Chief.'

'Yes?' Harpur replied.

'The local paper. The *Alert*.'

'Yes, I know it.'

'You understand what they're like up here about publicity, do you?' Maud said.

'They hope to what is called "manage" it, I gather. Sometimes they're keen, aren't they – to launch new proposals and laws, that type of thing.'

'Not the *Alert* kind of stuff. The tone.'

'It's the gossip column you mean, is it, Maud? "Talk of the Town"? That kind of journalism is usually done in a light-hearted, perky style, surely?'

Iles nodded perhaps to agree, perhaps to indicate he'd been right to guess the caller was Maud.

She said, 'Treats Iles as if he's a complete buffoon. A cuckold right for craziness every time he hears a key word such as "fret" or "lust". He's like someone who's been hypnotized and can be put back into a trance if he gets a cue. Did you ever see the original *Manchurian Candidate* on the movie channel? Like that. People here – well, they feel he exposes them to attack for selecting him, exposes the Department to attack. I'm referring to people as far up as the Secretary himself. Our press office fears the nationals and even TV news will get interested in the situation. They already have Cass, the murdered reporter, to wonder about and focus on, haven't they? There could be a Question in the House. I don't know for how long I can support Iles – support, in fact, the investigation itself. I *want* to because I picked him and you for the job, but I'm aware of increasing opposition.'

After the nod, Iles, alongside Harpur, remained utterly silent and still. Harpur couldn't tell whether he was able to pick up some – all – of what Maud was saying. He could probably guess most of it, anyway. He'd closed his eyes, as though relaxed and dozing. It might be to maximize concentration, though, or to dream hate schemes against Dathan.

'You'll wonder why I'm ringing *you* about it,' Maud said. 'He's your superior and I shouldn't be discussing him in this way with a subordinate – excuse the term. It's against protocol. Why I said "delicate". But I feel that you and I, Col, have—'

'I don't think the people above you there appreciate properly how Mr Iles functions,' Harpur said. 'Even you, Maud, might not realize this in full. People of immense talent often have their little quirks and foibles. It is part of their unconventionality. I've called it talent. Some might say "genius". Think of that artist who cut his own ear off.'

'Van Gogh.'

'The one.'

'You consider Iles is in that league?'

'As to the mysterious scope of his abilities, maybe.'

'Mysterious?'

'The way he can intuit, the way he can sense the essentials of a situation, a problem,' Harpur said. 'Often, it's phenomenal.' Iles didn't open an eye.

'In what regard?' Maud said.

'Mrs Young.'

'Leo Young's wife, Emily? I remember her name from the original inquiry,' Maud said. 'What about her?'

'Some strange behaviour, perhaps promising behaviour from our point of view.'

'Yes?'

'Mr Iles discovered – don't ask me how – that she had been on a night visit to the murder house on Elms.'

Maud was silent for fifteen seconds. Then she said, 'To what purpose, Colin? What's the significance?'

'She went solo but met Mrs Mallen there.'

Another pause. 'Leo Young's wife met Tom Mallen's widow at night on Elms?'

'Right.'

'Why?'

'At the Jaminel house,' Harpur replied.

'They both entered the Jaminel house?'

'No, they talked outside. Only Mrs Young actually went in.'

'Why?'

'Her shoes and clothes were not suitable for such a visit, but she'd brought a torch. This would seem to show intent. There's loose boarding that provides a gateway,' Harpur replied.

'Did she meet Mrs Mallen by arrangement?' Maud asked.

'Unclear at this stage.'

'Iris Mallen would have driven quite a way, wouldn't she? From a different police patch. Doesn't that suggest a rendezvous?'

'She had a separate purpose – separate from the encounter with Mrs Young.'

'Separate in which sense?

'Iris Mallen was there to look for a kind of memento of her husband.'

'Which kind?'

'Apparently, a Biro.' Iles remained completely still.

'A Biro pen?' Maud said.

Was there any other kind of Biro? 'She'd left it in the ground to show the spot where her husband died. A kind of marker, but a marker with a sentimental status, because it used to belong to Tom. She was afraid that, if construction picked up because of more quantitative easing as they call it, by the Bank of England, the Biro might get overlaid and lost.'

'Mrs Mallen trekked to Elms at night to look for a pen? Did she find it?'

'Apparently not.'

'Did Mrs Young help her look?'

'Unclear at this stage.'

'Mrs Mallen expected to find a Biro left there in mud and rubble months ago?' Maud asked.

'She's probably still in shock and not too rational after the loss of her husband.'

'So you must have been told all this by Mr Iles himself,' Maud replied.

'Absolutely,' Harpur said.

Another pause. 'And do you find it credible – not a further . . . a further example of Iles once more in the grip of his talent, his genius, as you describe it, this time fabricating a sequence around the Jaminel house?'

'Absolutely not,' Harpur said.

'All right, suppose it's as he says: we come back to the question, what's the significance?'

'I don't know yet. But that's the point, isn't it, Maud?'

'What?'

'He might get an intimation, a hint, from his remarkable mind about the significance – from his *subconscious* mind, possibly.'

'An intimation, a hint, from his subconscious?' Maud replied. 'As to what?'

'This is the kind of exceptional, sort of instinctive, insight that your masters and mistresses up there don't allow for. They should be told of it, Maud, and in strong form. I hope you believe enough in Mr Iles's splendid, inspired competence to take this message

effectively to them. It must be made plain that removing Mr Iles
from the inquiry would be a terrible error, an act of destructive folly
just when things seem about to open up, to open up under his
astonishing, unique influence.'

'Open up in which regard?' Maud asked. 'Why do you make so
much of his knowledge of the Jaminel house visit? He might have
been in or around the house when Mrs Young and Mrs Mallen
arrived there, and merely observed them. A total fluke.'

'Certainly he might have been,' Harpur replied. 'He hasn't said
so, but, yes, he might have been. That begs a considerable question,
though, doesn't it?'

'Does it?'

'If he was around the house at that time, *why* was he? There
would be nothing more to learn there so long after the crime. The
house has been examined and re-examined exhaustively. Or, at least,
there *appeared* to be nothing to learn there. You see, Maud, if he
were there, I would identify this as another of those inexplicable,
thrilling aspects of his work. A kind of amazing telepathy. When I
call it inexplicable, I mean inexplicable to basic thinkers like myself,
and, perhaps like your honchos up there. Oh, no doubt they have
fine incisive thoroughly trained minds, but they are fine, incisive
minds trained in dealing brilliantly with the tangible, the factual,
the practical. At times, though, Mr Iles is far outside those categories.
He is pure flair, he is consummate hunch and sharp sixth-sense.'

'OK, OK, but—'

'You're still concerned about the significance of all this,' Harpur
replied.

'If I'm going to convince people here that Iles is indispensable
to the investigation I'll have to—'

'Because I'm so used to Mr Iles, I can make a guess at how his
thoughts might develop. It will be *only* a guess. I emphasize that.
I don't have the kind of gifts we've been talking about as special
to him. I won't call them magical—'

'Thanks,' Maud replied.'

'But occasionally beyond the natural.'

She gave a short groan. 'OK, OK, again.'

'Here's how it might seem, then, to Mr Iles. Emily Young goes
to the Jaminel house. It would appear from the way she's dressed
and shoed that she didn't want Leo to know of her intention. She's
chair of the museum committee, isn't she, and might be in the right

gear for that, but will fit in the Elms trip as an extra. Why the deception? What's going on here? What's the psychology? Mr Iles would confront these puzzles. Mr Iles would see connections, see links, see likelihoods. He might wonder whether she's been asking herself lately if she knows all there is to know about her husband's business. This is an intelligent woman, used to the world, able enough to head that museum committee. She's not blind.

'Perhaps she even wonders about the death of Tom Mallen-Parry, on the face of it an employee of her husband, really an undercover cop. She might ask herself, why had this officer targeted her husband's companies? Did they warrant that? Where exactly did the constant, glorious profits come from? And, did Leo find out somehow what Tom really was and decide to do something about it, such as have him guided on to Elms and slaughtered? The Jaminel house possibly came to represent all this darkness and evil in her thinking, her pondering. A kind of exorcism was needed.'

'The subconscious *and* an exorcism?'

'Did she resolve to get along to Elms and confirm it was just bricks, mortar, bay windows and potential dinky front and back gardens?'

'It is all those, but can still be a sharpshooter post,' Maud said.

'Of course it can. But Mr Iles, seeking to explain her behaviour to himself, might conclude that this was a woman who'd suddenly experienced great and monstrous stress – her husband a possible killer, or accessory. She might have deliberately switched off such awful speculation until now. Something had made this no longer feasible. Horrifying ideas attack her. She makes a grab for whatever can bring some stability to her mind and life. The house? It could be so, couldn't it? Maud?'

'Could it?'

'This was what I meant by opening up,' Harpur replied.

'What?'

'A way into things – as long as Mr Iles remains in charge.'

'Mrs Young?'

'She might be vulnerable. This unusual behaviour – an indication of weakness. It could be exploited by someone with that kind of extraordinary skill and perception.'

'Desmond Iles's kind of skill and perception?'

'Absolutely.'

Maud went silent once more. 'I'll talk to the people here,' she said eventually.

'Warn them against hastiness. Warn them against seeing only the trivial drawbacks and minor snags in Mr Iles's personality, and not the astonishing overarching excellence.'

'If you think so much of him, Colin, why were you shagging his wife? Wasn't that what brought on the display of trivial drawbacks and minor snags at the play?'

'I'm confident your colleagues in the Department will see the dangers to their reputations and careers if they do anything to obstruct the progress of this inquiry so efficiently led by Assistant Chief Iles,' Harpur replied.

TWENTY-TWO

Iles drove them out towards Midhurst. He said: 'As a matter of fact, Col, I wondered why you'd been badgering the big computer for owner's name of a car reg that turned out to be Mrs Young's. Now I understand.'

'You're the sort, sir.'

'Which?'

'The sort who have some confidential means – some *very* confidential means – of finding out who's been visiting the computer with that type of very confidential question.'

'Now and then I get a tip-off from one of the people running it.'

'*Now* rather than *then*, in this case.'

'He calls me if he thinks I'd be interested in who's asking.'

'Me?'

'This is a service that took a long time to establish, Harpur – not a doddle, you know. And people get moved on, or retire, or are promoted, so the business negotiations have to start all over.'

'Effort, patience – they're worthwhile?'

'This kind of arrangement doesn't come cheap, Col.'

'Cop cross-palming cop. It's probably rare. A long-term investment, though,' Harpur said.

'I think you'll agree it's necessary when I have some shitehawk on my staff carrying out, in secretive, furtive fashion his own private programme of inquiries.'

'You'd see it as part of man management, I imagine.'

'A yellow and black Mini Cooper,' Iles replied. 'Licence due for renewal in March.'

'I thought it best to make out to Maud that it was you rather than myself who'd gathered all this problematical stuff about the women at the Jaminel place.'

'Why?'

'You've done the same for me sometimes, haven't you, sir? Attributed breakthroughs to me that were actually made by you.'

'Have I?'

'Certainly.'

'I probably pitied you, thought you needed it – needed some boost. It's not difficult to pity you, Harpur. Or, to put it another way, it's difficult not to pity you.'

'Perhaps I felt *you* needed a boost.'

'In which respect?'

'After all that sad carry-on at the theatre. People in the Home Office stalking you. So, I laid it on pretty thick with Maud, such as your "splendid, inspired competence" and "astonishing over-arching excellence". I had these phrases ready in case ever needed. I think I might have collected them from a book about D-Day and the leadership skills of General Eisenhower. Forgive the flowery extravagance of the compliments, sir. I know praise embarrasses, even sickens, you. It *is* necessary. We have to try and annihilate the impression of some who work with Maud – who possibly give Maud her orders – that you are a gibbering, loony wreck, a disaster who could bring disaster on them. This is not an easy aim, taking into account your behaviour and the fact that it's been reported by the Press in chuckling mode. But above all we have to keep the investigation intact, sir. You head the investigation. Therefore, I had to build you into something formidable and gifted, regardless. High civil servants worry about their careers, gongs and pension. They dislike getting caught supporting some flagrant plonker. It taints them.'

'*You* had to build *me*?'

'In Maud's estimation.'

'Regardless of what?'

'Essentially, she's on our side, but needed some backing, some help in convincing others.'

'And do you think she'll *really* try?'

'Certainly, sir. Why not?'

'She might want *you* to lead the investigation. Get rid of Ilesy, replace him with Col. It would be her way of buttering you up. This is a woman with a fine education. She knows how to be devious. She'll have read about Robespierre in the French Revolution – admirable in many, many ways, and hooked on plotting and ruthlessness.'

'She's one of your greatest admirers and—'

'I didn't like the way you dithered over the terms "talent" and "genius", when discussing me,' Iles replied. 'I detest indecision.'

'I think the vividness of the Van Gogh ear reference and the comparison of him to you will stick in her mind. That means she'll think of you in the genius category, like the artist, and not merely talented.'

'I take it we're seeing one of your customary egocentric, smelly tricks, are we, Col?'

'Which, sir?'

'We're on strange ground but you've already found an informant who talks only to you. He or she witnessed that night activity around the Jaminel house involving Mrs Young and Iris Mallen, did he or she?'

'The house is certainly a magnet,' Harpur replied.

'If I'd been there, Harpur, I'd have gone to Mrs Mallen and said, "Do you see this injury on my cheek? That's where your husband's damn Biro dug in deep. This was quite a zonk, more than touché, I can tell you. Thanks so very, very much for leaving it there, available to this thug, Harpur. If you'd had a poniard about you I suppose you'd have left that, and then he could have done a real job on me."'

'The wound's healing very well,' Harpur said.

'It would still have been visible, even in the dark.'

'I don't know what attitude she'd take to that, sir.'

'"Overarching" in which sense, Col?' Iles replied.

'That's the kind of word they're fond of in the Home Office. It's a stupid word, anyway. Arches are always over, so "overarching" is to say the same thing twice.'

'You were always a language purist, Col.'

The Youngs lived in a large converted Victorian farmhouse with grounds. The set-up reminded Harpur of Panicking Ralph Ember's place, Low Pastures, back on their own territory, though Ralph's was a genuine manor house and older than Midhurst. A Spanish consul and, later, a Lord Lieutenant had lived at Low Pastures way back. One of the gates had a plaque on it from an earlier ownership with a quote in Latin meaning something like 'a man's mind is what he is'. Harpur had heard that Panicking cleaned it every few weeks to make sure it stayed legible. He probably thought his mind pretty good and that this plaque contained his potted biography. Drugs tycoons liked to settle stylishly in the country, though not all would have classical plaques. They wanted some distance between the city streets and dives, where they made most of their money, and the spread they bought with it, where they raised their families. Big-time industrialists now and in history did the same: lived somewhere leafy, well away from their factories or mines.

Midhurst wasn't the only reminder of Iles and Harpur's own police patch. A smart housing estate known as the Elms Enclave existed there. But those properties were built, completed and quickly sold in the good times. The Elms development here languished, only part done. Harpur thought a parable about Britain's changed financial state showed clearly in the two Elms projects. Harpur liked to get a widish idea up and running in his head occasionally. He didn't let the notion out of his head, though. He wouldn't speak of it to Iles because he'd piss on it, saying the thought was obvious, banal and trite. Iles didn't care for competition in the ideas area. He'd told Harpur that at Staff College he was known as 'Thinking-cap Desy'.

Iles parked near some stone outbuildings to the side of the house and they walked across a gravelled forecourt to the front door of Midhurst. It was opened before they reached it, though, and Leo Young came out into the porch smiling a grand welcome. He had a small, congested face, but he could find room for what was undeniably a smile on it. They'd met him, of course, on the previous investigation here: Tom Mallen-Parry had masqueraded as one of his firm. 'Leo,' Iles called. 'This *is* a treat. You're looking great! The porch sets you off. But you should have Labradors gambolling around you. And I trust Emily is well. You'll remember Col Harpur. He has his own way of approaching things, but where would we be if were we all the same? Oh, deary me, yes. North Korea?' Young shook hands with both of them.

'But you got an injury, Mr Iles,' Young said.

'Par for the course in our line of work, Leo,' Iles said. 'Ask Harpur.'

'Mr Iles is always out there in front,' Harpur replied.

'Col's never far behind. Behind but not very far behind. Modesty prevents his saying that, Leo, but it's so.'

'Shall I tell you what I don't think is fair in this, like, situation, Mr Iles?' Young said.

'A good deal of life is not fair, Leo,' Iles said.

'People – they don't understand you, Mr Iles,' Young said.

'Which people, Leo?' Iles said.

'The press,' Young said.

'What about it?' Iles said.

'I wonder if you seen what's called "Talk of the Town" in the *Alert*,' Young said. 'But why do we jabber out here? Come in. We'll go to the drawing room, shall we?' Panicking had a drawing room, too, and would mention it in a similar offhand, classy style.

Young led the way. His wife was already in the room, standing near the big fireplace where half a dozen logs burned. Iles exclaimed delightedly, something about there being no smell so delicious and enlivening as smouldering larch. Emily Young, too, shook hands with Iles and Harpur. Young said: 'I mentioned that "Talk of the Town" to Mr Iles, Em. The word I used was "unfair".'

Mrs Young didn't say anything.

'A mockery note – am I right?' Young asked. 'Was this appropriate re a senior police officer? Never! That word, "appropriate", is around quite a lot lately meaning OK. This was *not* appropriate. I got to mention it. It don't say well of a city if it treats an officer from another city in that dis way. What I believe is, people don't understand you, Mr Iles. I don't know if Em feels the same, but that's my own opinion.'

'Which people?' Iles replied.

'When I say unfair, this got to be worse when it's someone with a wound,' Young said. 'Inconsiderate. Kicking someone when he's down on account of an injury. What I think of you as, Mr Iles, is someone who responds. Whatever the circs you will respond, because it's built into you, like a damp course in a property, what's known as "integral", whether it's in a theatre or anywhere else. All right, you start talking to the actors on a certain topic during some play. That's what I mean – you respond. Dialogue means two-way. All right, so you gave them some back. That's responding.'

'I heard this Duke figure going on about abused heart strings and his fret and it must have touched something off in me,' Iles explained.

'Why I say you respond,' Young answered.

'Harpur here was banging my wife in all sorts of illicit or crummy situations not long ago and so I'm ever a prey to influences contained in terms like "abused heart strings" and "fret", Iles said. 'They come at me like an assault. If I were one for tattoos, these would be words on my forearm.'

'We can sympathize with that,' Young said. 'I'm sure I'm speaking for Em as well as myself here.'

'Harpur thought I shouldn't have gone to the play a second time, but he would, wouldn't he, because he'd know a repeat might lead to such a reaction?' Iles said. 'My nose getting, as one might say, rubbed in it.'

'Almost bound to happen,' Young replied.

Leo stayed on his feet. The rest sat down. 'What we're here for, Leo, Mrs Young, is to sort out what kind of organization was behind Jaminel and the murder of Detective Sergeant Mallen and, most probably, the journalist, Cass,' Iles said. 'We had a notion you might be able to help in this regard. I'm not sure whether you're familiar with the Mallen killing, Mrs Young, but it took place on a stymied housing site of executive dimension properties known as the Elms.'

'This *is* a problem – the what you might nominate "behind the scenes" aspect,' Young said. 'I should think the authorities picked you out for this task because of that ability I referred to previous, the ability to respond. And you have to bring support – so, Mr Harpur. Like a team.'

'One of the Home Office women has the hots for him,' Iles said. 'There's a sexual theme to much of his life. He's giving it regularly to some undergraduate not much older than his daughters when we're home. She sleeps at his dump in Arthur Street more often than in her student accommodation block. God knows what her parents would make of it – quite decent people as far as I can discover. They're going to turn up one day, unannounced, as a lovely surprise on the campus looking for their daughter and someone will say, "Oh, she's over with her bit of the fuzz as almost ever."

'Maud, the Home Office piece, hopes to retain me on the investigation, despite "Talk of the Town", and the Chief here, because she wants access to Col. Or that's one way of assessing the situation. It's something like Humbert Humbert wooing the mother so he can get at her daughter, Lolita: not an analogy I'm fond of, though, because it makes me into a dumbo frump played by Shelley Winters.

The other possibility is that she's only playing at backing me because she wants to favour Harpur and win him top-dog position in this inquiry.'

'I'll get us tea, shall I?' Young said. He went to the kitchen.

Iles said: 'A lovely home, Mrs Young, with upkeep and heating an expense, I imagine, in inflationary times, even if the logs are from fallen timber on your own grounds. And do I remember right – two boys away at prep school?'

'Why are you here?' she replied.

Iles said: 'As I explained, Mrs, Young, we—'

'Yes, yes, the organization behind the Mallen killing. But why are you here, at Midhurst, at our home?' she said.

Harpur felt surprised by her tone. It wasn't aggressive or confrontational – not hissed as if they had no right to be here – a tidied-up version of *Why the hell are you here? Bugger off.* She really wanted information. It was as though Mrs Young, too, longed to know about the organization behind the Mallen killing, suppose there *were* an organization. Perhaps some of the fiction he'd given Maud to explain Emily's reasons for going to the Elms house was not fiction at all, but right.

By briefing her laboriously just now about 14 Davant, Iles had given Emily a chance to say she knew it, had been there, had run into Mrs Mallen there. *Yes, yes, everyone who reads a paper or watches TV news is familiar with the house. In fact, just to check it was nothing but what it is, an amalgam of the customary construction materials, I popped over there and did a bit of a survey the other night. Verdict? Solid. Not complete but, as far as it's gone, solid. The standard recipe of bricks, wood, plastic, mortar. No glass yet. It would be stupid to include the easily breakable. But glass will come in its due time.* However, she'd stayed blank.

Harpur had guessed the visit was secret, and this looked like confirmation. As he'd suggested to Maud, it might have been secret because she felt troubled about Leo's business and his possible part in the Mallen execution. Maybe she *had* needed a reminder that the house was only that, a to-be-one-day, ordinary residence, not a dark symbol of something brutal and rotten in her husband. So, had Harpur's spin to Maud been more than spin, truer than spin? She might have lived for years with the suspicion that Leo got most of the money for Midhurst, and the private boarding school fees, and the Mini Cooper, and his own cars, and Emily's top-notch clothes, by brilliant crookedness. Now, for reasons not entirely obvious yet, she had possibly moved beyond suspicion. From Iles and himself she seemed to be seeking insights that would take her towards terrifying certainty. Could she be turned – turned into an ally, which would, most probably, entail turning herself into a traitor to Leo?

Iles said: 'Wide-ranging, you see, Mrs Young.'

'What is?' she replied.

'Our purpose this time. It's not just a murder, but the context of that murder, and its possible connection with a later murder, the journalist, Cass. You, as I understand it, Mrs Young, are the chair of a museum committee,' Iles said. 'In that role you will deal with many single exhibits from ancient periods. Such exhibits are significant in their own right. But also, and perhaps even more significant, you will wish to see how they fit into their background; their context. Ours is a similar quest.'

'You think Leo is part of that context?' she said.

'Wide-ranging, as I've already declared it, Mrs Young. We are seeing many people.'

'And perhaps major, even commanding, in that context?' she asked.

'Wide-ranging,' Iles said.

'It's a kind of attrition, isn't it?' she said.

'What?' Iles said.

'You put a disguised spy into Leo's companies.'

'Not I,' Iles said. 'I haven't that kind of power.'

'I mean the police, the authorities, the Home Office. They have decided – I don't know why – that there is something to investigate and ordinary methods are not adequate. A spy is needed.'

'We don't normally care for the term "spy". It's from a different profession. We call it "covert surveillance". The word "surveillance" is neutral. It makes no assumptions: something might be found, nothing might be found.'

'Bullshit,' she replied. 'You wouldn't put an officer into that kind of dangerous situation if you didn't feel more or less certain there *was* something to be found. It's a judgemental act. What was it then that made Leo's business a target? This is why I say attritional. You – the police, the Home Office – place a spy in the firm and then, when the spy is killed, you decide that not just the man with the gun is to blame, but others who put the man with the gun up to it, because the spy might destroy their racket. And so you come to our home with politeness bordering on smarm but actually intent on wearing Leo down.'

'Wide-ranging, Mrs Young. We'll be calling at quite a few homes. You mustn't feel Leo is being victimized,' Iles replied.

And then the combativeness and hostility left her, left her again, and when she spoke it was with a question that simply and maybe desperately sought information. 'Why was this officer put into Leo's companies in the first place?'

'Covert surveillance is a recognized police procedure and is carefully supervised,' Iles said.

'I dare say, I dare say, but . . .'

Leo came back into the drawing room with a teapot and crockery on a plain wooden tray.

TWENTY-THREE

Leo was about 5' 5" with fair wavy hair worn long, and a fair moustache. He had a very small head and face, and Harpur thought his eyes, mouth, nose, chin and cheeks looked cruelly jam-packed in this limited area, like passengers on a rush-hour tube train. Young's decision to nab some of the scarce skinscape for a moustache seemed half mad: an unnecessary extra that increased the impression of clutter. Harpur guessed Leo to be in his early forties. Emily might be a little older. Harpur and Iles had both observed a kind of uncertain cockiness about Leo's body language. Iles had offered two comparisons. He said Leo's short, stocky build put him in mind of the classic physique for a dauntless Welsh rugby fly-half, but, in Leo's case, one who had lost his bearings after concussion in a game and scored a try at the wrong end of the pitch, against his own side. Or Iles saw him as a milkman who picked the career because, being short, he wouldn't have far to bend when doorstep delivering, but who'd then found this did not compensate nearly enough in winter for having to get up in the dark.

Leo fussed over serving the tea, with special care to get the milk and sugar, or no sugar, absolutely right for Harpur and Iles. The fine points of hospitality seemed important to him. In a splendid house and grounds like Midhurst, Leo might feel a kind of *noblesse*

oblige, though his personal strain of *noblesse* wouldn't get him into
Who's Who. He said: 'Mr Iles, Mr Harpur, some would resent a
visit at their residence by senior police in a major murder inquiry.
They would regard it as unjustified finger-pointing. But not us.
Emily and I understand.'

Nonsense, at least in part. Emily did not understand the reason
for the visit, or said she didn't. *Why are you here, at Midhurst, at
our home?* She'd quizzed Iles and Harpur, hoping for information.
Using that 'deconstruction' trick taught him by Denise, Harpur
decided Emily's question fell into two bits. *Why are you here at
Midhurst?* That is, as he'd speculated earlier: *How have you got the
fucking nerve to come nuisancing and ferreting at our place of
status and distinction?* And *Why are you here at our home?* That
is, *How have you got the clodhopping gall to come disrupting our
quiet, rural domestic existence?* Iles had fobbed her off, telling her
the inquiries were *wide-ranging* (no hint of what the width covered)
. . . in search of a . . . *context* (no definition) . . . *we are seeing
many people* (no names).

Leo said: 'We are proud to be listed among those regarded as
possibly useful in this new inquiry. Naturally, absolutely naturally,
everyone connected with Tom Mallen, also Parry, is likely to be
called on. Routine. Unavoidable. *Not* to make them calls would be
downright slackness. And, for definite, we did have a connection.
How could it be denied? He worked for our firm. He was welcomed
more than once into this very property on a warm and friendly basis.
He had a favoured position. He had seemed to merit that. But then,
the shocking Elms death and in due course the trial revelation of
his true identity – a police identity.'

Emily said: 'What we don't know is why he was ever sent to
snoop on Leo's business secretly from inside.'

'It could be the result of an anon, dirty tip from someone – a
business enemy, maybe – wanting to damage us by putting in this
bad word to the authorities, suggesting confidential checks should
be done; the kind of rotten commercial smear tactics that so very
regrettably sometimes occur,' Young said. 'Or like in the Soviet
Union, as was, when someone might send an unsigned letter to the
secret police saying a neighbour had called Stalin a shite.

'But, in any case, as of now it don't matter why he was sent.
When the trial took place, after that horrible murder, nothing illegal
or even slightly off-colour came out about the Young firm. Many

foolish tales re involvement went around, but all of them discarded, dismissed. We was totally in the clear then, and the same now. Very much so. Even more.

'We are glad, Emily and me, to give all the help you think you might need, Mr Iles, Mr Harpur. Your mission is a good and vital mission, a cleansing mission. The public are grateful for it, as they should be. We know you will do things totally right, and the slight malarkey at the theatre got nothing at all to do with whether you, Mr Iles, are someone fit for this kind of work when liable to certain mental surges. The theatre and plays affect people in so many different ways – joining in with the actors, for instance. I think of kids at the panto who shout a warning to their hero or heroine on the stage, "He's behind you!" Yes, our two, away now, have done that at the King's. Them children were in the drama as much as the actors! Same with you, Mr Iles, also at the King's.

'Or a member of the audience might get reminded by something in a play of very unpleasant facts in their lives, such as, with all respect, Mr Iles, the matter of your dear wife, mother, I understand, of your child, a daughter. This could clearly cause sudden distress. I hope, Mr Harpur, you will forgive me mentioning this, but it do seem to be part of the general picture. However, I believe, you are no longer having it away with Mrs Iles in various locales and vehicles, and you and Mr Iles are now more or less good mates for much of the time. There might be occasional rough moments, true, but that can happen to any pair of good friends, especially where one's been shagging the other one's missus surreptitious and it comes to light. This is what's referred to, I believe, as "a bone of contention", but that bone is only brought out now and again to be nibbled at, not by any means continuous. For quite long periods nobody watching would be able to tell how bad you, Mr Iles, have been hurt by your wife's carry-on. Restraint – that's what you often got, a true strength.'

'This is the kind of hearty and generous endorsement of our work that Col appreciates enormously, Leo,' Iles replied. 'Also myself, of course, but Harpur, particularly, longs for approval by the community. In him it comes close to egomania, but is more or less tolerable, and it does have its pathetic aspect, also.' Iles gave a small wave with his cup. Harpur felt this was meant as a sign of fellowship, despite his ego and pathetic need for approval by the masses.

They were in capacious, very comfortable brown leather easy

chairs, what Harpur thought of as gentlemen's club chairs, though he had never been in a gentlemen's club. Back home, Panicking Ralph Ember would have liked to think the club he owned, The Monty, of Shield Terrace, might one day deserve that title, but the transformation would take a while, plus exclusion of almost all the present membership, including those locked up, or recently released, or between stretches locked up, or on bail or probation. The Monty was the only club Harpur knew at first hand. He and Iles would look in there now and then, trying to eavesdrop and/or sense anything about current and future projects – wedding receptions, robberies, beatings, christening parties, protection schemes, acquittals, territory campaigns. And because they were fond of Ralph.

Iles said: 'It's that bright, Home Office babe called Maud who's interested in what we've dubbed the "context" of the Mallen death, Leo. Her job is to take the global view.'

'That's the way of them up there in London, isn't it, Mr Iles? Trends. They're concerned with trends. Something occurs and they're not bothered about the thing that's occurred as such but they ask theirselves, "What does this thing that happened tell us about trends?" They're entitled to ask this because trends are meat and drink to Whitehall people. Meat and drink. If they think it's a good trend they'll try to help it along. But if it seems bad, they'll want to kill it off before it gets to be more than a trend and is . . . and is what it is, like.'

Young's drawing room looked out on to the gravelled front yard and then beyond, towards the sea. Emily's yellow and black Mini Cooper was parked near the front door. Outbuildings to the right had been well restored and roofed with genuine slate. Framed floral prints hung on the drawing room walls, bland, unvivid. A fine, rosewood antique bureau and long mahogany chiffonier stood opposite Harpur's chair. The floor was varnished hardwood strips covered here and there with Persian-type rugs, their prevailing, background colour a dark, warm red. Leo or Emily had some taste. In Harpur's experience, Leo always dressed formally and had on a grey three-piece suit, button-down collared blue and white striped shirt, and azure silk tie, black lace-up shoes.

'Maud's persistent,' Iles said.

'Clearly, we could of asked for a lawyer to be present at this interview, a "sit-in" as they're known, watching out for questions that might do damage, and putting the block on same for the clients' sake, such as us.' Young stopped and took a few seconds before he resumed. 'But, no, no, not "interview".' He gave that a hard, confrontational, deep probe tone. '"Interview" sounds too cold and official – it should be "at this *visit*", like of a hearty, cuppa-based social nature. We decided, Emily and me, that a lawyer would not be appropriate in these circs. There's that word again – "appropriate". Or, in very truth, we could say its opposite, "*in*appropriate". This is how we regard the idea of a lawyer: inappropriate. Like an insult to all of us – an insult to you for suggesting you could be hiding something harsh and unfriendly behind a mock-up happy get-together under our roof; and an insult to us for seeming to brand ourselves, Emily and me, scared and needing an LLB in the room for protection.

'What, I ask, have we to be scared of in this meeting? The answer comes *so* easy – nothing. In fact, the total reverse.' Harpur thought Leo sounded delighted by the neatness of polar opposites. 'This is an occasion where common interests can be discussed in reasonable, relaxed fashion. These interests might not be wholly the same on both sides – your side, Mr Iles, Mr Harpur, our side, Emily's and mine – but nor are they head-on opposed to each other. There is plenty of agreement, and this can be improved and extended, which we'll all agree, I'm sure, is desirable.'

'Maud has a certain idea, Leo,' Harpur replied.

'That's another kind of item they're interested in – ideas,' Leo said. 'An idea can lead to a trend, and the other way about.'

'Maud believes that one of the drugs outfits had a business arrangement with some police, and that's why Mallen and the journalist probably got it – they'd started looking for evidence of this alliance, perhaps discovered some early fragments,' Harpur said.

'That's an idea, but a terrible, evil idea,' Leo said. 'This would probably mean police corruption.'

'Yes, most probably it would,' Iles replied.

'People who should be looking after the law would be rubbishing it,' Leo said.

'That exactly,' Iles said.

'We wondered, Leo, if you'd heard anything around the business community of this kind of abuse,' Harpur said.

Emily put down her cup with a hard smack on the wood floor. 'How would Leo hear something of that sort?' she asked. 'You're talking about drug-dealing businesses, aren't you? What would Leo have to do with *them*?'

Although it was said in an attack-defence voice, Harpur thought it sounded again, not like someone trying to kill off the topic with a question that suggested what he'd said was too ridiculous to need an answer, but a wife asking for real insights about her husband's business – though at the same time scared of those possible insights, and wanting to correct them, bury them.

'There are often ripples of gossip, rumour, speculation about these criminal firms which reach out even as far as eminently straight businesses such as, for instance, Leo's,' Iles said.

'Rumours of what kind?' she said. 'And I thought the police didn't deal in gossip, rumour and speculation. I understood you wanted hard evidence.'

'One reason it's called hard evidence is it's sometimes hard to find,' Iles replied. 'Gossip, rumour, speculation can offer a starting point.'

'None of this – the rumour and so on – has reached any of my companies,' Leo said. 'I'm sure such material would have been passed on to me if it had come to them.'

'Maud has a detailed scenario of how this corrupt scheme would be organized,' Iles said.

'But, obviously, this is only what we been discussing just now – one of them *ideas*. Yes? A scenario would be like an idea, wouldn't it?' Leo said. 'Scenarios are Hollywood. This is not fact or the arrests would already of been made. This is imagination. It might be clever imagination, which is what we'd expect from people in London doing that kind of flashy desk job. But it's still only imagination.'

'Maud sees it this way,' Iles replied. 'The management board of one of these criminal firms takes a decision to recruit some officers from the local force on to the staff in a "facilitator" role. The facilitating would be to do mainly with making things easier and safer for the firm's pushers. The board's street people, or disco or rave people, should be able to advise which officers looked likely and could be approached and talked terms with. Maybe some had already been taking sweeteners as payment for blind-eyeing. That would be on a small scale, though. This new arrangement would be more substantial and solid. Officers might be offered a salaried position, possibly pensionable, or be paid on a fee-per-task basis, non-pensionable. The choice would be theirs. An officer with dependants might prefer the long-term benefits of settled salary and pension. Their pension from the firm would, of course, be in addition to the fine police pension and lump-sum upon retirement after thirty years' good service, so Maud says some would regard this as an excellent double career path, and double income after ceasing work. But other officers might prefer the alternative of large, *ad hoc* fees as and when, and eventually rely on the police pension only.

'Anyway, whichever form their appointment takes, once they have received any part of it they're caught. They have to continue. They've become elements in a system, and the system can function properly only if *all* its elements are in place and operating efficiently. If they try to get out they're in danger of execution because the firm, and the officers who stay on, will fear the renegade might blow the whistle. He or she must be silenced. The renegade's family would also be in peril. There are very powerful pressures and, on the other hand, inducements to stay with a firm.

'Inducements? Yes, some very positive aspects exist. For instance, Maud says most firms of any size hold substantial reserve and contingency funds. These would cover such expenditure as (one) private health and anti-addiction treatment in the Betty Ford-style clinic for any member of the firm who becomes an uncontrolled user of company products. This is particularly relevant to police members because symptoms of junkiedom in an officer could lead to very prejudicial inquiries as to commodity source, and, therefore, a possible link to the firm.

'(Two) Organizations will keep a comparatively large amount of cash ready to subsidize families when someone on company business is arrested and jailed, leaving the household potentially destitute. All worthwhile firms recognize a responsibility in such cases and are ready to cough up: "Sustenance Subsidies", as this support is known. The convicted member of the firm will be aware, naturally, that such support terminates if he/she talks to the police. And there might be other reprisals, including, possibly, against children.'

'Monstrous,' Emily said.

'Disgusting,' Leo said.

'Thus, the Jaminel buttoned lips,' Iles replied. 'He could tell us so much. But the risk for him is too severe. Others, similar.'

'My God, it's awful,' Emily said.

'Terrible,' Leo said.

'So, what duties for the firm would the bought officers be expected to provide?' Iles replied. 'Maud proposes (one) to forewarn of any planned special anti-drugs drive by the police, and its locality – city district or club or pub; (two) to allow trading by the firm without

interference in those areas where the officers supposedly represent
law and order; (three) to move heavily and often against competing
drugs firms through prosecutions, with tactfully planted material if
required; (four) to act sometimes as secure couriers, taking supplies
to nominated pushers.'

As far as Harpur knew, Maud had never spoken in such precise,
exhaustive terms about that kind of crooked career scene. This would
be a commercial profile created entirely by Iles himself and, as
would be expected from him, brilliantly thorough and probable. But
to present it as his own thinking could scare Leo too much and
make him clam up. Iles must be hoping that, as long as Leo stayed
sociable and wordy he might – just might – accidentally reveal
something which could be followed up, worked on, developed. By
attributing the ideas to Maud he allowed Leo to regard them as just
that – London ideas, a scenario, imagination, part of Whitehall's
obsessive, high-falutin', woolly search for trends. He could remain
reasonably relaxed and devious.

'I expect you find all this a trifle out of proportion, Mrs Young,'
Iles said.

'What out of proportion?' she said.

'One bad moment at a house on the Elms, and then all this
subsequent activity and turmoil. There's a danger the house might
take on a kind of symbolic status,' Iles said.

'That's absurd,' she replied. 'It's a house, a part-finished house,
I gather. Nothing more.'

'Yes, you're right, I expect,' Iles said. 'I've been there myself.
It's as you say – a stalled bit of building. I imagine the same
depressing symptoms are on view all over the country.'

'Emily's not at all interested in that kind of grim spot,' Leo said.

'I'm sure she's not,' Iles said.

'Museums – that's Em,' Young said with a terrific pride-throb.
'Ancient caves and cottages, not half-done modern villas. Her
colleagues, who are themselves much qualified in the historic and
really historic stuff, think so high of Em that she's the chairperson,
meaning she has knowledge of all sorts – spinning jennies, cross-
bows, flints, millstones. You show her a millstone and she'll tell
you the century straight off, by looking at it, not Googling. It's in
her head. Same with ink and paper. She can tell their age. She would
never of been fooled by them Hitler diaries, so called, conning top
editors here and in Germany. Em would of said right at the

beginning, "Them notebooks are not the sort of notebooks that was around in Adolf's time."'

'How do you get on with the car, Mrs Young?' Iles replied.

'Car?' she said.

Iles pointed through the window at the Mini Cooper. 'I think that's yours, isn't it?' Iles said.

'It's fine. What's that to do with anything?' she said.

'Good,' Iles said. 'Maud sees a pattern in these corruption schemes,' Iles said. 'The basic organizational and financial factors are constant from case to case. (One) Obviously, all payments to officers, whether as salary or fees, are in cash with twenties the highest denomination. No fifties: they draw attention. Also there is an acute forgery risk. If a fifty was identified as dud there'd be no knowing where the inquiries might go. (Two) Sales in a notorious drug-dealing street, disco, club or rave must take place with maximum speed and discretion. Pushers from other firms might be nearby and spot such transactions. They'd possibly do some of that anonymous broadcasting of hostile information you spoke of, Leo, aimed at hurting, even dismantling, the competition. (Three) Payments should not be banked or placed in a building society, or share-invested, or used to upgrade housing in this country. All such displays of wealth could excite curiosity. Private schooling expenses are reasonably OK. Likewise university. Properties abroad in slump countries – Greece, Spain, Portugal – might also escape notice, and, incidentally, should be cheap.

'Maud thinks new car purchase has to be allowed, because it would probably take place even if forbidden. People are sort of conditioned: a windfall equals a better model. But the need for some moderation would be stressed – no Porsche, no Bentley. The money probably wouldn't run to that level anyway. (Four) Bonus provision: officers on a salary and pension from the firm could be granted an extra one-off payment for some especially useful piece of cooper-ation, say, getting another firm's chief executive sent down for at least ten years. Officers enjoying the other reward system – fees as and when – could receive an especially raised extra in the same circumstances, possibly doubling or trebling the customary amount.'

'But why are you telling us this?' Emily said.

Once more, Harpur reckoned it not a reproach but a request for guidance on how it could affect her and Leo.

'I thought it might interest you to know the kind of sophisticated operation Harpur and I – and, of course, Maud Clatworthy – are up against,' Iles said.

'I think I see what Mr Iles is getting at. He's talking about a very tricky task, Em,' Young said. 'He would appreciate help with it – help from you and me as responsible, alert citizens, committed to aiding the community in every way possible. All citizens have such a responsibility, it's true, but us maybe more than most, owing to distinction in that community, such as the museum committee and the property here. This help will definitely not be easy, but I have already said we would provide all of it that we can. I stand by this, Mr Iles, Mr Harpur.'

'Thanks, Leo,' Iles replied.

'Are you saying the Maud woman is responsible on her own for this grand survey of corrupt forces?' Emily asked.

'Who else?' Iles said.

'Well, yes,' she replied.

As Harpur had suspected all along, Emily Young's acumen didn't stop at putting a date on old millstones. She and Leo came to the front door with Iles and Harpur when they left. Iles went and had a close-up look at the Mini Cooper. 'Lovely little vehicle,' he said. He peered at the windscreen. 'And it's all right, Col, you needn't fret. It's licensed until March.' He turned with a kindly chuckle towards Emily and Leo. 'Show Col a vehicle he's not familiar with and he has to check the road tax disc. It's a sort of twitch picked up when he was in the Traffic Division.'

TWENTY-FOUR

When Harpur and Iles had gone, Emily did what she termed 'a bit of mulling' over things said in the drawing room get-together just now. Or, to use another term, she tried to 'deconstruct' some of the talk. She'd heard this word used a couple of times by a local, undiffident Eng Lit prof on the museum committee. As far as she could make out, it involved searching for all the possible meanings hidden in what had seemed at first sight a simple, clear statement, spoken or written. Most likely you always had to do that for anything said by the police.

She returned to the drawing room and squeezed another half cup of tea from the pot. Leo went to look at repairs being done on one of the outhouses. She felt he wanted to salvage some of his aura and calm. He must have exhausted himself concocting so much likeability for Iles and Harpur. Inspecting the stonework he'd be reminded he was Leo Young of Midhurst, a property with grounds and outhouses, one of them converted to take an indoor heated swimming pool; another stabling the family's horses. He was all backbone and reliability, wasn't he? Well, wasn't he one of those responsible, alert citizens keen to aid the community, whom he'd mentioned with a true boom to his voice when promising help to those dangerous visitors?

She'd asked Iles why he said so many of the ideas and analyses came from Maud – 'Maud says this', 'Maud says that'. He hadn't really explained though. Nowhere near explained. But she thought she could possibly see an answer. He wanted to keep Leo relaxed and ready to chat. If Iles had said, 'This is what I believe, Leo,' or 'This is what Harpur believes,' it would show they'd been really doing a hard scrutiny of Leo's companies and that could scare him, make him super-cautious. She felt Iles wanted plenty of friendly discussion so he and Harpur could fix on some of it and find what they wanted to find there. If Iles successfully pretended it was London Maud who'd been doing the thinking, she'd get blamed for all the long-distance nosiness and dirty hints, and Iles and Harpur could go on being chummy, encouraging the wordy word flow, not always grammatical, but that wouldn't bother Leo. God, all the chunter about 'trends' and 'scenario' and 'appropriate'!

And there *were* dirty hints, weren't there? What was it Maud said about the corrupt get-together of police and dealers – according to Iles? Something like, 'She thinks one of the drugs firms has a business alliance with police officers, and that's why Mallen and the journalist had to die. They'd been poking about and had started to get somewhere.'

Why tell Leo about this supposed theory of Maud's? That's what Emily meant by dirty hints. But maybe 'hints' was a feeble word for these tactics, though 'dirty' would do. Emily felt a disgustingly blatant suggestion had been made – that the firm Maud and/or Iles and Harpur meant was Leo's firm. Iles had spoken of Jaminel's silence, enforced by the need to keep the family support cash coming from its shady source while he remained locked up; and by terror of what might happen to him even in jail, if he coughed all to detectives. Was Iles saying, without actually saying, that he thought Leo provided the hush handouts, and the terror? Did Harpur and Iles want to see how Leo reacted to difficult parts of the signal from Maud; allegedly from Maud?

Might they even have wanted to see how *Emily* reacted? Well, she'd asked for more information, hadn't she? That had been her main response. She'd questioned how Leo, the eternally straight businessman, could possibly have heard about a crooked pact between a drugs baron and some police. She'd wondered aloud why Iles was telling them about all this organizational stuff. And, of course, she'd let them know that the tricky way Iles had presented all this material hadn't worked. Her last query had been along the lines of: 'Are you really telling us that Maud of Whitehall produced this great slab of analysis on her own?' Iles had replied, 'Who else?' And she'd said: 'Well, yes.' Enigmatic Em! Ironic Em! But he'd pick up, wouldn't he, that she thought the frank answer to his 'Who else?' was 'Iles' or 'Iles and Harpur'. They weren't the only ones able to get subtle and oblique.

But, yes, those two, Iles and Harpur, could also do some. They'd wonder what lurked behind her questions and occasional bits of near enmity. Emily knew what lurked behind, naturally. It was the half-belief, the fear, the dread, that the firm Maud suspected of a crooked partnership with police officers really *was* Leo's firm. Or, to put it more accurately, Harpur and Iles suspected this, but for tact and trap reasons, and to lull Leo, they spoke as if they were only messengers from Maud, bringing her 'ideas' and 'imaginings'.

Now and then during the meeting with those two she'd allowed some of her deeper anxieties to show themselves. She'd accused Iles of talking 'bullshit' when he claimed that placing an undercover officer in a firm – in Leo's firm – was a neutral ploy, with no presumption of guilt. She'd called it 'a judgemental act', and she believed she had that right. Police put someone in undercover, with all the risks and rigmarole that meant, only when they felt sure the undercover officer, by persistence, clever duplicity, crafty integration, luck, would find something criminal that could be brought to trial.

Despite such moments of aggression from her, though, would they have sensed she was agonizingly uncertain about Leo's business life and that the uncertainty had begun to deepen? It had shaken

her when Iles spoke about the possible symbolic status of the house
on Elms. She'd dismissed that notion as flimflam, but, of course, it
was exactly the notion that had taken her there the other night. She'd
wanted reassurance that it was just a part-finished house, nothing
mystical or fantastic. And she'd wanted the reassurance because at
times she *had* stupidly, childishly, come to regard the house as
something more than itself: something radiating an evil, lingering,
perilous influence which might one day bring Leo down – Leo and
therefore herself. Today, the appalling suspicion had come that Iles
somehow knew she had been down to Elms and the house, and was
teasing her. Could he even have guessed Emily's motive – the acute
longing to dispel her doubts about Leo? But that had to be impossible, didn't it? Didn't it? Iles might be brilliant, but he wasn't
psychic.

She heard Leo's footsteps approaching on the gravel driveway
and felt almost ashamed, as if, sitting alone, having her private mull,
she had been not just idiotic but disloyal in her thinking. He came
into the drawing room and sat down. She decided now that, if he
really had hoped to lift his morale by inspecting the outhouse work,
it had failed. He appeared uneasy. He appeared hunted. Now and
then during their marriage she'd seen this hunted look on his small
face before. It still shocked her. 'Are they making a good job of
things?' she asked.

For a moment he seemed baffled by the question. Soon, though,
he got his mind working properly again and said: 'Oh, yes, fine,
fine.'

She left it at that for a minute and then said: 'What's wrong,
Leo, love?'

He kept the pause going for a few more seconds. He seemed to
be wondering whether he could tell her what troubled him. 'Your
car,' he said.

'What about it?'

'Iles playing about like that – checking the licence.'

'It was OK, up-to-date.'

'Of course it was OK. Not the point, Em.'

'What *is* the point?'

He went quiet again. But then seemed to decide he had to say
what troubled him. She saw that a big change in their relationship
might be under way. This pleased her – and scared her. 'Look, Em,
for quite ordinary business reasons I have an arrangement with

someone running the national police computer that holds reg numbers,' he said.

'An *arrangement* to get classified information from the police computer?'

'It can be important to check someone's ID, or get the history of a used vehicle we might want to buy. We wouldn't like to become accessories to a theft, would we, not even accidentally?' He put a sort of jokey spin on this.

Yes, sort of, she thought. 'You have an arrangement with a police officer running the national computer?' Emily said.

'Yes, as a business facility, like I said.'

'It's illegal, isn't it? You pay him or her to give you confidential, stored information. You bribe him or her?'

'There has to be payment. I'm asking the officer to do extra work on my behalf.'

'And to risk his or her job on your behalf, and possibly go to jail on your behalf.'

'There's a word for this kind of payment, Em, which means it's not wages, and it's like there's no payment at all, just a . . . well, just a simple "thank you". I expect you know this word, Em.'

'Backhander?'

'No, a sweeter word than that; much sweeter.'

'A sweetener?'

'No, again.' He shut his eyes to think better. 'It got like honour in it. It shows there's nothing too bad about it.'

'An honorarium,' she said.

'That's it!' He grinned, eyes open again. She saw he was delighted with her skill and speed at coming up with the answer, and delighted English had a word that made a bung sound like a medal. He said, 'It's a minor thing and doesn't happen very often.'

'But you keep paying the retainer, do you?'

'There's got to be what is referred to in commercial things as continuity. I never know when I might need this service, you see, Em. It's like insurance.'

'Yes, I see. So there's a sort of non-stop standby fee?'

'That sort of deal, yes.'

'Paid how? Brown envelopes in the post?'

He ignored this. 'The car,' he replied.

'What of it?'

'This lad on the computer – he got a similar sort of arrangement going with Iles,' Leo said. 'Well, no, not totally similar. Obviously, a high officer like Iles can ask for info about a reg any time he likes, and he's entitled. But *his* arrangement is round the other way, like. Iles wants to be told by the computer lad about any queries he gets that might be useful to the Assistant Chief.'

'Iles is paying him, too?'

'It's an extra facility, isn't it? This is not just Iles starting something with a request to him, which is, like, positive and part of the normal police use. The computer officer's got to be what's known in the business scene as proactive in this special role for Iles. The officer is the one who got to get things going.'

'So, another honorarium? Extra boodle from all directions. How do you know he operates for Iles like that?'

'He told me, didn't he?'

'Did he? And will he tell Iles he operates for you?'

'No, never that. He'd be admitting an offence. He knows I'm always interested in any requests he gets from Iles, or from Harpur, while they're here on the investigation.'

'But *why* are you interested, Leo?'

Of course, she thought she could see why: Leo must know he was a target for Harpur and Iles. That's why they'd been out here today. Naturally, she'd suspected this, and felt certain of it now. It was part of that changed relationship she'd sensed earlier. Leo seemed to have decided to tell her more or less outright that some of his life was crooked and complicated. Maybe he thought she must be half aware of this already, and so secrecy had become absurd. Whatever he meant about her car might have pushed him a bit further on with his frankness and disclosures. But what was it with her car?

'Harpur at the beginning,' Leo said.

'Harpur what?'

'Harpur calls in for a check on a registration number he's got from somewhere. The computer officer knows Iles likes to keep tabs on Harpur as much as he can. He tells Iles of Harpur's request, and, naturally, gives Iles the number that Harpur had asked him about. A Mini Cooper, yellow and black, road taxed until March, owner, Mrs Emily Young of Midhurst, etcetera.'

'My God,' she said.

'That's what the bit of fooling over the licence was about when they left. Why are they focused on your car, Em?' His tone had become sharper. He sounded like someone who ran a firm, and a firm that had seen a lot of trouble, might see more, and needed to be vigilant. The little trip to the outhouse refurbishment hadn't done much for his mood, but the Mini-Cooper puzzle prodded Leo's leadership qualities back into play. 'What I mean, Em, is have you been anywhere unusual in the car?' he said. 'Anywhere that would make them curious?'

'From here to Waitrose and back. From here to the museum committee and back.'

'Nothing else?'

From here to the Ritson Mall multi-storey when she went to the Elms house. This she didn't say, though. She'd thought there might be someone in the house, hadn't she – why she'd retreated in a hurry? Could the someone have tailed her, returning to Ritson and noted the car number as she drove away? Hell, the house was back in her thoughts again as more than a house – a jinx. 'Let's eat out, shall we, Leo? I feel like a break, with non-police voices around.'

TWENTY-FIVE

Harpur drove off this police domain, Larkspur, and out to the Mallen house at Wilton Road on Carnation. He'd arranged by phone to call. The visit had been suggested by Maud. She thought it a necessary courtesy to keep Iris Mallen informed face-to-face of developments, now parts of the original investigation were up for review. Harpur agreed. Iles agreed. 'Go about matters with some gentleness, Col,' he'd said as Harpur prepared to leave.

'Well, of course.' They were in their room at Larkspur HQ.

'You can be so fucking galumphing, Harpur. Face-to-face is all very well – the human touch – but what we have to remember is that one of the faces will be yours, rather compromising the human aspect. Yet, this is a woman trying to put her life together again.'

'I realize that, sir.'

'We don't want to bring her any further shocks.' Iles gave a powerful, throaty scream lasting about five seconds. He was standing and rotated his body through 360 degrees. 'Is there time for you to get a decent haircut? Don't take flowers.'

'Right.'

Iles had repeated the scream at the same pitch and with the same spin of himself. Then he said: 'Flowers equal death. She's had enough of that.' The screams were an Ilesean tactic. He revolved so all parts of the room got a share. He calculated that, if this nominally private and secure room had been bugged at some point or points, people listening would believe Harpur must be trying to kill him and they'd have to come fast and intervene – so confirming the bugs' presence. Iles thought they might have noticed the wound in his cheek and, when they got the profound, earphoned screams from whichever hidden spot or spots in the room, would assume it could have been given by Harpur – rightly assume it could have been given by Harpur – and that he was now finishing the job, probably with a fair-sized serrated knife. Nobody arrived, though. Harpur decided this did not necessarily prove the room clean. They might *want* Iles killed. Now and then Harpur came across folk who obviously did.

The ACC had taken two twenties from his back pocket. 'There are a couple of kids, aren't there? Give only when you're leaving. We're not buying anything – not friendship, information, gratitude. We're seeking to make the best of an awful job. There is no best, really, but let them have one each. If they refuse, respect that. Some children have a lot of pride. But, Col, you're aware of this. Your own, for instance. I trust this will not sound vain, but I think they take pride in knowing me.'

'Your trust is barmy then, sir. Of course it sounds vain,' Harpur replied.

'I'd go to Carnation myself, but I want to look into a few things said at Midhurst.'

'Which?'

'Make my apologies to Mrs Mallen.'

'Most probably you'll have heard of this, sir, but lately I came across a different way of looking at words, by getting behind what they seem to say and discovering other stuff. It could be applied to extracts from the Midhurst session.'

'Deconstruction.'

'I was sure this would be your sort of thing, sir! In fact, I've heard people say, "That Mr Iles, he's well into deconstruction,

although an Assistant Chief.Whenever I hear the word 'deconstruction', I think of Mr Iles.'"

'Which people?'

'Oh, yes. Perception was their long suit.'

'That undergraduate Denise you're shacked up with for most of
her time has been giving you some literary theory coaching, has
she, in exchange for what you've been giving her?'

'She told me one of her professors is writing a book on negative
capability.'

'Some of them have a lot of that.' Iles must have read things
differently from Harpur and, because no rescue party had come to
deliver him, he decided the room was bugless and began to talk
more openly. 'We don't need deconstruction to tell us that Mrs
Young's beginning to get a horrifyingly clear idea of what her
hubby's business is, and what it requires to stay healthy – murders,'
he'd replied. 'It's in the droop of her jaw, Col. It's in the frailty of
her voice, the despair of her questions, the pitifulness of her little
spurts of anger. Possibly Leo has come to suspect this. Hence the
halt and lame claptrap to fill the time. Hence, also, that sudden,
violent switch of subject to museums and Emily's outstanding,
chairperson's flair with Ice Age pencil sharpeners, and other
antiquities.'

'But what you're doing now – this survey *is* a kind of deconstruction, isn't it, sir?'

'Just sense.'

Mrs Mallen and her children lived in a wide, suburban road of
between-the-wars, semi-detached villas facing one another across
an island of well-tended, litter-free grass. The houses and front
gardens were well-tended, too. Harpur liked the look of the area.
The people here set themselves standards. He considered them
good standards, although Harpur himself lived in a less spruce
district back in Cowslip. Iles was continually at him to make a
change – possibly to somewhere like this. But his daughters liked
Arthur Street. They could walk to their school, John Locke compre-
hensive, and to the bus station caff, a social hub for them and
their friends. The Arthur Street house had off-street parking on
hardstanding at the side of the front garden, ideal for Denise in
her Fiat. The fact that the car could be seen there, very obvious
and very often, pleased the girls. It proved there was nothing
furtive about Harpur's relationship with Denise: no leaving the car

somewhere discreet and sneaking into the house on foot. Altogether, Harpur found the ties with Arthur Street too many to think about a move. 'Get amongst the jumped-up and jump higher, Col,' Iles had said. 'Switch to aspirational from stick-in-the-mud.' Harpur had promised to consider it, and did, but stayed put.

He'd met Mrs Mallen several times before, during the original inquiry into her husband's death. He'd found her bright, brave, forthright. She opened the door at 11 Wilton Road now and took him into a sitting room. She was tall – about 5' 8" – very pale skinned, her face long, aquiline, expressive, not hostile but showing some tension, some suspicion, some toughness. He would have expected all those: the police had put her husband into danger and to that extent had caused his death, and Harpur was police. She probably wouldn't differentiate between one cop and another, nor make much of the fact that he and Iles were trying to get the people who'd ordered her husband's slaughter. Yes, police were police. She'd prepared some cheese sandwiches set out on a Pembroke table with a couple of cans of Bass beer. She opened these now and filled two glasses. They ate and drank and talked about the journey for a while. She was sitting opposite him, both in beige moquette arm chairs.

Then she said: 'Do you know, Mr Harpur, I used to resent – really resent – the way Tom had to become someone else, had to ditch his authentic self. But, of course, when it all ended like that I wished he'd managed to become that someone else even more thoroughly and efficiently than he had. He was tugged two ways, wasn't he? He had to make himself the real, gangster article. And he was also still a husband and dad. Maybe he sensed my hostility to this new job of his, and didn't give the undercover side maximum effort. If he had, he might have still been doing it. I was stupidly possessive and impatient. After all, the new identity wouldn't have been permanent. The other is.'

The other being death. But Harpur understood why she couldn't say that direct, even now, months after.

'Shall I tell you what I don't understand, Mr Harpur?'

'There's quite a bit *I* don't understand.'

'Tom ceases to be Mallen and becomes whatever it was he became and gets a place in a drugs firm. He apparently settles in well, but is then found out and it's all over bar the shooting. There would seem to me a link between the firm he infiltrated and . . . what

happened to him. Yet nobody from that firm was convicted. Another
police officer was. The firm presumably is still operating.'
    'We failed there,' Harpur said. 'Mr Iles blames himself. I blame
*my*self.'
    'But they stick with you – the Home Office sticks with you,
although you failed?'
    'We were answering other urgencies then,' Harpur said. Christ,
what verbiage, what shit.
    'Which other urgency?'
    'A successful arrest and trial for the crime.'
    'But surely the crime should have been seen as part of something
. . . something complex and carefully, ruthlessly, organized.'
    'It *was* seen like that. We'd been brought in because the Home
Office believed that what happened to your husband – tragic in itself
– also indicated a wider disorder. But we couldn't get close.' He
realized suddenly that she might think he and Iles had become part
of the plot not to investigate properly, instead of exposing it: police
were police; police took care of police. They didn't always stick
together, or Jaminel wouldn't have been nailed. But generally they
did. It was central to their training. How would anyone outside
know when those mystical bonds of absolute loyalty might be
suspended?
    Harpur could sympathize with her distrust, but, of course, longed
to correct it. He was unsure how to manage that. He recalled Iles's
instruction to take things gently with a woman who had to rebuild
her life. Iles could turn very tender. It confused people. It could
still confuse Harpur. Tenderness was not Iles's most obvious quality.
    In his pocket now Harpur carried the expired Biro which had
made that very timely pit in the ACC and quietened some of his
more usual characteristics: mad ferocity, merciless contempt, malicious scheming. Harpur had brought the Biro as a gift for Mrs
Mallen, in the hope it might provide some comfort and solace. She
had been searching for it at the Elms house – an item to commemo-
rate her husband.
    Harpur would not mention to her the honest, bloodletting jab it
gave to Iles, of course. Sensitive omissions were required. Although
Harpur had thoroughly cleaned away any fragments of Iles from
the Biro, it would diminish its value as poignant keepsake if she
knew the pen had been part of a brutal, muddy encounter on that
sad slice of ground in front of the Elms house, when Iles had seemed

likely to strangle him, on account of Harpur's affair with Sarah, Iles's wife. Despite episodes of tenderness, Iles was brilliantly accomplished at bearing grudges. He devotedly, expertly, refurbished his hates.

Harpur wondered now about the Biro. Had he been simple-minded in thinking she would be delighted to receive it from him? She had obviously wanted it badly, and had driven all that distance to search the Elms soil. But what would she make of the sudden disclosure by Harpur that he knew of the journey and her unsuccessful scour?

Emily Young had met her there by accident. Although she had refused to give her name, might that very refusal point to her identity? Iris Mallen was sharp. She'd notice the expensive clothes and expensive shoes. Why would a prosperous, middle-aged woman come out at night to this cursed estate unless she had some connection to the Mallen-Parry case? Iris might guess that the only person to fit this bill was the wife of the chief of the firm where, as it came out at the trial, Tom had done his undercover work?

If Mrs Mallen did get to that conclusion, would it look as if Harpur had gathered his information from Emily Young? He hadn't. It came from Hill-Brandon. But Iris might not know about him. Would she decide that the interlocking concerns of the the police and the villains, and the villains' wives, still prevailed, even though Harpur and Iles had allegedly been sent, and resent, to expose this cop-crook relationship? She already suspected the police of being devious and unscrupulous. The Biro might seem to her like a cheap piece of trickery aimed at soothing her, and at persuading her not to make trouble about what she saw as at least dud, and possibly corrupt investigations.

It was late afternoon. Her children, Steve and Laura, came home from school. Iris Mallen did the introductions. 'A Detective Chief Super?' Steve said. 'But why? I thought it was all over. The trial sent him down for life.' Steve was an early teen, his sister a few years younger.

'No, it's not all over,' Harpur said.

'We want to forget it,' Laura said. She was near tears.

'I can understand that,' Harpur said.

'So, what do you mean, it's not all over, Mr Harpur?' Steve asked.

'Others involved,' Harpur said.

'Well, of course,' Steve said. He was fair-haired and thin, like

his father. 'But police can only go so far, can't they? It's always
the same. There's one thing or the other. The big boys stay in the
clear.'

'No, it's not going to be like that,' Harpur said.

'You sure?' Steve replied. The boy had developed some adult
cynicism, perhaps inevitably after what had happened to this family.
He and Laura went to the kitchen to make themselves a snack.

'I'll be away, too,' Harpur said. He had the Biro in a sealed
envelope wrapped in tissue, so that the shape of the pen wasn't
outlined. He took the envelope from his pocket and put it on the
table. 'A present. Open when I've gone,' he said.

TWENTY-SIX

That visit to Midhurst by the two investigative police had
stoked up Emily Young's unease about her husband, and how
her husband made their money. The presence of this pair,
Iles and Harpur, had seemed to define for her things she didn't want
defined – had, perhaps, deliberately avoided getting defined: too
much information. Her job in the museum was to do with defining:
say specifying the date and provenance to within a century or two
of some pottery shard or coin. At this she was first rate, and
renowned. But it didn't mean she'd fancy the same sort of scrutiny
and precision applied to her life in general, and particularly not to
the coin area: that is, how exactly Leo earned their comfy keep,
and possibly – oh, God, yes, possibly – possibly disposed of those
who threatened it. That thought hounded her now.

She had felt at the time that the officers knew much more than
they let on. Well, of course, of course: they were police, weren't they?
She couldn't work out what was the purpose of the call, and what
they took away, beyond Leo's would-be-likeable, anti-grammatical
chatterboxing. There had been moments when she thought she was
being played with, made fun of, especially by Iles. She'd wondered
whether he'd discovered, somehow, that she'd been down to the
Elms house. He'd pretended to believe she might be ignorant of Elms
and had offered guidance. Absurd. Mickey-taking? He'd said he
couldn't be sure whether she was familiar with the undercover man's

death, but it had happened on a housing estate – a 'stymied' estate he'd dubbed it, meaning strapped for cash. But everybody in the city able to read a newspaper, listen to radio or watch local and network TV news knew about the house after so much trial coverage. Plus, it was a trial to do with the death of one of her husband's business associates. So, naturally, Iles would realize she needed absolutely no explanation of the circumstances, as if she'd just woken up from a lost decade binge.

Why would he fool about like that? Did he *want* her to recognize the mockery? Was he telling her not just that he knew she'd gone to the Elms house, but also that he could intuit or deduce the reason – obviously something centred on Leo? And what could it be about Leo but a suspicion, dread, in Emily that Leo was connected with the clever gunfire from this house? Did the connection go beyond the fact that the man murdered here had been, on the face of it, a business mate? Had Leo been implicated in the wipeout of that supposed business mate who was, in reality, a police spy?

Probably not even Iles would be able to chart the full, high-falutin', possibly mystical motive for her Elms jaunt – to rid the place of its symbolism and foul, unnerving aura by concentrating on and handling the banal bricks and mortar: builders' materials, not a doom-touched figment. But Iles would possibly guess her Elms jaunt was to inspect a murder site because her husband might have helped set up the ambush. Might have done more than help. Might have devised it.

Emily did wonder whether she was reading too much into Iles's words and tone. She hoped so. If not, it would explain why the officers had come to Midhurst. This would be about Leo, yes, but also, slyly, obtusely, about her. They'd watched her and noted the flavour of her questions. Had they placed those questions in a background that included her night sortie to Elms? Did they decide she was acutely troubled about Leo and therefore worth focusing on as a means of ultimately getting at him? Plainly, he was their target. She knew she shouldn't have been surprised at this. But the confirmation depressed her. Definition. Undesired definition. Were they in touch with Mrs Mallen? Was that where their information came from?

What she longed for was someone who could restore a portion of the happy, concocted, mental blankness about Leo and the firm that she'd enjoyed for so long. Her job required the strong light of brainpower and learning to shine on the past. Away from the museum, though, and particularly in her marriage, she hankered after soothing, protective, impenetrable shadows. Where could she get them?

Emily thought of Mrs Jaminel. She'd never met Mrs Jaminel, but she'd been mentioned now and then by the press and broadcasters during and after the trial. The mentions were only as Jaminel's wife. Emily knew nothing about her beyond this. Might she be able to say something, though – anything, however slight – but something to indicate, hint, speculate, that her husband had acted alone and from private motives; was not merely an executioner taking orders from Leo and Leo's advisers and board members?

There were no Jaminels in the telephone directory. Some people did without a landline now and relied on their mobiles. Or the number and address could be ex-directory. She'd probably been harassed by offensive calls. Emily went to the municipal library and looked out back-numbers of the local paper at the time of the Jaminel trial and conviction. One of the reports said he'd lived at Collit, a seaside suburban village just outside the city. It gave a picture of a country cottage with a distinctive, flat-roofed extension to the side, a scarlet burglar alarm box above a bedroom window, and the sea and Orville island with its squat, white-painted lighthouse visible in the distance.

Emily drove out to Collit on a shopping afternoon and along the sea front. She found the cottage easily enough.

A woman was in the front garden, crouched forward, working on a border: dumpy, almost fat, dark hair cut to shoulder length and grey-flecked. She wore heavily framed spectacles. She'd be in her late forties, Emily thought, her gardening movements slow and methodical. The garden gate on to the street carried a name plate: 'Axbridge'.

'Mrs Jaminel?' Emily asked.

'Who is it?' The accent was not local, possibly West Country. She sounded guarded. She'd probably had a lot of pushy media people here with their nagging, brutal questions when Courtenay Jaminel was found guilty. Mrs Jaminel stood upright now, facing Emily, her arms down at her sides. She wore yellow gardening gloves, a trowel in her right. The attitude struck Emily as like a sentry's stance. A 'who goes there?' stance. Mrs Jaminel had on tan trousers and a beige cardigan over what might be a man's shirt, white with green and gold thin stripes.

Emily pointed at the name. 'Axbridge. Somerset? Are you from there originally?'

'Who *are* you?' Mrs Jaminel replied.

'I'm Emily Young.'

'*Mrs* Young?'

'Yes, Leo Young's wife.'

'Oh, I see. Well, you'd better come in, Mrs Young.'

It wasn't the reply she wished for. She would have preferred bafflement when she gave her name and Leo's, or at least indifference. Emily had yearned for a reaction that said Leo had nothing to do with this household, and particularly not with her husband.

Mrs Jaminel leaned forward and opened the gate with her free hand. Emily thought she saw deference in the act. She felt feudal, like the lady from the Great House come to make a kindness call on a labouring tenant. She loathed this impression. It suggested, didn't it, that Mrs Jaminel felt indebted to Leo – and perhaps to Emily also – because he and the firm looked after the Axbridge mortgage, the Axbridge provisions bill, the Axbridge electricity and gas, and perhaps other outgoings. The newspaper reports said Jaminel had a daughter, Astrid, studying at a northern university: would Leo take care of the fees and student loan? Might Mrs Jaminel think Leo had sent her to see things were OK, woman to woman?

And another question: might Mrs Jaminel mention to Leo, or to one of Leo's emissaries, who brought her the regular wherewithal, that Emily had been here? Emily realized, of course, that this notion showed she had more or less decided by now that she definitely wasn't going to get the kind of response she'd hoped for from Mrs Jaminel. Emily began to assume exactly what she had feared: Leo and the firm looked after Mrs Jaminel so as to keep her husband quiet about the removal of the undercover policeman. Axbridge equalled silence.

They went into a room at the back of the house with a view through French windows to the pebble beach, the island and the sea. The room contained a mahogany table with six dining chairs around it, and nothing else. Mrs Jaminel did not sit down nor invite Emily to take one of the chairs and sit down herself. In their straight-backed tidiness and, for today at any rate, their non-use, they announced to Emily that the era of boisterous, liquored-up, exuberant dinner parties here was over, the former host, Inspector Courtenay Jaminel, behind bars and his wife not inclined to entertain. And

even if she did want company now and then, would company come
to socialize with the wife of a much-publicized killer cop?

Or – second thoughts – perhaps the table and chairs didn't look
like part of a household at all, but the ex-boardroom of a small,
defunct company, possibly in the sand and gravel or wide shoe line.

Just the same, Mrs Jaminel had picked this venue for their talk,
perhaps to keep things inhospitable and unleisurely. She had charge.
Emily felt the atmosphere of their meeting change. That feudal role
she'd imagined for herself vamoosed. There was no deference from
Mrs Jaminel, not even defence; instead, a kind of aggro. She still
had the gardening gloves on, still held the trowel. Emily saw something elemental about her now: Mother Earth. The gloves and trowel
gave the message that this encounter was a distraction, to be quickly
stifled so the crucial frontal weeding could get going again. Mrs
Jaminel might reason, 'OK, this is a tainted house, so all the more
reason to keep it looking properly cared for and up to scratch. This
property, *qua* property, will continue to be a credit to the Collit
neighbourhood.'

'I don't know why you've come here,' she said, mildly enough,
but with her eyes behind the hefty spectacle frames fixed full and
direct on Emily's.

Emily wanted, craved, to believe this: it signified, didn't it, no
connection between Jaminel and Leo, or no connection Mrs Jaminel
knew of. To be totally sure, Emily wanted to say, 'But the mortgage
for this lovely cottage – who pays it?' And, 'The running costs, the
food and drinks costs, who takes care of these?' And, 'The university
costs and jail visiting costs, who forks out for these?' But Emily didn't
put the questions. It would be to ask Mrs Jaminel to turn Emily's
guesswork into fact – the sort of fact she had come here to kill and
bury. And if, as Emily hoped, Leo was *not* shelling out to her and her
daughter, Mrs Jaminel would feel hurt, insulted, enraged.

She said, 'It would be foolish of me to pretend there were not
rumours – all kinds of rumours – at the time of my husband's trial,
Mrs Young. Perhaps you heard some of those rumours and have
kept them in your memory. Probably, they are what brought you to
this house today. But they *were* only rumours.' She repeated that,
her voice calm, matter-of-fact. 'Only rumours. I take it you come
to Collit now because you've begun to wonder about your husband's
business, and from there to wonder also whether he had some part
in the death of the undercover officer. You are not involved in your

husband's commercial activities, if we may call them such, and it is to your credit that you suffer anxiety about the true nature of those activities; though some might think you've taken a long while to reach the position.'

Emily felt battered by the language, its fluency and poise, its bluntness: *if we may call them such*; *some might think you've taken a long time to reach that position*.

'I presume you would like me to assure you that my husband was the only one involved in the killing. You imagine, do you, that I have some evidence to prove this, evidence I have never disclosed? But how can I help you in that fashion when I believed absolutely in my husband's defence at the trial, and believe it now – that he did not kill Mallen-Parry, either on orders, or as a private, work-alone figure? I consider the case against him was manufactured by two visiting police officers under severe pressure somehow to achieve a conviction and, in this way, allay, finish off the fears among senior law people in the Home Office that the original investigation into the murder was weak and dilatory because some local officers were accessories to the killing.' She raised the trowel, as if eager to get it back on duty. 'I think that's us done, Mrs Young,' she said.

'Yes,' Emily said. What else was there to say? Mrs Jaminel had produced an impasse.

She said, 'I'd prefer that you didn't come out here again. You might be followed. I want no involvement with all that. These people are very wary, very resourceful, very ruthless.'

'Involved with all what? Which people?'

'Please, stay away.' Mrs Jaminel led out into the front garden and stood aside so Emily could open and pass through the Axbridge gate.

Emily closed it behind her and, before making for her car, said, 'Goodbye, Mrs Jaminel.'

She nodded in reply, did not speak, might have been formulating in her mind some suitable eternal, farewell, such as 'So, now fuck off, Mrs Young. Go home to your murdering hubby.'

As Emily drove away she glanced towards the cottage, but Mrs Jaminel was out of sight, bent over a flower bed and hidden by a stretch of privet. Emily recalled that pay-off line from the play *Candide*, by Voltaire. '*Mais il faut cultiver notre jardin*' ('But we must cultivate our garden'), meaning get on with necessary, basic chores and leave the vaguer, grandiose matters alone. Did Mrs Jaminel realize she was following a famous French theatrical character's recommended creed?

For a moment or two she felt pleased with this snippet of applied scholarship. This was education, and education fashioned to illuminate an actual, nowish situation: a jailbird's wife making the best of a horrible, painful predicament. It was the kind of mental trick that justified the existence and cost of museums, wasn't it? They were full of ancient exhibits and these relics showed how our modern tools, machinery, weapons had their beginnings.

But then she thought this amounted to pretentious crap. The slice of Voltaire was so well-known it hardly counted as scholarship. Clichédom more like it. God how patronizing to ask, 'Did Mrs Jaminel realize she was following a famous French theatrical character's recommended creed?' Emily feared her smug sojourn into French literature had stupidly preoccupied her and taken some of her concentration off the road. But only some. She looked in the Mini's rear-view mirror and saw a Renault Laguna saloon not far behind. And she had a notion that she had more or less subconsciously noticed this vehicle earlier sticking close, though her main attention then had been on Mrs Jaminel in her garden and *Candide* in hers.

She did a more purposeful stare into the mirror now. She didn't recognize the car and it stayed too far back to get a proper view of the driver – a man, who seemed to be alone. She'd seen television crime dramas where one of the characters had to deal with a vehicle that seemed to be tailing him or her. The technique was to take a couple of turnings and see if the car behind followed. That would confirm, or not, if it was a tail or just a vehicle by chance doing some of the same route as the one ahead.

She took two lefts and then a right and the Laguna remained with her. In this manoeuvring the Laguna unintentionally came a little closer and twice for half a second she had a slightly better view of the driver – someone not tall, sitting low in the driver's seat. 'My God, my God!' she yelled to herself. 'It's Leo.' The idea that he might dog her like this, pry like this, infuriated Emily. Had he hired that Laguna to fool her? The sly sod. He wasn't at home when she left for Mrs Jaminel's. Could he have been waiting somewhere near Midhurst to see whether she would drive out in the Mini? That information he'd received from his contact at the national police computer about her car must have disturbed him, made him suspicious of her. It suggested a life he had known nothing of. Had he been behind her on the way to Mrs Jaminel's as well as after, but unnoticed?

She longed to confront him, show him her rage and contempt. The planning, the elaborateness, the car disguise appalled her. She took another left turn but stopped immediately in the new road, expecting him to pull in behind her. This was *not* something she had learned from TV cop dramas, though. It was a piece of crude, dangerous retaliation. Leo had lagged a little and, trying to make up the distance, came round the corner too fast, possibly afraid he'd lose her. He was putting his foot down when he should have been easing it back. Maybe he didn't know any more about the techniques of vehicle tailing than she did. He would have hit the rear of her car hard, perhaps injuring her or worse. Instead, he swerved out to go around the Mini and met a garden services lorry head-on. Through the driver's window she saw Leo's head jerked back by the impact and then he fell forward hard on to the wheel.

'Leo!' she screamed. 'Sit properly. Please!'

The Laguna and the lorry were alongside Emily's car, their fronts shattered and locked together, the Laguna gushing steam from under the sprung bonnet. She had just enough room to get out. She pulled at the passenger door of the Laguna. It was buckled and wouldn't open, but then did, a fraction. 'Leo,' she whispered. 'Oh, God.' He managed to lift his head from the driving wheel. He turned towards her and said absolutely clearly: 'Howie will see you and the boys are all right.' It might have been the reference to the children that made her think now that she'd never seen him look more like a hamster called Stanley once owned by their younger son, Grenville.

'Howie?' she said.

'Yes, Howie.' She could tell there'd be nothing more from him.

TWENTY-SEVEN

Harpur was back home with the children and Denise when verdicts in what had become known as 'The Howie' case figured in the television news. Howard Lambert and three other police officers including a Constable Silver and Sergeant Quick were sent down for their part in a corrupt business arrangement with the Leo Young drugs firm.

'That was you and Ilesy done it, wasn't it, Dad?' Jill said.

'Did it,' Harpur said.

'Yes, you two did it,' she said.

'We were there. I'm not sure we did much. It was Mrs Young,' Harpur said.

'Ilesy wouldn't admit something like that,' Jill said.

'He'd want the *gloire*, wouldn't he?' Hazel said. 'That's what the French call it – the glory. Or "We must have distinctions" as one of the Napoleons said. Desy Iles would go for any distinction available, wouldn't he?'

'Not always,' Harpur said.

'US cops in movies call it the collar,' Jill said.

'Little *gloire* or glory about,' Harpur said.

'Your dad's doing his modesty act,' Denise said.

'That's what I mean,' Jill replied.

'What?' Harpur said.

'Des Iles doesn't do modesty,' Jill said.

'It's that poor woman, widow, Mrs Young, I think of,' Denise said. 'I've been reading about her in the papers. As I see it, she was a woman with quite a bit going for her – in the career and social sense, I mean. And then she obviously comes to wonder what her husband does for a living, and fears it might be something horrible, so she starts her own inquiries.'

'Yes, like that,' Harpur said.

'Respectability is a very powerful quality,' Denise said. 'Reputation. Shakespeare is on about it in *Othello*, isn't he?'

'Is he? Harpur said.

'"Reputation, reputation, reputation," Cassio says. Without it he's a beast, he reckons. Social standing. It sounds bourgeois and prim, but is a great motivator and deeply democratic, because it values the opinions of others. She wanted it. She was on some museum committee, wasn't she? That would be full of worthies, I bet.'

'You'll be like it one day, I expect, Denise,' Jill said. 'A degree. Or maybe more than one degree. Full of learning and conversation.'

'Emily Young would imagine those snide museum colleagues guessing what her husband's life must really be like,' Denise replied. 'And it wouldn't be a very difficult guess.'

'Yes, I think she had some guilt,' Harpur said. He bought the *Epoch* next morning to see what they made of it all. There was a full court report but also a piece by the journalist Philip White under the heading 'An Unsatisfactory End'.

This article comes to you today in the style of a post script
– a post script to our previous tribute to David Lee Cass which
we, as well as many other newspapers, published at the time
of his death; and a post script, also, to the court case involving
corrupt police officers which is reported on pages one and
seven. I was David's editor and went not long ago to the police
area coded as Larkspur to see if I could establish that David's
death had helped rid the city of this vile debasement of a police
force. I talked to many people there, some of whom had been
in contact with David and remembered him favourably. I talked,
also, to the two officers who had been sent to investigate, or
re-investigate, the force, Assistant Chief Constable Iles and
Detective Chief Superintendent Colin Harpur. They assured
me it was the killing of David on the assignment that horrified
Mrs Young and made her determined to discover whether her
husband had any part in the crime. We cannot know the answer
to that, because he died. But it was as a result of what Mrs
Young told them, and later told the court about her husband's
last words – 'Howie will see you and the children all right'
– that the two officers decided to revisit Lambert and begin an
interrogation that led to his and his associates' conviction. It
comforted me to hear that in a roundabout fashion David had
contributed to this outcome, and I'm sure many readers of this
paper will feel the same.

He took the paper home in the evening. Denise had driven the children to their judo club and would pick them up in half an hour. She read the news report and the White article. She said: 'In a way Leo Young was a gallant figure.'

'Yes, in a way.'

'In a couple of ways,' she said.

'Yes?'

'He pulls out to avoid crashing into the Mini and Emily.'

'Crashes into a lorry, instead,' Harpur said.

'That's what I mean,' Denise said. 'A sort of self-sacrifice.'

'He could have killed the lorry driver.'

'Less likely than killing Emily in a small car. And, anyway, the lorry driver is OK. Young must have had time to calculate which was best to do.'

'You're a romantic,' Harpur said.

'And then, as he's dying in the Laguna, he thinks of Emily and the kids: "Howie will see you and the boys are all right."'

'Howie was Mallen's handler.'

'I realize that,' Denise said.

'It's a kind of almost holy relationship,' Harpur said. 'We have to assume Mallen told him stuff that Howie Lambert saw would scupper the business, if Mallen were allowed to continue. He must have found out a dangerous amount about "the arrangement" but, obviously, not enough for Mallen to know Lambert was the main man on the police side in the dark alliance. But Lambert feared this might be the next Mallen discovery. So, silence him – or get someone to silence him: Jaminel, another member of the corrupt police group, a trained marksman. Success!

'Everything goes quiet after the Jaminel conviction. Dathan, the Chief, is content to let matters rest. He doesn't want any more hostile interest in his team. But then, suddenly, there's a new snooping bugger about, this time David Lee Cass, plus the return of those two other snooping buggers, Iles and Harpur. Dathan tries to get rid of Iles following a quaint disturbance at the theatre. And Lambert believes Cass has begun to unearth too much, just like Mallen. Lambert fixes a remote rendezvous with him, supposedly to spill secrets, and Cass walks into it, the way Mallen walked into the other trap on Elms. This time, Lambert didn't depute the killing, though.'

Denise looked shaken. 'What happens to Mrs Young and their children, then, Col?'

'You mean Howie won't be around to see them right? The firm's extinguished.'

'Yes.'

'Not our concern, Denise.'

'But she helped you.'

'I've said thank you to her several times,' Harpur replied.

'What about Iles?'

'He might have, too. He can occasionally turn quite soft.'